Praise for *2030*

A *New York Times*, *Los Angeles Times*, and *USA Today* Bestseller

"Albert Brooks is a keen and critical social observer. . . . His first novel is an inspired work of social science fiction, thoughtful and ambitiously conceived, both serious and seriously funny." —*The Boston Globe*

"With *2030* Mr. Brooks has made the nervy move of transposing his worrywart sensibility from film to book. Two things are immediately apparent about his debut novel: that it's as purposeful as it is funny, and that Mr. Brooks has immersed himself deeply in its creation. *2030* is an extrapolation of present-day America into the not-so-distant future, and it is informed by the author's surprisingly serious attention to reality. Unlike the fantasy writer who foresees a gee-whiz future full of alluring gimmicks, Mr. Brooks has dreamed up escapism about problems we cannot escape." —*The New York Times*

"Comedian and filmmaker Brooks welcomes the reader to the year 2030 in his smart and surprisingly serious debut. . . . Brooks's mordant vision encompasses the future of politics, medicine, entertainment, and daily living, resulting in a novel as entertaining as it is thought provoking, like something from the imagination of a borscht belt H. G. Wells."

—*Publishers Weekly*

"An intriguing vision of America's future." —*Library Journal*

"Required reading!" —*New York Post*

"Brooks's vision of the future is credible and compelling." —*Booklist*

2030

ALBERT BROOKS

The Real Story of What Happens to America

 St. Martin's Griffin New York

This is a work of fiction. All of the characters, organizations, and events portrayed in this novel are either products of the author's imagination or are used fictitiously.

www.stmartins.com

The Library of Congress has cataloged the hardcover edition as follows:

Brooks, Albert, 1947—.
2030 : the real story of what happens to America / Albert Brooks.
p. cm.
ISBN 978-0-312-58372-9
I. Title. II. Title: Twenty thirty.
PS3552.R65858A614 2011
813'.54—dc22

2010054560

ISBN 978-0-312-59129-8 (trade paperback)

First St. Martin's Griffin Edition: April 2012

10 9 8 7 6 5 4 3 2 1

For my wife, Kimberly, and my children, Jacob and Claire

CHAPTER ONE

It was a normal day, or so it seemed. Actually, nothing in 2030 seemed normal, not to Brad Miller anyway. Brad was surprised at how many people showed up for his eightieth birthday. Surprised because he had these friends in the first place and surprised at how healthy they all were. This was not what people in their eighties were supposed to look like. Sure, the lifts helped, along with the tucks and the hair and the new weight-loss drug, which, while only seven years on the market, had become the biggest-selling drug in the history of the world. That's what happens when a chemical works almost one hundred percent of the time, in everyone. *But still,* Brad thought, *these folks look good.*

And they did. They were thin, healthy, all looking better than their parents were at forty. The only thing missing were younger people. Brad couldn't remember the last time he'd seen a young person at his birthday. Other than his son, whom he never talked to anyway, he didn't even know anyone under fifty. Nor did any of his friends. There was just too much resentment and too much fear.

As the lights dimmed, the customary "life" movie played in the middle of the room, holographic style. People were getting tired of these. It was one thing to watch home movies of someone else; it was another to feel like you were in them. It was like boredom squared. But people watched; they laughed and told Brad how much fun it was to see him "age." He, like many of them, actually looked better now than he had ten years ago. But it was funny. Where once that was a compliment relating to how you lived your life, whether you ate well or exercised enough or got a good night's sleep, now it was just about what you could afford. And once cancer had been cured, the youth business went crazy.

Most people in that room were only in their twenties when Richard Nixon declared a war on cancer. Like all the wars going on at the time, this one seemed to have little success. The progress was so slow. Still, people held out hope that when they got older there would be a cure for what ailed them. But when the year 2000 rolled in, there they were: bald, fat, and ugly. And there was still cancer.

But everyone in that room, probably everyone in the world, remembered where they were when they heard the news. Oh, there had been so many hopeful stories over the years. So many false starts. So many mice that were cured, but when the human trials started, people dropped dead of all kinds of things that had never bothered a mouse. But then it happened. And like all of the greatest discoveries, from Newton to Einstein, Dr. Sam Mueller's cure was so exquisitely simple.

Dr. Mueller was no genius. He grew up fairly normal, in Addison, Illinois. A big night out was going to Chicago for pizza. After graduating Rush Medical College, Sam Mueller interned at Rush-Presbyterian-St. Luke's Medical Center and then, realizing that making a living as an internist was going to be tough at best, he started looking elsewhere. He thought of concierge medicine, which was all the rage, but decided to take a fairly lucrative position at Pfizer. He figured he would do that for a while and then something would unfold. Oh my, did it unfold.

Mueller had always been interested in the immune system. So much in medicine was pointing to the body's own defenses as a cure-all, but the success rates were modest at best. He was assigned various projects at Pfizer. Some were interesting, some he hated. He never understood the Viagra-for-women thing. Every woman he ever knew could go all night, have a bowl of cereal, and go for another afternoon, but he worked on it anyway, and when it happened it was huge.

The team got big-time bonuses and raises and all kinds of rewards. They were even sent to Hawaii, where Sam Mueller met his wife. She wasn't Hawaiian, she was an assistant on the project whom he had never really gotten to know, but then one night on Kauai they both got drunk, walked on the beach, watched the most beautiful sunset in the world, and fell madly in love.

Maggie was a great companion for Sam. Smart, easygoing, and very supportive. He could talk to her about his ideas and she would not only listen but also encourage him. The idea she liked most was an interesting one. Something about using a person's own blood to attack cancer cells. Sam was convinced that if a person's blood was combined with someone else's blood that wasn't compatible, if the combination of the two was just right, one person's blood cells would fight not only the other blood cells but the foreign bodies in their system as well, including the cancer. But the real break came when Pfizer merged with a Swiss firm and Sam was let go. Thank God he never told anyone there about what he was working on or they would have owned it.

With Maggie's help, Sam Mueller raised three hundred thousand dollars, took on a partner, and started Immunicate. His blood idea was in the right direction but it didn't work properly; it knocked out cancer cells but attacked the other organs, too, and the body's immune system went into overdrive, killing everything. Something had to be done to make the blood combination work against the disease without working against the rest of the body. The answer turned out to be common amino acids.

Sam and his partner, Ben Wasser, spent an entire year injecting the blood with different aminos. With the help of computers they tried millions of combinations. There were so many months where they felt it was not going to work. And then on the night of June 30, 2014, they put together alanine, isoleucine, proline, and tryptophan. Four common amino acids that had never been combined before, certainly not in this precise measurement.

Two years later, over ninety-four percent of the participants in the human trials were cancer-free. There were still rare cancers that did not respond, but all the big ones were knocked out, and the success was so overwhelming that trials were stopped early and the drug was available to the general population by the spring of 2016.

CHAPTER TWO

Kathy Bernard was just five years old when she heard about the cure for cancer. It meant very little to her, although she wondered if her grandfather would benefit. She didn't really like her grandfather, but she didn't really like anyone. She was voted angriest girl in her sixth-grade class.

Some of the reasons were obvious—divorce, a lot of fighting in the family, a stepbrother who was a freeloader, a verbally abusive mother—but there was something else. Something that she felt even as a small child watching her family move down the ladder. Her father and mother both losing their jobs, owing more money than they had, her birthdays becoming less and less of an event. She simply felt that her generation was getting the short end of the American dream. And she wasn't the only one her age who felt that way.

Kathy started hanging around with a gang when she got into her teens. Not a typical gang—these kids didn't kill each other or go to prison or even get arrested. They were smart and pissed. They all felt they were getting screwed by their country. They didn't hate any particular race, although if you mentioned the "legal" illegals, you would start a fight. What they really hated the most was the whole idea that their lives were going to be tougher than those of their parents—something that had never happened before in America.

When Kathy was very young, her father, Stewart Bernard, seemed secure in his job, but that was only because she didn't really understand the situation. He worked, like his father before him, for General Motors. But unlike his father, the last ten years of Stewart's employment were filled with uncertainty. The family moved from Missouri, where he had a job building Chevy vans, to Kansas, where he worked on Malibus, to Tennessee, where he had the misfortune to build Saturns, which GM decided to just stop making altogether.

The whole concept of an American car for which there was no haggling on price, for which the dealers were like your friends, and for which the craftsmanship took on a European feel had been such a rush when it was first introduced in 1990. And twenty years later Stewart Bernard was on the factory floor the day they announced the brand was finished. For all intents and purposes, so was he. The family moved again, this time to Indianapolis, where Stewart took a job with Goodyear Tire & Rubber. After five years, when that job ended, he was out of options. He wound up working at a Jiffy Lube, and then one day Kathy saw her dad dressed in that stupid outfit, his hands and face covered with grease, and she snapped. *How in God's name did this happen? And what does this mean for me?*

At a quarter to ten Brad Miller's birthday party ended. The older folks didn't much like to stay out past ten-thirty. They also didn't travel alone. It was a rare sight to see anyone past seventy driving by themselves. Several companies even marketed something that people had tried twenty years earlier to get into the fast lane on freeways: the fake passenger. But these new ones looked really good. You could get them in any color, though mulatto and Hispanic were still the favorites. They had the most realistic faces you could imagine and they were lightweight, so they could easily be taken from the car to the home. You would have to touch one to know it wasn't a real person, and you certainly could never tell in a speeding car.

When placed in a house, the fakes made the residence look occupied. In the beginning they deterred almost any burglar, but as the bad guys got hip to the fakes, the fakes had to be improved, and the moving mouth was a big step forward. If people looked through a window and saw a large figure talking, most didn't want to break in to find out if he was real.

The fake business in general had become huge: fake protection, fake friends, fake life, and fake love. It was getting so good that the word "virtual" was virtually dropped. If someone said he was going to Tahiti for a week, the first question was usually, "The real one?"

New kinds of fakes were coming on the market all the time, and some of them were children. People who could afford it found a Japanese company that made children who were as real as pets. They didn't grow; you could buy them at age five and they would stay that way. However, an unexpected issue popped up: People fell in love with them but got bored at the same time. Apparently, if the child didn't get older, the adult would lose interest. The company tried putting out a model that gradually aged, but the cost was prohibitive.

The pet children also presented another problem: pedophilia. Certainly pedophiliacs could enter virtual worlds or buy any number of artworks or movies or photos to titillate their fancy. But people drew the line at their owning a fake child. That was why a law was passed that required a permit to purchase a robot that looked younger than eighteen.

Fortunately, Brad Miller had no propensities toward children. The only fake person he owned was Lola, a six-foot-tall Hispanic woman whom he would either put in his passenger seat or prop up in his kitchen. Robot research proved Hispanic females were as effective a deterrent as a man. The studies were done by a company that specialized in fake Latino women, but still.

As Brad headed home with Lola in the front seat and two of his real friends, Herb Fine and Jack Eller, in the back, his mind started to wander. He missed his wife, who had died seven years earlier, but he felt great physically, certainly for his age, and he had no real material wants. He owned his condo outright, and with Social Security, plus his retirement from the Los Angeles Department of Water & Power, he could pay his bills. The hair transplants that had cost him a fortune in his thirties turned out to be his best investment. Fifty years later he still had something to comb. And his posture was still that of a younger man; the older-age stoop he had always been afraid of had never come.

He did desire a girlfriend and felt something might be wrong with him when he occasionally looked at Lola the wrong way, but other than that, he was doing as well as could be expected. Sometimes, though, he cursed the memory drugs that were making Alzheimer's a thing of the past. It was funny how people could get nostalgic for anything, even a disease. "Remembering the bad things," Brad would say, "is not such a plus."

"Hey, schmuck!" Herb said. "You're going past my complex, wake up!"

Brad pulled over to a gated apartment building. Almost everything was gated where the older folks lived. Some places had a human inside a guard shack; other complexes, like the one Herb lived in, had gates and cameras and sometimes a robot figure, but no live person.

Brad drove up to the camera. Herb rolled down the window and looked straight into the lens, and after a second the gate opened. "I swear to God," Herb said, "these eye things give me the worst headache. They can't be good for you."

"They don't do any harm," Jack told him. "If you've got a headache, you're not peeing enough."

"I'm peeing fine! What are you, the Internet?" Herb got out of the car. "Happy birthday, Brad."

"Thanks, Herb. Are you going to play golf tomorrow?"

"Seven o'clock."

"Meet you at seven." And Brad drove off, leaving Herb to go through one more eye check to get in the door.

"You're going to give me a tumor!" he yelled at the machine.

Jack Eller didn't live in a gated anything. He was the poorest of Brad's friends and still lived in a retirement home with no protection and no real services to speak of. Eller had never married. He'd lived with a woman for twelve years and helped raise her son, but when that relationship broke up he never met anyone else. It didn't bother him that much—he was one of those people who were okay being alone—but Jack made a fatal mistake moneywise. He did not diversify. He put all his retirement back into the company he worked for, a successful energy business based out of Houston, Texas. When its stock went from 190 to 3, Jack was wiped out. And when the company was sold for nothing, that was exactly what he was left with.

He found other employment, but it never compared to the good years, and now he waited each month for his Social Security check. It was his lifeline.

One day, years earlier, when Jack Eller was turning sixty, he ran into the boy he'd helped raise. The boy, now seventeen, didn't recognize him at first, but even when he did he showed no interest. Jack couldn't get over how angry the kid was and he had no idea that the boy had joined the "resentment gangs"—the same gangs Kathy Bernard hung out with. By 2023 you could find them in every city in America.

Kathy Bernard would be considered pretty by almost any standard, but she certainly didn't feel that way herself. At nineteen years old she looked twenty-four, stood almost five foot eight, and weighed 118 pounds. She had beautiful black hair that she wore long, and with pale skin and light green eyes, she looked almost European. Kathy seemed to go out of her way to play down her looks, but the few times she let it all out, it even surprised *her*.

One of those times was when she went with Brian Nelson, her boyfriend, to a frat party. Kathy had met Brian a year earlier and liked him; nothing amazing, but he was cute and he went to college, something Kathy could not afford at that point in her life and something she envied. Kathy's situation at home was pretty bleak; her father barely had enough money to pay his mortgage, so when she graduated high school, furthering her education was not even discussed. She went to work in a restaurant, which was miserable, but at least it brought in some income. She was determined to get a real estate license one day and made that her goal, but for now her life was all about tips and dreams.

That night, waiting for Brian, Kathy came downstairs dressed in a short black skirt, high heels, and ruby red lipstick. Her father almost had a heart attack. "Where are you going?" he asked, already knowing, but that was all he could blurt out.

"You know where."

Stewart had mixed emotions. He wanted to tell her never to dress like that again and to always dress like that again. He knew Kathy was no girly girl and sometimes he even wondered if she liked boys at all. But when he saw this side of her, he was amazed. She looked like someone else's daughter. "You look beautiful, Kathy. You look beautiful and mature."

"Thanks."

"Has Brian seen you dressed up like this before?"

"Yes."

"Has he seen you undressed?"

"What?" Kathy heard it but couldn't believe this would be the time for *that* discussion.

"I just meant . . ."

"I know what you meant. Don't worry about that. I'm the last woman on the planet that wants to bring a kid into this world."

Her father said nothing. It's funny how an answer can relieve you and bother you at the same time. He knew she was saying that she hated the thought of being a mother and wouldn't have a baby no matter what. And yet he didn't understand her dark side and felt helpless that he couldn't do anything about it. This was one of the big disadvantages of not having a woman in the house. But Kathy's mother had never had a clue how to raise a kid, so neither Stewart nor Kathy were really surprised when she left. Someone else might have been nice, but her father had never met that person.

At that moment the door announced who was there. Stewart opened it and looked at Brian Nelson. *Another angry prick,* he thought, but he had to admit Brian was not as bad as some of the others.

"Hello, Mr. Bernard."

"Hello, Brian."

"Is Kathy here?"

"No, you're going with me." Brian just looked at him.

"What?"

"That's a joke, Brian."

"Oh. That's a good one."

Before Brian had to think of something else to say, Kathy came out from the kitchen. "Holy shit!" was what Brian almost blurted out. Fortunately, all he managed was "Hi. You look very nice."

"What time are you going to be home?"

"Late," Kathy said. "And don't track us. Please."

"Don't be silly," her father answered, but of course he would. GPS had been embedded for years into every gadget and appliance in the world. You had to make an effort *not* to know where people were.

Brian put his Chinese sports car in "D" and floored it. The whine of the electric motor replaced the eight-cylinder growl of years back. These cars could do zero to sixty in under three seconds.

After years of accident rates declining in America, the dominance of the electric car reversed that. They were so fast off the line that many of them came with governors on the motor to reduce speeds from a standing start, but guys would remove those for three hundred bucks. As Kathy was forced back into her seat, she asked, "What's the difference between this and the Japanese one?"

"Twenty thousand dollars."

"Jesus, so why would anyone buy the other?"

"They're not."

The difference between Japanese, Chinese, Korean, German, and the one American nameplate was negligible. You could still pay more for finer leather and real wood, but the basics were the same. The robots that built them were all alike and the parts were interchangeable.

Parts in cars had been reduced from hundreds to just a few. One electric motor and one gear, and it either worked or it didn't. It was really hard to distinguish what was under the hood anymore, although the very upscale car companies—Rolls-Bentley, for example—claimed they used gold wiring in their motors that conducted electricity faster and didn't heat up as much. All a waste of money. But really rich people bought it, the same kind of people who paid thousands of dollars for gold speaker wire when that was still available.

The one area where money *did* buy you something in an automobile was safety. Advanced materials, the kind used in jet fighters, provided better protection in a head-on crash, and you paid extra for that. But even the cheapest car was safer than anything made before, and although the accident rate was up because of excessive speed, more people survived.

"I thought you were going to buy the one with the solar roof?"

"This is all my dad wanted to spend. And as long as I'm living at home, I don't give a shit about the electric bill, so this is fine."

"It's a nice car," Kathy said. "I wish I had one."

CHAPTER THREE

For Sam Mueller's fifty-fifth birthday, his wife was planning a surprise party at their house on Turks and Caicos. It was hard to fly in a hundred friends and keep it a secret and the fact is, she hadn't, but Sam pretended he didn't know. He told Maggie he was going to play golf and wouldn't be home before six. The private planes had been arriving all day. The guest list was as prominent as one would imagine for someone who had cured cancer—a few longtime friends, but mostly dignitaries and senators and some entertainers. There was even a holographic message on the way from the pope.

Dr. Mueller had never had another breakthrough that rivaled the cancer cure, but what would one expect? After the theory of relativity, didn't Einstein basically putter around the rest of his life? Mueller did try some other combinations of aminos on mental illness, but came up short. With all the advancements made in medicine, there were still too many people walking around just plain nuts. When science thought they had solved one thing, like the miracle drug that helped cure schizophrenia, something else crept in. The newest malady was called "virtual dementia"; people who had it could no longer distinguish between what was real and what wasn't. Scientists had known this was coming, they'd seen glimpses of it since the beginning of the new century, but no one realized just how serious it was. It was one thing to try to get someone to stop playing games and talk to the people standing in front of them; it was another when they absolutely couldn't. People with this disease didn't even seem to register when real people were there; it made them frightened and angry.

Sam Mueller worked on a cure for that for years, but with no success. He still went to Immunicate's headquarters every day, but mostly he was just a big celebrity, drawing huge crowds at speaking events, universities, and pay-per-view holographic presentations. He wished he had another big thing in him, but still, deep down, it very much pleased him that when he died, his obituary would read THE MAN WHO CURED CANCER. That always made him smile.

He was also rich beyond anything he could have ever imagined. Unlike a product that would make billions for a number of years and then go generic, his cancer cure was a code. A combination of common substances that could never be used without paying a royalty. In 2020, Immunicate was offered $130 billion from a German-French pharmaceutical giant for forty-nine percent of the company. After everyone was paid out and all taxes taken care of, Dr. Sam Mueller walked away with $40 billion, and still owned the company to boot. He bought homes, gave to charities, set up foundations and scholarships, bought more homes, and was one of the first five people to own the Gulfstream 10A, the "jet that flies itself." And that wasn't just a slogan. This was the first private aircraft in the world not to require an onboard pilot. The plane could not only fly itself from start to finish, but as a backup it had remote pilots in Denver checking every minute of the flight and intervening if necessary, which it never was.

Dr. Mueller's two children—Patty, fifteen, and Mark, thirteen—did not attend his birthday party. Mark was at a fancy private school in Switzerland that the Muellers had learned about when they sold their company. They had made a lot of German, Swiss, and French friends and adopted some of their rich habits, including sending their child to an elite boarding school 140 kilometers from Geneva that the most privileged children in the world attended.

Patty was in school in the States, but she didn't want to miss classes. She was also a little embarrassed about being the daughter of the man who cured cancer. Normally that would be something to be proud of, but to many young people, the same kinds of kids Kathy Bernard hung out with, the cancer cure was a major factor contributing to the never-ending lives of the older generation. One of them even taunted Patty, saying, "If it wasn't for your dad, my grandfather would be dead by now, but instead we're paying for him to eat through a tube. Thanks a lot." Patty was still proud of her father, and she certainly was not like any normal kid—she would never have to worry about money for the rest of her life—but she wanted to be cool. And the cool kids hated the "olds."

As the guests arrived from all over the world, they were impressed by Sam Mueller's spread on the island. And these people had seen everything. There was a main house that was approximately twenty-five thousand square feet and two guesthouses close to twenty thousand square feet each. The Muellers could easily accommodate two hundred people in the type of luxury reserved for heads of state. Each private suite consisted of three bedrooms, a living room, a den, three bathrooms, and a butler. There were complimentary health screenings performed by doing nothing more than giving one drop of blood from your finger, although not everyone chose to do that. Guests were treated to any sport they desired and the meals were legendary. People would say, "What in God's name is this guy going to do when he turns sixty? Buy Italy?"

But what Sam enjoyed the most were the rousing discussions that took place after dinner on a large veranda that overlooked the Caribbean. This was where the movers and shakers told all: what the future held, what to invest in, doomsday scenarios—the whole damn thing. This was where Sam Mueller had first gotten the news of the biological attack that had taken place twelve years earlier.

In the summer of 2018 two things happened. A heat wave swept over the East Coast, unprecedented in the United States, and caused temperatures to remain close to 105 during the day for almost six weeks. Global warming was not challenged anymore, not after the Lambert Glacier in Antarctica melted three hundred years before anyone thought it would. Sure, there were a few scientists who would say man had nothing to do with it, but it didn't matter anymore, it was happening. Sometimes during very cold winters, there were still people who pooh-poohed global warming altogether.

"Look outside, it's a blizzard," they would say. But of course the terrible winters were a sign of even further erosion. And when the eastern seaboard had forty-five consecutive days above one hundred degrees, the skeptics melted away, along with everything else.

And something else happened late that summer. The United States had always said that the likelihood of a nuclear or biological attack was greater than fifty percent. And people always thought about it the same way they thought about earthquakes: They knew something was coming, but what could they do? Well, it wasn't a nuclear attack, but on August 15, 2018, people started getting sick with flulike symptoms in San Francisco. Before anyone realized it, a smallpox virus had contaminated the city. The government's best guess was that five or six terrorists had come into the country already infected with the disease and worked their way through crowded streets, department stores, schools, supermarkets—everywhere it could be spread. Before it was over, twenty thousand people were sick, the city came to a halt, the stock market fell fifty percent, and the fear level increased tenfold.

The government made a point of catching who they could and claiming it was an isolated incident, but it had happened nonetheless. Most of the country was relieved it took place in San Francisco, and not New York or Los Angeles, but they felt it was only a matter of time before it happened again, and this time in a much bigger city. The Department of Health and Human Services poured hundreds of millions of dollars into developing a new smallpox vaccine that could be given instantly to large populations. A new kind of delivery system.

Immunicate was one company that was awarded an $80 million contract to try to come up with an idea. The smallpox vaccine had been around for over a hundred years, but since the disease was cured, no one received it anymore. Now that smallpox had reared its ugly head again, the government thought there must be an easier way to immunize people.

Mueller's company worked on several fronts—putting it in food, spraying it as an aerosol, using it in an eyedrop—but nothing took off. The old vaccine was as good as it was going to get, and as each year passed with no further attacks, the government stopped the program. They just went back to inoculating people the same way they had in the 1930s.

Brad Miller, after dropping off his friends, finally pulled up to the guard shack of his retirement community.

"Good evening, Mr. Miller."

"Hello, Jose."

"Happy birthday."

"Thanks. When's yours?"

"Not until December."

"Well, make sure to remind me so I can get you something."

"I will, sir. There's a package for you. I had it scanned and I put it in your receiving slot."

"Who's it from, do you know?"

"I know, sir, but it's a surprise for your birthday. It's safe, don't worry."

"Thanks, Jose. See you tomorrow."

Brad continued the drive to his small condo, nestled among three hundred others in one of the more upscale retirement villages in the area. The garage read the info on his car and opened quickly. He drove in but still was surrounded by cement until the eye detector recognized him. Then a second door opened and he drove into the real garage.

The one thing Brad had never liked about his home was the smell. It was too clean, like someone had just been there with deodorizer. It was the materials used in construction. Every item was stain proofed, which produced a chemical odor that was very hard to get rid of. Many older folks had lost their sense of smell to the point of not being aware of such things, but not Brad. He had always had a great nose.

He went into the kitchen and checked the receiving slot near the side door. There was a package nicely wrapped, but he didn't see a card. Was it from the condo association? Maybe one of his friends back east? He took off the paper, opened the box, and there was a blue sweater. He held it up to see what it would feel like. It was wool, which he hated. Wool made him itch, so it must be from someone who didn't know him very well. Then he saw an envelope with the word "Dad" on it. *Of course, who else?*

Brad had not spoken to his son, Tom, for almost two years. They had even stopped leaving their once-a-year recorded birthday messages. No big moment had caused it, at least not one that he could think of.

Tom was forty-five, married with one child, with whom Brad had almost no contact. Even though his granddaughter lived in San Diego, he had only seen her twice in the last five years. Brad had never liked Crystal, his son's wife, and she felt the same way about him. He made the mistake of telling Tom on his wedding day that he was marrying the wrong woman. That put a crimp in their relationship.

Dad, the note said, *I hope you're well. Happy 80th, enjoy the sweater. Love, Tom.*

His father had mixed feelings. He liked the thought, hated the gift. He had complained about wool his entire life; did his son have no idea about that, or was this some sort of message? He decided to call Tom and thank him personally. When he told the refrigerator, the appliance where all central communications were located, to get his son on the line, it quickly told him that all the numbers it had for Tom Miller were no longer active. *What a prick. He doesn't even give me his right number.* Brad put the sweater back in the box. It would be an early birthday gift for Jose. He hoped Jose didn't hate wool, too.

CHAPTER FOUR

Matthew Bernstein woke up at 5:35 A.M. He didn't need an alarm. No matter what time he went to bed, he still got up within three minutes of the same time every day he was in the White House.

President Bernstein was the first Jew to be elected president of the United States. The election of 2028 had been a contentious one. A woman, Margaret Sandor, was the favorite, but she did much worse in the mini-debates than anyone had predicted, and one time, when she was sure she was out of range, she said, "That's a Jew for you." Even though more people agreed with that sentiment than not, the remark revealed a dual personality and that turned off voters, who still would rather have some-one they thought they knew, even if it meant that person was a Jew.

Bernstein had always played down his Jewishness. His mother was Catholic, and he was never bar mitzvahed. He didn't look, act, or seem Jewish in any obvious way. His friends called him Matt, and there was even a time in college where he was going to change Bernstein to Barnes, but he didn't. In the Jewish religion, if your father is Jewish but your mother isn't, theoretically you are not a Jew. But if you're running for president of the United States, even living on the same street as a Jew makes you one, so having a Jewish father was more than enough to get into the history books as the first Jew to hold the highest office in the land.

Before he entered politics, Bernstein had made and lost a lot of money in the private sector. He founded a solar panel company that built new generation panels for home use and did very well for about five years. But he turned down an offer to sell and then watched an Indonesian company come up with a newer technology that overnight made what he did almost obsolete. He eventually sold his business for half of what he had turned down and took what money he did make, then ran for Congress in 2022. He won, rose quickly to chairman of the Finance Committee, and then became the first Jewish Speaker of the House. The first "Jewish" was something he was hearing a lot in politics, so why not try for the presidency?

He met his wife, Betsy, in college. She was an economics major and both of her parents were Jews. Matthew loved going to her house; he loved her mother; she was the mother he always wished he had. "She's so supportive of you," he would say. "Are you sure she's Jewish?"

They married young and both of them went to work. They seemed like the perfect couple, lookswise. Neither was especially attractive. Betsy stood five foot four and had brown hair and brown eyes, which were closer together than she liked. She thought it made her look more ethnic than her friends, but Betsy had a very good instinct about what she could change and what she couldn't, and spacing her eyes out was not an option.

Her husband had no ethnic features. A very average-looking man, five foot eleven, a hundred and eighty pounds. Before he was president, people always guessed he was an accountant. His hair thinned out early, but he never lost it, and unless someone saw his bald spot first, they would think of him as a man with hair. Bernstein wore glasses, not because he had to—there were all kinds of options to see clearly without them—but because he thought they made him look smarter. And they did. He wasn't handsome, but he did look smart.

A year after they married they had a child. The baby was born with a rare genetic defect. The little boy's heart was not fully developed and quit working before he reached the age of one. Betsy got pregnant again two years later but lost the pregnancy, and that was it for kids. They chose not to try again.

Betsy never loved the idea of her husband running for president, but she turned out to be his strongest asset. She was whip smart and probably gave better stump speeches than he did. And when Margaret Sandor let out her

"Jew" comment, it was Betsy who would not let it die. Her husband played it down, always taking the fake high road, but Betsy made it her mantra. "Have we learned nothing as a country?" she would say. "Do we really want a president who has hate in her heart for *any* American? How would you know that she didn't hate *you*?" The people loved that line.

On election night they both watched in silence as Matthew Bernstein became the forty-seventh president of the United States. Polling had become so precise that it took all the fun out of elections, but there was always a chance, remote as it was, that something unexpected would happen. In this case it was exactly as the polls had predicted, and at 11:30 P.M., Eastern Standard Time, Ohio put Bernstein over the top. Obviously he was very happy, but he also felt somewhat powerless.

By the quarter-century mark, almost three trillion dollars was going just to pay the *interest* on the national debt. There was no longer room for any meaningful programs; it seemed that the president's job was just to keep the ship afloat. Initiating any great changes had become impossible. It was just too expensive. And Bernstein, still in his early fifties, also sensed that the younger generations were losing interest in their country. It had always been warned that the giant debt would fall to them, but until it actually did, young people still held out hope for the American dream. Once they were being taxed higher, earning less, and receiving less government assistance than their parents, the resentment level soared. Bernstein tried to address this in his campaign, promising to ease the burden on the young, but if you pissed off the seniors, you didn't get elected to anything, so it was difficult to take too strong a stand. He wound up where all presidential candidates did, somewhere in the mushy middle.

Brad Miller woke up at three in the morning with a pain in his chest. *It must be indigestion,* he thought. His last tests had all been fine, and although he didn't have perfect arteries, he was on so much advanced medication that the thought of a heart attack was far from his mind.

He got up, had some water, sat down, and waited for the pain to subside. After ten minutes he pressed the emergency button on the fridge and a man appeared on the screen.

"What is the nature of your emergency?"

"How do you know if you're having a heart attack?"

"I can tell you. Place your right hand in the sending device and sit comfortably." Brad placed his hand in the silicone sleeve and sat down, his chest feeling very tight. After two minutes the man was back. "You're not having a heart attack."

"It sure feels that way."

"Where's the pain?"

"Where do you think? In my foot."

"I mean where *exactly* is the pain? In your chest, in your arm?"

"Right in the center of my chest."

"Sir, I want you to jump up and down ten times."

"Are you crazy? I'll die!"

"You're not having a heart attack. Please jump up and down ten times."

Brad did as he was told. He felt like an idiot jumping up and down in his kitchen, but after the eighth time he let out the biggest belch of his entire life. It was so loud he thought his neighbors would hear it. The man on the screen smiled. "Do we feel better?"

"I don't know about you, but yeah, the pain seems to be subsiding."

"Is there anything else I can help you with?"

"No. Is this paid by insurance?"

"Yes, sir. There is a five-hundred-dollar deductible but everything else is covered."

"I'm curious, how much is the whole bill?"

"Two thousand, sir."

"Wow. Well, I guess it's worth five hundred to know I shouldn't have pastrami with orange juice."

"I would concur. Do we need anything else?"

"I'm okay, how about you?"

"I'm sorry?"

"Never mind. Let's hang up before it costs me another five hundred."

The screen went blank and Brad returned to bed. He lay there not quite understanding how the government could afford fifteen hundred dollars because he ate like a pig. No one else could understand it, either. It was a magic trick whose magic had faded decades ago. But as long as they paid, so be it. That was the mantra for the older folks.

CHAPTER FIVE

It was one o'clock in the morning when the frat party broke up. Brian and Kathy went to an after-party, mostly consisting of college seniors, and Kathy drank a little and tried smokeable steroids, which made her feel all-powerful and quite angry for about ten minutes before she got dizzy and came down. The boys liked to orgasm on it; the girls just got irritated.

Kathy listened as everyone there just bitched about what was coming next. All generations were disillusioned, but for different reasons. Kathy's grandparents had rebelled because they didn't want money, they wanted free love and a free life. Her parents never had time to rebel, mainly because her grandparents got their wish. Her generation had different issues. They *did* want money, they wanted it all, but knew they could never get it. They were growing up in the flat world, and it was obvious that America had to move down to meet everyone else halfway. They were the first ones riding the pendulum back, and they hated it.

Even after college, kids were living with their folks or grandparents, longer than ever before. America was becoming like Italy, where if parents didn't throw their children out, chances are they would never leave. Some parents liked that, but most wanted their life back and couldn't stand the sound of the retro subwoofers rumbling through their house.

Brian was too drunk to drive Kathy home. It wasn't a decision; the car simply wouldn't start. All cars now came with a Breathalyzer. You could defeat it by getting someone else to blow into the steering wheel, but the penalties were so great that people refused. A man in Buffalo blew for a kid and the kid killed someone, and they arrested the man and put him in prison for life. No one tried to fake out a Breathalyzer after that.

Kathy breathed into the device and the car started, but even though the car thought she was fine, she didn't want to drive. The steroids were screwing with her vision, so Brian took the wheel. "I'm really okay," he said, "I'll take you home." And then he backed into a garbage can.

"I'll call my dad."

"No, he already hates me. Telling him I'm too fucked up is not a way to make him feel better about us."

"I won't tell him that." Kathy pressed the dash and her father answered, sounding like he was fast asleep.

"Hello?"

"Daddy?"

"'Daddy'? What kind of trouble are you in?"

"I'm not in trouble."

"The last time you called me 'Daddy,' I had to go to the police station."

"Brian and I had a glass of champagne and I just thought it was safer if you picked us up."

"A glass of champagne? Will the car start?"

"Yes, but I thought it was safer." Her father wasn't buying this.

"Take a cab."

"We don't have the money. We weren't expecting to pay for that."

"Tell them I'll pay when you get here."

"They don't do that anymore. It's all in advance, remember?"

"Jesus, Kathy, it's two o'clock. If the car will start, drive it."

"Dad, don't make me beg."

Kathy and Brian just sat in the car until her father got there. Brian couldn't help but stare at her, she looked so beautiful that night. "Troubled beautiful" is what his friends called her, but they were all jealous. Kathy was the most interesting girl at the party, by far.

Possibly because he was drunk, possibly because he couldn't help himself, Brian leaned over, kissed her, and told her that he was in love with her. That was the first time he said it. She smiled, gave him a quick kiss back, but didn't say the words. Now he felt terrible. *Why did I say it? Did I ruin it forever?* He was so angry at himself. At that moment her dad arrived. She got out of the car and asked Brian if he wanted to be taken home.

"No, thanks. I'll go back inside until the champagne wears off."

"Champagne, my ass," Stewart said. "Go inside and sleep it off."

Kathy and her father drove home without talking. He was too tired to make obligatory conversation and she was still feeling the effect of the drug, even though it was supposed to last only a few minutes. It made her feel extra angry. Not at her father—after all, there he was, unemployed, no future, and still getting out of bed at two in the morning to pick her up. She was angry at everything else.

Her grandfather used to tell her how he stopped the war by rioting and filling the streets and how it really meant something. But it was different then. You had options in a war. You could lose, win, declare victory even if you didn't win; you could turn the fighting over to the country you invaded. Lots of options. But now, massive debt was something else. All you could do was pay it off or not. Or you could keep delaying the problem, hoping that the next generation would invent something to take care of it. But as advanced as science was becoming, no one had come up with a debt machine. Finally Stewart spoke. "I won't be home until late tomorrow night."

"Why?"

"I've got a new job."

"Really? That's wonderful! What kind of job?" Kathy sounded so hopeful. Her father was dipping dangerously into his life savings and really needed a break.

"It's not that great."

"What is it?"

"They're adding a person to the automated security staff at the city college."

Kathy wanted to cry. A security guard? In her mind that was worse than a grease monkey, but she tried her best to sound positive. "Wow. That's good news. It'll give you something to do."

And they drove the rest of the way home in silence.

When Brian Nelson woke the next morning he felt awful. Physically and mentally. Hungover, hating his crummy college, knowing it would only buy him a few more years before the shit hit the fan. He had a car his parents had given him and that was it. One possession.

College had become meaningless to so many kids. The few who had privilege went to the expensive ones and that was still fun, and it was good to have a degree if you were going to work in a white-collar job, but it guaranteed you nothing. If the parents couldn't pay, most kids didn't go. The student loans took so long to pay back that young people really had to examine if it was worth it. There were all kinds of calculations that would tell them exactly how much they had to earn and how many years it would take to pay it back, and many kids decided that a lower-paying job, in the long run, would earn them more than a college education and a huge debt.

Brian had no idea what he wanted to do with his life. His father was a pharmacist, but he couldn't do that; that job was being replaced by pharmaceutical assistants monitoring automated dispensing machines, and the pay was terrible. He didn't want to drive a truck, the way his grandfather did. His grandfather was always going from company to company and bitched about never having any security. Besides, Brian had never liked his grandfather and certainly did not want to emulate him. And he resented that whatever he wound up doing, a portion of his earnings was always going to go to his grandfather and all the rest of them. "He never even sent me a birthday present," Brian would say, "and now I have to pay for his wheelchair."

CHAPTER SIX

Sam Mueller had received so many honors in his life, he had a separate bungalow just to house them. And he knew all the living presidents—in fact, two of them were alive because of him—but he had yet to meet Matthew Bernstein.

President Bernstein liked to make calls himself. He got a great kick out of appearing on someone's screen. No secretary, no Secret Service, just him. Many people thought it was a joke. There were pretty good devices that had come on the market around 2018 that could change your appearance when you made a call. You could even change your sex if you wished. So when Bernstein called Dr. Mueller the very first time, Mueller thought someone might be playing a prank. Like the call he got a year earlier from Marilyn Monroe. "How did you get my number?" Sam asked.

"I have everyone's number," President Bernstein replied.

"I don't have time for this. But I must say, this is a very good program. It has the voice and face down pat."

"That's because I'm real." At that moment Allen, one of Dr. Mueller's assistants, came rushing into his office.

"It's him!"

"Who?"

"The President!"

"How do you know?"

"There's no digital manipulation. We just got confirmation. And I called a special number and the Secret Service verified he's talking to you . . . *now*!" Dr. Mueller motioned for Allen to leave.

"Mr. President . . . I'm sorry, I thought it was a joke."

"So does everyone," the President laughed.

"Well, it's an honor to talk to you. How may I be of assistance?"

"Are you going to be in Washington anytime soon?"

"I wasn't planning on it, but I certainly could be."

"How about Wednesday?"

"You would like me there on Wednesday?"

"Yes. I always ask people if they are going to be in Washington anytime soon. It's more polite than saying, 'Be here on Wednesday.'"

"What time, sir?"

"How's noon?"

"Is that another question where the answer is meaningless?"

"Yes, please be here at noon. I'm going to have a lunch for a few people in the health industry. I would like to talk over some new ideas. I'd love you to be present."

"I'll be there."

"We'll cover all costs."

"That's fine, sir, I'm happy to cover it myself."

"Well, good. You have more money than us anyway. By the way, I just decided, this is the last call I'm making myself. The thrill is gone."

"Well, I hope I'm not the reason."

"Of course not, you just happened to be there when the fun disappeared. See you at noon on Wednesday." The President smiled and the screen went blank. No matter who you were, whether you liked the man or not, it was still a thrill to get a call from the president of the United States.

Maggie Mueller was very excited. "The White House? What do I wear to the White House?"

"He didn't say anything about spouses, honey."

"Oh, screw you," Maggie half joked. "I'm going. I don't have to sit in the meeting but I'm going to the White House." At that moment Dr. Mueller's watch buzzed. It was one of his assistants. Sam never could get over this. His father had given him old comic books when he was a young boy to encourage him to read. His favorites were *Richie Rich* and *Dick Tracy*. And now here he was, almost as rich as Richie and with a watch exactly like Dick's. What would have happened if his father had given him *Wonder Woman*? In any case, there was his assistant's face on his wrist, always starting out with the same question.

"Am I bothering you, sir?"

"What is it?" Mueller asked, making sure he had nothing in his hand when he turned it to look at the watch. As silly as it sounded, when the device first hit the mainstream, people would get so excited they would forget they had coffee in their hands and dump it into their laps like in a Three Stooges movie. On the very first watches, Apple T&T even had a video warning before the face would appear, just in case someone scalded himself, but people hated that. The company changed it to a warning on the box: "Make sure hands are free before answering." That was sufficient to release them from liability.

"The White House called to confirm the fifteenth at noon," Mueller's assistant said. "The invitation is for both you and the missus."

The one bad thing about the watches was that people could hear both sides of the conversation, unless the recipient wore an earpiece, which no one did. "See!" Maggie said.

"Thank you, Sarah, I'll make sure my wife is informed."

"Thank you, Dr. Mueller. Good-bye." And his watch went back to displaying the time. Sam put his arm around Maggie.

"I wouldn't go without you, you know that."

"You're so full of shit. But I'm still excited."

Why anyone wanted to be president of the United States became more and more of a mystery. Campaigns were endless, and the bubble one lived in was more like an MRI machine. It seemed that the entire job was raising money and trying not to say anything that could be construed as remotely controversial. And most of all, the ability to change the world was no longer part of the job.

Money makes the world go 'round and debt makes it stop in its tracks. Sure, a president could still fire weapons and was still commander in chief and the official spokesperson for the nation, but that wasn't the fun part. The fun part was making real changes that could affect generations to come. But that took money. A lot of it. Money that was no longer there.

Bernstein longed for the days of FDR, or even Barack Obama, where it was still possible and Congress would go deep into debt to give a president trillions to try to make things happen. But now the rules were changed. After the national debt passed one hundred percent of the gross national product, stiff new regulations were imposed on the executive branch.

Congress had always had the last word. But in previous administrations, the president still had the power of persuasion. Now the majority of Congress was elected with the promise of taking that power back. Successfully blaming past administrations for continuing to run America into the red, people running for the House or Senate convinced their constituencies that the White House was too powerful. That *that* was the cause of the problem. It was all bullshit, of course, but it led to a new era in gridlock. It was as if every member of Congress ran for his or her own presidency. Candidates never aligned themselves with the White House anymore, or even with their own party. They ran as individuals, on the notion of returning America to the people. What it really did was introduce a new kind of motionless government. Nothing got done. Denying new spending provided the House and Senate with the illusion of expressing the people's voice. But the people didn't want their lives and the nation's infrastructure to rust away. What they really wanted was somebody to make tough choices, really tough choices, which took a leader. And the one thing the legislative branch could never be was a leader. That was the president's job, and that was why Matthew Bernstein ran. And even if it was getting impossible to change things, he still wanted to try.

CHAPTER SEVEN

The first time it happened, no one thought anything more about it than they did about the random acts of violence that always occurred. In January of 2026, someone boarded a bus on its way to an Indian casino near Palm Desert, California, and shot twelve people, killing nine and injuring three. The odd thing was that the bus had thirty people on board, and anyone who appeared to be under forty was left untouched.

The shooter was a young man, twenty-six years old, and he was killed by the driver, so no one could ever talk to him to find out what was in his mind. His family and friends were interviewed and they came out with the usual stuff: "He seemed so quiet." "He was such a nice guy, a great neighbor." The couple who owned the Korean bakery even said they thought of him like a son. But upon further questioning it became clear they meant he was the *size* of their son, they weren't referring to how they felt about him.

Violence in 2026 was really the same as it had always been. There were gangs and murders and domestic disputes and robberies, all the stuff that never changes. The one group that did seem to grow in stature was the neo-Nazi gangs, the skinheads. These people hated everything America had become. And where blacks and Jews had always been number one and two on their list, the newly legalized Hispanics made them even more nuts. The "last of the true white people," as they called themselves, they realized they were never going to get America back, and all they could hope for was to make it really unpleasant for everyone else to live there.

But the bus massacre had nothing to do with that group. The shooter was white, but not a skinhead. Educated, with at least two years of college, he'd never been in trouble before. Everything ever written on his mobile devices was analyzed immediately.

In the new world, actually going to someone's home and seizing property was done last, since every single bit of communication lived forever, and all that was needed was a judge's order and it was all downloaded and scrutinized in the blink of an eye. People knew this, of course, and if they really wanted to communicate and have it never be known, they would do what their great-grandparents had done and write a letter, or meet in person, or just not tell anyone anything. But even if they didn't write down their intentions, the software used to analyze their communications was getting ultra-sophisticated. And where years ago someone who was going to murder his spouse might put the word "chloroform" into a search engine and have that as evidence in court, now programs were designed to come up with that same kind of incriminating evidence from everything you ever looked at.

If you committed a crime, every piece of reading material, every store you ever went to—either real or virtual—and everything you ever bought was analyzed at such lightning speed that law enforcement would have three really good theories before they ever went to your home. In the case of the bus murderer it was easier than most, as he wrote angry letters to his congressman complaining about the outrageous taxes he had to pay for health care even though he was never sick a day in his life. They also found old-fashioned letters to his mother saying that he could no longer give money to help with Grandma, as he had been demoted and his pay had been cut. That, along with his obsessive interest in everything Peter Pan, helped the computers come to a conclusion: This guy hated everything old.

Brad Miller hit the ball straight down the fairway. It went almost three hundred yards. Herb had just hit into the trees and was sixteen over par by the fifteenth hole. "I shouldn't have bet," Herb said.

"Don't worry, there's three holes to go. You want to press?"

"You're seven strokes ahead. You would actually need a real stroke for me to win." He took out fifty dollars. "Here, let's stop. I lose."

"Come on, finish the game," Brad said, taking the money. Brad pressed the button and the sixteenth hole lay before them. This hole was always windy, with a dogleg on the right and a huge sand trap on the left of the green. Brad addressed the ball.

"Wait," Herb said. "Let's not play with the wind today."

"Okay with me." Brad went to the control wall and turned off the breeze.

The Golf Depots, as they were called, were springing up everywhere. Invented in Japan, where space was always at a premium, they were open-air golf centers that consisted of one 350-yard hole. Every time someone completed it, he turned around and started the next. The putting green on hole one would become the tee on hole two. Scenery would change, wind would increase or die down, sand traps would emerge in different places, and you would get the exercise walking back and forth on the same hole. The centers, which took up approximately three square acres, could let ten foursomes play at the same time, all playing from the center outward.

The cost was minuscule compared to real golf, and what was also great was that it was safe. There had been some incidents in the past few years on public courses. Younger people hassling the "olds" for taking too much time or, in some cases, for even showing up at all. The Golf Depots had great security, welcomed an older clientele, and were a bargain compared to actually joining a club, which not only had prohibitive costs but didn't much like members over fifty.

When the game was finished they got into Brad's car. Brad had always liked to buy American, although that had become impossible. Even with the Ford-GM merger that took place years earlier, so many parts in those cars were made overseas that they were American in name only. Still, Brad felt good about driving his electric vehicle with the familiar two logos from the car companies he grew up knowing.

As he slid into the seat, which was molded to his body, the belts retracted, and a pleasant female voice asked him where he wanted to go. "Do you want to get something to eat?" he asked Herb.

"Sure, I could go for a pastrami sandwich."

Brad knew of one place somewhere toward downtown that had great pastrami, but he wasn't sure of the name or where it was. That's where Susie came in. That's what he called the voice of his car. "Susie, what's the name of the delicatessen somewhere off the Ten freeway near downtown?" Susie dutifully named off three delicatessens but none of them sounded familiar. "That's not it." Then Susie named another place that rang a bell. "That sounds familiar. Call them."

A voice came on the line, Hispanic sounding, but then again, every voice on the phone sounded Hispanic to Brad. "Is this the place with the great pastrami?"

"I can't hear you," the man said.

"Forget it." Brad hung up. "That's the right place. I recognize the accent. Take me there, honey." And Susie displayed the route, traffic conditions, alternate routes, time to destination, average speed, weather, and three rest stops along the way, something the dealer programmed in thinking Brad would need, which he really didn't.

"That's amazing," Herb said. "How did she figure out the restaurant?"

"She'll take all the restaurants in the area, look at their menus, check for reviews, and if pastrami comes up a lot, she'll tell me."

"Can you fuck her?"

"You actually can, but that was another four grand. And you have to stick your dick in the lighter."

About fifteen minutes later Brad's car pulled into a parking lot next to Amigos, a beat-up-looking diner, crowded to the gills, with a line snaking out the door. "This is the place?" Herb asked, a little reticent.

"This place has the best pastrami in town. Trust me, it's gotten raves. That's why there's a line."

"There's a line at the doctor's office, but no one's raving about that."

"Do you not want to go in?"

"No, I do. Come on."

They got out of the car and stood in line. They seemed to be the only ones over fifty. Certainly no one in that diner was anywhere near eighty years old. People made no eye contact with them, and as the line moved slowly toward the counter, Herb wondered if they should go elsewhere, but he didn't say anything. After thirty minutes they were facing the menu board, about to be served. "What are you gonna have?" Brad asked.

"Tuna fish."

"What?"

"What the hell do you think I'm gonna have? You think I stood in line for an hour for peas?"

They both placed their orders, two large pastrami sandwiches with cole slaw, pickles, and a dipping bowl of beef juice that would make the sandwiches fall apart in their mouths. They were told to go to a table and the food would be brought to them. They found a small table near the window and sat down, and at that moment two Hispanic men in their early twenties walked over. One of them said to Brad, "Get the fuck out of here, old man, this is my seat."

"No one was sitting here," Brad said.

Herb stood up. He was not in the mood to argue. "Maybe it *was* their seat."

"It wasn't. The table was empty."

"Get the fuck out of here, did you not hear me?"

A waitress appeared with the sandwiches and put them down, oblivious to what was going on. One of the young men picked up a sandwich and took a bite. "What the hell are you doing?" Brad was getting angry. "That's mine!"

"I don't think so, man. This is our table and it's our sandwich."

"I'm calling the manager."

"You fucking do that, Grandpa. Good idea. And when you're through we'll talk about it outside."

"Brad, let them have the sandwiches. I've lost my appetite."

"They're not having my sandwich. I paid for it, it's mine."

Brad went to find someone. Herb just wanted to disappear. He stood there not saying a word as Brad brought back a heavyset man, also Hispanic. Brad showed him the receipt. "We paid for these; these are ours."

The man looked at it and said something in Spanish to the young men. The three of them laughed and the two men decided to leave. "Eat your sandwiches, you old fuck," one of them said. "We'll see you later." They walked out of the diner. Herb was panicking.

"They're going to wait for us outside."

"Just eat," Brad said. "There's a lot of people here, they can't do anything."

"What are you, crazy? There are a lot of *Mexican* people here. They can do anything they want. I knew we shouldn't have come."

"Bullshit. It was your idea."

"It was my idea to get pastrami. Your goddamn car sent us to a prison."

Brad bit into his sandwich. He was worried about his safety but didn't show it. "Wow, this is good."

"It better be. It's our last meal."

They ate in silence, staring at the car through the window. They couldn't see the men; they were hoping they had left. This wasn't the first time Brad had felt picked on because of his age, but it was becoming more frequent. Herb, meanwhile, made up his mind never to try a new restaurant again. *Better to have the same old thing and not be stabbed.*

At ten o'clock at night, Stewart Bernard saw an alarm light go off that told him someone was breaking into the school gymnasium. The cameras confirmed it. It looked as if six boys were forcing the door open; one of them had a basketball in his hand. Stewart thought how silly this was. It was dark in there; how did they think they could play without lights?

He got on the Shuffle, the three-wheeled cart he took on his patrols, and headed down to the gym. When he arrived the door was open, and he heard the sound of a basketball and saw some dim lights. The boys had brought electric lanterns with them. Stewart stood there and smiled. This was harmless. They weren't stealing or disturbing the peace; they were just playing basketball. But he had a job to do, so he threw on the switch and the overheads lit up. The boys stopped and looked up to where Stewart was standing. "The gym is closed, boys. You're not allowed in here."

"We're just playing basketball," one of them yelled.

"I'm going to have to ask you to leave."

Stewart felt it before he heard it. A sharp pain in his collarbone. As he reached for his chest, he heard the explosion ricochet throughout the building. The kids were running up the stairs to the exit. Stewart dropped to the floor, feeling as though he was going to faint.

"What the fuck did you do that for?" he heard one of the boys say to another as they ran by him. Stewart really wanted to hear the answer but he blacked out. He lay there in a pool of blood until one of the robot vehicles sensed there was a door open and came to take a look. The next time he opened his eyes, he was in an operating room.

Kathy was home when her reading device blinked red. She knew what that was, but had never seen it before. All handheld devices had an emergency chip that could either send or receive an urgent message. The device displayed the words "Contact St. Peter's Hospital. Your father is hurt."

She was hoping against hope that maybe it was a prank, but hacking into an emergency chip had severe penalties and she didn't know anyone who would do that, anyway. She was frantic. She called Brian. They were both at the hospital within fifteen minutes.

Kathy looked pale and scared. Brian didn't know what to do other than support her. He hated hospitals—the smell literally made him sick. When Brian was five years old, he fell off a scooter and skinned his arm so badly he needed stitches. The doctor did it poorly and it became infected, and he had to spend a week in the hospital, sharing a room with a teenager who had broken his neck skiing. The infection wasn't what spooked him; it was seeing a boy in the bed next to him wearing a full body cast. It left an impression that hospitals were to be avoided at all costs. *Better to just die.*

When they opened the door to the emergency room they could not believe the number of people waiting. It was more crowded than the Department of Motor Vehicles. Probably three hundred people at least. There was so much sneezing and coughing that if someone walked into the room healthy, by the time he got to the front of the line he would need medical attention. Those who could walk were lined up in one of those S-shaped rope lines. Kathy had always thought that was one of the great inventions in all of human history: a way to keep people lined up in a small space while giving them the illusion that they were getting closer. *Who thought of that?*

People were slowly moving toward two very haggard-looking nurses sitting behind a glass partition. There was also an S-shaped wheelchair line. Fifteen people who couldn't even walk wheeling around their own ropes. Kathy kept looking at the crowd to see if she could find her father. "I don't think we're in the right place," she said.

"Did they say he was here?"

"They said he was in the hospital."

"I don't think we have to wait in this line. Let's go to admissions."

They went into the main entrance and there was a line there, too, but a much smaller one. When they got up to the admissions desk, Kathy told a woman who she was and the woman repeated the information into her headset. She waited for the answer on the screen below her. After a moment she said, "Are you the next of kin?" Kathy was panicked. That sounded devastating.

"Yes."

"He's in surgery."

"What?! Why?"

"I can't give you that information. Please sit over there and someone will come and talk to you."

"Is he okay?"

"I don't have that information. Someone will come and talk to you."

Brian lost it. "Jesus Christ, what are you good for? How much do they fucking pay you?"

Fortunately for Brian, the woman behind the desk did not respond. Someone newer might have had him arrested. Behavior that could get you thrown off planes decades earlier now got you thrown out of every public building in America. People just didn't take outbursts. They would call security at the slightest hint of anger. There was so little human-to-human contact now that people were just not used to a display of actual emotions; it all came across as hostile.

"Come on," Kathy said, taking his arm, "let's sit down."

She and Brian waited for what seemed to be thirty minutes before a woman in a business suit came out of the elevator and walked over to them. "Are you Miss Bernard?"

"Yes." Kathy was scared.

"Is this your husband?"

"No, my friend. He drove me."

"I'm Sue Norgen. I'm with the hospital administration. Normally I just talk to family members."

"Why? Is he dead?"

"No, he is just out of surgery. He will be okay."

"Thank God," Kathy said. She reached for Brian's hand and squeezed it so tight he thought she would break it.

"We need to discuss some issues," Sue told her. "If you'll follow me, we can go to my office."

"Can I see him?"

"He can't have any visitors now. He's in intensive care."

"Oh my God! That's bad, right?"

"That's where everyone goes after surgery."

Kathy realized that she still had no idea what was going on. She couldn't believe so much time had gone by and she still knew nothing.

"What happened to him?"

"He was shot."

Kathy thought she was going to pass out, but instead tears poured from her eyes. Brian put his arm around her and Sue Norgen extended her cold hand, offering zero comfort. "He's going to be all right, dear, that's the important thing. Would you like a cold drink?" Kathy nodded. "Let's go to my office and we can discuss everything."

CHAPTER EIGHT

People always wonder about the transition period of the American presidency. What exactly happens during the two and a half months between winning and taking office? What does the new president find out that he or she hadn't known before? For Matthew Bernstein, it was a bit overwhelming, to say the least. He was given security briefings when he was officially the candidate, and those by themselves gave him pause. They were certainly more detailed and authoritative than the available news of the day.

There were no trusted sources of newsgathering anymore, no voice of one news organization or one reporter that people believed over another. It was a combination of professionals, amateurs, citizens, gossip, pictures fed to a world from billions of handheld devices; a whole slew of information that people had to somehow slog through and decide for themselves what they thought was true. There was even a site that claimed to know what the CIA daily briefings were. Surely that wasn't true—or was it? So many things on that site came to pass, and every time it was shut down it reopened somewhere else.

But when he became a candidate, Bernstein started to get the same briefings as the president. This was the information that had to be perceived as real. To paraphrase Nixon, "If the president hears it, it must be true."

What he *wasn't* told was what the president already knew. He was only privy to what was happening at the moment, but the real stuff, the stuff that a president had to take office to find out—that was still out of reach.

After the election, around November 20, Bernstein was told that he was to go on a week's retreat to a beautiful spa on the Cayman Islands. His wife was allowed to come, and he was told this would be about "filling in" details. He knew of these retreats—they were given to all incoming presidents—but he had had no idea, no idea at all, what he was about to hear.

It started out slowly. The first day was basically rest and relaxation, along with the daily briefing, which now took on an air of more significance. The candidate had been told for many months of the current threats and future threats and potential threats, but he was never given serious enough information in case he lost the election. From November 8 onward, the briefings got longer, and more privileged, but it was still nothing like the week he was about to have.

In the first official meeting on the Caymans, Bernstein sat down with three men, two in military uniform and one dressed in a suit. One of the military men started by asking him if he had any questions. Were there things he had always wondered about that were never satisfactorily answered?

"My God," Bernstein said. "Are you kidding? Where do I start?"

"Fire away, Mr. President-elect. We're at your service."

"Okay. Here's something I've always wondered. Did spacemen ever land here? What was Area Fifty-one?"

The man in the suit laughed.

"That's almost everyone's first question. No, Mr. President-elect, no one has landed here. There are no space creatures hidden anywhere, but something did go on in Area Fifty-one. The United States was testing an entirely new way of flight propulsion, and it was saucer-shaped. It crashed. People saw that. And the government at the time decided that an alien story was far better for our national security than to let our enemies suspect we had even a remote knowledge of what we were trying to accomplish."

"What kind of propulsion was it?" Bernstein asked.

No one said anything. After a few seconds one of the military men spoke. "No one here is qualified to answer that, sir, but we will get someone to explain it to you."

Bernstein just blinked. Was this whole week a waste of time? Were they going to tell him *some* things but not others? His next question was "Who really runs this country?"

"I beg your pardon, sir?"

"Who really controls this country?"

"You do, sir, starting in January."

"I don't believe that. There must be continuity that has nothing to do with presidents. Who has the ultimate power in the United States?"

"The Supreme Court?" one of the military men asked.

"This is not a test," Bernstein said. "I'm asking you a question. Maybe the right way to put it is, is there a shadow government?"

The man who had given him the answer to the Area 51 question smiled.

"No, sir. There are very wealthy individuals and family dynasties that have controlled a great part of the world for hundreds of years, but they do not, as far as I know, have greater power than the government."

"As far as you know?"

"Yes, sir, as far as I know."

"Who killed John Kennedy?"

"Lee Harvey Oswald, sir?"

"Okay." The President-elect got out of his chair and went to get a glass of water. "So those were my three questions. Why don't *you* talk now?"

He wondered if these men were the ones who knew the secrets and, if they did, were they telling him? And if they didn't, why wasn't he meeting with the ones who knew?

What they did tell him over the next week was still more information than he'd ever wanted to know. The threats to the country seemed more severe than the daily briefings had made them out to be when he was just a candidate. The debt crisis sounded worse; the health care and child care and education systems all sounded as if they were beyond repair. Day after day he was shown figures, charts, data, algorithms, predictions by think tanks, names of famous people who might be trying to overthrow the country, bridges that were about to collapse, hurricane predictions, and on and on and on.

At the end of the fourth day he told Betsy he believed these transition periods were only set up to take the wind out of the sails of any new administration. "If there is a shadow government, this would be one way to make a new president feel powerless."

Betsy took another approach. "You have nothing to lose. If it's that bad, all you can do is make it better. Does the First Lady still get her own staff?"

"Of course."

"There you go. Things are looking up already. What about the spacemen?"

"I asked. There aren't any."

Kathy and Brian sat on a couch in Sue Norgen's office. Sue again suggested that maybe the conversation should just involve direct family and she was told again that Brian could stay. Sue never made it her decision. If family members wanted others present at times like these, it was their choice, and quite frankly she didn't really care. She pulled up a chair and faced Kathy, only occasionally glancing at Brian.

"Your father was shot at work, as you know."

"I don't know anything! This is the first information I'm hearing."

"He was shot at the school, one bullet in the left collarbone."

"Oh my God."

"Fortunately, it did not go into his heart, but he has lost a lot of blood, and the bullet was so deeply lodged that they had to remove quite a bit of bone to take it out. The nerve in his left shoulder may or may not have been damaged."

"What does that mean?" Kathy was trembling.

"It means that we won't know for a while if he is going to lose any movement or feeling in that area."

"How much movement could he lose?"

"I don't want to speculate. It may be fine or he may lose the ability to move his arm."

"Oh, no. Oh God."

"I think it's much too early to speculate. I'm just giving you the details that we have now and the information that will pertain to his recovery. He will need to stay in the hospital for a week and then he might need extensive physical therapy."

"I understand," Kathy said. "Whatever he needs."

This was the part Sue didn't like. Kathy did *not* understand. No one did until they were told. For the most part, Sue liked her job, but she never understood why the task fell to her to explain basic economics. So many people thought these expenses were just paid for out of thin air. *Do they teach nothing in high school anymore?* "Kathy . . . may I call you Kathy?"

"Yes," Kathy said, knowing that that expression never led to anything good.

"Your father does not have a comprehensive insurance plan." Kathy's face was expressionless. She knew what was coming. But it was much worse than she thought. "As a matter of fact, he has no real insurance at all. His universal coverage lapsed a year and a half ago when he stopped making the minimum payments."

"But he was going to make those payments up. That's why he took that job."

"I understand, but he didn't. If you let your co-pay go unpaid, the government guarantee of health care is void. It is everyone's responsibility to keep that payment going."

"Well, can I get the money somehow and pay the co-pay myself?"

"It's too late for that. When the government saw that too many people simply stopped their end of the bargain, just waiting until they got sick to resume their payments, they passed very strict laws regarding co-pays. It's really the same as a mortgage. If you miss your mortgage payment, you lose your house." Kathy was getting angry.

"We got behind in our mortgage and we didn't lose our house."

"How many months did you get behind?"

"Two."

"Well, your father let his insurance payment go for almost a year and a half. Even two months would have been a problem, but at eighteen months there's nothing I can do."

"So what does this mean?"

"Well, the good news is, we are going to treat your father for the time he is in the hospital. We will have no ability, though, to get him physical therapy if it turns out that that's what he needs. You will have to arrange that."

"Okay," Kathy said. That didn't sound so bad to her; maybe her dad wouldn't need therapy, maybe he would be okay. Then Sue Norgen continued and Kathy heard it, but didn't. Her brain could not comprehend what came next.

"Kathy, the hospital bill will need to be paid." Sue looked down at her small screen, confirming the figures before she said anything further. "The bill, including the surgery, including one week of care, no more, will be approximately three hundred and fifty thousand dollars."

It was Brian who spoke first. "What did you say?" Brian was now standing.

"The surgery and the one-week stay will be approximately three hundred and fifty thousand dollars." Brian started pacing like an animal. Kathy just sat there, still not comprehending what this meant.

"He has universal care; it can't be that much!" Brian said.

"He had no care. He let his payments lapse," Sue replied.

"But he was *going* to pay them; that's why he was working at such a shitty job!" Brian raised his voice. "That's why he got shot!"

"I know it sounds unfair, but I do not make the rules. My job is to collect money so the hospital stays in business."

"We don't have the money," Kathy said. "Are you going to kill him?"

"Of course not, you know that." Sue got up and went back to her desk. "I am going to send to your screen various plans where you can take out a medical loan, much like any other loan. This can be dealt with in that fashion. Did you ever take out a student loan for college?"

"I didn't go to college. I had to work."

"Well, this can be paid back over time by anyone you choose—your father, you, anyone." Kathy got up. She looked terrible. No color in her face, no expression.

"So I have to borrow three hundred and fifty thousand dollars?"

"Yes."

"What if they won't loan us the money?"

"Didn't you say your father owned his home?"

"Yes, but I think he owes more than it's worth."

"Kathy, the medical loans are a bit more lenient because the expense has already been incurred, so I'm sure as long as someone has a job and is willing to make a serious attempt, you will get the money."

"And what if we don't?"

"You're a healthy young woman. Even if your father can never work again, I'm sure you can, or someone else in your family can. And I am sure over time you can pay it back. But I'm not the lender; my responsibility is to the hospital. So when you get home, look over your choices. I can't imagine that something won't work out."

"Can I see my father?"

"Not while he is in intensive care."

"When can I see him?"

"Go home for now. Look over the material I've sent and I will call you and let you know when your father can have a visitor."

Brian was furious. He wanted to punch this woman in the face. Kathy walked to the door. She honestly felt that if she didn't take care of the money, she would never see her father again.

CHAPTER NINE

The President had asked for a meeting with several prominent health professionals for Wednesday, the twelfth of June, but something was about to alter his plans.

Wednesday morning, Jack Eller, Brad's poorest friend, got up early. He had a terrible pain in his right foot. His insurance was the barest-bones coverage the government offered. For a low premium, he was allowed one doctor visit a year, and one visit to an emergency room every three years. Major surgery was covered if three separate medical sources wrote that it was absolutely necessary. Ambulances were not covered, home nursing was not covered, physical therapy was not covered, and the overall deductible was five thousand dollars.

The result of such a stringent plan was that patients simply stopped asking for help. If they passed out in their own home, they would be lucky to be taken to the hospital by a private car so they didn't start out the visit owing three thousand dollars for the ambulance ride. If they were luckier, they woke up in a bed with at least two approvals for whatever it was they needed, a third approval at that point being pretty much guaranteed. Many patients died waiting for these approvals, but the government held firm.

As Jack was sitting on his bed rubbing his swollen foot, he glanced at the clock. It was 6:35 in the morning. The pain was so bad he thought maybe Brad could pick him up and he could use his one emergency room visit—he hadn't had one in almost four years. He didn't want to call Brad too early, so he hobbled over to the kitchenette and pressed "brew" on the coffee machine. As soon as he pressed the button, it started: a small shaking that either would be gone in a second, or not.

Living in Los Angeles, people were used to this from time to time, and most of the time it was nothing. The last sizable shake, which was in Palm Springs in 2020, measured a 7.1 and was felt throughout the Los Angeles area. Immediately after that quake, experts came on the news and declared that it wasn't "the big one." What did that mean, "the big one"? Everyone thought about it, but nobody had lived through a "big one," so people could only imagine.

Jack waited for the shaking to stop. It didn't. It had only just begun. After about twelve seconds it seemed to double in intensity, and then it tripled, and then everything fell down. Jack ran to hide under his bed. He didn't make it. A beam from the ceiling hit him in the forehead and that was it.

Brad was literally thrown out of bed. As his ceiling started to come down, he ran to the doorway of the bathroom and just stood, expecting to die. Every piece of glass broke in his condo, everything came out of every cabinet, and the refrigerator-communication center fell over. The framed picture of Brad and his wife meeting Bill Clinton was shattered. The Lalique crystal water faucet he was given at his retirement lunch was smashed into a hundred pieces.

The electricity ceased after the first fifteen seconds. Handheld devices now communicated directly with satellites, so Brad reached for his watch, but he didn't know who to call or what to do. He called Herb. There was no answer. He called Jack. No answer. Then *he* got a call. It was his son. The fact that they never spoke didn't matter now; he was grateful to talk to anybody.

"Dad?" His son sounded panicked.

"Tom, are you all right?"

"No. We've had a terrible earthquake." That his son lived near San Diego, two hundred miles away, and thought the earthquake was centered there, gave Brad an indication of just how big this was. "Are you all right, Dad, is it bad there?"

"It's bad here," Brad said. "You have to protect yourself from the aftershocks."

There was no response. "Tom?" Nothing. "Tom, can you hear me?" The connection was gone. Now it was impossible to get anything on the watch. There were too many people using the satellite system; it was overwhelmed.

Brad made his way outside as soon as the initial shaking stopped. And then he felt the first aftershock. It was an aftershock worse than any earthquake ever recorded in California.

So this was "the big one." This was the one scientists said in 2010 had a fifty percent chance of happening in the next thirty years. Fifty-fifty. Red or black. The San Andreas Fault had not moved substantially in over three hundred years. "Overdue" was an understatement.

The initial shake was a 9.1. The first aftershock was an 8.7. The second was an 8.2. The third, an 8.0, was bigger than anything that had ever been predicted.

It was funny. Brad remembered a science show he had seen years earlier that talked about the San Andreas Fault. "Compared to other faults," the show said, "the San Andreas is only capable of something in the high sevens." And yet the show *did* point out that in the next million or so years, Los Angeles would be somewhere north of San Francisco. Brad had wondered at the time how scientists could be so sure that a fault would never go higher than a certain magnitude, since obviously it was in the process of moving hundreds of miles. *Couldn't they be wrong, just once? Couldn't the earth decide, one afternoon, to move a little faster than geologists agreed on? How could someone be that sure about the earth's crust? They don't even get the weather right.* Brad remembered thinking how presumptuous that was, and today he wondered if the guy who hosted that program was in the city. To have your life destroyed *and* be wrong—well, *that* would be a bad morning.

Los Angeles was not prepared for this. No city could be. No freeway was drivable, no buildings were okay, and many came down completely. Ninety-eight percent of the property in Los Angeles County was severely damaged.

The death toll was close to fifty thousand and the number of injured was incalculable. First reports said up to half a million people were seriously hurt. Hospitals could do nothing. They were damaged beyond repair; all they tried to do was keep the patients who were already there alive.

And then, after all was said and done, after all of the damage and death and destruction, there was one looming issue. Where in God's name would the money come from to fix America's largest city? For a country so deeply in debt, this seemed like an impossible task.

The nation's largest insurance company simply declared bankruptcy. It had liability in the great quake of more than a trillion dollars. It couldn't pay a hundredth of that. That was the problem with earthquake insurance: It was a good bet in a small quake where *your* house was damaged but the house down the street was fine. Then, after paying a large deductible, you were likely to see some money. When all the houses in the entire city were damaged, that equation didn't work. State and federal aid would be bare minimum at best. To fix the highways alone would cost fifty times more than it did to build them.

But all that would have to wait. This was a true humanitarian crisis, the worst the United States had ever faced. In images beamed instantly all over the globe, California looked like a third-world country. People were lying in the streets, bodies piled up along the sidewalks; fires raged all over the city, and the possibility of severe outbreaks of disease grew by the hour.

The earthquake occurred at 6:36 A.M., Pacific Standard Time. At 9:36 A.M., Eastern Standard Time, President Bernstein was in the Oval Office drinking coffee, eating a jelly doughnut, and reading the morning briefings. His chief of staff, John Van Dyke, felt a tingling on his wrist. His communicator was set on "tickle" and he immediately looked at his watch. He gasped. Bernstein stopped reading and looked up. "What's the problem?"

"A colossal earthquake."

"Where?"

"Here, sir."

"Here? I didn't feel a thing."

"In Los Angeles. A nine point one."

"Come on. No. Jesus Christ!"

Bernstein pressed a button and the wall in front of him changed instantly into multiple screens. He could see anything he wanted. Every news outlet, his Joint Chiefs of Staff, NORAD, live cameras placed on top of government buildings in every city in America, images from space—it was his choice. For three minutes he just watched the same images being fed to every other American. Devastation not seen before by a U.S. president.

Bernstein was known for his calm. He didn't show emotion in public very often and he even tried to keep it from his staff. But he felt he was losing it. He started to sweat and he could feel his heartbeat accelerate. "My God, John. What has happened? Is everyone sure this was an earthquake?"

"What do you mean, Mr. President?"

"Could this have been a nuclear explosion and people assumed it was an earthquake?"

"No, sir. It registered a nine point one on the Richter scale."

"My God. My God."

That's all the president of the United States could muster as he watched one image after another of America's biggest city in ruins.

Dr. Sam Mueller's G10 landed at Reagan International Airport at eleven A.M. He had been in flight when the earthquake happened, and as soon as he touched down, he, too, watched the screen in the private terminal along with dozens of other rich people. His mind was racing. *Will there still be a meeting? Can I do something to help? Is there an invention to be hatched here to deal with this crisis?* It would sound cold to some, but Mueller's mind had always worked that way. He hated when he saw tragedy and thought of business, but he convinced himself that was how the brains of brilliant people worked. *Don't beat yourself up for being brilliant.*

The government was in full crisis mode. President Bernstein ordered half the National Guard to California. Every army base in the western United States sent all available manpower and resources to the coast. He asked General Robert Roscoe, assistant head of the Joint Chiefs, to get to Los Angeles as quickly as possible and coordinate the rescue effort. Bernstein wanted the army to set up as many temporary hospitals, which were really nothing more than large tents, as it had. He wanted them up and running immediately, and even though there wasn't enough staff for all of them, he felt it was important for the public to see those images.

The first country to offer help was Canada. They sent thirty doctors, over a hundred nurses, and supplies. Mexico also offered assistance. Bernstein had to make a decision about whether he should go to California immediately, but it was felt that it would be best to let the military get its foot in the door and then he would fly out and tour the area. It was such a production to transport the president of the United States, and he didn't feel Los Angeles needed to give its attention to him at this moment of crisis.

There was another major issue that required him to stay in Washington. In a disaster this size there was always a higher likelihood of trouble from either inside or outside the country. Individuals, even nations, can take advantage of a weakened adversary, so the President ordered the United States on highest alert. Police in other cities were on twenty-four-hour watch for suspicious activities, and the Strategic Air Command went to DEFCON 1, its war footing. America was immediately turned into a no-fly zone: For forty-eight hours all commercial flights were grounded, and it was ordered that anything in the sky would be shot down. Los Angeles was so crippled that even a small attack during this time would destroy it for good.

The President was leaving the Situation Room when John Van Dyke reminded him, "We have the health team all assembled here. Do you want to cancel it?"

"No," said the President. "Make it for later, but don't cancel. This isn't exactly the health issue I wanted to talk about, but their advice will be important. Make it after lunch. Feed them, show them around, take them to the zoo, whatever you have to do, but give me a few hours to deal with this. Why don't you make it for three o'clock?"

"Yes, sir."

The President returned to the Oval Office and just watched the screens as they displayed devastation never seen before. *At least this wasn't my fault.*

Kathy Bernard and Brian Nelson were sitting in her home in Indianapolis, watching the disaster. "I've always hated Los Angeles," Brian said. "A bunch of rich perverts. They deserve it."

Normally Kathy would correct him when he made those kinds of gross generalizations, but this was the last thing on her mind. All she could think about was her dad. "It's not fair," she said. "He was trying to make his payments. He's still young, compared to all those fucking boomers who won't die. Why should we pay the health care for someone who has already had ninety years of life and not my dad?"

"I'm with you," Brian said. "I say kill all those old fuckers."

They went back to watching the earthquake. Kathy felt a bit selfish watching such devastation and thinking only about her own problems, but to her a $350,000 debt was the same thing as a 9.1.

The watch on Dr. Mueller's wrist lit up. It was his assistant in Florida.

"The President's appointment secretary just asked if you could stay later. The President would like to meet at three."

"Sure," Sam said.

"What do we do in the meantime?" Maggie whispered, overhearing the watch. His assistant heard her.

"You are welcome to come to the White House now for lunch and a tour with the First Lady, or you can spend the day however you wish and arrive there shortly before the meeting."

"We'll go now and do the lunch and the tour," Maggie said.

"You heard her," Sam replied. "That's the decision."

"All right, sir. A driver is waiting for you. Did you see the earthquake in Los Angeles, Dr. Mueller?"

"Yes. Horrible."

"Our office building and lab there were completely destroyed, but nothing dangerous was released. And thank God it was early, so no one was in the building."

"I know," Sam said. "Bob called me an hour ago. It's lucky for us they make it too expensive to do business out there or we would have lost a lot more. I'll check in with you later."

Sam and Maggie got into the limousine.

"Where to, sir?"

"The White House." That felt really cool. Some things never got old.

The Situation Room was fully active now, as if the country had been attacked. They watched secure feeds of information flowing in, getting the most up-to-the-minute counts on the dead and injured, and watched close-up pictures from space.

Bernstein could never get over these pictures. They weren't new technology—this had been around for probably fifty years—but they kept getting better. Stupendously clear photos of the smallest objects, with the best sound you ever heard. You could read a Vehicle Identification Number on an automobile from fifty miles up. And you could hear the conversation in the same car. The government had to go through the motions of getting judicial approval to hear what people were saying, although visual spying was allowed—it was odd, you could see someone in bed, you just weren't allowed to hear him without a court order—but the orders were easy to obtain, and most of the time the government listened anyway and got the permission later.

Today, however, they weren't interested in conversations. This wasn't about a conspiracy. It was about a catastrophe. The worst the nation had ever seen.

CHAPTER TEN

The United States had always felt it was just a matter of time before a nuclear device went off somewhere in the country. But its worst fears—that of a full-fledged bomb exploding—had not yet happened. When a dirty bomb exploded in Chicago in 2023, it was handled well. The thing about dirty bombs is that they leave large parts of real estate uninhabitable, but they don't kill on a large scale.

People were scared to death when it happened, but the explosion itself was over before anyone knew there was radiation involved. The area, about one city block, was sealed off, and remained that way for five years until they were able, with the help of new chemicals, to cleanse the buildings of any measurable contamination. Still, no one moved back there. They almost had to give the land away and they were forced to put up a big electronic Geiger counter, like a billboard, that always registered zero, just to put people at ease. The area was affectionately known in the city as the Hot Zone, and some strip clubs and dance clubs actually made money there, with strippers known as "Xray" and "NewCleo."

Other parts of the world were not that fortunate. People had always expected the first nuclear explosion to be in the Middle East when Iran got its weapon, or Pakistan or North Korea. But North Korea surprised everyone.

When Kim Jong Il died in 2013, the country fell apart and into the hands of the south. Over the next few years the two countries became one Korea with not only no resistance from the north but almost an attitude of gratefulness. The people in the north had nothing, knew almost nothing about the world, but knew from messages that had gotten through to them from relatives who had escaped a long time ago that they had it as bad as it could get. And once change was offered to them, they ate it up like starving animals.

Israel waited through 2011 as the United States talked to Iran and tried to present a face of progress, but Israeli spies knew the truth. Weapons were being constructed at the rate of one a month starting in January 2012. With help from double agents inside Iran and secret help from Egypt and Jordan—two Arab countries more scared of Iran than Israel, if that was possible—a massive strike was undertaken to set back Iran's nuclear ambitions by at least a decade. It unleashed a conventional war that went on for almost six months, with tens of thousands of casualties and Arab nations fighting one another. The United States supplied weapons but refused to officially enter the conflict.

Fighting was brought to an uneasy truce toward the end of 2012, and for the foreseeable future Iran, other than by buying one off the black market, was not going to have its weapon. The odd thing was that as soon as fighting ceased, Israel went back to the same strained relationship it had had with Jordan and Egypt. They were there for each other in times of absolute crisis, but barring that, Jews were Jews and Arabs were Arabs, and that was not going to change.

Pakistan and India were not as lucky. By 2013 there was complete chaos in Pakistan. The Taliban, fighting the United States and NATO in Afghanistan, in a war that was making Vietnam look like a quickie, made their move to take over Pakistan once and for all. Slowly, each year, they gained the support of more of the people. Pakistan, unlike India, never distributed its wealth, and as the population got poorer and less educated, the Taliban took over more hearts and minds. The news reports that the Taliban had been driven out were true. Driven out of one place, but welcomed into another. Not dead and not gone. And when they'd become quiet for a few years, people made the big mistake of thinking the worst was over. But all they had done was go back into the population and fester. They cemented themselves with the millions of impoverished people and the thousands of soldiers who wanted a more religious state.

The Taliban made their move on Christmas Eve 2013, a date that meant nothing to them, almost as if to say to the Christian world, "Merry Christmas, you fuckers." It was quick, coordinated beyond anyone's wildest imagination, and because of the help they had within the army, relatively bloodless. By New Year's Day 2014, Pakistan's nuclear arsenal was under Taliban control. The remaining government basically surrendered without a fight. The rest of the world watched in horror as Sharia law was imposed on an entire nation. The Taliban immediately organized military parades, as they wanted Pakistan and the world to see thousands of people cheering for them in the streets. An Al-Qaeda bomb—actually, seventy of them—was finally a reality.

The United States went on highest alert, and war plans were discussed in case Pakistan had to be attacked before any of these weapons could be fired. But it was India that was truly petrified. Yes, the Taliban hated the U.S., but they hated India more. And, like all Pakistanis, they wanted the land they believed was rightfully theirs.

It only took two months in power before the first clash came in Kashmir. India noticed immediately that the Pakistani soldiers fought with a new intensity. Accompanying the fighting were strong warnings and threats coming from the Taliban government: "Give us this land, or else." The last thing India wanted to do was now its only option.

Secret meetings were held with the United States, Germany, France, China, Japan, Russia, and the UK. None of these countries liked the new Pakistan, and only China and Russia, among the major powers, thought they could do business with its new government.

India said, and the intelligence backed them up, that it was going to be attacked with nuclear weapons and it had to strike first. The United States thought it was the right thing to do. China and Japan thought India should give it more time. Germany and France, with their large Muslim populations, were mixed in their reactions. They knew an attack would cause an uprising in the streets, but they were more scared of Taliban influence spreading into their own society.

The United States thought that India could dismantle Pakistan's ability to strike back if it hit key facilities first, with bunker-buster nukes. These were still nuclear weapons, but they were exploded deep in the ground, not in the air, and they did phenomenal damage without catastrophic radiation release. There was no way to prevent Pakistan from firing something, but with advanced defense missiles and a population large enough that it could afford a million or so casualties, India convinced the rest of the world that it was now or never.

India kept the fighting up in Kashmir to divert attention and, in late 2014, it launched a preemptive attack on the Taliban's nuclear facilities, along with sending in a million men to try to take hold of the country. The plan mostly worked, although five Taliban rockets were launched with nuclear warheads. Two landed in unpopulated areas, but three landed near cities, with one landing twenty miles outside of Delhi. Three hundred thousand people were killed instantly, with hundreds of thousands more getting sick over the following weeks. But India had secured Pakistan and now occupied it. The Pakistani people were shocked by how quickly their country was taken over, but they didn't love the Taliban enough to rise up, and the Pakistani army was leaderless and too disorganized to put up any further resistance. With India now in control of the Taliban's nukes, plus its own, it would be impossible for Pakistan to fight them and win.

India's first job was to try to put a government favorable to it in power. It found some Taliban who were friendlier to the idea than others and cultivated them, along with leaders in exile whom the people still had some affection toward. But no new government was going to get the nukes back. Those went to the victor, and for the first time in fifty years Pakistan had no weapons of mass destruction.

The nuclear explosions that took place during this conflict did one positive thing, if one could call it that. They gave the world a chance to see firsthand what nuclear devastation really looked like. A nuclear bomb, to the majority of people alive in 2015, had meant nothing. It was a weapon that signified something terrible, but virtually no one had any experience or memory of it, or even read books on Hiroshima any longer. There were still some aging baby boomers who remembered hiding under their desks in grammar school, as if that would have saved them when their schools heated up to three thousand degrees, but short of that, nuclear war was just a lingering threat.

Then people finally were able to see for themselves what a nuclear bomb really did, and more people than ever before were determined not to let it happen again. On the other hand, it also confirmed that there was no better weapon of terror ever invented.

And that's what Los Angeles looked like. As if a big fat fifty-megaton hydrogen bomb had been dropped in the center of the city. The same devastation without the radiation. Thank God terrorists didn't know how to start earthquakes.

CHAPTER ELEVEN

At 2:45 President Bernstein finally left the Situation Room and went upstairs to the residence to take a shower and change clothes before his meeting with the elite of the medical establishment. His original idea for the meeting, to discuss a range of issues including the problems inherent in unabated longevity, now seemed unimportant. And yet the country's business still had to go on. There were still forty-nine states with no earthquake.

The President had one question that he wanted a real answer to. Put simply, "Are people living too long?" He had to be careful how he phrased it, just as he had had to be when he was running. It was something the other side loved to get ahold of and distort. CANDIDATE WANTS SENIORS DEAD, one headline screamed during the election. But Bernstein knew that this was an issue that *had* to be dealt with by someone, so it might as well be him.

The United States had already pushed the retirement age to seventy-three, trying to stave off the Social Security debacle. They raised premiums on Medicare and cut the coverage to bare bones, but nothing really made a difference. The cost for these programs had overwhelmed the country, and the bigger question was always looming: At what price life?

When Bernstein was in high school he had been on a debate team, and one of the debates was pro-choice versus pro-life. He was assigned pro-life even though he wanted to debate for the other side. But he got all of his talking points straight and tried his best. He argued that life began at conception and other humans had no right to take a life, and asked, What if they'd aborted Jonas Salk or Winston Churchill? And he was winning. Then someone from the other side said, "The pro-life movement only cares about the human while it's still in the mother. As soon as it's born, the pro-choice people have to take care of it." And Bernstein couldn't answer. He agreed. And he lost the debate.

He believed that many of the pro-lifers never thought about life as an entire journey. Just get the human beings here any way possible and the rest will be figured out. Who would do that? Who would figure it out? Maybe now that he was president, he could at least start the discussion for real.

"And at this very desk, Harry Truman made the decision to drop the first atom bomb on Hiroshima." Betsy Bernstein loved giving the tours almost more than anything else.

Here she was, a plain girl from Detroit, showing the people who cured cancer and muscular dystrophy and Alzheimer's exactly where former presidents had sat as they determined the fate of the world. She showed off the White House as if it were her own home, and she had done a lot to make it that way. The famous Blue Room was no longer blue, it was now off-white. In another room she replaced all of the antiques with a retro design, furniture made in America from the 1950s. She took out many of the Persian carpets that had been there for over a hundred years, and in their place put Indian rugs and added Southwestern touches throughout to give the famous home a different feel. And for the most part people liked it. There was the normal talk of too much expense, but she made sure that the items were donated and made sure to let everyone know that.

The Muellers were enthralled with the tour, as were the other guests. Betsy took them to the elevator and said, "Now, because you're such a special group, if you would like, I will take you up to the residence. That's something not a lot of people see." Everyone thought that was a fine idea, and when they got to the second floor and walked down the hallway,

Maggie Mueller couldn't believe her eyes. One of the bedroom doors was open and the room was a mess. She nudged her husband.

"Look in there," she whispered. Sam looked in the door but didn't see what the big deal was.

"So?"

"The room looks like it hasn't been made up for days."

"So what? Maybe his messy brother is staying here."

"Still," Maggie said, "it's the White House. You would think the room would be cleaned as soon as someone is out of it."

"Maybe they're still in there, honey." Sam was now smiling. He loved these discussions about nothing.

"They're not. You can tell."

"Maybe the CIA makes them invisible during the tours."

For one-tenth of a second Maggie thought he was serious. Before she could even laugh, Betsy Bernstein opened a door and said to the group, "Now, for the piece de resistance, the Lincoln Bedroom." And when she stepped aside there he was, Abraham Lincoln, sitting in a chair, reading, looking as alive as could be. Lincoln looked up and said, "Hello, and welcome." The people on the tour were giddy.

What started out seventy-five years earlier as crude animatronics at Disneyland had transformed into a machine that looked one hundred percent human. It was as good as any robot produced in 2030. The robot Lincoln had stories to tell, would take questions, and then, after the presentation was over, said, "If you don't mind, I'm a little tired, I think I will lie down." And with that, the tour was over. Lincoln didn't stand up. The very fact that he was not required to walk saved twenty million dollars, but anyone on the White House tour who was important enough to go upstairs never forgot that moment. They felt they'd actually spent time with Abraham Lincoln.

One of the scientists during the question period thought he would be funny and asked Lincoln about John Wilkes Booth. But of course the creators knew that that question would come up, so what did Lincoln do? He looked puzzled, thought for a moment, and said, "I don't know who that is. Remember, you're talking to me while I'm still alive." It got a great laugh and made the questioner feel like an ass.

At three o'clock the visiting dignitaries were led into a meeting room in the West Wing of the White House. They were told to make themselves comfortable, and that the President and the chief of staff would arrive in a few minutes.

Everyone there knew each other; several of them had either won or been nominated for a Nobel Prize. Besides Mueller there was Sidney Nash, the man who was credited with curing muscular dystrophy (with, of course, plenty of help from the late Jerry Lewis). There was Heather McMillan, who was given the most credit for curing Alzheimer's, although a new kind of memory loss was starting to occur in the elderly that did not respond to medicine. Bennett Friedman, who headed the largest pharmaceutical drug company in the world, was there, as was Cynthia Lowenstein, secretary of Health, Education, and Welfare, and of course, Patricia Twain, the surgeon general. Several other people were at the table whom Sam did not know, but they knew him. Everybody knew the guy who cured cancer. They all made light conversation before the President arrived. "How's business, Sam?" Bennett asked.

"You'll have to talk to the accountants," Mueller said. "I don't get into the business end very much anymore."

"I heard the growth spray was a bust."

"Was it?" Sam smiled. "That's not what I heard."

This was a spray they were all working toward. A safe way to administer a small amount of human growth hormone to improve the overall well-being in older people, but with none of the previous side effects. The so-called "feel goods," the drugs that served no purpose other than to make you feel younger, were the toughest to come up with. They always had a rebound effect. You couldn't go up without coming down, which was always a problem, and many of the drugs that sailed through clinical trials showed side effects years later.

One in particular that didn't show its dark side for almost a decade came to market in 2019, synthetic caffeine. It gave people the jolt they wanted with none of the irritating side effects. People had energy, their thinking was clearer, their moods were improved, they didn't have jitteriness, and at the end of the day it wore off completely and actually assisted in sleep.

Clinical trials went perfectly. The drug was approved in 2022 and was marketed under the name Alert. It became the third-best-selling drug of all time, and then people's kidneys started to fail. It was something that didn't show up for years, but when it did, it affected almost twenty percent of the users. Global-Pharma, the company that manufactured the drug, paid out twenty billion dollars in damages.

But still, the companies continued their research. To have success with the "feel goods" was to own the goose that laid the golden egg. "Imagine if someone had the patent on coffee," they used to say. Just to think of it made businessmen swoon.

They all stood up when the President entered. President Bernstein was not a hand shaker. Early on, he adopted an Indian-style nod with his hands clasped together. It was odd at first, but it became his trademark and many other politicians followed suit. The Chinese and Indians knew something about shaking hands. There was no reason to get a person's cold just from greeting them. And Bernstein thought adopting this Eastern way was not only healthier but had a peaceful ring to it. It was also better than having two assistants following him everywhere with hand sanitizer. People hated that image, the President shaking your hand and then, moments later, washing you off.

"Thank you for coming. The reason I wanted to meet all of you today was to discuss various issues regarding health, but of course with the largest natural disaster in our history striking the country this morning, I feel we need to discuss what can be done to keep Los Angeles from severe outbreaks of cholera and other communicable diseases. Quite frankly, I can't even believe I'm using the word 'cholera' in 2030, but here we are."

Of course, the people at the table knew there had been an earthquake, but they could see on the President's face that it was worse than they had even imagined. Bernstein continued. "As I say, this was not the point of the meeting, but since you're here, I thought it would be irresponsible not to share any ideas you might have that could help in this crisis."

He listened to everyone's opinions about what could be done. All of their suggestions—temporary hospitals, an infusion of medicine, sending in the military, ensuring fresh water—were already being implemented.

The President heard from each person and when they were all through he thanked them and then changed the subject.

"I would like your opinion on another very important matter." He paused. He wanted to say it properly. "Are we getting too good at longevity? Is there a point at which life is not worth pursuing?"

The people at the table just stared at him. They were not expecting this question.

"I am raising a subject that must be talked about at some point, though possibly this is not the best time. It was brought up in the election but was shot down before it could really be analyzed. We have to ask ourselves if science has exceeded our ability to handle the elderly population. I thought the people in this room would have valuable opinions on the subject."

No one at the table had ever heard this put so directly by a sitting president. Sure, people talked about this issue, a lot. Even the companies that came up with new longevity products would joke, "Who the hell will take care of these walking corpses?" But it was always someone else's problem. Now the President was asking *them*.

Before a real discussion could start, a woman walked in and handed Bernstein a note.

"I'm sorry," he said. "I've got to go. Thank you for your ideas on Los Angeles, and I would appreciate it if the longevity issue would remain confidential. We will meet again soon, hopefully under different circumstances, and I would like to really delve into this discussion."

And then, backtracking so he didn't appear too callous, he said, "Of course, it is a true achievement when science helps people live a longer life, and we must always strive for that. My own mother is ninety-four and for that I'm grateful. I just wanted to hear your thoughts on the ramifications of life extension. Thanks again for coming today." And with that, the President was gone.

Bennett Friedman turned to Patricia Twain. "What the hell was that about?" The surgeon general was a big Bernstein supporter and came to his defense.

"It's something that needs to be discussed. The President knows this is a serious issue with the younger generation. It must be addressed."

"Are you sure that's the reason?" Friedman asked. "Maybe he just hates his mother."

And the whole table laughed, including Twain.

After the meeting with the foremost health minds in the country, the President prepared for his address to the nation, really to the entire world. When deemed important enough, which this was, the President appeared on every single device that could transmit voice and picture. And it was available in real time around the globe. With instant translation, a laborer in China or a construction worker in Kuwait could watch as the president of the United States talked to his people. At eight o'clock, Eastern Standard Time, Bernstein solemnly faced the camera and spoke:

> "Good evening. As you know, early this morning the United States of America experienced the worst natural disaster in our history. A nine-point-one earthquake, followed by several severe aftershocks, hit Southern California, doing unimaginable damage. We have already dispatched thousands of our finest military and medical personnel to ease the pain and attempt to get things back to some reasonable semblance of normal. I promise you tonight, we will make tremendous strides in a very short time to get America's biggest city back on its feet and to get its great people the help they need. Let no nation on earth think that we are weakened by this event. Our country not only has the capacity to deal with whatever crisis is thrown at us, but in the end it bonds us as Americans and strengthens our will as a free and democratic people. I wish to thank all of the countries that have offered their help; your concern and your generosity are greatly welcomed. Nature does not tell us when or why she makes her decisions, but we must accept them and try to let them transform us into a stronger and better people. And to Los Angeles, your best days are ahead. I assure you of that. May God bless us all. Thank you."

When the President was through, he just sat very still behind his historic desk. John Van Dyke said, "It was brilliant, sir. I couldn't have imagined a better speech."

"Too bad it was a lie," the President said. Van Dyke knew what Bernstein meant. America did not have the funds to fix this disaster. Where would these "best days" come from? But that didn't have to be discussed tonight. Van Dyke thought the administration had acted perfectly during the first day of the crisis, and he had learned from his years on Capitol Hill that if you didn't enjoy the moments when you performed your job in an admirable way, you would find no joy of any kind in public service.

The President left his office and went upstairs to the residence. Betsy had watched the speech and thought it was perfect. "That was all you could do for now," she said.

"I feel so helpless. I don't know how to make this okay."

"You have to let it go tonight. Give yourself a little break and you'll figure something out. Are you hungry?"

"Starving."

"I'll have Henry make a deep-dish pizza. Maybe you should go mountain climbing." The President smiled. Mountain climbing was one virtual experience he absolutely loved. He would climb on the machine and it made him feel as if he were in the Alps, or any other mountain range he programmed in. It took his mind off everything.

When they had first made the mountain-climbing program for the President, they had put in virtual Secret Service agents climbing along with him. Bernstein was furious. "What the hell did you do that for?"

"Well, Mr. President," the genius Indian programmer said, "we wanted to make it as realistic for you as possible."

"Are you crazy? Get them out of here."

"Yes, sir. Do you want *anyone* there?"

"Other mountain climbers, people who have no idea who I am. Maybe Lincoln."

"Yes, sir, I understand now. I forgot, sir. I was just going for realism."

CHAPTER TWELVE

Stewart Bernard was moved out of intensive care and into a room shared by six other people. When Kathy came to visit him, she had no idea his room would be so crowded. It looked like an army barrack, for God's sake. She sat by her father's bed and tried to keep up a positive attitude. He didn't bring up the money issue, so she certainly didn't want to introduce it. But that was all that was in the back of her mind. *How the hell will we pay for this?* She forced herself to make light conversation.

"You look great."

"Thanks," her father said. "I don't feel that great."

"The doctors said it went perfectly. You'll make a complete recovery."

"I can't believe I almost died just keeping some kids from playing basketball. I would have done the same thing myself when I was their age."

"You can't think like that. You were doing your job. For all you know, they might have been hurting someone."

"Yeah, me. Did they catch the kids?"

Kathy didn't know the answer but she knew what to say. "Yeah. They got 'em."

"I can't believe I got shot. I just can't believe it. That's something that never would have happened at GM."

"Don't get nostalgic for GM, Dad, they were pricks. They were the reason you had to take this stupid job." As soon as she said it, she realized it was mean. "It wasn't stupid, it was just beneath you, that's all."

"I know what you meant, honey. It *was* stupid. But it was work." Her father yawned and let out a groan.

"Why don't you rest now. I'll come see you tomorrow."

"Thanks, honey. I love you."

"I love you, too." She gave her dad a kiss.

As Kathy walked out of the hospital she ran into Sue Norgen. At first Sue didn't recognize her, but after a second she remembered. All Kathy said was, "I'm trying to get the money."

"I wasn't going to ask you that. I was just going to ask how your father was doing."

"They're one and the same, aren't they?"

"Kathy, I don't make the laws, I try to enforce them on behalf of my employer."

"Oh, why didn't you tell me that before?" Kathy said sarcastically.

Sue nodded with that small smile people give when they have nothing more to say. As she walked away Kathy almost felt like apologizing, but she didn't. She still had no idea what she was going to do. She almost felt jealous of her father because, at least for the time being, his brain was not consumed with this insurmountable debt.

When Kathy parked her father's car in the underground garage of the office building, she began to sweat. It wasn't that hot; she was just anticipating the meeting that was about to take place.

She had gotten the name of a lawyer who possibly could help out with the medical bills. Many people missed payments and still were able to recover some insurance money, or so she had been told, so it was certainly worth a meeting to see if this firm could intervene. They advertised that if they couldn't, there would be no fee, so what was the downside? Kathy thought about waiting until her father was out of the hospital, but it would be horrible to be shot and come home to a $350,000 bill. Maybe she could make some headway here and actually give him some good news.

She took the elevator to the sixth floor and walked down the hall to the office of Payton, Grace, and Osborne. These were medical lawyers who advertised heavily. She felt a little stupid going to someone whose commercial she had just watched, but she thought that if they had enough money to advertise, they must be good. And again, if they couldn't help, it was free. She opened the door and the waiting room was empty. There was no live assistant. A face on a screen welcomed her and asked, "May I help you?"

"I'm Kathy Bernard. I have an appointment."

"Yes, you do. Have a seat, please."

Kathy sat down and waited about fifteen minutes. She picked up one of two readers and scanned various news sources, not really paying much attention. It was all about the earthquake anyway, and she had seen enough of those terrible images. As she put down the device, the door opened. "Miss Bernard?"

"Yes?"

"Kevin Booker. Won't you come in?"

Kathy walked down the hall to Kevin Booker's office. Kevin was a paralegal, not even a junior partner. *Where's the guy in the ad?* Kevin's office was small but comfortable.

"Have a seat."

"Thank you."

"Some earthquake. Can you believe it?"

"It was horrible." This had now replaced the weather as the official conversation among strangers. It was how people would greet each other for months.

"Too bad we can't sue God, huh?" Kevin laughed at his joke. Kathy smiled and wished she were dead. "So tell me in a nutshell, how can we help you?"

"My father lapsed in his health coverage, and he was shot on the job, and now they are saying that universal care will pay nothing and we are stuck with the bill."

Kevin looked genuinely concerned. "I'm very sorry. Is he all right?"

"Well, they think he'll live, but no one knows how much care he'll need."

"What is the bill now?"

"Three hundred and fifty thousand."

Kevin nodded. "It could be worse. We just had a client who owed three million and their son was still a mess. Let me ask you the most important question. How long did he go without paying the premium?"

"Eighteen months."

Kevin let out a low whistle. The kind of whistle electricians give when they open a junction box and know without doing a thing it's going to cost you twenty thousand dollars. "Kathy, I've got some bad news for you."

"Bad news?"

"We can't do anything if it's over a year. If the premiums were not paid for a month or two, or maybe three at the most, we might be able to establish just cause, but a year and a half is too far over the limit. I'm sorry."

"That seems so unfair. He paid in all his life, he took this new job so he could continue to pay."

"Where did he get shot? What kind of job?"

"He was a guard at the city college."

"Damn," Kevin said. "Of all the employers, the city is protected the most from lawsuits. I'm sure his contract is rock solid in their favor."

"So what are my options?"

"I'm afraid you'll have to borrow the money. Have you contacted any of the medical loan companies?"

"Not yet. I was hoping to talk to you first."

"I'm going to forward you some names that are reputable. It's not pretty out there, the interest rates are off the charts, but you will get the money, providing you have some assets. Does your father own his house?"

"It's heavily mortgaged."

"Well, you're young and I'm sure there are ways to show these companies that you're serious about paying back the money. Hopefully your father will recover completely and continue working."

"Right," Kathy said, getting up. "Hopefully he'll get better enough to get shot again."

"I'm sorry, Kathy. Believe me, I wish I could help."

"I know you do. Thank you." Kathy started to leave the office.

"Excuse me, Kathy, do you want to pay now or should we take this directly from your account?"

"What?" Kathy couldn't believe it. "The ad says if you can't help it's free."

"That's only if we take a case and have no results. It does not include consultations."

"Well, how much is that?"

"Normally a consultation is a thousand dollars, but seeing you're in a bind, I will only charge you five hundred." She wanted to shoot him, but all she could do was hand him her card. He ran it through the scanner and handed it back. "Believe me," Kevin said, "no one gets charged this little. I could get in trouble."

"You're a saint." And Kathy left his office without actually saying, "Fuck you," which was very, very difficult.

Kathy called Brian and told him. He was furious. "You're kidding!"

"No. Five hundred for nothing."

"What a son of a bitch. Listen, try and forget it tonight. What are you doing later?"

"Feeling sorry for myself."

"Come to a meeting."

"What kind of meeting?"

"I'm not sure. A guy told me about this group that's trying to do something about health care."

"I can't sit through any more of this."

"It's not what you think. It's a lot of younger people who have some radical ideas about how to change things."

"What things?"

"Exactly what you're going through. Come on. Come with me."

"What time?"

"It doesn't start till nine. We'll get something to eat first."

Kathy was silent for a moment. Brian asked her again. "Come on, if it's boring we'll leave."

"Okay. Come get me at seven."

Euthanasia was legal in only three countries, and the United States was not one of them. Several of the states had allowed medical intervention to end life if there was great suffering, but the federal government wouldn't make it official, and there was always a chance someone could be prosecuted by the Justice Department, although the current administration was not active in that area. The matter went before the Supreme Court in 2020, but in a five–four decision they threw it back to the states, and it remained in the same gray area it always had. Certain states looked the other way and other states just banned it.

Oregon was the most lenient and, for a time, so many people went there to end their lives that the tourist bureau seriously thought about using that as an incentive. One of the slogans they tossed around was "See Oregon before you die." But better heads prevailed and they decided that advertising for a snuff job was a little crass. Nevada was also lenient, as were the states of Washington, Montana, North Dakota, North Carolina, and Florida. Florida out of necessity.

California was still not quite sure. No one would question a doctor letting a patient go in peace if there was great suffering, but in 2023 a lawsuit was brought against a physician by the family of a seventy-five-year-old woman with Lou Gehrig's disease. She was slowly losing all movement of her body and she begged the doctor to end it. He did, and three days later one of the big medical journals announced a possible cure. Even though the cure was years away and had not even started trials, the family sued. And won.

A jury got very emotional and ignored the woman's suffering. They sided with hope. The doctor's insurance company had to pay twenty million dollars. That decision scared other physicians in California away from the practice of euthanasia, and this left a void in the state. Hence, Walter Masters.

Walter Masters was a seventy-year-old science professor who watched his wife lie in a coma for six years before she died. Every doctor had said there was no chance of recovery, but she was not brain dead and no one would pull the plug. Masters was a mild-mannered man who lost it. Flipped out. And after that ordeal he decided he was put on the earth to keep other families from the same kind of interminable suffering, aside from draining all of their resources. The sad thing in his case was that for years he and his wife had talked about their feelings on this matter. He knew she didn't want to be kept alive by machines, but she never wrote it down. He had always told his students that whenever something was important, *write it down.* And in this one case he didn't follow that advice.

So there he was, a modern-day Kevorkian, but friendlier looking. With a shock of gray hair and a small mustache, Masters looked distinguished and somewhat mad at the same time. And he became famous in the underground world of euthanasia.

Masters took no chances. He would never end life if all the immediate family members were not on board, or if he sensed any ulterior motive, and he would not do the actual deed. He set up a drip system that would start five minutes after it was inserted. He insisted that the family be there and that they, or the patient if the patient was able, start the drip. Or they could stop it, but no one ever did. People didn't go to that much trouble and then change their minds.

Walter also said no occasionally. Once there was a man who was forty-five and a quadriplegic—a skier who took a wrong turn and fell down a mountain. No doctor would ever end a quadriplegic's life if his brain was functioning, not even in Oregon. So the man called Masters and asked for a meeting.

When Walter got there he was very understanding of the man's condition, but told him that he thought the man could make something out of his life since his mind was intact and there were so many new devices that would allow him to get around. Walter said he would have considered it thirty years ago, but with all the mobility the man was offered, he refused to terminate. The man begged. "Please, my wife left me and took my children and moved out of state. I'm all alone. I want to die."

"I'm sorry," Walter said. "I think with some counseling you can still lead a good life. And you don't want your children to be without a father. I cannot help you, but I will give you the name of someone to talk to."

"I have no money for that."

So he treated the man to ten sessions with a psychologist. It was a wonderful gesture even though it came to nothing. The last he heard was that the man was still living and got just enough movement back that he could inject himself with heroin. *You can't win 'em all.*

Walter felt the strong shaking of the great quake even though he lived in Kern County, almost two hundred miles north of Los Angeles. But what really affected him was the number of people who contacted him after the disaster. So many people were severely injured that the first thing they or their family members did, after realizing that help was not coming, was try to put themselves or their loved ones out of their misery.

Masters didn't quite know what to do. He was receiving fifty contacts a day. Fifty. He felt sorry for all of these people, but he explained that even if he was willing, he couldn't get to Los Angeles, as there was no way to travel there. No roads were open.

People begged. One man asked if he could do it over the phone. Walter, who had to have a dark sense of humor to do what he did, actually thought about telling the man to sit in the bath and make toast. But all he really could do was take their information and tell them that when it was okay to travel to Los Angeles he would check in and see how they were doing. Most of them would not be alive by then.

Brad Miller still could not really comprehend the damage to his condominium complex. He actually was lucky. Being on the first floor, his ceiling came down, but the condo above did not fall on him. A closet, the one where he kept Lola, collapsed, and Brad was sad when he saw her head lying next to her body. Sure, she was a robot, but it was amazing how you became attached to these things. He actually laughed for a moment, thinking what it would look like to a potential burglar to see a headless woman sitting in the kitchen. *Now, that would scare them even more.*

As he walked around the grounds, Brad saw several units, especially those on the second and third floors, that were leveled. Large solar panels and air-conditioning equipment on the roof that weighed thousands of pounds had fallen through the ceilings into the top-floor apartments.

At night Brad would sit outside on the artificial lawn with some of the other residents who remained, and they compared stories of who they knew was all right and who was not. Brad had not been able to contact Herb or Jack and had no idea if they were even alive. A neighbor he had a small crush on was nowhere to be found. Another man who lived next door had been killed in his sleep.

The scary thing was that all over Southern California, as people were assessing the extraordinary damage, they understood that no one was coming to help them anytime soon. There was just too much devastation. So people helped one another the best they could. If someone still had a room, they would take in an injured person and try to keep him alive. If people had extra food, they would share it. And everyone was on the lookout for looters, who, until the National Guard was fully in position, simply ran wild. The residents who had weapons were now considered the smart ones.

Brad had never bought a rifle, although he had been tempted to when the new laser guns were available for home sale. These fired a beam of light that would burn a hole in someone's skin from fifty yards. Brad's friend Herb had bought one but Brad said, "I've got a security guard right next to my place. Let him handle the bad guys."

When the security shack was leveled, the guard just ran away. Brad hoped he at least shot someone on the way out.

CHAPTER THIRTEEN

Brian and Kathy left the Charge N' Eat and went to the meeting, which neither of them knew anything about.

A new infrastructure had been built up around the electric car. One of the things that really caught on was the modern-day drive-in, known as the Charge N' Eat. Gasoline could only be sold by the oil companies, but electricity could be sold by anyone, and it was. Gasoline stations had done everything they could over the years to give people something else besides gas—the market, the fast food, the arcade, lottery tickets, anything that could fit—but no one ever wanted to eat in their car sitting in a gas station. Electricity was a different animal.

The first Charge N' Eat opened in 2016 in Phoenix and was an instant hit. As their cars were charging, customers could order food, and cute roller-skating girls delivered it. It was a throwback to the very first drive-in restaurants that had all but disappeared, but this time around it caught on big.

If people needed to get going in a hurry, they could charge their cars with the ultrafast electrical pumps, but that cost more, like premium gas. So most people opted for the cheaper thirty-minute slow charge, and they had to have something to do while they waited. Why not munch burgers and fries? It was a perfect fit. The people who came up with the Charge

N' Eat also tried to bring back drive-in movies, but that idea went nowhere.

"I think we're lost," Kathy said.

"Who gets lost anymore? The car knows where we are."

"Screw the car; have you ever been anywhere near here before?"

Brian looked out the window. It was farmland that seemed to grow nothing. All of a sudden his navigation voice told him he was on private roads and it could no longer confirm his location. "Shit."

"I told you."

"She never gets lost."

"What are we looking for?"

"A church. Or something that looks like a church. Supposedly the town is very small."

At that moment the navigation came back to life and informed him he had three miles to go. "See!" Brian was so proud of his car. "She never gets lost."

After another ten minutes they drove through a one-stoplight town and, sure enough, there was a building that looked like a church, but it also looked as if no one had gone there for years. It had a stained-glass window that was broken and boarded up. Kathy had never seen that before. She'd always assumed that stained glass was never left broken, that that would be almost sacrilegious, but obviously she was wrong. There were a few cars parked outside, along with several motorcycles. Kathy was thoroughly confused.

"Who told you about this?"

"This guy."

"What guy?"

"A guy who works in security."

"What do mean, security?"

"He's a bouncer, but he's a nice guy. Really smart."

"Jesus," Kathy said. "You met a guy in a fucking bar?"

"He's a nice guy. I was telling him about your dad and he suggested I come to this meeting."

"Why are you telling bouncers about my dad?"

"You're making too much of this. This guy is in the same situation as you. Paying off his mother's health care. He bounces to make extra money."

Before Kathy could say anything else, two motorcycles roared up behind them and the biggest guy she had ever seen recognized Brian. He yelled, "Hey, man!"

"Hey, Louie. I came."

"I wish I'd cum!" Louie laughed at his dirty joke.

Louie was basically a skinhead. About six-five, 290 pounds, quickly running out of any more room for tattoos. They had perfected laser treatment that could remove tattoos and leave the skin looking normal, but what they found was that most people who had their tattoos removed eventually put a new one in its place. Louie had the words FUCK YOU tattooed on his right forearm. He had it removed, but a year later he added MOTHERFUCKER. He always kicked himself when he realized he only had to remove the YOU. By just adding MOTHER and ER he could have saved three thousand dollars. This was the guy Brian called really smart.

They all walked in together. There were about thirty-five people standing around getting high and talking a mile a minute. Kathy, who was no prude when it came to altered states, didn't feel comfortable enough to lose control tonight. When she looked around the room, she had mixed feelings. Part of her felt that Brian was an idiot to get talked into something that he knew nothing about, and the other part was drawn to these people like a magnet. There was something all of them had in common. The anger.

A blond-haired guy stood up. He looked to be in his early thirties. Kathy couldn't help but stare; he was gorgeous. Six foot two inches. Two hundred pounds. He looked like a poster boy for being in shape. And a handsome face. Not movie-star handsome, more like Olympic-ski-team handsome. He introduced himself. "Hey, everybody, my name is Max. I'm originally from Maine. I've lived here for three years and I'm bored out of my fucking mind." Everyone laughed. "I think we all showed up for the same reason. This fucking country no longer cares about us. We're only here to pay the debt of the olds and it's time to say no. We are *not* going to pay their fucking bills any longer." The whole group broke into applause.

Kathy was wet. She was in love with this guy. Like crazy. She actually looked at Brian and felt sorry for him. His simple idea to go to this meeting was going to change their relationship forever.

Kathy had never been a love-at-first-sight person. As a matter of fact, with the feelings that she was experiencing at this moment she wondered if she had ever really been in love before. *This is crazy. Just listen to what he has to say and tomorrow this will all be nothing.* But as the meeting continued she felt closer and closer to these people. They were different from the kids in the resentment gangs. It was not just that they were more articulate; they were actually experiencing what she was—having to work for years to pay off a medical debt—or else they were sick themselves and couldn't get the proper care.

One woman, Sandy, had a damaged heart valve and was always tired, even at twenty-five years old. Her mother's health plan was so meager it would not pay for her operation, so Sandy lived her life with the energy of someone three times her age. Another young man, Robert, lost his vision in his left eye after a carjacking. If he could have gotten care quickly enough, his sight might have been saved, but his parents were divorced, and when his father remarried and had a son, Robert's health care vanished. It was something in the law that Congress always wanted to fix, but didn't.

People, one by one, stood up and told their stories. Brian told of his grandfather's illness and how it cost his parents a fortune, but he spoke quickly and did not make much of an impression. Kathy didn't feel she wanted to speak. But when she stood up and told the story of her dad, everybody was mesmerized. No one more so than Max.

She found it to be a great release. She could vent and cry and maybe even do something about it, though at the moment she didn't know what that was. No one had gotten to that part.

When everyone finished, Max stood back up and said, "Tonight is a starting point. It's important to know our stories and how we feel. Next time we'll talk about what we can do. The only thing worse than what we are going through is to feel helpless. So it's time to take back some power." Again, people applauded. No one really knew what he meant, but the words sounded so good. Everybody agreed they would meet again.

Kathy didn't want to leave. She wanted to talk to Max all night. She went up to him and said, "You were so great. We'll see you at the next meeting." Max gave her a hug.

"Feel better," he said.

Kathy stared at Brian as Max had his arms around her. She was aware of her expression. *Don't swoon. Look like it's your uncle.*

"Thank you," Kathy said, breaking the embrace so it wouldn't lead to anything more serious. Her tone of voice was all for Brian's sake. She sounded as matter-of-fact as possible. "We'll see you again sometime."

As Brian and Kathy were driving home, Brian was the first one to speak. "That was sort of boring, I'm sorry I dragged you there."

"I didn't think it was boring. I thought it was fascinating."

"You don't want to go back, do you?" Brian knew the answer.

"Are you kidding? I want to hear some solutions. Don't you?"

"I don't think that group is really going to have any solutions."

"Why not? No one else is doing shit."

"So we should go back?"

"I'm going back. You don't have to."

"No, that's all right. I'll go back."

And they drove for a while in silence. Brian reached over and pressed a button and music filled the rest of the ride home. Neither of them spoke until he dropped her off. Kathy beat him to the question of whether or not he should come in.

"I'm exhausted. I'm going to read for a bit and go to sleep. Thank you so much for taking me. I loved it." She gave him a quick kiss and opened the car door.

"I'll call you tomorrow," Brian said.

"Great," Kathy answered, hoping she sounded as if she meant it.

CHAPTER FOURTEEN

Shen Li had a grand celebration for his fortieth birthday. He flew his parents in from Hunan province and treated all of his childhood friends from home to an airplane ticket and a hotel room. Most of them had never been on an airplane, and certainly none of them had ever stayed anywhere as nice as the Beijing Hyatt.

Li's success story was legendary in his hometown. He had gone to the same rundown school that all of his friends attended, but from early on he showed ability as an organizer. At sixteen he got his prefecture's president to organize a protest against a factory that was poisoning a local stream. His younger brother, Hue, was diagnosed with cancer at the age of ten, and Shen was sure the stream was the reason, since his brother, more than anyone else in the family, was a swimmer and loved to dive into the water day or night, no matter what the weather.

When his brother died, Shen vowed to teach the factory a lesson. At sixteen, all he could do was protest. But at twenty-five, after graduating law school third in his class, he sued Matchuta Manufacturing and won a rare verdict against a company that fought everything and was always victorious. Shen's reputation grew, not only as a brilliant litigator but as someone with a future in politics if he wanted it. It was highly unusual for a person to come from his humble background and rise so quickly, but he had a gift.

Shen's mother, who still did her laundry in that same stream, looked at her son's birthday party as if she were on Mars. She was so proud of him and occasionally thought, *This can't really be my son; someone must have switched him at birth.*

Li's father was like a kid in a candy store. He had never seen a hotel buffet before and the Hyatt did it up right for the party, with all the delicacies that his parents loved but almost never got a chance to eat. Steamed wax gourd and straw mushrooms. Cheese-baked prawn, and one of his father's favorites, fish heads with the eyes sautéed in vinegar.

His mother loved frogs. Not the legs, the whole frog, boiled, cut into pieces, and mixed with onions and peppers. And although they were not drinkers by nature, the cocktails were so tasty that both of his parents got tipsy and rambled on about how their son had paid for all of this and how he was famous and beloved in Beijing. He wasn't really famous, but he certainly was heading in that direction.

Shen Li did not want to stay in law. It was not exciting enough. He felt he could succeed in business in a spectacular way as soon as he found his passion.

While still a lawyer he invested some money in a company that made pencil phones. As the name implied, a communication device, along with a camera, was put into a regular pencil without adding any bulk or noticeable weight. The company made them for a dollar and sold them for seven. It sold ten million in two years, and Shen made a small fortune. But he wasn't interested in gimmicks. He wanted to make money at something more important. And probably because he always thought of his brother and how someone who was so full of life was deprived of it so early, Li felt that something must be done to get health care to the masses. In 2022 Health Care for All was formed, with Shen Li as its president.

The concept was simple, even though the execution was not. Hundreds of millions of people throughout China would see a doctor, if they were lucky, two or three times in their life. Once, maybe, when they were born; once when they started school; and once if they enlisted in the People's Army. And decent medical care was still located in just the big cities.

In a rare instance an employer might pay to have a very valuable employee taken to a hospital in Beijing or Shanghai, especially if there was any thought that the company was responsible and could be fined. But mostly the poor got little or no help. Shen was convinced that if enough people paid pennies, small clinics with nurse practitioners who had access to current medical data could be set up around the country and bring care to people who would otherwise simply live with their illness or, in many cases, die from it. He knew that helping someone with pneumonia was not only cheap, but kept other people around them from getting the illness, and the result was that people were sick less and could be more productive. When the government saw that a little went a long way in keeping the population healthy, it became the biggest investor in Health Care for All.

So Shen Li wound up creating something that was one of the most successful public-private ventures in modern China. And he, in the process, became one of China's richest men.

President Bernstein was in the middle of his morning workout when John Van Dyke walked in. Bernstein was given a look that said, *I need you in private.* The President asked his trainer to step out. He wiped the sweat off his face and took a swig of water. "What is it, John? Another earthquake?"

"Your mother is in a coma." The President didn't say a word for what seemed like a full minute.

"When?"

"A half hour ago."

"Where is she?"

"They took her to Lady of Mercy."

Bernstein had a contentious relationship with his mother. He thought she never treated him like an adult, certainly not the adult he was, the most powerful man in the world. Well, not the most powerful anymore, but right up there with the Asian countries. He also blamed his mother for killing his father when she up and left him after fifty years of marriage. His dad got up one morning and found a note. An old-fashioned note, handwritten, in an envelope with his name on it. He had had no idea what it was, not even a clue. When he read that his wife had been unhappy for two decades, it wiped him out. It made him question everything he ever knew. He thought his whole life was a sham and wondered if everybody felt the same way about him.

Bernstein was Speaker of the House at the time and was so busy it made him angry that he had to come and take care of this mess himself. He let his dad come to Washington and got him an apartment, but his father died within the year. The President never forgave his mother, who came to the funeral with a date. She claimed the man just drove her because she was too upset, but Bernstein saw them holding hands.

John Van Dyke knew all about this, so he was not surprised to see his boss basically emotionless.

"I guess I have to visit her," the President said.

It was odd. He now had to act more distressed than he was, simply because he was president. The President was the griever in chief and if he didn't look sad that his own mother was in a coma, it would confuse the country. "Set it up, John. Put me through the paces. Let's leave today. We'll get there and do what we have to do."

"I've already arranged it, sir. Do you want to look at your statement?"

"No. I know what I said."

When the President arrived in Chicago, the press was waiting. Betsy didn't like his mother any more than he did, but when they got off the plane, they both could have been contenders for an Academy Award. She even had tears. The President approached the reporters and said, "We have no further information at this time. My mother is still in a coma and we are rushing to the hospital to be with her." One reporter actually yelled out, "Were you close, sir?" Bernstein almost laughed. What a ballsy question. This guy deserved an answer.

"Very."

When the motorcade got to the hospital, there was a slew of press waiting there, too, but they avoided it by going into the garage. They were taken to intensive care, where his mother was obviously being given special treatment. She was all alone in a large room designed for at least fifteen people. The President asked where the other patients were, and he was told they had been moved to other hospitals or different floors so she would be secure. This actually made him upset. He didn't think people who were in critical condition needed to be moved just so his mother could have all the machines to herself, but of course he said, "Thank you."

He looked at her face. She had no expression. Three doctors were standing by to answer any questions and, of course, to be near the president of the United States. Bernstein took his mother's hand and squeezed it. She didn't squeeze back, but no big deal, he was used to that. After a few minutes of touching her forehead and rubbing her arm, he asked to talk to the doctor in charge. A heavyset man introduced himself as Dr. Martinez.

The President was always amazed at how fat doctors were. *How can they ever give you medical advice when they need to lose a hundred pounds? And why don't they take the weight-loss drug? Do they know something we don't?* He asked to talk to the doctor privately.

They went into a small office and the President said, "Give me the truth. Real information. How long will she live?" Martinez didn't hesitate.

"She could live for years, sir, as long as the machines are connected."

"Really?" the President asked flatly. "Can she come out of the coma?"

"At this age and with the extent of the bleeding, I would say no."

"Is she brain-dead?"

"No."

"So she is not brain-dead but will remain this way?"

"So it seems, sir."

"And whose decision is it to keep the machines running forever?"

"Did she have a DNR, sir?"

"I know a lot of abbreviations," the President said, "but remind me what that is."

"'Do not resuscitate,' sir."

"I don't know if she did. Would that be in her will?"

"In her will or special instructions, Mr. President."

"I'll see. We'll look into it and let you know. Obviously she can't take up the intensive care unit forever. What will happen to her?"

"She would go to a facility."

"That's wonderful, it sounds so inviting. She can have lunch with Ariel Sharon." The doctor didn't laugh. He didn't know who that was.

Bernstein was on the plane back to Washington when he broke down. He wasn't crying for any simple reason. He was sad about the coma, he was sad that their relationship had deteriorated to such a degree, and he was sad that at the very moment in his presidency when he wanted to approach the subject of keeping dead people alive, it was taken from him by his own mother. Then he started to laugh. *Do not resuscitate. How funny.* He actually thought his mother might have had an "RAAC," "resuscitate at any cost."

CHAPTER FIFTEEN

It took about fourteen days for the military to get completely in place in Southern California. The work was so overwhelming that no one knew exactly where to start, but the first order of business was to bury the dead and to try to locate and attend to the injured. One hundred triage stations were set up in strategic points around Los Angeles. The U.S. Army Corps of Engineers worked day and night to restore as much electricity and water as possible. Generators were installed where landlines were completely destroyed, and electricity was fed neighborhood to neighborhood, if there were still standing buildings that could receive it. Water mains were repaired where the damage could be seen, but there were so many breaks in the system that even when large mains were fixed, nothing flowed.

Hundreds of trucks with drinking water were sent around the city, and people stood in line to get their few gallons. It was like Bangladesh, with the people of Los Angeles lining up with buckets and thermoses waiting for fresh water and precooked food. Helicopters flew over the city with loudspeakers directing people to the food stations, and the army tried to space things out so no one would have to walk more than four miles.

The government was trying to help the physically injured, but mental illness was not on the radar. The thought was that if they could get food to people and keep disease away, that would be ninety percent of the game. But what happened when people lost hope and gave up? That was never really planned for, certainly not on a scale this size. Here were millions of people who had had the life literally shaken out of them, with no one to tell them it would get better. There was a general sense of chaos, except chaos was slowly being accepted as the norm. It was amazing how fast the unthinkable was taken for granted.

Walter Masters eventually made his way down to Los Angeles. He visited some severely ill people whose friends or relatives had contacted him, and he performed about fifty procedures to end their suffering. When word got out that he was functioning in the area, people started begging him. Some people who were physically okay but financially wiped out wanted to end their lives, but that was not Walter's game. He ended genuine suffering, not horrible bad luck or going broke. *My God, if I opened my practice to financial catastrophe, I would have the world waiting in line.*

Brad Miller's condo was finally red-tagged; he could no longer live there, even though his walls were still standing. He slept in the bedroom for almost a month, feeling the air at night that came in through the holes in the ceiling.

One day someone knocked on his door, someone who looked like a cop or an army private, he couldn't tell which. He informed Brad that he would have to go to the shelter that was closest to him, in Pasadena.

"Pasadena?" Brad asked. "I don't know anyone there. Can't I just stay in my bedroom?"

"No, sir. These properties are going to be leveled over the next several months."

"What happens to my investment?"

"That will be handled by another department, sir."

"But it was a condo. I don't own the land, just the building. Now it won't be here. Do I get my money back?"

"There will be people to talk to in Pasadena, sir. That is not my department. You are allowed to take one suitcase."

"One suitcase? I can't fit my life in one suitcase. What do I do with all my memories?"

"I'm sorry, sir. Pick out what is most valuable to you that will fit in one suitcase. I'll leave you some information that might be of help. You will be moving on Thursday."

"That's two days. I'm not ready." But before Brad could say any more, the man was gone. He left a sheet of paper. At the top it said, *One Suitcase Only*. And there was a list of suggestions of what to put in his suitcase for the rest of his life. Brad threw it away. He didn't need the government to tell him how to pack.

He went outside and sat under the tree. There were only twelve people remaining in the complex and they met there each night at dusk and drank and cried and reminisced. They had all been informed that they were being relocated. Brad was surprised that they were not all scheduled for Pasadena. The army guy had made it sound like everyone from this area would go to that one place, but apparently their system was based on something else. Brad hoped it wasn't Jews.

As the folks sat under the tree for what might be the very last time, someone brought up Walter Masters. A woman's sister's husband had been relieved of his suffering just two days earlier, and Masters was talked about like some Pied Piper of death. "What did he do?" asked Brad.

"Put him out of his misery," the woman said.

"How?"

"I don't know. Some kind of shot."

"What kind of shot?" another man asked.

"A shot right to the head," Brad joked.

The woman said she didn't know what the shot was but it was quick and painless. "Is that legal?" someone else asked.

"Who gives a shit?" the woman answered. "Who would care? Do you think they want more of us to take care of?"

She had a point. And Brad was glad he didn't have access to the shot at that very moment, because the thought of going to Pasadena with one piece of luggage for the rest of his life—well, he just might have used it.

CHAPTER SIXTEEN

The Mueller family was vacationing at their home in Vail, Colorado. They loved to ski there in the winter and bike around the magnificent pine trees in the summer months. Sometimes Dr. Sam Mueller looked at his children and thought they were spoiled. Patty was turning into a real beauty and Mark would have been a heavy child in another era, but with a simple pill each day he looked quite fit, if not as handsome as his sister was pretty. Their mother did her best to make sure they knew how fortunate they were and tried to instill a sense of "giving back," but they didn't really have anything of their own, so giving back was just watching some of their parents' millions going to other people instead of them.

Sam Mueller always admired the very wealthy who claimed they were leaving their children nothing so they would not lead a life counting on their parents' riches, but "nothing" to these kinds of people meant fifty million dollars instead of a billion. Sam had not gone that route. His will left the bulk of his estate to his wife and children. But when he got very angry with his son, which was rare, he would threaten him with no inheritance. A thirteen-year-old boy doesn't really respond to that, especially when the threat is issued on the family's private island.

The night before, in their eight-thousand-square-foot villa, had been a little tense. After being served dinner, the family decided to watch a movie. Before they did, Sam scanned the major news outlets and got immersed in watching footage of Los Angeles, which now had its own channel. "I hate seeing this. It breaks my heart," he said, to no one in particular.

"It's their own fault for living there," his son said.

Sam snapped. "What the fuck did you just say?"

"Honey," Maggie said, "take it easy. He didn't say anything." Mark got nervous. He knew this side of his father and didn't like to provoke it.

"That's not what you say when people are devastated to this degree," Sam shouted. "That's a spoiled brat talking. Do you think people have choices like we do, that they can just live in any mansion they want?"

"Dad," Patty said, "I don't think he meant it that way."

"Stay out of it, Patty. How *did* you mean it, Mark?"

"I don't know. I didn't think about it that much."

"You have to learn goddamn empathy."

"Honey, he has empathy."

"When? Where? I've never seen it. He feels sorry when one of his friend's boats breaks down."

Mark got up and stormed out of the room, stifling a cry. He ran upstairs and slammed the door. Maggie got up and followed him. Sam tried to stop her. "Leave him alone, honey, let him think about it."

"He doesn't even know what he did."

Patty was left alone with her father. She moved closer to him and took his hand, which was still shaking with anger. "I don't think he meant it that way, Dad."

"Does he know what we have, Patty? Do you?"

"Yes, of course I do. You know how grateful we are."

"I don't want you to be grateful. I want you to care about people deep down. I don't want my success to spoil you rotten." Patty smiled at her father. She knew how to wrap him around her finger.

"Dad, I didn't come into this world expecting anything. I lucked out being your child and I always know that. Mark knows that, too."

Sam gave her a hug. All of a sudden he felt guilty. Maybe this had nothing to do with his son's comment. Maybe if he had cured schizophrenia, he would not feel like a one-trick pony. Even though the cancer cure was the greatest trick there was, he was always amazed at how not following it up could make him feel like a failure.

Sam came downstairs early the next morning and his son and daughter were having breakfast. He gave Mark a hug. "I lost my temper last night. I'm sorry."

"That's okay. I didn't mean what I said to sound like I didn't care. I just always thought it was stupid to live on a giant earthquake fault."

His father laughed. "I can't disagree with you. It is pretty damn stupid." They all had a chuckle over it, then Sam brought up a proposition to his son. "Marky, I have a speaking engagement next week. Do you want to take a ride with me?" Mark looked at his father. This was an unusual question, as his dad never asked him to travel on business.

"Where are you going?"

"Chicago."

"Do I have to?"

"Of course not," his father said, obviously disappointed. Mark realized he should have just said yes.

"You know what, Dad, I'll go. It might be fun."

"Don't worry about it. You can decide later."

"No, no. I'll go. It will be fun."

His father was pleased. "I think so, too. We'll have a great time. Father-son stuff. We'll have a ball."

When Stewart Bernard came home from the hospital, he appeared to be making a recovery. But one Monday morning he got out of bed and fell on the floor. He didn't trip; it was almost like fainting. He lay there for a minute and then got up and went about his day thinking that maybe he had just eaten something bad or had a cold or something. He decided not to tell Kathy because he didn't want her to worry, and he also felt guilty that he had now become such a financial burden. The last thing he wanted was to dump more problems on her.

Kathy was already up and sitting at breakfast when he walked in. She looked at him for a long time. "You don't look well."

"I'm fine."

"You look white as a sheet."

"No, I don't. By the way, I have a job interview this week." Kathy was surprised, and excited. Money was such a big problem now that additional income would be extremely helpful.

"What kind of a job?"

"Construction coordinator."

"What's that?"

"I'm not sure. Bob Seagram called me and said he heard of an opening and thought I had the kind of experience that would be a plus."

"I don't remember Bob Seagram."

"Bob worked with me at Saturn and moved to Toronto five years ago. Loves it there."

"What do you mean, Toronto?"

"What do you mean, 'what do I mean'?"

"The job is in Toronto?"

"Apparently."

"You can't move out of the country."

"Why not?"

"Because what am I going to do?"

"Honey, I'm a burden to you here. Financially and every other way."

"I don't want you to leave this house. You can find a job here; you don't have to move out of the country."

Her father loved her so much. She really did care for him. He got up to give her a hug and that was the last thing he ever did. He blacked out and fell on the floor, and Kathy became hysterical. She called Emergency and described the situation, and they said they needed to confirm a beating heart before they sent a resuscitation team. In the new world, if the patient was already dead, there was no hurry; they would just ask the caller to cover the body, leave the room, and wait. Only if the person had a real chance at surviving would someone come.

Kathy was asked to put a transmitting device, a device that every residence was required to have, on her father's skull. Through the transmission of medical information they would tell her what their decision was. After sixty seconds Kathy heard what she was most afraid of. A passionless voice told her that the person lying there was dead. She was told to cover the body with a sheet or a blanket and wait in another room. She started screaming and throwing dishes and smashing her fist against the wall. "What the fuck! What the fuck!" And then she started to weep uncontrollably.

She covered her father as instructed and left the kitchen. And then the strangest thing happened. She looked up Max Leonard. She had not seen him since that meeting, but he was whom she wanted in her life at this critical moment. Her father had died less than a minute earlier and she wanted to be held and comforted and told everything was going to be okay by a man she'd only met once.

Max Leonard had just turned twenty-eight. He was born into a lot of money, raised in Maine, and the irony was that his parents, who were still living, were rich enough to take care of themselves and would never be a burden to him. But he had always been different. He was rebellious before he even knew what the meaning of the word was. And he wasn't like his other friends who had dough. Most of them were either spoiled or drugged out or in business with their families. Max thought it was all bullshit.

When he quit college, much to his father's dismay, he had joined CareCorp, a group of young people who worked for a year with underprivileged families within the United States. He was sent to a town in West Virginia. He had had no idea when he was summering on the beaches at Bar Harbor that people lived like this less than a thousand miles away, and Max became very close to his adopted family.

He learned about life in a way that schools didn't teach. For example, it appeared to him that people who came from great poverty seemed closer. Less divorce, no screwing around, more loyalty. It seemed that luxury brought with it a type of behavior he abhorred.

Max was with this family when the father died of cancer, having no access to the cure. The mother was never well, drank too much, but still tried to take care of four children, and Max wound up being their surrogate dad for a period of eight months. After his year was up, the mother had gotten worse and the kids were now living with relatives. Max felt as if he had accomplished nothing, except that he had. He had changed forever. He officially rejected the destiny his parents had planned for him and vowed to be one of those people who made a difference. And he was serious.

Instead of going back to college, he traveled. He worked with several community organizations and became a charity bum, helping out groups in different cities, seeing the world, and trying to find out what was in his soul.

He worked in Indianapolis for a charity that helped underprivileged children, and he liked it there. The vibe felt right. So Max bought a small farm on the outskirts of town, did some sculpting and painting, and spent time with the underprivileged kids, basically living like a retired person, but it suited him. At twenty-one he inherited enough money to last him a lifetime and all that was left was to find his passion. He knew one thing: The children he was working with had lost all hope. They were not excited to grow up. They felt overwhelmed, and at such an early age. Max knew this was wrong and it had to change. That was why he held that meeting, the meeting where he met Kathy. He could get any girl he wanted, but he had never really fallen for any of them. Until now.

Max was lifting weights when he heard her voice. He was listening to music in his earpiece and it was interrupted by the call. "Did I bother you?" Her voice was so clear, he actually looked around the room to see if she was there.

"Who is this? Kathy?"

"Yes, how did you know?"

"I just did. What's wrong?" She didn't get much out before Max left to go to her house. In what seemed like ten minutes, he was standing at her door and she was crying in his arms. Her father was still in the kitchen.

"How did it happen?"

"He stood up and that was it."

Max walked in and took off the blanket. He stared at her dad. "He was handsome. He was a good man."

"How do you know?"

"You. I know because of you." And then they kissed. Right there, with her father on the floor. *How insane,* she thought. She was madly in love with this man, his tongue deep in her throat, and her father lying there, dead. She almost laughed.

"What a strange way to ask for permission to date," she said.

Max looked in her eyes. He didn't laugh or frown or make any facial expression. He just knew that this was the person he was waiting for. And at that moment the doorbell rang.

"Dead body?" one of the men standing in the doorway asked.

"In the kitchen," Kathy said.

The other man took all of the relevant information. He asked Kathy if he could take a quick brain wave from her. It took five seconds and nothing had to be worn, just something passed over the temple. The PTS, or Portable Truth Scanner, had been in use for almost five years. It was not admissible by itself in court, but if you failed you would be asked to take an old-fashioned lie detector test, which *was* admissible. And if you refused the PTS, you were thought guilty by that very fact. Even in the product's literature they pointed out how in ninety percent of the cases that people refused to be scanned, they were lying. Refusal equaled deception.

Kathy passed her test. They removed her father and told her he would be cremated unless she had other plans. "Other plans?" she asked. "Can you bring him back to life?"

"No, ma'am. Of course not."

"Then cremate him. That's fine."

Kathy went into the living room and sat down next to Max. She put her head on his shoulder and cried. One man was gone and another man had arrived. *God, life is strange sometimes.*

CHAPTER SEVENTEEN

These were the meetings the President hated the most. Anything to do with budget issues always ended badly. When he entered the room, everyone was already seated: the secretary of the Treasury, the chairman of the Federal Reserve, the director of the Office of Management and Budget, and twelve others who always looked like the sky was falling.

A decade and a half earlier, in 2016, the dollar's run as the world's reserve currency ended. It was not replaced by another, but instead a complicated shared currency went into effect in which the banks of the world, which previously held their reserves in dollars and euros, now used the renminbi, the rupee, the dollar, the euro, the pound, and a rising star, the Korean won. It was not only a complicated mess, allowing shrewd traders to profit from trading one currency against another, but Bernstein always felt that it weakened the United States. As long as the dollar was being diluted so severely, why not get rid of it in favor of a world currency?

Bernstein had addressed the world currency issue in his campaign, but it seemed to scare people. The official demise of the dollar, too many people felt, would end the United States as a power once and for all, even though that demise had already taken place. But the very idea of the word "dollar" leaving the language was too much for most people to handle. And economists could not be certain that a world currency would make Americans richer, though the President strongly disagreed. Bernstein felt that if all of these currency conversions were eliminated, trillions of dollars could be saved. He kept telling anyone who would listen that if there were a single currency, the trading in money would be stopped forever. The President hated that a few people around the world could decide each day what the dollar was worth. *Why should money be traded as if it were coffee or sugar?* But once the President got into office, a cascade of issues fell on his head, as they do on every president's, and the world currency campaign took a backseat. He still wanted to revive it.

As he sat down, his chief of staff opened the meeting. John Van Dyke was smart. He knew a little about everything and in many areas he was an expert. He hated the debt that America's engine ran on, but like everyone else, he had no idea how to solve it. The debt affected every single person now, not just the rich or the old or the young or the poor, but to solve this problem, everyone's life would have to change so radically that no one wanted to deal with it. And the worst thing about the debt was that it was now accepted as part of American life. When it finally surpassed the gross national product, people running for office stopped saying, "It's time to wipe out the debt." Now all they said was, "Elect me, and I will keep it from going higher."

One candidate in the 2016 election actually came up with a World Forgiveness Day, a day when the entire world would forgive all debt and everyone on the planet could start from scratch. It got some traction; people loved the idea, and it made for rousing speeches. Until, that is, someone actually analyzed it and came to the conclusion that the rich people would lose the most as banks would go out of business, since banks made all of their money on debt. Ideas that put banks out of business generally went nowhere and this one was no exception.

The President turned to his secretary of the Treasury, Morton Spiller, and asked him to begin. The President thought Spiller was smart, but the more they worked together, the less he liked him. He was impressed by Spiller's career in finance as head of GoldmanSachsofAmerica (GSofA) for six years, during which time the company had made more money than any other financial institution in the world.

Spiller had never worked in government but could not refuse when the president of the United States asked him to take the job. He had one request: He wanted to work four months of the year from his farm on Nantucket. With communications being so sophisticated, the President agreed, but began to resent it when everyone else was suffering through the summers in Washington and Spiller was relaxing at home in his pajamas.

Bernstein had so many meetings where Spiller was on a screen dressed in a sharp blue suit that he became sure the suit was fake and Spiller was really naked or at best in his underwear. Before Spiller spoke, the President said, "Good to see you're actually here, Morton. Where's that suit?"

"I beg your pardon?"

"Nothing. Just making conversation. How's the farm?"

"It's doing well."

"Good," the President said. "Give my best to the family. How long you here for?"

Spiller could hear the sarcasm in Bernstein's voice and didn't want to get him more annoyed than he was going to be after their meeting, so he played dumb. "I'm here for a long time, unless you need me to go somewhere."

"That's fine," the President said. "I like seeing you in the flesh. So what's up?"

Van Dyke answered. "We've run numbers on California. They're not good." Bernstein turned to Spiller.

"Spiller the beans, Morton." It was a joke he had used before, but the people in the room chuckled. A lot had changed over the course of the history of the United States, but the one thing that always remained the same was that people laughed when a president made a joke. A bad joke, an incomplete joke, a repeated joke, it didn't matter. It was the original form of ass kissing. Bernstein would even comment on it to his wife. "They laugh at everything. I bet all leaders go through this. I'm sure when Moses made a bad joke they stopped working on the golden calf and chuckled." His wife laughed at that and he even wondered if that was fake, too.

When Morton Spiller was finished with his presentation on the dire economical state of postearthquake California, he sat down and waited for the President to speak. All Bernstein said after looking at the charts and graphs and a screen full of numbers was, "What does this mean?"

"It means we can't fix it," Spiller said. "We have never had a disaster of this kind. Never before has a city even close to the size of Los Angeles been basically leveled. It's worse than a war. Even a nuclear device would not have done this much damage. To rebuild would cost twenty trillion dollars, and that might be low-balling it." The President let this sink in.

"Twenty trillion? What about the insurance companies?"

"No insurance company can come up with money even close to this," Spiller said. "They'll all go out of business unless we bail them out. There is no way people will get reimbursed from their insurance."

Someone else at the table gave an example. "It's as if every vehicle in the United States had an accident on the same day. No insurance company ever figured that into their equation." Bernstein got angry.

"Bullshit. Insurance companies knew damn well this would happen. It was always predicted. They just didn't give a shit. They should never have insured these people to begin with if they had no intention of paying. That's against the law, isn't it?"

"It might be, sir," Spiller said, "but I'm afraid that's not the issue. They do not have the money. We don't have the money. Courtrooms at this point are not going to help anyone. We need to figure out a way to deal with this." The President turned to the secretary of the Interior.

"What's the current situation at this moment?"

"We're just trying to keep everyone's head above water now, sir. Tending to the really sick, leveling buildings that are on the verge of falling, supplying water and food—that's all we can do right now."

"And even that is costing five billion a week," Spiller said.

The President rubbed his forehead with his right hand and let out a groan. "So what the hell do we do?"

Van Dyke had a thought. "We should first rebuild the hospitals so the people can get better treatment over the long run. Right now all we have are the triage units, and the best they can do is sew someone up or help with the spread of disease. We need better facilities."

"I understand that," the President said. "I'm asking about the larger issue. How do we rebuild our West Coast?"

There was no answer. Finally, after what seemed like five minutes, Spiller said, "Maybe we don't."

"What?" the President asked.

"Maybe we don't fix it. Maybe it returns to the way it was before they built it up."

"You're kidding, right? You want fifteen million people to roam around orange fields? That's a joke, right?"

"No, sir. I didn't mean that. But maybe we relocate people to other states, and return to an era of a much smaller population out West with far fewer structures. Something like that."

"Good, Morton," the President said. "Can you take a hundred thousand people on your farm?" Everyone laughed except Spiller. He looked away. He was angry, but certainly was not going to show it in front of the others.

"I'm just trying to help, sir."

"I understand," the President said, "but we can't move millions and millions of people and build them homes and provide a life for them. Wouldn't that cost the same as rebuilding the city?"

"I don't know, sir. I haven't run those numbers."

"Well, run them if you like, but I think we have to concentrate on how to restore Los Angeles. Our other major cities are crowded enough and we're not going to send everyone to a desert island, so let's start thinking of ways to rebuild. Maybe there are ways to do it for less, or use some kind of new construction or something we're not thinking about at this moment. John's got the best architectural minds in the country working on this. How's that going?"

"They need more money, sir."

"Of course they do." Bernstein got up. "Listen, I wanted to talk more about the world currency but I don't think today is the best time. Let's break for now. Los Angeles will remain the top priority. We need more ideas. From everyone. Morton, come to the Oval Office for a minute, please."

And with that the President left the room. Spiller walked over to John Van Dyke. "What's this about?"

"I don't know. Believe it or not, he actually makes decisions on his own."

When Spiller walked into the Oval Office, the President was seated on the couch. "Have a seat," Bernstein said. "Morton, you're a good man, but I don't want to do the farm thing anymore." Morton knew instantly what the President meant, but acted as if he didn't.

"The farm thing?"

"I need my secretary of the Treasury here, permanently. A vacation now and then is fine, but four months away is too much. It's setting a bad example."

"Well, Mr. President, you did make the agreement as part of bringing me on."

"I did," the President said, "but I don't want to anymore."

"Well, sir, I have to talk to my family. May I have a few days to think about it?"

"No. We are in a serious crisis and I need people here who are putting the country first."

"That's not fair, sir. I love this country."

"And you should. You have more money than God. But possibly you are in a period of your life where your farm beckons you, and that's okay. But I need twenty-four seven."

"I've always given you that, sir."

"I need twenty-four seven here, in Washington."

"So you want me to resign?"

"I want you to make a decision now."

"I can't do that, sir."

"I know," the President said. "I'll tell you what, take two hours. You know what's ahead for us. Only stay if you think you can run another marathon in your life. I will understand if you can't. And if you leave, you and John will craft something that sounds reasonable. I don't want people to get more scared about their money than they already are."

"I understand. I'll make my decision before dinner."

"Thank you, Morton."

As Shen Li continued to watch the news of the devastation in Los Angeles, he was amazed that the nation that had for so long been the leader in everything now looked like it was handling one of nature's worst disasters as if it were a third-world country. Seeing people lining up for food and medical care, it looked to him like a disorganized version of what he did much better. Being a concerned citizen of the world and someone who also loved making money, Li wondered how he could get involved in this. Branch out, so to speak.

The one area where Li thought he could really contribute was mental health. He had learned a long time ago that when people who were not used to trauma or even regular medical care needed attention, the emotional component that went with that was substantial. Calming people down became a science, and if done right, would make their treatment much easier.

For example, Li had had scientific studies done of what kind of music worked best, although he knew he might have to alter that for the Western world. He knew what colors and temperatures worked, he knew the perfect things to say to people who were in great stress, and he knew how to recognize when someone was so far gone that it was best to administer psychiatric drugs immediately, before anything else was even attempted.

One of the things that the Americans did not do was "work the line," as Li called it. In times of great stress there were always lines of people trying to get whatever help was needed. Li had done many studies that proved the effectiveness of having trained people make physical and verbal contact with patients waiting on line. It might have sounded simple, but before Li it had never been done, not in China or anywhere else. People were only attended to when they finally got in the door. But crowds could create terrible conditions for themselves if left alone, and Shen Li figured that out. Simply having people working the line made everything go better.

Li didn't know how he could export an entire program or philosophy to the people of Los Angeles, especially since he wasn't asked, so he started with something small. Something for the children to do while they waited with their parents. He had created small handheld devices with hundreds of problem-solving puzzles that were not just for play, but were designed to take a child's mind off of the calamitous world they'd been thrown into. The child not only was occupied, but the device communicated with other children in the same line or in the immediate area, so a communal effect was generated, starting with the kids. And it worked wonders. Instead of having hundreds of children who were all strangers and more scared than their parents, a community was immediately hatched simply by having them interact. This—along with line counseling and the right music and feeding people, and a magician or two—well, it made waiting for help almost fun.

Li donated the handheld devices. He had them programmed in English, found out what department in the U.S. government would accept such a gift, and then shipped one million of them to Los Angeles at a cost of approximately a dollar each. And this was how he got his foot in the door of America. The largest provider of private health care in China was, for the first time, talking to the American government. Li saw this not only as an opportunity to do more business with the United States, but also as the first real test of his Eastern methods working successfully in the West.

CHAPTER EIGHTEEN

Brad Miller looked at his one piece of luggage and couldn't really grasp that eighty years of living was coming down to this. He did not want to leave his condo. No one would tell him what was to happen with his property. This was his biggest investment. How could the government just ask him to leave without giving him a check, or a promise, or something?

He opened the door for the last time and walked out to where a bus was waiting. He watched as some men put up police tape around the entire complex, signifying that people were not to cross—the structure was unsafe, and to enter would be punishable by a fine or jail, or both. He had to laugh. *What jail? There is no jail. That collapsed in the first minute. Where are they gonna put me? Jail. What a joke.*

He boarded the bus and looked back one last time at the place he loved. He then took a seat and that was it. He didn't want to think about it again, but he could think of nothing else. He wanted money. Were they going to rebuild and let him move back in? Were they going to offer him a check in Pasadena?

As the bus pulled away, Brad noticed that it was only a third full. But soon enough it stopped at one place, then another, and another, until it was packed, all with people carrying one suitcase.

A fat older man sat next to Brad. He had body odor. *Thank God we're just going to Pasadena, this guy smells like a salami.* The fat man immediately fell asleep and snored loudly. Brad looked at the man's belly sticking out from his golf shirt. *He couldn't afford the pill? Maybe he had a rare condition and couldn't take it. Maybe he took it and decided he liked being fat better.* Brad started to laugh. This was what his life had come to. Guessing about a fat guy on a bus. He laughed so loud, the man woke up.

"What's so funny?" the fat guy asked.

"Oh, it's nothing. Just the way I deal with stress."

"Tell me about it," Fatty said. "This is beyond stress. The only thing that makes me feel better is to eat."

"Really? Have you ever taken—"

"Of course I have." The fat guy stopped him; he was used to the question. "You know the one-tenth of one percent it doesn't work on?"

"Yeah."

"You're lookin' at him."

"Really? I've never met anyone it didn't work on."

"Well, I lost weight, but the side effects weren't worth it."

"What were they?"

"Paranoid thoughts, sweating, heart palpitations, interrupted sleep, the whole nine yards. Everything it said on the package, I got."

"I'm sorry."

"Sorry for what? That I'm fat?"

"No. Sorry you had side effects. I'm sure being paranoid was not fun."

"Listen . . . what's your name?"

"Brad."

"Brad, being overweight is the least of my problems. I'm divorced, I don't see my kids, they moved back East and what did I do? I chose to stay on the goddamn San Andreas Fault. So now I have nothing. And I'm going to some concentration camp."

Brad got scared.

"What do you mean? Where are we going?"

"I heard it was like where they put the Japanese in World War Two."

"You're kidding. What do you mean?"

"You know, barbed wire, that kind of thing."

"Who did you hear that from?"

"Someone on line at the food bank."

"They can't do that! They don't have the right to put us there!"

"I don't know, we'll find out soon enough. Do you have a protein bar or some cake or something?"

"No."

"Well, I'm gonna try and go back to sleep. Punch me if I snore too loudly."

And as his seatmate snored again in less than twenty seconds, Brad just stared out the window.

Before the quake (BQ), a trip from Brad Miller's condo to Pasadena would have taken twenty minutes, half an hour at most. After the quake (AQ), the trip took almost four hours. Since every road in Los Angeles was severely damaged, decisions had to be made about what to fix first, how much of it to fix, and how permanent the fixes would be. Mostly, with the help from the federal government, roads were patched that were considered the most vital arteries in the city. Where a twelve-lane freeway had once stood, now only one or two lanes were functioning, so people just didn't travel unless it was an emergency.

When the bus finally pulled into Pasadena, it moved at one or two miles an hour, as surface streets were in just as bad a shape as the freeways. A town like Pasadena, which had hundreds of streets, now had only one or two that were passable. And then Brad saw the sign: ROSE BOWL 2 MILES.

"They're putting us in the goddamn Rose Bowl!" he said out loud. "I'm not living in the Rose Bowl! I'd rather sleep in the park than sleep in that crummy old place!"

Fatty woke up. "They can't be putting us in the Rose Bowl."

"Why?"

"Because it fell down, it was leveled. I saw pictures. That and Dodger Stadium, they were both destroyed." And then, as the bus turned onto the Rose Bowl grounds, they saw their new home. A tent the size of a football field.

The Rose Bowl had indeed been leveled, and one of the first construction projects the Army Corp of Engineers completed was to push aside the crumbled cement and put up a temporary structure. It wasn't really a structure; it looked more as if the biggest circus in the world was in town. It was designed to house up to four thousand people.

Inside were rows of bunk beds stacked four high holding three hundred people on each level. There were one hundred toilets, four areas of food service, and eight designated areas where people could sit and watch images coming from one of the ten large screens. It was noisy, but had no real odor. The one thing they had perfected over the years was how to properly ventilate these kinds of temporary structures, but it was still hot.

Brad just couldn't believe it. *How long is this for?* He was a goddamn home owner, for Christ's sake, not a kid going into the army. Were they just going to keep him there forever? He wanted answers. He wanted out of there. He hoped he was not going to share a bunk with Fatty, although he sort of liked the guy. Anybody who could sleep on a bus as he was being driven to a concentration camp couldn't be all bad. But right now all Brad really cared about was information. *What is the plan? Do I get my money?* Every employee he asked told him the same thing: "That will be addressed later." The only real information he was given was his bunk number and the rules of the tent. He was also given a food card and a key to a small chest of drawers. He went from anger to confusion to a sort of passive state, which lasted only ten minutes, until he saw the line for the bathroom.

"There are people I need to tell about my father," Kathy said as she sat holding Max's hand, never wanting to let go.

"I understand. Can I help you?"

"I need to tell Brian."

"I'll give you some time alone. Will you call me when you feel like it?"

"I feel like it now." They walked to the door and they kissed. So passionately, so beautifully, she just couldn't get over how life could deliver so many emotions in one day.

When Max left, Kathy sat down. She started to cry. For her dad, for herself, for breaking Brian's heart. For everything.

"Hello?" Brian said, looking at his watch.

"Hi."

"Where have you been? I've been trying to reach you."

"My dad died."

"What?! You're kidding? How? When? I'm coming over."

And before Kathy could answer, he disconnected. Not that she would have tried to stop him anyway.

Brian was there in ten minutes. The door was unlocked and Kathy was in the kitchen, where she was making tea. Brian walked over and gave her a hug. He didn't try to kiss her and she wouldn't have let him anyway. "I'm so sorry," he said. "How did it happen?"

"Just suddenly. It happened right here. He was having breakfast."

"Breakfast? It happened at breakfast? Why didn't you call me?" Kathy said nothing. She took her tea and went into the living room. Brian followed her. He asked again. "That was six hours ago, how come you didn't call me?" Kathy sat down and tears began welling up. "I'm sorry," Brian said. "I don't want to see you cry. I just wanted to be here to help. That's what people do when they're close. I just wanted to be here. You should have called me."

Kathy couldn't hear this anymore. She took advantage of her state of mind and just blurted it out. "I don't love you."

"What? What did you say?"

"Brian, you're the most wonderful guy and I have had some amazing times with you, but I don't love you."

"When did *this* happen?"

"I don't know. It happened." In the past it was moments like this when Kathy would say something like, "I'm just confused right now," or "I just need time to think." But she didn't. She said, "I'm in love with Max Leonard."

And now Brian had a moment that everyone goes through at least once. A moment when someone is told something that he already knew but never wanted to hear, and when he does hear it, he is forced to act shocked, as if it were a surprise.

"What? What the fuck? The guy from the meeting?"

"Yes."

"When did this happen?"

"It just happened. Probably instantly, I don't know."

"So you called *him*?"

"That's not important."

"It is to me. Your father died and you called *him*?"

"Yes."

And that was the worst thing Brian could hear. He knew it was over. He knew how significant that was. He was so torn. He wanted to say something mean to try to hurt her for hurting him, but her dad had just died, and more important, he knew that nothing he could say would change a thing. He got up. He made a small attempt at keeping his dignity, using probably the most overused line in breakup history: "No one will love you like me, Kathy. No one you will ever meet." And then he left her house and cried all the way home. He was so crazy about that girl.

CHAPTER NINETEEN

His wrist made a small vibrating noise. Robert Golden looked down and saw a disturbing story. Almost two years had gone by since the bus massacre where old people were killed for no apparent reason, and now it had happened again. This time in Arizona, near a retirement community. A young man had boarded a city bus and shot eight people he thought were over the age of sixty. Seven were; one was a forty-six-year-old man who had obviously had a long night. Just when the first incident had slowly faded from people's memory, here it was again.

Robert Golden had recently turned sixty-five and, as head of AARP, was one of the go-to people regarding anything involving aging. AARP had grown from an organization that claimed thirty-five million members in 2010 to one that had almost a hundred million in 2030. Their power in Washington, always legendary, was stronger than ever, and whenever they felt threatened by laws that would impinge on their age group, they went into action. They were excellent at organizing protests and bothering Congress and everything that one does to remain the squeaky wheel.

Golden called into his office his trusted underling, Paul Prescott, one of the few younger people on the board. Paul was fifty, no spring chicken, but he was considered the link to the younger generation, which of course he knew nothing about. A gay man with no children, he would brag about how his nieces and nephews loved him to death but he basically hated everything that young people did and had always felt old even when he was a kid.

"Did you hear about this?" Golden asked.

Paul looked at the screen and replayed the story. "This was at an Indian casino?"

"No," Golden said, "a retirement home. People are trying to say it was an isolated incident, but it sure looks a lot like the one two years ago."

"I never believe in isolated incidents," Paul said. "I don't think the human race is capable of those."

"What do you mean?"

"People aren't that unique. It would be impossible for only *one* person to do something, no matter what it is. A person needs other people to even think of an idea, whether it's art or an atrocity or anything. Single, unique events are really nonexistent." Golden was impressed. Maybe it was the fact that Paul made the dean's list at Harvard or that he had written some of the most popular articles for *AARP* magazine, but whatever it was, Robert Golden thought he was a genius.

"I never thought of that," Golden said. "But what about the *Mona Lisa*?"

"What about it?"

"Well, no one ever painted that again. Wasn't that unique?"

"No, Bob. Of course not. For that to be unique it would mean that people stopped painting altogether. Just because no one ever captured an unhappy woman in quite the same way, it doesn't mean that thousands didn't try."

"I get your point," Robert said, wanting to get back to the subject. "Why don't you look into this incident and see what you can find. See if there might be a trend. I'm hoping it's just a copycat crime and it won't amount to much."

"Copycat crimes usually come in the first few months. Two years later doesn't suggest copycat."

"Fine. So maybe it's bigger than a copycat. Check it out. I'll want you to write something to put the members at ease. Let's not let this blow up if we can help it."

"I hear you," Paul said. And he left the office.

What a brilliant guy, Golden thought. *If I were gay, that would be my kind of man. Actually, I probably would go for a body-builder type. I don't know, maybe . . .* and before he could continue with his once-every-six-months who-would-I-like-if-I-were-gay thoughts, his intercom rang. "Yes?"

"Dr. Mueller's lawyer wants you."

"Thank you." Robert prayed Mueller wasn't canceling. He swiveled his chair to face the wall screen. "Hello, Carl, what's up?"

"Hi, Bob. Sam is bringing his son to the lecture in Chicago, so either change his suite to a three-bedroom or get a suite for the kid."

"That's all? No problem."

"He also wanted to confirm that he was doing the 'Aging Without Pain' lecture."

"That's right."

"Fine. Are you sold out?"

"Everything but some balcony seats way in the back, and those will be gone, too, I'm sure."

"What does the gross look like?"

"A million and a half, not including downloads."

"Great. Sam will be pleased. He'll see you Friday."

"Thanks." And with that Robert clicked off. He still thought Dr. Sam Mueller was greedy. *Ninety percent of the gross.* Hell, here he was arranging for everything, doing all the advertising, and only getting ten percent. *Bupkis.* But then he reminded himself that this was the man who'd cured cancer. By simply doing that, Sam Mueller single-handedly added fifty million people to AARP. *Just give him what he wants.*

Kathy and Max were sitting outside of her home in the early evening. She felt so guilty for hurting Brian, but Max handled it perfectly. He was not just a charismatic speaker, he knew when to listen, and he let her vent her feelings without saying a word. And on her own she always came to the same conclusion, that she didn't love Brian and therefore wasn't leaving one person for another, and that Brian had never been the right one anyway. Of course, she *was* leaving one person for another.

Most times, if a relationship is not finished and someone leaves for someone else, it colors the new relationship and everything falls apart.

But once in a great while, people leave people for someone new and stay with that new person for fifty years. Max pointed that out and Kathy asked, "Are we the fifty-year couple?"

"It sure feels like it to me." And he kissed her and her guilt just washed away. "Do you want to do something interesting on Friday?"

"Of course," she said.

"The guy who cured cancer, Sam Mueller, is speaking in front of thousands of olds in Chicago. Want to go?"

"Sure, I guess. Why do you want to hear him?"

"I'd like to know what he has to say. He's one of the main reasons the country is so fucked up. Guys like him who extend life for others get to be billionaires and then stick the bill for everyone that they cured on us."

"Interesting. I never thought of it quite that way. I'd love to go. I hate him already."

"Great. We can make a fun road trip out of it."

Then Kathy thought a moment. "Do you think it's too soon after my father died?"

"I think it's like a tribute to your dad. If they had spent some money helping your father instead of giving it to all the ninety-year-olds, we would still have him."

"You're right. They treated him like shit."

"Resources going to all the wrong places," Max said. "By the way, what do you want to do with the ashes?"

"I don't know. I thought I would put them on the mantel or something."

"I have a great idea. Let's put them in the backseat and take them with us to Chicago. It'll be like he's on the trip, too. Then we can find a beautiful spot on Lake Michigan and let him free."

Kathy just looked at this man. "You're so amazing. God."

And they kissed again. Softly. Not a crazy, passionate kiss, but a kiss that suited the conversation. It was terrific.

The pilotless jet turned onto the runway at Eagle County Regional Airport. Sam Mueller liked to fly, especially in the privacy his wealth afforded him, but these smaller airports that serviced resorts like Vail were not his favorite. He looked over and saw Mark. This was unusual. They had not had very many father-son activities over the years, and even though Mark might be bored, Sam thought it was great that he was coming to Chicago to hear his dad speak.

Sam Mueller had so many strangers worshipping him, but it never translated to his children. Maybe a little bit with Patty, but Mark seemed unimpressed. Possibly it was the way he was asserting his own identity entering into his teen years, but Sam wished his son looked up to him more. So just the fact that Mark decided to take this trip was a good sign. Maybe he needed a healthy dose of watching thousands of people applaud his father.

The jet made the final turn onto Runway Two Five and stopped for one minute. The face of the captain monitoring the plane back in Denver came on the screen. "Are you all set for takeoff, Dr. Mueller?"

"All set," Sam said.

"We should have an uneventful flight. If you need anything, Elaine will get it for you. Have a nice trip."

"Thanks."

Mark turned around and smiled at Elaine. She smiled back. *Jesus, she's hot. She looks like a model. How cool to have a beautiful woman like that bring you crackers.* And then Mark wondered if people had sex with her on the plane. After all, no one else was here. An empty cockpit. *Who would ever know?* He then asked his dad, "Can the pilots hear you or see you?"

"Only if you want them to. Why?"

"I was just wondering if it was two-way."

"That's the passenger's choice. I like when they can see, but some people don't."

"They can't see in the bathroom, can they?"

"Only if you wanted it."

"Who would want to be watched going to the bathroom?"

"Probably nobody, but if you had a problem in there they could see it and help."

At that moment the jet roared down the runway. This new generation of Gulfstream was ninety-nine percent soundproof. The jets at full power sounded like the hum of air-conditioning. Mark watched his screen in front of him, which he set to "cockpit controls." He could see everything the remote pilot saw. It was awesome. He couldn't help but pretend he was flying the plane, although he didn't want the gorgeous Elaine to think he was a child. "How long have they been flying without pilots?"

"Almost two years," his dad said.

"Were you scared the first time?"

"It was a little disconcerting, but the systems are so reliable and so redundant that you don't really think about it. Remember, this plane can do everything itself from its own computers. It doesn't even need contact with the ground, so having the guys in Denver, you just don't think about it."

"Really? But if I wasn't here you would be all alone with Elaine. Wouldn't you think about that?"

"What did you say?"

"Nothing," Mark said, and grinned a little.

Sam was torn. He was a man who did not screw around on his wife, and yet he felt a small male bond with his son over this remark. He was tempted to tell Mark that he didn't think about other women, but they had so few moments like this, he didn't want to ruin it. He made a decision to simply answer as if he were Mark's buddy, instead of his dad. He looked at Elaine and then back at his son. "I guess I *would* think about it. A lot."

Mark smiled. A private moment between two guys. For that instant his dad became accessible. He knew it wouldn't last long, but he loved it.

CHAPTER TWENTY

Betsy Bernstein was livid. She had just read the Morton Spiller resignation letter prepared by John Van Dyke for the President's approval. She thought it sounded far too condescending toward her husband. It said that Spiller admired what the President was trying to achieve but, due to policy differences, he thought it was best to allow the President to bring on someone more in sync with his line of thinking. She got John on the phone. "This is bullshit."

"What's wrong with it?"

"What's wrong with it? He makes the President sound like a child that didn't understand the workings of the economy. And it sounds like it was Morton's decision."

"We had it thoroughly tested and people seemed to think there was just a disagreement and the President wanted someone else."

"Well, it doesn't read that way. I think he should be honest and say that he didn't want to come to town and get messed up in politics, that he liked staying on the farm."

"We can't say that."

"Why not?"

"Because people will criticize the President for even making that deal. They will perceive him as weak for agreeing to Spiller's demands."

Betsy hadn't thought of that.

"Well, why can't he at least say he wants to spend more time with his family, like they all do?"

"It's been so overused, people think that sounds more suspicious than giving an actual reason."

"The resignation was tested?"

"Thoroughly."

"What were the numbers?"

"Fifty-five percent thought it was a basic disagreement in philosophy, twenty percent perceived it as Spiller wanting to get back into the private sector to make more money, ten percent thought he was a bad choice in the first place, and fifteen percent didn't know who he was."

"Okay, then. But I wish we could get something in there that suggested the job was more than he could take."

"He would never sign off on that. Let's just get rid of him and start fresh. We have some very good prospects."

"Like who?"

"Well, we're giving the President a list this afternoon. I'm sure he will share them with you."

"I'm sure he will."

The President's closest advisers sat around the Oval Office going over the names for Morton Spiller's replacement. All the usual suspects. Men from banking and finance and a few CEOs of big accounting firms. All of them seemed the same to Bernstein. "What's wrong with this list?" the President asked.

"It's boring?" Van Dyke answered.

"Not just boring, but what else is missing?" They all stared at it but didn't see the obvious. "There are no women."

And the men who were gathered there realized Bernstein was right. As a matter of fact, this remained the very last cabinet position in the United States government that had never been held by a woman. "Why don't we make history and bring in a sharp gal who can figure out Los Angeles and maybe get the world currency going," the President said.

"Well, sir, we have to find someone who can get through Congress. That may not be easy."

"Congress is not going to turn down the first female Treasury secretary unless she's a half-wit. Get me a list. Take two days and have fifteen great names. This is a real opportunity. It's always fun to make a little history."

The music was too loud at Chelsea Bar, but Paul Prescott liked that because no one could overhear any other conversations. Since he had been in a relationship, which was celebrating its six-year anniversary, he didn't much go to the bars anymore, although he found them an endless supply of gossip, which he readily admitted he was addicted to. A gay bar in the heart of Washington—God, there was just too much information there.

The first time he saw a congressman dancing the night away, it was such a big deal, but over the years seeing big shots in the bars became routine. Senators, judges—the running joke was if you came in often enough, you'd see the president. Paul was amazed at how sexual urges trumped everything else. And even though the appearance of prejudice seemed to subside with each generation, Paul always thought that was all it was, appearance. Being gay was different from being black or Jewish or Hispanic. When people hated those people they weren't afraid of becoming one; they just hated them. But hating gays, or at least not being comfortable with them in high office—well, that had more to do with one's fear of his own sexuality. People who hated gays feared that one morning they might wake up as one, or at least with one. No one who hated black people thought their skin would change color.

As Paul sat down at the bar, his ego was stroked by how many guys were giving him the eye. At six foot one, with all of his hair, he looked thirty-five and was extremely fit.

Over the decades muscle stimulator machines had come and gone, some a gimmick, some not, but they never really caught on big until the early 2020s, when they were made matchbook size and could be worn under clothing. The little stimulators would send a small electrical current into the muscle, tighten it up, and then release, so while you were at work or driving or watching a movie, you would be doing the equivalent of a thousand sit-ups. Not everyone used them, but anyone who wanted that type of physique found them an easy, painless way to get a six-pack. And Paul loved having a six-pack.

Tonight, however, he was only interested in one thing. He wanted to ask around and find out what people knew about the second bus shooting. He immediately saw a guy he recognized, someone he had seen before at several Washington events. He walked over and introduced himself. The man, Jack Willman, was friendly, but seemed guarded. When Paul sat down Jack blurted out, "This is my first time in the club."

Paul laughed. "I don't care if you live here. You don't have to apologize to me. Before I was in a relationship I came here every night."

"Are you in a relationship now?"

"Six years. What about you?"

"I was married for three years."

"To a man?"

"A woman."

"I understand. Don't worry about it. Find out who you are, have fun doing it, that's my advice."

"Thanks. That's good advice. So what do you do?"

"I'm one of the heads of AARP."

"Wow, you look so young!"

"I'm not a member, I just have a great job there." Paul laughed.

"That's one powerful lobby. I've heard my boss bitch about it often, how you can't get anything done unless AARP signs off."

"Who's your boss?"

"Hernandez."

"Hernandez? At Justice?"

"That's the one."

"Wow. Big-time boss. Whoever thought he'd bitch about little old us."

"Right. Little old us. Everyone worries what you guys think. So what are you doing here tonight?"

"I'm actually trying to find out some information, and so many people in the know come here I thought I could score . . . information."

"What are you looking for?"

"Do you guys know much about the latest bus massacre?"

"That's all we've been dealing with the last few days."

"What can you tell me?"

"Gee, I don't think I can tell you anything. I could get in a lot of trouble." Then Paul did something that might have backfired big time, but it didn't. He leaned over and gave Jack a kiss. On the mouth. No tongue. But a real kiss. Jack was blown away, not just at the kiss but at the balls of this guy. Then Paul finished it off with some words of wisdom.

"Listen, there's something you have to know. Our kind of people stick together. We always help each other—anonymously, of course, but that's how Washington works. There are thousands of people who trade information, and one way to distinguish who to talk to is by who goes through the same shit all the time. And we do. That forms a trust. You help me, I help you, no one knows anything, but we're bonded. Bonded by who we are. Does that make sense?" Jack's answer showed Paul that it did.

"It looks like there might be a conspiracy," Jack said, "although it's in the infant stage and right now there is no organization. It's just hostility coming out here and there, but we think it will only get worse. And more organized."

"What kind of conspiracy?"

"Some young people are reaching the breaking point. They feel burdened and angry. It's not widespread yet, but it's growing. We expect the violence to ramp up."

"And what's the solution?"

"Nobody knows. Maybe the government has to step in and take some of the pressure off."

"How would they do that?"

"I don't know. That's your department."

"Any names? Any groups?"

"I haven't heard a name of any group yet. Right now we're looking at individuals."

Paul reached into his coat and gave Jack a card. With all the new technology, the simple business card had made a surprising comeback. It was so retro. People had them in wild colors and with holograms, and sometimes they smelled like the ocean or the forest.

"Call me if there's something I really need to know. And I will return the favor with anything I can do for you."

Jack took the card. "Okay. That sounds reasonable."

"What is your name?"

"Jack Willman."

"Thanks, Jack. You don't mind if I call you from time to time?"

"No."

"I appreciate it. And maybe we'll have a meal, all four of us."

"I'm single now."

"Well, that won't be a permanent condition. You seem like a great guy. If I meet someone I think you'd like, I'll set you up."

"Not another woman."

"No, I gathered that."

The smell inside the tented Rose Bowl was horrible. The ventilation system was broken and no one had come to fix it. Brad Miller lay on his bunk and stared at the springs on the one above him. He was so depressed. For days no one would give him any meaningful information. He was told his concerns would be attended to, but that was not happening.

A woman came by once a day and asked people how they were feeling. It wasn't so much out of concern for the actual person as it was to anticipate a flu that could spread through a tent like this in an instant.

So many medical wonders had taken place over the years, curing some of the major diseases of the twenty-first century, but the flu wasn't one of them. It was just too smart. The flu virus could not only adapt instantly, it lived in the mucosa, not the genes, so there was no real fix. There were drugs to reduce the severity, and shots to give immunity, but every few years a virulent strain swept down and took over the human body and nothing could be done to stop it. There was also a growing fear that in the race between the virus and the cure, if the virus got too far ahead it would wreak disaster. Since each new strain was immune to the drugs that came before, there were many scientists who were convinced the flu virus would one day win and be immune to anything medicine could come up with. So with all the medical breakthroughs, the flu was still something to be avoided at all cost.

"How are you doing today, Mr. Miller?"

"Not well. I'm feeling depressed."

"We can help that. Let me take a drop of blood and see what medication can make you feel better."

"I know what medication I need."

"Fine, what is it?"

"Money. I need to be injected with the money you stole from me by throwing me off my property. You got money on you?"

The woman smiled and told him the same party line. "Someone will deal with that at the appropriate time."

"What time is that? Before or after I die?"

"Thank you, Mr. Miller. If you need anything else, tell us."

As she walked away, Brad yelled after her, "Money! I need money! Give it to me in pill form, I don't give a shit!"

Brad lay down on his cot and fell asleep. When he woke, a young man in a suit was standing over him. "Mr. Miller?"

"What happened? Is this heaven?"

"I'm Steven Collard. I'm with the Department of the Interior. Would you come with me."

"Where are we going?"

"Just to talk in private. To the office structure, outside."

"Are you the guy that can help?"

"I can certainly try. Let's talk."

They exited the giant tent and walked three hundred yards to a temporary office building. It was three stories, made out of steel that could be put together like a LEGO toy, and it looked very active. Each office was occupied. Brad followed the younger man up the stairs to the second floor, went down a hall, and stepped into a cubicle. It was tiny, just enough room for a desk and a small couch. Collard sat down behind his desk and motioned for Brad to sit. Brad said he preferred to stand.

"Mr. Miller, if it's any consolation, I know exactly what you are going through. I have an uncle in your same situation."

"Is he here?" Brad asked.

"No, he's staying with us. He didn't come to Pasadena."

"Well then, he's not in my same situation."

"I meant financially. He also had a condo that was leveled and has nothing to show for it."

"Great. So how does that help me?"

"Well, first of all, you did have insurance, correct?"

"Of course. American Life."

"And what do they say?"

"They say nothing. They don't answer. They claim they are overwhelmed, and I'm hearing in the tent that they, and all of them, are going Chapter 11. Without Uncle Sam we're fucked, excuse my French."

"Well, they're not all going out of business, but many of them are, yes."

"So what do I do?"

"The plan is to make you whole. The government doesn't want to see people who had insurance get nothing, but it's going to take some time. I know the President has stated that people who were insured should get their money; we just have to figure out how that can happen."

"The government can write me a check and then go after my insurance company, how about that?"

"It's not that easy. But I just want you to know that people are thinking of you and at some point in time there will be a solution."

"At some point in time? Well, what the hell am I supposed to do to get to that point?"

"We can keep you here for as long as necessary and feed you and take care of your medical needs."

"My boy, I had a condo! I owned it outright! I don't need people feeding me or housing me; if I did, I would have moved into a nursing home. I am owed that money! As a citizen of this country, I am owed that money!"

"I agree, Mr. Miller. My uncle feels the same way."

"Well, good for him. Hey, does he want to trade with me? I'll live with you for a while and he can stay in my bunk."

The man smiled. He realized there was nothing more to say. "Mr. Miller, I just wanted you to know that you are not invisible. We are trying to come up with real solutions to a problem that has never existed before."

"Well, that makes me feel better. Hey, would you like to stand in line with me for two hours? I have to take a piss."

Kathy and Max were on the road to Chicago. It was a beautiful day in the Midwest: mild temperatures, blue skies. It would have been the best day of her life if her father's urn weren't sitting on the backseat.

Max's car was a lot nicer than one would have thought listening to him at that first meeting. Max Leonard came across as someone who had no finances and who had to bum rides with someone else, or who had a broken-down car that was twenty years old. That wasn't the case. He had a German sports sedan with everything on it. Huge electric power, auto drive, a sound and visual system that would rival a home setup. You could cruise along at a hundred miles an hour and actually forget you were in a car, especially if you chose the auto drive. The advanced radar systems were so good, they would simply not allow you to get into an accident. The sensors could see front and behind up to a mile, and off to the side up to a quarter mile. If someone was about to sideswipe you, the car would take evasive action, and then ask you to take over. Other than that, it would never bother you. It could easily turn corners by itself and stop before anything got in its way. If an animal or a human ran in front of it, the auto drive would stop the car faster than if it were being driven by a person, so driving was more about having something to do than for safety.

As they cruised along Highway 41, Max told Kathy his life story and how he'd gotten to this point, and as he talked she couldn't believe that she'd found him. This was her dream man. A rebel with money. Someone who could offer actual comfort but still want to change the world. *What a combo.* She hoped she wasn't too materialistic wanting this kind of guy, but screw it, why not? She wasn't asking him to pay off her loans. She wasn't asking for anything. That was why it seemed great. The love came first and the other good stuff just happened to be there.

Max was aware of her $350,000 debt and he brought it up on the trip. "You know what I think is really fucked?" he said.

"What?"

"That medical loans have to be paid off even when the patient dies."

"Let's not talk about it. It's beyond fucked."

"What if you just don't pay it?"

"I don't know. Jail, I would imagine."

"Maybe there's a way around it."

"Let's just have fun. I don't want to talk about it in front of my dad." Max looked behind him at the copper urn.

"I understand. But from everything you've said about your father, I bet he would be the most angry of all."

Kathy picked up the urn, rubbing it as if a magic genie would appear. "He would really like you," she said.

CHAPTER TWENTY-ONE

The President's mother, Bernice Bernstein, had been moved to a facility in Baltimore, a sophisticated recovery center where people rarely recovered, mostly living in a coma forever, mostly on the government's dime.

Bernice was in suite 401. It was a large room, overlooking a parklike setting, with six machines working 24/7. She lay there with her eyes closed and no expression on her face, and to look at her, one would have no idea if she was even alive, but the machines confirmed that she was.

The President came a week after she was installed, as he liked to put it, and sat in the room and allowed a few private pictures—nothing for the press, just photos taken by the White House photographer for the family. There were shots of him kissing his mother's forehead, holding her hand, sitting on the end of her bed, and standing at the window, looking reflective.

When he left the room he told Betsy that he never wanted to go back. That it made him sad and angry and his emotions were so complicated, he just didn't want to deal with it. He also knew that the image of a ninety-four-year-old rich person being kept alive with taxpayers' money would not play well. If someone was a great person, like a pope or a Mother Teresa, someone who did a lot of good for the world, maybe then a nation would want to keep them going, but family members of important people still came across to the masses as the spoiled rich who had too much in life and now, too much in trying to sustain it. And the President felt the same way. But what could he do? He couldn't pull all the plugs. And he couldn't let it seem as though he didn't want his mother to survive. If only she had a DNR. Maybe she did; maybe they just hadn't found it yet.

John Van Dyke came into the Oval Office with a huge smile on his face. "Read this," he said. The President saw one name on the screen: Susanna P. Colbert.

"Why does that sound familiar?" Bernstein asked.

"She's one of the most successful businesswomen in the country, former CEO of HomeInc, one of the founders of The Card, retired, but raring to go. She would make the perfect first woman secretary of the Treasury."

"Did you talk to her?"

"No, I was waiting to make sure it sounded as good to you as it did to me."

"How does she vote?"

"Republican, most of her life. Voted Democratic in 2008 and 2012, but that was it. It makes it even better. It will look like you're irresistible to work for."

The President laughed. "It will, huh? How old is she?"

"Seventy."

"No shit?" The President looked at her picture. It must have been taken a long time ago because this woman did not look seventy years old.

"Do you want me to see if there is an interest?"

"No. I want you to see if there is anything, *anything* at all in her history that could bite us in the ass, and when you give me the all clear, I'll cold-call her."

"Then call her now."

"She's clear?"

"Clear as a baby's butt."

"What? What does that mean?"

"Clear."

"That's a terrible analogy. You can't see through a butt no matter how young the person is. A baby's butt is not clear."

"Okay. Okay." Van Dyke made his way to the door. "Don't go nuts on me. I meant clear as the skin on a baby's butt."

"Have you ever seen diaper rash?"

"I hate you," Van Dyke said. "Cold-call her, it will blow her mind."

The President asked Annie, his primary assistant, to get Susanna Colbert on the line. He wanted voice only, no picture this time.

Annie always got various reactions when she called people on behalf of the President of the United States. Invariably, if the President made the call himself without his assistant, people thought it was an impersonation. But even when Annie called and said, "I have the President of the United States for you," it played with people's minds. Just as they were thinking it was a prank, there he was and their hearts were racing. That is what happened to Susanna. Before she could say, "Is this a joke?" she heard Bernstein's voice.

"Susanna . . . may I call you Susanna?"

"Of course, who is this?"

"This is Matt Bernstein, and right now I happen to be the president. How long it will last, no one knows." Normally that would get a laugh, but Susanna was still feeling her way through the call. Then the President said, "Here's a number, call me back right away. I have some important matters to discuss with you, okay?"

"Okay," she said.

And the President disconnected. This was something he loved to do, asking someone to call back through the White House system and be put through directly to the Oval Office. People slowly realized it wasn't a trick. Annie buzzed him in less than a minute. "Ms. Colbert is on the line."

"Thanks for getting back to me," Bernstein joked.

"Well, hello, Mr. President."

"I'd say call me Matt, but I like Mr. President." He got a little laugh out of her. "Where am I reaching you?"

"I'm in Arizona."

"You live there?"

"Most of the year, yes."

"That sounds great. Can you take a day or two and come see me?"

"When, sir?"

"How's tomorrow?"

"That would be fine."

"I'll give you back to Annie; she will make the arrangements. I really look forward to sitting down with you."

"May I ask what this is about?"

"If we like each other and we get along, I'm going to offer you a job. A good job. A great job. That's all I can tell you now."

"Okay. I'll be there. See you then."

This was a good sign. If she was really retired and had no interest in returning to work, she would have balked or asked more questions. He liked her voice and her attitude. He purposely did not want visual communication on this first contact; he would wait until they were face-to-face. It always made a bigger impression that way.

The Chicago Center would be filled to capacity. Almost ten thousand people, all over the age of seventy, and most over eighty. This was the typical Sam Mueller audience. He was one of the preeminent speakers to the older crowd. Some thought the experience of hearing him speak was almost evangelical. Maybe because he cured cancer, *they* would be cured of something, just by being in his presence. It was why his lectures always sold out.

He and his son were driven to the Chicago Town House, a small, very upscale boutique hotel located just two blocks from the event. They were taken to the fifth floor, where they had one side of the hallway for themselves. The hotel had joined all of the suites together so they had a total of five bedrooms, three living rooms, and three master baths with steam rooms and whirlpools. Plus kitchens and a gym and a gorgeous player piano.

Sam, no matter how rich he became, was always knocked out by this stuff. He just never could believe this was where he had wound up. Mark was a different story. This was all he knew. His father was disappointed that this didn't wow his son in the same way, but he accepted it. "What do you think of the spread?"

"Cool," Mark said. "I'll take the room at the end."

"Why don't you take the suite next to mine? Why go all the way down there?"

"I don't know, I like it down there."

"Fine. Are you hungry?"

"No."

"Well, I'm going to take a little nap. If you go out, be back by six so we can walk over together."

"We have to walk?"

His father tried not to lose his temper. "Mark, it's two blocks. I *want* to walk."

"Okay, that's cool."

"Thank you." His father closed the door to his suite. *This is my fault. They have too much. It's my fault.* And as he lay down for his hour nap he started to think of ways to correct it. *No inheritance? Military school? Change the shrink or the medicine?* He didn't know what to do. Maybe Mark would snap out of it, although with each passing day in the spoiled kingdom that seemed less likely.

Kathy and Max arrived at the event early. They left the urn locked in the trunk. They had a momentary thought that it could be stolen, but what was the worst that would happen? That someone would discard the ashes somewhere else? Maybe they would even put them in a prettier place, like a golf course or a garden, or the aquarium. But of course, no one was going to steal it.

They bought the cheapest seats, which were in the last two rows of the balcony. They were four hundred dollars each, which in 2030 was considered a bargain. They wanted to be the first ones in the auditorium so they could watch the crowd. See who all of these older people were who idolized this man. See exactly who it was who would pay big bucks to hear a lecture called "Aging Without Pain."

There were so many new medicines for pain; it was one of the largest aspects of the big pharmaceutical companies. The science of pain medicine had advanced over the years and now had become specific in nature. If your elbow was hurting, you could take something targeted to that. The high had been engineered out of most pain medications, which kept the addiction rate lower. Older medicines like Vicodin were replaced with newer ones that helped your back but didn't make the world seem more loving. So, of course, people were still addicted to getting rid of the back pain, but they didn't have to take more and more just to keep the high going, since it hadn't been there to begin with.

There were still drugs like morphine for severe overall pain or to end suffering, but for the most part the new class of drugs targeted specific neuro pathways. The same way a person can move a hand without moving an arm was the way these medications worked, almost replicating the signals from the brain.

Many people were upset by the diminishing choices of drugs that made them feel like they lived on cloud nine. But in one area, the area of depression, the drugs got so good that they were now the most abused. Even if someone never experienced panic or bipolar disorder, taking drugs for these conditions would produce euphoria in most people. That is, until their brain chemistry got so screwed up that they actually created the depression they hadn't had. And then the drugs could not help them. It was a complicated dilemma: Feel great for five years and then wake up bipolar, with no means to cure it. Not a good scenario, but people still did it; the high was just too powerful. No matter how much humans advanced, it seemed the need and desire to alter one's state of mind remained constant.

Dr. Mueller woke up from his nap at six-twenty. He didn't like to arrive too early for these events; standing around made him nervous. He thought if he got there at seven-thirty, a half hour before the lecture, that would be perfect. He showered and dressed leisurely, and at seven he opened the door of his suite and called for his son. There was no answer.

"Mark," he called again, "let's go, we gotta leave."

No answer.

Instead of being worried, he was angry. *Why is everything a problem with him?* He continued dressing and looked at the clock. It was seven-fifteen. At that moment Mark's face appeared on his father's watch.

"Hey, Dad."

"Where are you? Do you know what time it is?"

"I'm here. I'm at the lecture."

"You're there now?"

"Yeah. It's a nice place."

His father was relieved. "Okay. Do you want to wait for me backstage?"

"I'm just talking to some people. I'll come backstage when you get here."

"Fine. See you soon." Sam Mueller had to smile. In one moment he went from having a son who couldn't care less to a son who cared enough to go early and check out the auditorium. *Like a little road manager. How nice is that?*

Mark disconnected from his dad and walked back to Max and Kathy. As they were the only other younger people in the whole place, they caught his attention immediately and he went up to the balcony to see who they were. The three of them bullshitted about nothing in particular, but he did not tell them who his father was. Sometimes Mark liked to tell and other times he didn't.

"So what are you doing here?" Max asked him.

"I'm just hanging out. Thought I would see what this was all about."

"You're a little young for this, aren't you?"

"Not really."

"Are you in pain?" Kathy asked.

"Am I in pain? Why would you ask that?"

"Isn't that what the lecture is about?"

"Oh yeah." Mark felt he was digging himself into a hole. "My dad's in pain, so I came with him."

"I'm sorry," Kathy said. "Where is your dad?"

"I don't know. He went to the bathroom."

"Do you know the guy who is lecturing?" Max asked.

"Not personally."

"Do you know what he's famous for?" Now Mark was getting uncomfortable. Why had he lied?

"Yeah, he cured cancer."

"What do you think of that?"

"I think it's great, don't you?"

"It's great in a baby. I don't know how great it is in a grandpa."

"Why?"

Kathy interrupted. "Honey, I think he's too young to have this discussion."

At that moment someone who worked at the theater came up to the balcony. "Are you Mark Mueller?" Mark was trapped. He mumbled that he was. "Your dad wants me to take you backstage." Mark smiled and walked away without saying another word.

"What the fuck!" Max said. "That was his goddamn kid!"

"No. Are you sure?"

"Of course. Same name. Backstage. I bet the creep was sending his own kid out to spy on us."

"Do you really think so?"

"They're not stupid. They have to wonder why anyone under a hundred would even attend this thing. That was pretty sneaky to have the kid try and dig up information."

"Jesus," Kathy said. "I never thought of that."

As the auditorium filled, Kathy and Max were stunned by the age of the crowd. Even older than they had anticipated. "Do you see this?"

"I see it."

"These people are dinosaurs. The last generation that had it all. Now we take care of them. What's wrong with this picture?"

Kathy looked around. It was hard to hate older people she didn't even know, but these people had had so much plastic surgery and had so many new advanced drugs coursing through their veins that they didn't look as decrepit as she expected. They looked like they would live forever and keep taking and taking. *Why did my father have to die young and these people don't even look sick?* That made her angry.

When Sam Mueller was introduced, he received a standing ovation. His lecture lasted about ninety minutes. He showed many visuals and tried to keep everything from sounding too technical. He told of the exciting advancements in longevity that Immunicate was working on, and when he said, "We are on the verge of keeping the human being alive for one hundred and fifty years," the crowd went wild. This made both Max and Kathy the angriest they had been the entire night.

"That's all we fucking need," Max said. And yet as he sat there, he knew that being angry wasn't going to change anything. But what could he do?

When the lecture was over they stayed in their seats, watching the old people file out. After everyone was gone they walked outside and saw Sam Mueller and his son exit the stage door. Sam did not see them, but Mark did. His eye caught Max's and they stared at each other for a few seconds. Mark smiled. Max did not. And that was the end of their first encounter.

CHAPTER TWENTY-TWO

The private jet landed quietly at Washington Dulles International. A car was waiting for Susanna Colbert, and it took her to the Hay-Adams Hotel, a hotel she was very familiar with. She even had a favorite suite. When she was CEO of HomeInc she would come to Washington often, acting as her own lobbyist.

HomeInc was a builder of gated communities, a soup-to-nuts organization that procured the land and constructed everything. It started out building retirement centers, but noticed there was a need for high-end security housing. Many areas where rich people lived were accessible to anyone who had a car, and as time went on, people wanted guards. It was always thought that if someone had enough money, they would shy away from developments. But HomeInc read the market right, and luxury communities with prebuilt ten-to-fifteen-thousand-square-foot homes became its bread and butter.

They would provide their own financing, and their genius was that each community would look unique. People would not know there was a plan behind it from visiting just one development. All the homes looked absolutely original. But in different cities the development was exactly the same. Instead of duplicating homes in the same area, like most developments, they duplicated the entire gated community, so unless someone went from his street in Long Island to the same street in Palo Alto, he would never feel as if he were living in a luxury tract. This way the company kept the design and building costs to a minimum and its profits were enormous.

Susanna stayed with HomeInc for fifteen years and then started The Card. The Card was a superexclusive credit card that required a high income level and came with a large annual fee. For that, owners received special treatment in the world's finest hotels, restaurants, and resorts. The Card's slogan was "Knowing someone on the inside." And it really worked.

When a person's name by itself could not automatically get a great table in a five-star restaurant, having The Card would do the trick. The Card became more famous than the people carrying it, and it opened doors that no other credit card had ever been able to open.

Another interesting aspect of the The Card was that owing money did not cost the cardholder the outrageous interest rates that the other credit card companies charged. Whereas MasterCard might charge eighteen percent on unpaid items, The Card would charge ten. It encouraged its super-high-spending clients to get lazy about paying it off, so with a ten percent interest rate and a ten-thousand-dollar yearly fee, business was great.

The spending limit on The Card was also very high, three million dollars. And if someone took The Card to Macau and ran up a two-million-dollar gambling debt, they didn't need permission from the hotel. The Card would cover them automatically, providing, of course, they had liquid assets to back it up. Susanna's last major coup before she left the company was to make arrangements with the world's finest hotels to set aside entire floors for The Card members. That had never been done before, and the day Susanna retired there was a waiting list of twelve thousand rich folks hoping to receive notice that they'd been accepted to the world's most exclusive credit card organization.

President Bernstein knew that this woman had made her fortune dealing with the rich, and quite frankly he worried about that. *Would she have any connection to regular people?* He thought the new secretary of the Treasury should have a broad understanding of the people who lived in the United States, but that was the kind of discussion he wanted to have in person.

Also, previous secretaries had been rich or had come from big Wall Street companies and some of them turned out to be a good fit, so he wasn't going to make any judgments until he spent some time with her.

He called her at the hotel at eight o'clock just to welcome her to Washington and to tell her to come to the White House for lunch the next afternoon. The phone call lasted almost an hour.

Matthew Bernstein was a no-nonsense phone person. He figured that anytime he spoke with someone he was being recorded, and that caused him to keep his conversations short and to the point. So when he glanced at the clock and saw that he and Susanna had been talking for fifty-eight minutes, just talking, like friends, he was quite amazed. She was funny and smart and had that soothing sound of an older woman who has been around the block and has great stories to tell about it. They were to meet at noon the following day, and after he hung up he realized he hadn't even mentioned specifically why he'd requested that she come to Washington. And she hadn't asked. That was highly unusual.

When he went upstairs to the living quarters, he told Betsy how he had talked to this woman for an hour, and his wife looked almost jealous. She had never seen her husband stay on the line for that long. "What were you talking about?"

"Washington, business, growing up, just stuff."

"Does she sound like she'll be good at the job?"

"I don't know; she sounded like she would be a better mother."

"What does that mean, exactly?"

"She sounded wise. Sort of what you'd like your mom to sound like on the phone."

"Really? Well, if she's not good at Treasury, hire her as a shrink."

The President laughed. *If only I could have a shrink without the world finding out.* "I'm going to meet her tomorrow. I'll know more then."

"Sounds like you know now."

The President was excited when he got up the next morning. Who was this woman who kept him on the line and made his wife jealous? He would find out in a few hours.

When he went downstairs, Van Dyke was waiting for him. "We have a debt-reduction meeting in an hour and you have a meeting at one o'clock with General Marshal."

"One o'clock? I have a lunch with Susanna at noon; what if it runs over?"

"Well, if you can't decide in an hour you can meet her later in the day, but I think you'll have an idea in ten minutes."

"Does she know what job she is being offered?"

"You told me *you* wanted to tell her. She knows it's important, but you wanted to play this 'surprise me' game, so I didn't say anything."

"It's not a 'surprise me' game; I need to look into a person's eyes when they hear information like this for the first time. It tells me something."

"Couldn't you have seen that on the screen?"

"Listen," the President said, "we fired one guy because he was on the screen *too much*; I don't want to start out a new relationship the same way."

"I hear you. If an hour isn't enough, let me know by twelve-thirty and I'll push the general."

Bernstein went about his morning business checking the time every fifteen minutes. *My God, I haven't looked at a clock so much since I was in school waiting for recess. What's gotten into me?*

He was sitting at his desk signing some meaningless papers when Annie buzzed him exactly at noon. "Mr. President, Ms. Colbert is here."

He opened the door, and standing there was a class act. That was his first impression. A woman seventy years old, looking fifty, with gray-blond hair, very well styled, in great physical shape, slate blue eyes, wearing a teal-colored cashmere dress and a smile to kill for. The President extended his hand and she followed him into the Oval Office.

"I realized we talked for an hour last night and I never asked you what I was here for," Susanna said.

"I realized the same thing. Are you hungry?"

"I am."

"Hungry for what?"

"That's a loaded question, Mr. President. But if you mean food, a turkey sandwich on sourdough would be great."

"Do you like your bread toasted? Wait, let me guess. Yes."

"No."

"Damn it. I thought I knew everything about you."

"I like bread toasted but not sourdough. If I asked for rye I would have it toasted."

"Why not sourdough?"

"Because untoasted sourdough absorbs the flavor of the sandwich. Much better than other kinds of bread."

"You know, it's good that you know this, because the job I am offering you is White House chef." Susanna didn't laugh immediately. She had always fancied herself as a great cook, and for one millisecond the offer sounded wonderful.

"I accept."

"What else would you like with your sandwich?"

"Whatever you're having."

The President placed the order. Two turkey sandwiches on untoasted sourdough, pickles, tomatoes, and a dab of French mustard. And two coffees.

"Do you often order the same thing as your guest?"

"I already ate. I just ordered two in case you're really hungry."

She laughed. "You have a delightful sense of humor."

"Thanks." He paused a second or two and then just said it. "I've brought you here to see if you are interested in becoming the first woman secretary of the Treasury of the United States."

The offer hit Susanna like a right hook. Whatever she was expecting, this wasn't it. "Really?" was all she could come up with.

"Yes. Do you think it's something you might be interested in?"

"Yes. It's something I've never thought about, but when you say it, it sounds like it was always my plan."

"I've had that feeling, too," the President said. "I call it Déjà Beshert."

"What is that?"

"I just made it up. *Beshert* is Hebrew for 'meant to be.' And 'déjà' means . . . oh, you know what 'déjà' means."

"Well, I like the expression," she said. "And I am very interested in the job."

"Of course, you would have to move here."

"Not a problem. My husband travels frequently; I don't know that he would even notice. And my children are grown."

"What does your husband do?" The President knew, but he wanted her to tell him.

"He's an archeologist. He works with several universities. He's very good at it."

At that moment the lunch arrived and the two of them ate and talked effortlessly, and at the end of the hour the deal was done.

"Susanna, I don't expect any issues with the approval process, but I would like you to spend a few days with John Van Dyke so you can go over the details of the job and make sure you are as comfortable as you seem to be. When you go before Congress I don't want there to be any surprises. I'm sure it will all be fine, but I want the transition to be as free from stress as possible. Work out the schedule with John and at the end of that time we will make the announcement, providing you don't change your mind."

"I don't intend to change my mind."

"I know you don't, but you haven't seen the numbers. They're not pretty."

Susanna smiled. "I don't expect them to be. Thank you, Mr. President. Can I call you if I have any questions during this period?"

"You can call me even if you don't. Just not too late at night; I don't want any problems at home." Susanna laughed. Matthew Bernstein *loved* this woman. Not in a sexual way, but in a way that no other older woman in his life had ever quite filled.

CHAPTER TWENTY-THREE

Shen Li's gift to the kids of Los Angeles had gone over very well. He was even contacted by the governor of California, who wanted to thank him personally. But Li was frustrated. He still wanted to break into the United States health market, but he didn't know the exact way to go about it. Of course, health had become a global business, but Li didn't just want to buy into America, he wanted to change it.

When Anthem Blue Cross was sold years earlier to an Arab company, it created a small amount of uproar in Congress, along the lines of, "Should Arabs be taking care of Americans?" But since no national security was involved, the protest went nowhere, and the United Arab Health Group became the second-biggest provider of health insurance in America.

No one noticed any difference. The company's intent was not to change the system but to buy a profitable business and save money by combining accounting costs with its other businesses around the world. People thought Arab doctors would fill the hospitals, but the hospitals looked exactly the same. The same long lines. The same poor service. And this was exactly what Shen Li was not interested in.

Li always felt that what he created in China was the most efficient system in the world, and he just knew that it would translate everywhere. But America was not yet clamoring for his ideas.

In 2026 he was able to break into the Indian market, and he took that country by storm. India had already had solid heath care in its biggest and richest cities, but like China, that care simply disappeared in the smaller towns. And it was those places where most of the people lived. If people in those areas got sick, they would have to ride hundreds of miles to a small clinic, or do nothing. Li used the system he invented in China and began serving the India that no one had served before. His Health Care for All made its way into the parts of that country that had never even seen a doctor.

One of Li's original secrets—aside from letting nurses do most of the work with the help of virtual doctors—was robotic surgery. Obviously, surgery needed to be performed by trained physicians, but technology now made it possible for that to be done from anywhere in the world. And instead of buying superexpensive robotic units for each distant location, Li had them mobilized. They were constantly on the move so that none of the five-million-dollar robots was ever idle. It was like combining medicine with Federal Express. Each operating unit, as soon as it was finished in one location, was cleaned and on its way to the next place within an hour, either by truck, plane, or train, whatever was the most cost-effective way to move it.

These self-contained operating theaters could work anywhere, even where there was no electricity, so the concept of patients traveling a long way for major surgery was slowly becoming a thing of the past. If someone in a small Indian village showed up with an acute appendicitis, the operating unit could be in that location within a half a day. Certainly faster than getting that person to the nearest big city, which could be a thousand miles away.

Doctors in Hong Kong or Beijing—or whatever place Li had agreements with—would take out the appendix remotely, and only one nurse would have to be in attendance. Even anesthetic was given remotely, with everything monitored the same way as if the anesthesiologist was in the room.

Shen Li was the first person in the world to perfect this mobile system, and he was still the best at it. And even though he had a few doctors he partnered with in the United States who would sometimes act as the remote surgeon, the idea itself had not yet cracked the American market.

The American Medical Association was against it in principle, saying that Americans didn't live in small villages, that everyone in the USA was close enough to a working hospital where they could be seen in person and given personal contact. The AMA's real fear was that the mobile system would put doctors out of business. It was feared that one surgeon in South Africa, for example, could do seven or eight operations a day, taking business away from American hospitals.

The AMA spent a fortune on advertising trying to convince people that a physician in attendance was better. One ad that was especially effective showed a doctor on one side of the bed, soothing an older woman, and a robot on the other side, just making machine noises. The voice-over said, "Which one would you choose?" But worldwide results of robotic surgery proved that the robots were no better or worse than having the doctor there. Surgery was only about who was doing the procedure, and whether they were in the room or in Greenland, the result was the same.

As for America, Li needed a way in. So when he got his thank-you letter from the governor of California, he framed it, sensing it might be the start of something.

Max and Kathy stood at the north shore of Lake Michigan and opened her father's urn. "I've never done this before," Kathy said. "Do you say a prayer?"

"Only if you believe in God."

"Well, I believe in something, so whatever it all is I hope my dad becomes one with the universe and finds peace, along with adventure."

"That's great," Max said. "Peace along with adventure. What a great wish."

With that, Kathy raised her arms as high as she could, and spun around, flinging the ashes into the lake. Some of them fell by her feet, and she kicked those into the water, but most made their way onto the surface, where they eventually either sank or were blown away from the shore.

"Did your dad like to fish?"

"No."

"Did he like boating?"

"Not really."

"What did he like about the water?"

"He wasn't a big water person."

"So how come you chose the lake?"

"It was your idea."

"I thought you wanted it."

"I did want it. It's beautiful here."

"He must have liked something about the water."

"He liked fried clams."

"There you go. Soon he might be a part of what he loved to eat."

Now Kathy was having second thoughts. *Maybe this wasn't the best place. Maybe a bowling alley would have been better.* But it was a beautiful day, the sun was setting over the lake, and the idea of coming back as anything anyway was so remote, she felt she had given her father a proper send-off.

As they were driving home, Kathy sat quietly, looking out the window.

"What are you thinking about right now?" Max asked her.

"I was thinking about all those old people at the lecture. How happy they looked. Like they had crossed a barrier where worry and fear don't seem as important."

"Goddamn right. Because they're taken care of. I'd feel worry-free, too, if I had millions of young slaves attending to my every need."

"I keep thinking how unfair it was that my dad didn't get to enjoy any peace. He was always worried."

"Of course he was. He was the first generation that wasn't being coddled. And I'm telling you, and you mark my words: When we get to your dad's age it's going to be ten times worse. Those old fuckers will still be alive. We'll be paying for one-hundred-and-twenty-year-old people to be carried to the toilet."

"So what can we do?"

"We can kill them all."

Kathy stared at him and then smiled. "That's a joke, right?"

"I guess. I guess that would be impractical. But we certainly can present the case of the younger generations in a more forceful way."

"How?"

"I don't know, exactly. It's what I've been thinking about for years. But there has to be a final solution."

Kathy liked that phrase, "final solution." Of course, she had never heard it in its original context. Max didn't know what it meant, either; it just sounded good. "That's a good phrase," Kathy said. "Did you make that up?"

"I don't think so. I heard it. I think it comes from a war. It means taking care of business once and for all."

"Well, if anyone can come up with a plan, it's you. You're amazing and I feel a part of you."

"She's brilliant," John Van Dyke said to the President. "I have never seen anyone, except for you, who can take in tremendous amounts of information so quickly and with such understanding."

"That's what I thought." The President got Susanna on the line. "You still want the job after spending all that time with John?"

"Yes, sir. I do."

"Okay. Why don't you call your family and close friends and tell them you are to be the eighty-first, and first woman, Treasury Secretary of the United States."

Susanna let out a squeal. "Thank you, Mr. President."

"Get your life in order over the next week; we'll get you in front of the Senate and they'll fall in love with you like everyone else here. I think you're going to be superb. And Susanna?"

"Yes, sir?"

"Besides California, work on the one-world currency idea we discussed. Give me your thoughts on that as soon as possible."

"Absolutely. I'm thrilled. I hope I don't give you any problems with the Senate."

"The only problem you'll give me is that they'll want to keep you there."

"Thank you, Mr. President."

"See you soon." The President turned off his screen.

"Sir," Van Dyke said, "do you want help in wiping that grin off your face?"

"Does it show that much?"

"I think she's great, too."

"She's more than great. Except for you, she is the easiest person to talk to in this whole place. She might even be easier than you."

"Should I be worried?"

"Always. You should always be worried. But I'm telling you, John, her business acumen will come in handy. She is full of ideas and so persuasive, but in a good way. She makes you think it was your idea. That's an incredible gift. Quite frankly, I'm surprised she never ran for office. She would be impossible not to vote for."

"She was probably too busy becoming superrich."

"And that's another thing," the President said. "You absolutely forget that when you're with her, and when you're reminded of it, you don't care. She doesn't wear her money, which I love." At that moment Betsy appeared on the President's screen.

"How did it go?"

"We love her. She's in."

"I'm proud it was you who picked the first woman. It's important."

"Thank you, sweetheart. I'll see you later." Bernstein got up from his desk and walked over to the bowl of M&M's. "You mark my words, John, this country is going to fall in love with this woman. She'll be like a mother figure that you trust. I want a global currency to be part of my legacy. She's going to help me with that."

"I believe she will. But most important, maybe she'll have some ideas about Los Angeles that no one's thought of yet."

"Jesus Christ. Los Angeles. I can't go five minutes without hearing the name of that city. I don't even think they voted for me. What's going on this morning?"

"Every day is worse; it just gets worse."

"We need to go back out. Two times isn't enough."

"I agree," Van Dyke said. "Let's get her sworn in and we can take her with us. Pray God she can help."

The President smiled. "Maybe she can pay for it."

CHAPTER TWENTY-FOUR

Brad Miller, along with two thousand others in the Pasadena tent, was slowly giving up. There had been two suicides over the last week; one was a gentleman Brad had become friends with.

One morning, on the news, Brad saw that the President had just appointed a new secretary of the Treasury and they were both going to come and tour Southern California. There were also going to be several video town halls where people could ask the President questions in an orderly fashion. Brad went to one of the attendants and inquired if they were going to have a camera placed in the tent so he could ask a question himself. The attendant knew nothing about it but said he would find out and let Brad know. People always said that here. They readily admitted—almost boasting—that they knew nothing, as if that was some sort of badge of honor.

As *Air Force One* made its way across the United States, the President was in his flying office along with Susanna Colbert (who had been approved overwhelmingly by the Senate); John Van Dyke; and the secretary of the Interior, Franklin Little. They discussed what this trip might accomplish.

"Obviously we have no definitive answers on how to proceed," the President said. "So we'll take advantage of Susanna being new in office and say we want them to meet her, how brilliant she is, and how we will now lead a new charge in figuring out a financial solution to the biggest problem the country has ever faced."

"Should I answer questions directly?" Susanna asked.

"I don't see why not, do you, John?"

"I think if her answers are too specific it will hurt us at this point, especially since we can't deliver. So if you say that you've been working on this problem since the moment you've come into office and it's your top priority, I think that will be sufficient. But you can feel free to charm them."

As the presidential helicopter toured the city, Susanna was not prepared for the devastation. She had seen all the pictures and newsreels and immersed herself in this disaster, trying to come up with any possible ideas, but seeing it in person was overwhelming. "My God," she said. "It's as if a nuclear weapon went off."

"Not really," Van Dyke said. "A neutron bomb would have at least left the buildings. A lot of dead people, but a functioning infrastructure. Here, we have nothing."

The helicopter landed at one of the larger triage units. The presidential party greeted the sick and wounded and hopeless, and a press conference was held. Questions came in directly from various remote sites, but they were screened, as the President did not want this to be an event where he was just responding to furious people; he wanted real questions that he could give some reasonable answers to. The moderator began.

"The first question, Mr. President, is from Sally Maelstrom." An older woman appeared on the screen. She looked as if she'd had her hair done for the occasion.

"Mr. President, the condominium I owned is no longer livable. I have been relocated, they tell me temporarily, but what is your plan? Will my home be rebuilt? My entire investment is gone."

Brad Miller, watching the press conference in the Pasadena tent, leaped up from his chair. "That was my question!" he yelled. "That's the answer I want! Let's see what he says!"

"Sally," the President answered, "thank you for asking that. The property question is one of the issues that is foremost on our agenda. As you know, insurance companies that would normally handle this in a prompt manner have been so overwhelmed that they are not responding as they should. We are in talks with all major insurers and we are also looking into other sources of revenue, as the cost is so great, the government cannot handle this alone."

More bullshit, Brad thought.

"Sally, I want you to meet the new, and I might add, first woman secretary of the Treasury, Susanna Colbert. I have brought on Secretary Colbert because of her brilliant business mind, and as soon as we get back to Washington, this will be her first priority, rebuilding Los Angeles into the great city that it is."

Brad mumbled to himself, *You son of a bitch. That's the same answer the attendant gives me. Why don't you just hand out the goddamn money?!*

The rest of the press conference went pretty much the same way. Obvious questions with no real answers. But there was one moment toward the end that was unscripted, when a question was directed to Susanna. It was from a forty-five-year-old man. "Ms. Secretary, where is the money going to come from? The country doesn't have it, the insurance companies don't have it, do we just print it? Won't it be worth nothing if we do that? Where does it come from?" Van Dyke looked down at his screen. This question was not there. Susanna was on her own. And she answered without hesitation.

"We can't just print it, you're right," she said. "To print that much money would devalue our currency beyond repair. The time may be near to ask other countries for monetary help. It's up to the President, of course, but that may be what is necessary at this point in time."

Susanna glanced to her right, and both the President and John Van Dyke were not smiling. They had not formally introduced other countries into the mix, but now it was done. Susanna quickly added, hoping to repair any damage she might have caused, "I stress this is something the President has not decided on, but he has always put every option on the table and I'm sure he will make the right decision."

Before *Air Force One* even left the ground the headlines from the trip were everywhere and they were all essentially the same:

PRESIDENT TO ASK FOR FOREIGN AID

Susanna sat alone on the return trip. After an hour someone came to her seat and asked her to come to the President's office. She thought she was going to be the record holder for the shortest time in a cabinet position. She walked in and the President was smiling. "Sit down."

"I feel terrible," she said. "I seem to have put you in an uncomfortable position."

"Quite the contrary. You spoke what we have known from the beginning but were hesitant to say. The cat's out of the bag and it's about time. When we get back to Washington we'll put our heads together and figure out a way to borrow these unfathomable sums with the least amount of pain. My feeling is that, if possible, we can spread it around the world so no country holds that much more of our debt. The number is so great already that I don't really know how to borrow another twenty trillion, but that's why you're here now."

Susanna felt somewhat relieved. "Let me work on it. And I'm sorry if I caused headlines on something you weren't ready to deal with."

"I would never have been ready. So, in that regard, thank you. But Susanna?"

"Yes, sir?"

"Don't do it again. Don't give answers to questions that I don't know about in advance. Is that clear?"

"Yes, sir."

Susanna went back to her seat still not knowing if she was in trouble. What she did know was that she was numb. *Twenty trillion dollars, what does that number even mean?* The debt the country was currently paying off was already so large; how could it take this much more? She took a pill and ordered a whisky sour. She was going to either sleep or enjoy the flight. Susanna had learned a long time ago to use air travel as the one place to relax. If she crashed, what a waste of time worrying would be. About anything. And as she looked around she had to pinch herself; everyone did the first few times they flew on *Air Force One.*

Robert Golden was in a meeting when he heard the loud explosion. He thought a terrible accident had occurred outside his office window. Alarms sounded and a security official appeared on every screen. "Please evacuate the building through the emergency exits immediately. Do not panic. Everything is under control." Paul Prescott came running in.

"What the fuck was that?"

"I don't know. Let's get out of here."

As people filed into the street they could see a gaping hole in the side of the front entrance to AARP headquarters. It didn't look like a car had crashed, and there was no car there anyway. Apparently it was a homemade bomb: plastic, small, but it did a lot of damage.

After two hours the police determined it was safe to return to the offices, although most people chose to take the rest of the day off. Golden immediately ordered an internal investigation to see who had been fired recently, who'd been reprimanded, who was disgruntled, anything they could gather to put together a suspects list.

The first person Paul Prescott called was his new friend at Justice.

"Are you all right?" Jack Willman asked him. "Are you hurt?"

"You heard, huh?"

"I'm watching it right now. I was going to call you."

"What's going on?

"I don't know. This was a surprise."

"Is this related to the bus shootings?"

"I don't know."

"Christ, somebody is angry. That's a big hole out there."

"Maybe one of your members thought the dues were too high."

"Very funny."

"Sorry. So you're okay?"

"I'm okay. So how are you?"

"I'm fine. At least my building doesn't have a hole in it."

"Keep making fun," Paul said. "Seriously, let me know if you find anything out."

"You know I will. Have you been back to the club?"

"No. Not since you."

"Well, I enjoyed that night. It was fun talking."

"I agree. We'll do it again."

Paul walked back into Golden's office and found four people there. Two were from the FBI and two from the Secret Service. "Folks, this is Paul Prescott; he's my number one here." Golden then handed Paul a sheet of paper. It was the note left by the bomber:

WARNING—GIVE BACK. ALL YOU DO IS TAKE. YOU HAVE HAD YOUR FUN NOW IT'S TIME TO LET OTHERS HAVE THEIRS. WE WILL NOT STOP. THIS IS NOTHING COMPARED TO WHAT YOU WILL SEE IF YOU DON'T SHARE YOUR COMFORT AND YOUR WEALTH. WE HAVE NOTHING, YOU HAVE IT ALL.

And it was signed, YOUTH FOR EQUALITY.

Prescott sat down, not knowing what to say. He asked one of the FBI agents if they knew who that group was. They didn't. "So what happens now?" he asked. An FBI agent said they were aware of these kinds of groups but not this specific one. They were going to increase security around the building but do it in a way so as not to attract attention.

"How can you do that without attracting attention?" Golden wanted to know. "And maybe we *should* attract attention. Maybe we should let these people know they can't just attack us like this."

"There's a way to go about this, Mr. Golden. Let us do our job, and if we feel you or your people are at further risk, we'll step things up. The one thing we don't want to do is to act scared. That's what they look for and that will give them encouragement for more attacks. If it looks like it caused some commotion, but things promptly went back to normal, it will make them plan more aggressively, which is the best way to catch them."

"What if we don't catch them?"

"We will."

Paul asked a good question. "Did this note go everywhere? Does the news have it?"

"Yes," one of the Secret Service men told him. "It was sent everywhere."

"So how do we deal with that?"

"We will help you craft a statement that will be out within an hour, and you will do your best to avoid answering questions directly. If you are forced to do so, you will say you don't know anything, which is true, since you don't."

"And you think it's safe to work in this building?" Golden asked. The Secret Service agent gave him the best answer.

"Mr. Golden, my sister works here and I would tell her to show up as usual."

"Who's your sister?"

"Janice Eaton." Golden thought a moment and then went to his screen to check on the name.

"Oh, sure. She's wonderful. In accounting."

"She *was* in accounting; she was transferred to event planning."

"That's great," Robert said. "She is a valuable employee."

"She *hates* event planning. Any chance she could get her old job back?"

"Done. Tell her she's back in accounting." As if Golden was going to piss off the Secret Service.

When Max Leonard saw the news of the bombing and then read the note, he felt as though his life was coming together. At times he thought he was the only one who was passionate about this, even though he knew others were out there. But when he saw someone brave enough to make a big statement like this one, he knew he was on the right track.

Max was almost jealous. All he had done was to have meetings and talk about it, but here was someone who put those words into action. When he saw Kathy that night he was so excited. "I have to find out who this group is. Maybe we can join."

Kathy seemed excited, too, but she really hadn't thought it through like Max and she wasn't sure if bombing buildings was the best way to accomplish what they were trying to do. She expressed those feelings and Max listened, but he gave her such great answers that she started to see it his way.

"Baby, nothing is going to change without this. In every important revolution, shit happens and that's the way it is. The olds have to be shaken out of their stupor and realize that they share this planet with everyone else." Max then used the money she owed for her medical loan as part of his argument, and each time he brought it up, it worked. "Do you know how long you're going to be paying off that money? Forever. And the only reason you had to take out that loan is that there isn't enough to go around. The olds are getting it all. Do you think that's fair?"

"No," Kathy said. And she meant it.

"Goddamn right, no. They have the votes and they have the power and they're not going to give up a fucking penny without something being done. Everything important in human history needs a push, and sometimes the push is hard and people get hurt." Max wasn't sure that was completely true, but it sounded right and Kathy certainly bought it.

"You're a genius," she said. "You're like a true revolutionary."

"I wish. The guy who blew up that building is the revolutionary. Right now, I'm all talk."

"That's not true. You're just figuring it out. You'll figure out what the best idea is. Are you going to have another meeting?"

"I don't know. I was starting to think the meetings were a waste of time. But maybe now, with this news all over the place, we should try again. See if people are more committed."

President Bernstein was not surprised when he was informed of the bombing. He knew the hostility was out there. It was always just under the surface, and in the last decade it had been getting worse. A new generation was finding its voice.

In the late 1960s, the government acted upset when young people took drugs, but acid was a bureaucrat's dream. No one blew things up on acid or pot or Ecstasy. The officials had to act outraged, but they were grateful for any substance that kept the youth stoned and passive and with any kind of luck kept the older folks in their jobs longer because the young people were too loaded to take over. And once the military draft was ended, no politician ever wanted it back. It took away the main reason that caused kids to take to the streets. They didn't want to die in wars they disagreed with.

But the President never understood why the newer generations had waited this long to get angry about their issue. Debt. It's why he brought up the subject of living too long in his campaign, and it's why he was not happy that his mother was a vegetable, kept alive now at government expense.

Bernstein tried not to mention his mother's lingering condition, but occasionally, in a press conference, he was asked how she was doing. He would turn sad and say, "Not well. We hope for the best, but it looks very bad." He was always worried that the next question would be, "How can you spend so much of the taxpayers' money when she has no chance of recovery? Aren't there better uses for those funds?" But that question never came. Still, he wished his mother had left instructions on when to pull the plug. He thought it was so selfish that she hadn't.

And that was one more reason why he was drawn to Susanna Colbert. As rich as Colbert was, she wasn't selfish, not like his mother. As a matter of fact, Susanna was one of the least selfish people he'd ever met. Most ultra-rich were intolerable, spending all of their energy on their business, with little time for anything else. Susanna was nothing like that. At her swearing in, when Bernstein met her children, he was beyond impressed. *Right from central casting,* he thought. *Smart, humble, a good sense of humor, an obvious great love for their mother. How did this woman do that and still make so much money?* He was glad she was secretary of the Treasury. Maybe, just maybe, some of that magic would rub off on America.

CHAPTER TWENTY-FIVE

Sam Mueller was just about to give up the dream of one more great discovery when a face floated in front of his screen early one morning. Mueller was still sleeping when he rolled over and saw Dr. Peter Stern, one of Immunicate's leading researchers, staring at him. "Sam, get up."

"What is it?"

"We did it!"

Mueller knew what he was talking about. It was what everyone was working on all around the world and, if true, it would be the next big thing.

"Are you sure?"

"Come down here and look at the goddamn mice."

When he got to the complex his heart was racing. One problem that remained with older people were their bones. There were many medicines to take as a preventative for bone decay, but they did very little in the long run. As more people were living into their nineties and beyond, a simple fall in the shower always resulted in a broken something. Science had tried to find a way of regenerating bone and had succeeded somewhat, but it had always concentrated on speeding up the healing process once the bone was broken.

Immunicate was working on something different: regenerating

undamaged bone tissue. Bones that were simply weakened by age. By working with genes and new classes of stem cells, Immunicate finally showed that old bone could turn into new, replacing itself gradually, until a ninety-year-old's leg was exactly the same as when he was forty.

The trouble it kept running into was that the process did not stay in the bones alone, but spread to the other organs, causing them to try to regenerate, which resulted in failure. But it looked as if Immunicate had finally solved the problem. Stern showed Mueller very old mice that were running on a wheel at top speed. "There is no spillage. It's staying in the bone tissue."

Sam Mueller had learned over the years not to get excited too soon, but he couldn't help himself. He and his company needed this.

"If this works," Mueller said, "we'll have one-hundred-year-old people entering the Olympics! If the mice are fine, let's go to the dogs."

"Do you think I would have called you so excited if we hadn't done that already?"

"You did?" Mueller was shocked. There was an earlier time when that step would never have been taken without his knowledge, but those days were gone. The company was so big and diverse he wasn't in the loop on every single thing anymore. "And?"

"Same," Stern said. "Same fucking thing! Great bones, no spillage!"

"My God! How long does it take?"

"Substantial regrowth in three months, complete repair in half a year." Mueller thought he was going to faint. This wasn't as good as curing cancer, and it may not have been his discovery directly, but the company he founded was about to let old people run and play like kids.

"So when do we start trials?"

"We'll submit everything, hopefully in two months."

"I think we should blast it out to the world. Let everyone know that you don't fuck with Immunicate. Make it clear that humans haven't tried it, but also make it clear that these animal studies are a first, and you mark my words, every big drug company on the planet is going to be jealous. I love it!" The news made headlines all over the world:

IMMUNICATE HOPEFUL OLD BONES
WILL TURN INTO NEW

When Max Leonard saw that he went apoplectic. "Do you know what this means?" he said to Kathy. "This means the olds just got another twenty years of life, *minimum.* And if they find a way to regenerate the bones, all of the organs are next. These fuckers are going to live to be two hundred. They're never going to leave."

"Well, they haven't tried it on humans," Kathy said. "Maybe it won't work."

"It doesn't matter. It just shows you where their priorities are. And as that Mueller gets older, all he's going to do is try to fix up his own age group. Shit. This *has* to be stopped."

"How?"

"Let's have one more big meeting. We'll know what to do after that."

Brad Miller read the bone news, but he had mixed feelings. His bones were okay, and if he had still had his life and his home and his money, he would have been very happy, but what did he need better bones for? For the tent? He'd had enough of the tent. As much as he didn't want to, he swallowed his pride and called his son.

"Dad? Are you okay? Are you still in Pasadena?"

"Yes."

"We wanted to come visit but traveling there is still too tough."

"I know. That's okay."

"Hey, did you read about the bones?"

"Yeah."

"Pretty great, right? Are you excited?"

"I'm thrilled."

"Well, right now it's only in mice, but we'll keep our fingers crossed for you."

"Thanks," his father said sarcastically. "That means a lot."

"So how are they treating you?"

Brad decided just to stop the small talk. He held his nuts, a habit he acquired long ago when he had to say something he hated, and just blurted it out. "What about me living with you and the family?"

There was a silence on the other end that seemed to go on forever. If Brad hadn't been looking at his son's face, he would have thought the connection was lost. "You want to move in with us?" Tom meekly asked.

"You know what, forget it. It was just a thought. Forget it."

"No, I'm just surprised, that's all. Let me talk to Crystal. It's just such a surprise and we don't really have the room. You know it's tiny here."

"It's okay, Tom, it was just a thought."

"No, Dad, it's a good thought. Let me figure it all out."

"Fine. You figure it out. I love you." And Brad hung up, sorry that he had called his son in the first place.

The bone story circulated around the West Wing and was raised at the morning press conference. "Has the President seen the news on the latest breakthrough on bone regeneration?"

"He's seen it," said Elizabeth Foreman, the press secretary, "and he thinks it's very exciting, but we know from other discoveries that human trials are the most important, so we are keeping our fingers crossed."

"Is there an update on the President's mother?"

"No. Nothing has changed."

Then a question came from the screen above the podium. The White House press briefings now allowed for twenty percent of their questions to come from reporters in other countries. A man from Germany asked, "Did the President's mother leave instructions about end-of-life care?"

The press secretary not only did not know the answer, but she had to act offended, as if it breached some private boundary. "I have no idea and if I did, I don't think it would be appropriate to tell you. That's a personal family issue." She thought it would stop there, but the reporter continued.

"Isn't it a people's issue because of the great cost of these situations? Is the President paying for this from his own pocket? Does his insurance pay for this?"

The press in the room were silent. They had felt it was too soon to address these kinds of issues, but apparently the overseas reporters did not. Foreman tried to contain her anger.

"The President has insurance through his job, which covers his immediate family. That would not include a parent, as you well know. Mrs.

Bernstein would have to have her own coverage. Are you an insurance agent looking for a commission?"

She got the room to laugh a little and before the German reporter could ask anything else, she motioned for the screen to go black. Now all she was hoping for was that this did not open a Pandora's box.

The President watched the press briefing while exercising. He was surprised it had taken this long to get that question and even more surprised it had come from overseas. The fact was, he agreed with the reporter. His mother did have insurance, most of it from the government, and this was an overwhelming expense that was going to lead to nothing. But what could he do?

Bernstein had earlier called in his private attorney, Harry Cannon, and had what could be perceived as a borderline illegal discussion.

"Did you look over everything?"

"Yes, Mr. President. There's nothing there. She's left her estate to the children and various causes but there is nothing spelled out for this."

"Can a DNR be added?"

"I'm sorry, sir?"

"Let's say a child knows what the wishes were, that they heard the parent say it. Can it be added?"

"Did you hear her say that?"

The President looked at him. "I don't know, maybe."

"Don't you have sisters, Mr. President?"

"Yes."

"Did they ever hear that?"

"One sister doesn't talk to her and the other feels that life should be prolonged forever."

"I think unless all the siblings heard her wishes, it would be difficult to even contemplate changing the will at this point."

Bernstein realized he had to backtrack a little just so this conversation would not look bad when Harry Cannon wrote his book. "I obviously want my mother to have the best care, but I don't want her to suffer. I'm in a tough position. If the public thinks large amounts of Medicare are going to the President's mother, especially when there is no hope of recovery, well, you understand, don't you?"

"I do, Mr. President. Is she brain-dead?"

"No more than when she was alive."

Harry laughed. It was a good joke, even if it was a bit surprising. He wasn't aware of the details of the President's relationship with his mother, but he had heard stories from White House staff of the few times she came to visit. Apparently there was a lot of arguing. "Seriously, sir. Is she medically brain-dead?"

"No. In a deep coma. No chance of coming out. But there is brain activity."

"That's a tough one, Mr. President. If a doctor ended her life out of compassion and one of your sisters sued, he would lose everything. No doctor would do that. She really needed to have something in writing."

"What if there was something in a personal note somewhere? I know there are a lot of her things we haven't gone through yet."

Harry Cannon thought a moment. He didn't feel completely comfortable in this conversation, but as a lawyer he couldn't show that. "I guess it would depend on what the note said. If it was specific and detailed enough, it might have merit."

"Okay, thanks, Harry. We're looking over her personal stuff now. If I find something, I'll let you know."

"That's fine, sir."

When Harry left the meeting, the first thing he did was look at his own father's living will. His mother had died before the cure for cancer, but his father was one of the olds and Harry didn't want to face this same situation.

That night when they were lying in bed, the President and his wife talked about it. "Did you hear that German guy ask the question everyone is thinking?"

"Yes. I saw it."

"I'm now the poster boy for the one thing I don't believe in."

"I don't know what choice you really have."

"How about killing her? After all, I'm the President."

Betsy laughed, although there was a small part of her that wondered if her husband was serious. "She might just pass naturally."

"There's so much equipment in that room, she'll outlive us."

"There's nothing you can do, at least tonight. Maybe nature will surprise you."

"Yeah, maybe she'll be the first person in a coma who can still criticize."

Every day, AARP circulated to the senior staff any news story that could affect the organization. The question from the German reporter was right at the top, considering its implications. AARP's job was to service the older population, but they wanted to create the impression that they cared about younger people, too. It was all a ruse, since their loyalty was only to their membership, but they still spent a lot of money on public relations to make them appear compassionate.

For example, they did not play up the bone story as much as they would have liked. First of all, there was no reason to, since it had made headlines on its own. It didn't need their help. But they also didn't want to appear to gloat about discoveries that made life easier for them and not others.

When Paul Prescott saw the question from the German reporter, he immediately called the head of PR, June Scully. "What did you think of the question about his mother?"

"I had the same feeling you did."

"How do you know what my feeling was?"

Paul was smiling. He and June thought alike. She was ten years older than Paul and he was crazy about her—her work ethic, her sensibilities, everything.

"What I'm afraid of," June said, "is that this is going to come up over and over. You have a President who ran on questioning life extension and now he's in the middle of it. We have to hope this dies out."

"We have to hope *she* dies out."

June laughed. "Seriously, this could really be a problem, with the bombing and all. We sure don't need such a highly visible person sucking money out of the system."

"I know. I don't see a way out right now. Maybe something will develop."

"Maybe. I thought Los Angeles would take people's minds off the seniors for a while, but it seems to have gotten worse. The less money there is out there, the more they look at us."

"I'm so glad I'm not your age," Paul joked. "Keep an eye out, honey, see if this story goes anywhere. Even small-time stuff, let me know."

"I will, Paul. I'm worried, too."

CHAPTER TWENTY-SIX

Matthew Bernstein was a presidential historian, as most presidents were. When you belonged to such an exclusive club, you tended to know minute details about all the members. The most interesting of them all to Bernstein was Richard Nixon. Not because he thought he was the best president—far from it—but because there existed years of taped records of the man sitting in the Oval Office. Not before or since could someone just listen to the inner thoughts of the most powerful person in the world. Over the last ten years the remaining tapes had finally been released, and they were doozies.

Bernstein, being a Jew, wondered how Henry Kissinger could have ever worked for Nixon, as Nixon seemed to hate Jews as much as the Arabs did. *Maybe Kissinger thought it was love-hate.* But in thousands of hours of tapes there was no love. Just "Jew" this and "Jew" that and "gay" this and "gay" that. *My God,* Bernstein thought, *had Nixon never seen a Broadway show?*

And Nixon knew he was being taped. That was the amazing thing. To be so confident in his position of power that he believed the record of all he said would always be under his control, which it was, until Watergate.

And that's what Bernstein couldn't get out of his mind. Watergate. He would lie in bed at night and think about it, not in the context of stealing secrets from the other party, but in the context of someone successfully breaking in, accomplishing a task, and no one ever knowing. The idea of Watergate was a heady one. Maybe a similar tactic would be the easiest way to end his mother's suffering and thereby his own. Someone could break in and pull the plugs. Then he laughed. *Right, and look what happened to Nixon. I'll be known as the president who killed his mother. Great. Next idea.*

But Bernstein knew very well what was happening with the bus incidents and the AARP bombing. And he knew it would get worse. *If my mother is still being kept alive two years from now, could I even be reelected?* He hated those thoughts, but as president he had to think of everything, gruesome or not.

And then finally, before he fell asleep, the thoughts, as they always did, turned to California. This was the most pressing problem. This had no solution; no one's death would solve this. Tomorrow was the first full cabinet meeting with Susanna Colbert in place as secretary of the Treasury. She was going to formally present her ideas on Los Angeles. Maybe, just maybe, she had a way out.

The President's entire cabinet was immediately taken with Colbert. It was the deceiving nature of her being. She looked and sounded like a good-looking, churchgoing mother, someone Norman Rockwell might have painted. But when she got hot and heavy into the conversation, no matter what it was, she was the smartest person in the room. Not flauntingly so. She just was. Prepared, full of facts and ideas, a world-class listener, and a problem solver like a computer. Fifteen minutes into the full cabinet meeting, no one even thought of Morton Spiller.

The ideas were sparse. How do you rebuild? Do you just print more money? It was now common to live with a moderated form of hyperinflation, but if it got out of hand—more so than it already was—the United States would spin down the black hole of worthless currency.

It always came back to the same thing. Borrow. And the only country that really had the kind of money they needed was China. The thought was that since the Chinese remained the biggest lender to the United States, they would have to loan more or they would be at risk of not getting their investment back. The United States was comforted by being the original "too big to fail" institution.

Susanna thought, and the President agreed, that there should be a high-level meeting as soon as possible to discuss further lending. Susanna said there was no reason to borrow all of it. A few trillion would jump-start a real plan to rebuild, and when that was spent they could ask for more.

So the new secretary planned to go to Beijing to meet her counterpart and suggest a three-trillion-dollar emergency loan, specifically for Los Angeles. She would use all of her charm and everything else she could muster to try to get the most favorable terms possible. She would be accompanied by a slew of undersecretaries, but she would be the most senior cabinet member on the trip.

When the meeting was over and people were filing out, the President asked to talk to her alone. "Do you feel confident in this? Is it too soon?"

"No," she said. "I expected this when I took the job. I have been preparing."

"Have you used the Nextron before?"

"Yes. I love it. I was going to invest in it as a startup."

"Great. This will be hugely important. Obviously the better the terms you can negotiate, the more it will help us down the line, since we'll be coming back to this trough often."

"I know. I believe I will have success there."

Then the President, for some reason he didn't fully understand, blurted out a question that had no relevance to the topic. "Are either of your parents alive?" Susanna took a moment to change gears, but answered as if it were part of the discussion.

"My mother died at ninety but my father is still living. He's ninety-eight."

"That's wonderful. How is he?"

"He's well. He had some problems with digestion, went on a feeding tube for a while, but it's out now and he walks every day and still communicates his thoughts through a talk blog. He's got a lot of opinions."

The President smiled. "Does he have a DNR?"

Susanna looked at him for a second without answering. The President thought she didn't know what the initials stood for so he started to tell her. "A do-not—"

"No, sir, I know what it is. The fact is, I don't know the answer. I know his wishes are for no excessive intervention. He certainly feels that if he is unconscious for any length of time he doesn't want to be machined, that's for sure."

"Trust me, Susanna, you should make sure it's written down. Do it before you go to China. It's quite something how people avoid putting that in writing. It's as if they don't do it, it will never happen."

Susanna knew exactly what was on the President's mind. "Your mother has nothing like that?"

"No, she doesn't."

"When I get back from China, Mr. President, maybe you would take me to see her."

"You want to see her? Why?"

"I would like to see what you're dealing with. I know it's on your mind."

Bernstein stood there. *Look at this woman. Look at my new employee. A mother, a shrink, and hopefully the best Treasury secretary the country has ever seen.* And even if she wasn't, the first two were enough.

The next meeting of the—well, they really hadn't given it a name yet—was going to be held at Kathy Bernard's house. The house her father left her. The house still had a mortgage of half a million and that, plus the medical loan, put Kathy in the red for almost a million dollars. And she had no job. Her father did have a little money squirreled away, but all it would do was assist her in paying off the debts for a few months longer. Max wanted to help her. "I have the money," he said. "Let me at least pay off some of the medical."

"I can't do that."

"Why?"

"I'm in love with you, you know that, but it's too soon to feel indebted."

"You wouldn't be indebted. I have the money; it's what I want to do with it."

"Let me just take the offer to heart and feel good about that. I don't want you to do this right now. Maybe soon, but not now." Max understood. It was why he liked her.

"Are you sure you want to have the meeting here?"

"Why not? How many people came last time?"

"I don't know. Fifty."

"So even if we double it, we can put them in the backyard. We'll have hot dogs and drinks and it'll be fun."

People were informed about the meeting through the usual channels and on a Saturday at noon, with a hundred people at the most expected, three hundred and fifty showed up. Max was blown away. Kathy was a bit panicked. People were everywhere, walking in every room, filling the yard, waiting for the bathrooms. Her small house was overwhelmed.

It was an odd group—bikers and teachers and a lot of regular-looking people, more regular looking than last time.

At least twenty people had on T-shirts with a picture of someone Max did not know. He was told it was Walter Masters. Someone had heard about Masters from a relative and looked him up and loved his face, so the person made the shirts and gave them out at the meeting. People wearing them really had no idea who he was. When asked, they would say, "He's the exterminator of the old." No one knew what that even meant, but it sounded great, and one could see how folklore gets started.

"People!" Max yelled. "Could we get as many of you to come outside as possible? The rest, let's get into the rooms that face the backyard and we'll open the windows and try to have everybody participate."

Even though Kathy wasn't thrilled that so many people were trampling through her house, she *was* impressed by the turnout. She wondered exactly what had caused it. *What happened between the first meeting and now?*

Max started the proceedings. "I just want to make sure everyone is here for the right reason. We are trying to come up with solutions to make the spread of wealth fairer and give younger people the same opportunity as the olds."

"Who?" someone shouted. Someone else who knew yelled, "The olds. What we call the greedy old farts who take everything." People cheered at that. Max continued.

"Since we met last, a lot has gone down. I'm sure you know about the bombing at AARP." The crowd burst into applause. "As far as we know it had nothing to do with anyone here, so obviously there are others who are just as angry and trying to figure out a solution. Today we want to hear ideas, real ideas, on how to change the world."

Kathy was quite amazed at how violent the suggestions were, at how angry the group was. One man in his thirties actually suggested a civil war. Not between the North and South but between the Young and the Old. The crowd loved this idea. Max even thought it was interesting, although he questioned how they would start it.

The name of their group was settled on by the spontaneous chant that people burst into from time to time: "Enough is enough." People yelled it over and over and the name stuck.

Max realized that a group by itself was meaningless. Sure, they could picket or even get violent, but they would be shot down quickly unless they had a coherent plan. He appointed three people in charge, ones who were at the first meeting along with himself. They decided to meet in smaller groups over the next few weeks to try to give the organization a real direction. But everyone agreed that today had been a good start. Enough Is Enough was born.

During the afternoon Kathy looked around from time to time to see if Brian Nelson showed up. He didn't. She'd kind of hoped he would, just so she could put a period on the whole thing, but he didn't give her that satisfaction. The truth was, she didn't think about it for long—she was too preoccupied trying to keep hordes of people out of her closet.

At the end of the day, as the last few people left, Max turned to Kathy and gave her a bear hug. He was so happy. "This was fucking incredible! Could you imagine how many people we would get if we had the space and the resources to let the *world* know? I bet a million people would come to this. The anger is everywhere."

"You were great," Kathy said. "You're a natural leader. Now you just have to decide what you want these people to do."

"I know. That's the hard part. One thing I was thinking, maybe we should contact that guy on the T-shirt."

"Who is that?"

"Walter Masters."

"What does he do exactly?"

"He puts old people out of their misery."

"He murders them?"

"I don't know. I think he does it with their consent, but obviously something is going on there. Maybe he would join and have some ideas. I'm going to get one of the people who know him to put me in contact."

"That's a good idea," Kathy said, and she meant it, even though murdering large numbers of old people was not something at the top of her to-do list.

Walter Masters was back in his Kern County home after an exhausting trip to the earthquake zone. He had helped a hundred and ten people transition in Southern California, and now he was spent and a bit depressed and wondering what to do next. He couldn't really make a living out of this; people paid him for his expenses and a nominal fee, but it was never meant to be a business. It was born out of a need to help others, and now he was tiring of it.

He tried to keep up with his correspondence while traveling, but when he got home he had hundreds of E's waiting for him. He had standard one-key replies that thanked people for contacting him but graciously told them he was unable to help for whatever reason he chose, distance, type of illness, age of patient, and so on. He even had a reply for when he sensed the sender might be someone trying to make trouble; it simply said, "You have the wrong person."

He finally got around to an E from Max Leonard, who introduced himself, gave plenty of references, and asked if they could have a face-to-face at his convenience. Not a screen meeting, but a real one. Masters was not used to people Max's age asking for help, so he contacted him.

"Hello?" Max said, looking unshaven and almost as if he were asleep.

"Walter Masters here."

"Oh my God, hello." Masters saw the screen go blank for a few seconds and then Max came back with a clean shirt and his hair combed. "You caught me unprepared."

"Sorry, do you want to do this another time?"

"No. Not at all. I wanted to sit down with you and talk in person if you would do that."

"What's the matter with you?"

"Nothing. It's not about that. I just wanted to talk. I'm an admirer of your work and I wanted to meet you."

"Where are you located exactly?"

"I'm in Indianapolis."

"Gee, I'm in California. I have no plans to travel east at this time."

"May I come and see you?"

Masters thought a moment. He was a bit confused. "May I ask what this is about?"

"Mr. Masters, I am head of a group called Enough Is Enough." This was the first time Max had used the name and it sounded great. "We are concerned about the ongoing expense of allowing people to live beyond their natural lives, and you have many fans in this group. I want nothing more than just to sit in person and talk to you. I could be out there in a day."

"What do you mean 'allowing people to live beyond their natural lives'?"

"Please, I don't want to explain everything like this. Let me come see you. Just for an hour. I promise it will at least be interesting."

Walter stared at Max's face. The guy did seem smart and sincere and he had changed his shirt just to talk to him. "Come on Friday. I'll meet you at a restaurant in the town where I live." And Walter proceeded to give him all the particulars. He felt it was best not to invite Max to his home, but what could the harm be to meet him for an hour in a public place?

"Thank you, sir! Thank you!" And Max disconnected and let out a cheer.

"What is it?" Kathy asked.

"He agreed to meet me."

"Who?"

"The hero on the T-shirt. Masters."

"Wow. That's great. Should I come?"

"It's in California. He was so hesitant that if I bring another person he might freak out. Let me fly out for a day and see if I can make him comfortable."

Kathy understood. It made sense to her. "That's great," she said. "He sounds like a genius or something. Maybe he'll join the group."

CHAPTER TWENTY-SEVEN

As the Air Force jet touched down in Beijing, Secretary Colbert was, if anything, overprepared. She knew every trade agreement the Chinese and Americans had executed in the last forty years, all the way back to 1990. She knew how much debt the United States borrowed, at what true interest rate, not just the rates published for public consumption; and she knew her counterparts—their public and private lives, everything about them. She was to meet one of the vice premiers, Hu Lanchoi, someone she was quite familiar with and someone very high up when it came to matters of finance.

She and her party were met at the airport with dancing girls and beautiful flowers and taken to a private residence that was used for foreign dignitaries. Susanna had been to China more times than she could count. She even spoke the language fairly well, although on this trip everyone used the Nextron.

The Nextron was the breakthrough in translation that people had been waiting for forever. It made learning another language almost obsolete. Decades earlier, software was introduced that turned many devices, like cell phones, into translation machines, but they all had their share of problems. People had to speak slowly and carefully and do voice training, and the devices still made too many mistakes. The Nextron was the first stand-alone device that was error-free. People spoke normally, looking directly at the other person, and the small box, half the size of a paperback book, not only translated without mistakes but could project images, play music, record video, and do everything else one would need to do in a business environment. Travelers carried them around like a credit card, and in restaurants and hotels and meeting places all over the world one could hear the din of people talking in their native language, with one of six different voices that were available to choose from, translating perfectly.

When Susanna entered the meeting, along with her undersecretaries, the table was filled with Nextrons, supplied by the host country for those who didn't bring theirs, but people never forgot. It was the one true "Don't leave home without it" device. Susanna impressed her host by speaking Chinese in her initial greetings, but once the meeting started in earnest the Nextrons began whirring away.

After the perfunctory hellos and small talk, Susanna wasted no time. "I'm sure you have been following our great troubles in Southern California. Even you, who are used to earthquakes, can understand that such a magnitude in a city as populated as Los Angeles is something that can never be comprehended until it actually happens."

Lanchoi listened sympathetically, but he was thinking, *You should have been prepared for this; we are.*

And the Chinese were. They had suffered massive destruction over the last century by several devastating earthquakes in their smaller villages, and even though fault lines were less likely to erupt in their big population centers, the Chinese initiated retrofitting of buildings to an extent not attempted before by any nation. Every structure over three stories high had rubber joints and bearings fused to the foundation. When retrofitted, a building could sway up to four times more than it could with its original design. The friction would eat away at the rubber and leave the building itself intact.

All Chinese skyscrapers erected after 2017 had foundations and floor joints that could twist and bend like straws. They were built to withstand a 9.0 quake, which was something that was never expected in Beijing or Shanghai, but they did it anyway. Lanchoi wondered why Los Angeles, which was on a known major fault, would not do the same, but then again, the two countries operated in a totally different manner.

As Susanna made her case, which was basically, "We need three trillion dollars today and more later," Lanchoi smiled and nodded, and everything looked as if it were going to be a fait accompli. But when Secretary Colbert finished her "plea speech," as one of her assistants called it, they were all shocked at what came back to them over the Nextron. Hu Lanchoi spoke very, very fast, faster than a human translator could ever keep up with, but it was no problem for the machine. And the entire time he was talking he had a smile on his face.

"First and foremost, we understand the disaster that has befallen you, and if there is anything on the humanitarian side that we are not doing, let us know and we will fill in those gaps immediately. However, we can no longer lend the United States this kind of money."

When Susanna heard that, she didn't flinch. Maybe he meant they would only loan *two* trillion, which would be a disappointment, but at least it would be a start.

He continued. "We feel connected and close to your country, but the time has come to end the borrowing of these great sums. As you know, your debt to us is bordering on fifteen trillion dollars, and yes, you pay back with fair interest, but you are a bottomless pit and we no longer feel comfortable feeding it. There are other countries in the world that may feel more comfortable with such a large loan, but we do not. And we beg you not to take this personally. If any country came to us at this point in time and asked for three trillion dollars, we would be unable to accommodate them, so please, do not think this is just about you."

Susanna had to laugh. As if any country other than the U.S. would ask China for three trillion dollars, and as if any other country *but* China could loan that kind of money. The United States already owed India a trillion dollars and had even borrowed five hundred billion from Indonesia in 2022. Without China, there was no one left.

Susanna really didn't know what to say. She felt angry and would have lashed out if this was just an old-fashioned economic discussion, but it wasn't. She was representing the United States as its Treasury secretary and she had to be careful not to antagonize what was slowly becoming an unpleasant situation. "So let me be clear, Mr. Vice Premier. Is the number too large, or is the whole idea of further lending now soured? What exactly is the issue?"

"I would say both."

"Both? So China has made a decision to no longer be the lender of choice to the United States?"

"No, I would not say that. There are smaller amounts, a hundred billion here or a hundred billion there, where I am sure we could work something out. But for the amounts you are now talking about, I would say this is no longer viable."

For the first time Susanna looked visibly shaken. Lanchoi smiled in sympathy. "Madame Secretary, I am not saying we cannot offer help, just not in this fashion."

"Yes, I know what you said. You would be happy to offer more humanitarian assistance, but that is not what we are looking for."

"I would think we would be willing to offer much more than that, but no longer in the same fashion. No longer gargantuan amounts of borrowed money." Susanna laughed for a moment. To hear the Nextron pronounce "gargantuan" was funny, but she knew it was time to end the meeting.

"I thank you for your time. The President is anxious to know how things went today, so let me report back to him and we can discuss this at a future date."

"Madame Secretary, please understand one of the points I am trying to make. We are interested in providing the help you are looking for, just not in the same unproductive ways."

"I don't understand you exactly. What do you mean?"

"I think for that discussion my premier and your president should sit down together. This is beyond my, as you people like to say, pay grade."

"You're asking for a presidential summit?"

"I am authorized to tell you we would be happy to sit down at our highest level if you would really like to hammer out this issue."

"And how would we do that, Mr. Vice Premier?"

"In ways neither you nor I are authorized to talk about."

Now Susanna was intrigued. She had no idea what he meant, but he was obviously saying that when borrowing went this high, the two bosses needed to talk. She actually thought Bernstein would be amenable to that—after all, what choice did he have? "I will pass this along to the President, and I thank you for your time."

"It was wonderful to meet you. I am a fan of your work. When The Card came to China it was a big hit. I had one of the first ones."

Susanna smiled. "I know you did. I had to approve it."

Max Leonard had never been to Kern County, but unlike most people he had at least heard about it. His uncle was a big country music fan and used to talk about Buck Owens and how he owned his own city called Bakersfield. Buck didn't actually own Bakersfield, but he was one of its biggest landholders, and he had a nightclub there, the Crystal Palace. He certainly put Kern County on the map for a lot of people who would never have otherwise given it a second thought. Walter Masters did not live in Bakersfield; he lived about thirty miles west in a smaller town called Taft. And he was not a country music fan.

Before the earthquake, Max would have just taken a nonstop flight from Indianapolis to LAX and driven the rest of the way, but that was now impossible. Flying into L.A. was an ongoing nightmare, so Max took three connecting flights and landed at Meadows Field, the airport that serviced Kern County. He rented a car, drove to Taft, and thought he had entered a time machine.

This was one of those small towns that simply didn't change, as if it had been set in stone. The Wal-Mart looked as though it had been remodeled maybe once in the last thirty years. The two shopping centers both looked exactly the same, as if they'd been built on the same day in the last century. And there was one movie theater complex. That was the only structure that looked relatively new.

Movie theaters no longer handled film or video. All products were sent by satellite and nothing was stored in the actual theater itself. This led to the disappearance of the traditional projection booth. The new projector, which was tiny, was built into the back wall. There was no longer any need for a room behind it, so some movie houses had taken on a different look. Many theaters had rows of lunch counters in the rear, where the equipment once was. You could sit at the counter, order food, and watch sports or entertainment. Everything was holographic or advanced 3D, requiring no glasses. That's what people expected. No one was willing to pay sixty dollars to see flat images. Those days were long gone.

At the appointed time Max walked into Jennie's, a small diner that had been there, as the sign said, since '09. Walter had taken a table in the back where they could have some privacy. When he saw Max, he stood up to greet him.

"The funny thing," Walter said, "is that modern communication takes away all the surprises. It used to be fun to guess what someone would look like. Have a seat."

"I can only imagine," said Max. "I've been looking at people on screens forever. I don't remember it any other way."

"It was interesting. It made you use your imagination." They both sat down and Walter looked Max over for a few seconds. "So how can I help you?"

"Do you mind if I get something in my stomach? I'll think better. I don't want to waste your time by rambling."

"Sure. They'll send someone over if you want, but they like it if you just tell the kitchen yourself."

"Is there a menu?"

Walter pointed to the wall behind him. Max turned around and looked at an old-fashioned menu board. "The tuna sandwich looks good. Maybe that with a dinner salad and a Coke." Walter placed the order over the intercom; he ordered a peach cobbler and a coffee for himself.

"Do you want to wait until it comes or do you want to start now?"

Jesus, Max thought, *this guy sure doesn't waste time. You would think if you lived in a place like this you would want to waste time, but apparently not.* "I can start now." Max took a sip of water and gathered his thoughts. "It would be nice to find some common ground with you, so let me begin by saying that I also think there are too many old people taking up space."

"Who told you I think that?"

"Well, no one told me, I just thought that one of the reasons you did what you did was that you felt older people were being kept alive against their will."

Walter was intrigued. Young folks for the most part never had this discussion with him. "Part of what I do is so people do not suffer needlessly. I don't make judgments based on their age."

"Well, do you think people are kept alive beyond a reasonable time?"

"What do you mean, 'a reasonable time'?"

"Are people living too long?"

"Some are, yes."

"Mr. Masters, may I ask how old you are?"

"No. It doesn't matter."

"Well, whatever it is, you must know that the world has changed since you were my age."

"I know that. But why don't you tell me how it has affected you. Don't talk in generalities."

"It hasn't affected me. I have money. But anyone who doesn't is screwed. The debt on young people is too great to crawl out of. The girl I live with, for example, owes almost four hundred thousand dollars for a medical loan and her father is already dead."

"What does this have to do with me?"

"At a time when it's harder than ever to get a piece of the pie, the world has decided to keep its older population going forever. Who the fuck pays for that? Excuse my language. I do. And my friends. And five-year-olds who don't even understand it. I thought you also might feel the same way."

At that moment the food arrived. A pleasant-looking woman who obviously had no interest in the fat pill put the order down and said, "If you need anything else, just buzz."

Max scarfed down his sandwich and kept talking. "I lead a group of hundreds of younger people called Enough Is Enough."

"What do they do?"

"I don't know. That's one of the reasons I'm talking to you. We need a plan. The olds are—"

"The what?"

"We call everyone over seventy 'the olds.' It's just easier that way."

"I'll have to remember that. Go on."

"The olds have all the power and access to the money. Something has to be done. Even if violence is part of the equation."

"Mr. Leonard, I hear your frustration. And I agree with much of your thinking. But I don't know what I can do to help you."

"You could kill all of them." Max hoped, really hoped, that Masters had a sense of humor. If not, this was the end of their lunch.

"I don't have the time," Walter said, "or the medicine. I can only kill half of them."

Max was relieved. "Half would be fine, sir."

"Listen, my friend, I think you have real issues here and I think you are to be commended for trying to change a system that is impossible to budge. But unfortunately, I don't know how I can be of any help to you."

"So killing half of them was a joke?"

"Do you really want me to answer that?"

"So why do you do this kind of work that no one else does? Are any of your reasons like mine?"

"No. You and I both have a revolutionary quality to our souls. If I was your age, I would be in your group. But my reasons are different. I abhor suffering. But I don't do it to balance out the population. As a matter of fact, many times I have helped young people pass when there was no hope and the medical establishment would not recognize that." Max was silent. He didn't know what he had expected at this meeting, but it didn't sound as though it was going to be as helpful as he thought. And then Walter asked him that exact question. "What did you expect when you came here?"

"I wasn't sure. Maybe, I thought, if you felt like I did, you would help our group."

"How?"

"I don't know."

"Yes, you do. In your mind you thought I might step up the pace, right? Start eliminating the enemy?" When Max heard it that way, he knew Masters was right. And he knew it sounded truly crazy. "Listen," Walter said, "I understand why you wanted to talk. But you need to go in another direction. I don't prolong life, I do the opposite. You need to talk to the people who keep it going. The doctors and lawmakers and religious nuts who want as many minutes as you can squeeze out of this existence, at any price. That's where you're going to find some answers. Not here. Does that make sense?"

And at that moment Max could not get the image out of his head of all those olds worshipping Sam Mueller. "I guess it does. Yes. It absolutely does." Max got up and shook Walter's hand. "Thank you for meeting with me."

"You're a bright kid. If I were younger, I would be on your wavelength. Go change the world. I'll pay for the sandwich."

CHAPTER TWENTY-EIGHT

The tent in Pasadena felt more and more like a minimum-security prison. Brad watched new people move in as others left, some finally moving out of state to live with friends or relatives and some trying something completely different, the retirement ships.

Decades earlier this trend had begun with people buying luxurious homes on cruise ships and living there part of the year. It was very expensive and reserved only for the ultrarich. Then, in 2021, Royal Swedish Cruise Line took the concept one step further and introduced the first affordable retirement cruise ship, *The Retirement One.* In order to keep the price down, luxury was no longer an option. The ship held over two thousand people and had plain rooms, average food, and some entertainment and activities, but basically it resembled a standard retirement facility. Some people even referred to it as "a nursing home on water." Sometimes the ship wouldn't even move for months: It would dock at a Royal facility in one of six countries and stay there for the summer or the fall. The residents were guaranteed only three months of actual cruising, but still people loved the concept, and Royal constructed another ship, *The Retirement Two,* and then their third, *The Sunset.*

Five years earlier this was something Brad Miller would have scoffed at. He remembered telling his friend Jack, "Those poor people are packed in there like sardines . . . except sardines don't get seasick." Now, as he stared at the brochure, he wondered if this might be the way to go. Except Brad didn't even have the money to be a sardine. Everything was tied up in his condo, which was no longer there, and he couldn't even borrow against it. Here was a man who felt so vital on his eightieth birthday and now he thought, more often than not, about dying.

Some nights he would lie awake and imagine the letter he would write to Walter Masters, asking for his services. It reminded Brad of when he was a child and wrote to Santa Claus. Other times he would lie in his cot and stare at the brochure for *The Sunset*. The ship was starting to look better with each passing day.

One morning Brad was playing cards with three new arrivals when he heard his name over the paging system, asking him to come to the office. He had never been paged before and he couldn't help but feel a tinge of excitement. Maybe there was some good news.

When he walked outside he saw his son standing there, waiting for him. Tom hadn't told his father he was coming; he wanted it to be a surprise.

The first thing that struck Brad was how bad Tom looked. He had a potbelly, which now was unnecessary unless you really didn't give a shit about your appearance, and was balder than he remembered. His son looked defeated. *Jesus, I'm the one who lost everything and he looks worse than I do.*

"Hi, Dad."

"Hey. Why didn't you let me know you were coming?"

"I don't know. I thought I would just come."

"Well, it's good to see you."

"Yeah, same here." Tom offered his father a sandwich.

"What is this?"

"Cheese."

"Jesus, couldn't you bring something a little more exciting? Did you really think I wanted a cheese sandwich?"

And that little comment set Tom off. Years of suppressed feelings and anger and frustration just made him blow. "How the fuck do I know what you want? Can't you just say fucking thank you instead of criticizing the sandwich? Do you know how long it takes to fucking drive here with no fucking roads? What the fuck's the matter with you?"

Brad turned around and walked back to the tent without saying a word. His son ran after him. "I'm sorry. I'm sorry. I just wanted you to say thank you. Please, Dad."

Brad stopped. A wave of emotion swept over him. His son looked so sad, so crushed. *What is wrong with him?* He walked back to Tom and gave him a hug and apologized. He hadn't hugged him for so many years that it felt strange, but he wanted to stop his son's anger.

"Listen," Tom said. "I know you don't like it here. The only reason I haven't asked you to live with us is that we have no room, literally. You'd have to share a bedroom with Melissa; that would be too strange, don't you think?"

"Don't worry about it. I don't want to bunk with my grandchild. I know you would put me up if you could."

"Dad, I have made a lot of inquiries and I'm sure you'll get your property back."

"My property? Don't you know there's nothing on it? What am I going to do with my property? I don't even own the property. I have nothing."

"What I meant was I think you will get the money back."

"How?"

"The government has to come through. They just have to."

"And where is that written? In the Constitution or the Ten Commandments?"

Then Tom reached into his jacket pocket, and his father could not believe what he pulled out. A brochure for *The Sunset.* Brad acted as if he had never seen it before. He just couldn't bring himself to tell his son that he was thinking about the same thing. "What is this?" Brad asked, trying his best to feign surprise.

"It's a ship that you can live on and it's affordable, and I'm willing to take out a loan to help you do that, if it's something you think you might want."

And that was it. Brad just started crying. He cried so much that his son got worried. "Dad. Stop it. I'm sorry. I was only trying to help."

Brad shook his head no, trying to say that he wasn't crying because he was upset; he was crying for all the reasons in the heavens that made this moment happen. Finally, through his blubbering, he said, "You are very kind to offer me this. Can you even afford to loan me this money?"

This was the moment of truth for Tom. He couldn't afford it; he was almost broke. He could barely keep up with his medical insurance, and every day he prayed that no one in his family got hurt or sick. But the whole point of this offering was to make some kind of amends with his father, and if he told him the truth, the entire gesture would be meaningless. "Yes, I can afford it."

Brad took the brochure, continuing the charade. The same way his son wanted his dad to feel as if this was a true act of the heart, Brad wanted his son to think this was his idea and he would be a hero if it worked out. Brad opened the brochure and tried to look surprised. "May I keep this and think about it?"

"Of course. Keep it, it's a brochure, they don't want it back. Yes, think about it. If you think this is something that would make you happy, I will make it work."

"This is a grand gesture, Tom."

"It's okay, Dad. You would do it for me." And even as Tom said that, he knew damn well that if he ever got to his father's age, no one would do shit for him.

Paul Prescott was shopping in an actual store, something he almost never did anymore. There was a tchotchke store near his office at AARP and he had had an argument with his better half that morning, so he thought he would stop in and see if he could find something to ease his way home.

The security parrot was cute. It sat on a perch and looked very real and recorded everything it saw, and it could also make simple conversation. He also liked the virtual fishbowls. These had gotten so good that unless you knew, you would never suspect there were not six live guppies swimming around in a tank of water. They came to the side when you wanted to look at them, and they played and hid in the rocks and did everything real fish did.

Paul got neither. He bought a wine lamp, an art deco item that cooled a bottle of wine and used its contents to reflect light in a beautiful pattern.

Supposedly it also made the wine taste better, but that was still up for debate. While he was paying, his watch vibrated. It was Jack Willman. "Hi," Jack said. "Is this a bad time?"

"No, not at all. How are you?"

"Fine. I have some information I thought was interesting."

"Wow. What a pleasant surprise."

"I'm not comfortable giving it over the line."

Paul thought a moment. "I'm on my way home; do you want to meet somewhere?"

"Yes, that would be great. Do you know where the Mediterranean is?"

"I'm three blocks from there."

"I'll meet you in fifteen minutes."

The Mediterranean was a small restaurant that had wonderful food and was always busy. It was frequented by a younger crowd that worked in and around Georgetown. It had been there since 2010 and had gone through several chefs until it settled on one who turned out to be a genius. Its linguini with clam sauce was the best in the city, and its risotto al gorgonzola was legendary. People often met late in the day for drinks and always wound up eating more than they wanted to. The meal started with the bruschetta, which arrived at the table exactly at the same time the customers did, and once they ate that they had to order more, so late-day business meetings often turned into early dinners.

Paul and Jack had wine and made small talk. Jack looked better than Paul remembered. Certainly better in person than he did on the watch.

"Did you lose weight?" Paul asked.

"No. You thought I was fat?"

"No. But you look different."

"I had my eyes enlarged."

"Seriously? You had them enlarged?"

"Yeah. It's not a big deal. They burn out a small part of the upper lid and when it heals it exposes more eye."

"Really? How long does it take?"

"To heal or the procedure?"

"Well, both."

"The procedure you do at lunch and you wear shades for a week, at most. And then you look like you've slept twelve hours."

"Or that you're surprised at something."

"Does it look like that?" Jack sounded worried. "I didn't want that, I wanted to look rested."

"I was kidding. You look great. It's great to see more of your eyes; they're good eyes."

"Thanks."

"So what's the big secret? I can't wait."

"Well, it's not that big, but I told you I would tell you stuff as it comes through my desk, and we had one of our people attend a meeting a week ago in Indiana."

"Indiana?"

"Yeah. Indianapolis. Someone who works at a local office heard about a group that seemed to be revolutionary—at least that's the way it was presented. They're calling themselves Enough Is Enough."

"I've never heard of them. Did they blow up our building?"

"We don't think so, but there was a lot of talk of sympathy with whoever did, and this might be a splinter group. We now have the names of many of the people who were there. The guy who runs it is named Max Leonard. Ever heard of him?"

"No. Should I have?"

"We'd never heard of him, either, but these guys have to start somewhere. I would put his name in your database and be aware of it, and the name of the group."

Paul made a note to himself. "I appreciate that."

"We've devoted more time now to the violence. The bombing at your building shook a lot of people up at Justice and I think they're taking it more seriously."

"This is great information. I owe you one."

"Do you want to go out sometime?"

Paul smiled at him. "We're out right now, aren't we?"

"No, I meant . . ."

"I know what you meant. I'm in a relationship that isn't so great so I don't want to make it worse, but that doesn't mean that I don't want to or that it won't happen at some point. I just think that if I confuse things right now by adding another person in the mix, then I'll dig myself into a deeper hole."

"So that's a yes?"

"Yeah. I guess so. I'll call you."

On the flight back to America, Susanna Colbert was on the line with John Van Dyke. The President's chief of staff had already been briefed about the meeting with the vice premier by others in attendance, but he wanted to hear it firsthand from her. "Did you get any indication of what they have in mind?"

"No," Susanna said. "Possibly they want the President to ask for it himself. Perhaps it's too large an amount for anyone other than him to request."

"When you get back we'll sit down with the President and see where to go. I don't know if we're prepared to have a major summit at this point, but if we feel that's what it takes, we certainly can invite them here and see what it's all about."

"I think that's going to have to happen to get to the bottom of this. I feel bad because they might have been taking advantage of my short time in the job or that I'm not Spiller. You would know that more than I."

"Taking advantage of your inexperience, and I only mean that from their point of view, might have some validity. But trust me, Susanna, they hated Spiller. They told me so themselves."

"Well, maybe they treat people they hate with more respect."

"Those are the Arabs. The Chinese actually want to like you. Have a safe flight and we'll see you here. Good job, even though you didn't come back with the loot."

"I did get a couple hundred billion as walking-around money."

Van Dyke gave her a chuckle and disconnected. And then he thought about that for a second. When he was a boy, a couple of hundred billion dollars could change the world. Now it wasn't even taken seriously. It was moments like this, at least for him, that marked the passing of time.

CHAPTER TWENTY-NINE

Shen Li was on a friendly basis with every bigwig in the Chinese government. He spoke to them often about his desire to take his model of health care to the Western democracies and they were all for it, but they really couldn't offer assistance. They kept saying to him, "When they ask, you will strike."

Li had made the government a lot of money as he enriched himself. He also made the government look kinder than they would have without his genius. China's life expectancy ranking had gone from eightieth in the world to sixteenth. In 2030 the average Chinese citizen could expect to live to eighty-four, and much of this was due to Li's ability to get care to the people who had been bringing the average down. It was suggested many times that Li get into politics, but Chinese politics did not interest him. He loved giving speeches and getting the adoration, but he also felt that nothing was better than providing a great service and becoming unthinkably rich at the same time.

One night Li was having dinner with Zhou Quinglin, the current head of the Political and Legislative Affairs Committee. Quinglin was one of the highest-ranking members of the Politburo. He told Li about the meeting with Secretary Colbert and how China refused the request for three trillion dollars. Li was shocked. He had had no idea his government was finally putting their foot down. He also had mixed feelings. He completely agreed that the United States needed to break its addiction to Chinese loans, but he so desperately wanted into the American market that he didn't like the idea of alienating such a lucrative source. But Quinglin told him that the Politburo was certain the U.S. would come back and deal on terms that were heretofore unthinkable. "What do you mean?" Li asked.

"I can't say, but we feel that the opportunity has finally come to change the way we do business with the United States, and possibly the world."

"Oh, you must tell me what you mean. You can't hang that in front of me."

"I not only can, but I can also say that you might get your wish."

"My wish?"

"We might finally be able to help you crack that market. Your robots may one day be operating on American hearts."

"You're so mysterious. Are you planning an attack?"

Quinglin laughed. "Yes, we are going to invade the United States. Rockets are being fired as we speak. Listen, my friend, I've said too much already. I just wanted to make a point that things may be getting easier for you to go where it has previously been impossible. That's all I will say."

Li had no idea what was going on, but anything that could help make his dream come true was positive. So he decided just to enjoy the anticipation. They both drank well into the night and talked about their favorite subjects, women and money and cars. And music. Shen Li loved classical music, the old and the new. He idolized Beethoven. He also loved Aaron Copland. Sometimes when he was dreaming about conquering the West he would listen to "Fanfare for the Common Man." Every time the old woman who cleaned his penthouse heard Aaron Copland, she would say, "That's the devil's music." And that made Li turn it up even louder.

A high-level cabinet meeting was called the day after Susanna Colbert returned from China. She relayed in detail all of the information she'd gathered. The President listened intently. Having never been turned down before for economic assistance, he was in uncharted waters. "Do you think they want me to beg for this myself? That certainly is what it sounds like."

"I don't know, sir," Susanna said. "It sounds to me like possibly they want different terms to loan this kind of money. New terms."

"Yes, but Chen Biao does not want to sit with me in person just to ask for twenty percent interest. That could be relayed through others, don't you think?"

"Yes, sir."

Opinions varied widely. Secretary of State Bob Nugent was opposed to any top-level meeting at that time. "I think there's nothing that can come of it," he said. "It sounds like some sort of trap. Almost like they want to humiliate us and they need you there so they can feel good about it."

The President disagreed. "I think the question before us is how badly we need them. I am not above begging for three trillion. If they want it to come from me, so be it."

The vice president, Ronald Simpson, volunteered to go to China to see if that would be sufficient to secure the loan, but the President thought that was a bad idea. "We can't have another situation where they refuse us and demand again to see me. That would make us look weaker than if I just agreed."

"What if they came here?" Van Dyke asked.

"I think they would," Susanna told him.

"Then maybe we should set up a summit."

"No," the President said. "Not here; too much press. What about Camp David?"

"What if they *won't* come here?" the vice president asked.

"Then fuck 'em," Van Dyke replied. The President looked at his chief of staff.

"John, I would like nothing better than to fuck 'em, but we desperately need this money. We can't even get the goddamn lights back on without it. We are in no position to fuck anybody. If they don't want to come here, let's deal with that when they say no. They're either going to help or not, but obviously they want this meeting, so let's give it to them. Invite them to Camp David and make it sound like it's the most special honor we can offer. Which it is, by the way. I like that place to remain private; I don't want the Chinese crawling all over it, but I'm willing to let them. Make them understand it's a privilege."

As the cabinet members got up to leave, the President asked Susanna to remain. This was the second time this had happened. If it continued there would be talk, or at least jealousy. He pulled his chair up next to hers. "How did your first encounter feel? Were you nervous?"

"I wanted very much to succeed for you. I wish I could have come back with something real. They might have taken advantage of me."

"I don't think they took advantage of you, Susanna. I sent you for a reason. There were things that Spiller did that annoyed the hell out of them. He would have gotten nowhere; they would not have even wanted to meet with him. I made a gesture of sending you, which in their culture is a way of starting over. Apparently they took it a little too literally, as God knows what they want."

"I still feel I might have let you down."

"If you do, I'll let you know."

She smiled. "Thank you for making me feel better about it. May I ask how your mother is doing?"

"You may. Thank you. I really feel my mother is going to exist in this machine-like cocoon for decades. It bothers the hell out of me. I wish she would die."

Both the President and Susanna were surprised at how easily this came out of his mouth. What did this woman possess that he could say such a thing so effortlessly? And she was somewhat surprised that it sounded as natural as it did to her. "I know the feeling," she said.

"Do you really?"

"Well, not exactly, but I know I would have the same feelings if I were you."

"What can I do?"

"I still would like to see your mother. Would it be odd if we visited her together?" The President thought about it for a moment.

"I don't think you and I can go see my mother. It would be hard to explain. To the press. To Betsy. To everyone."

"I understand. Could I visit her myself?"

"You really want to do that?"

"Yes. So at least if you choose to discuss this with me, I will understand it."

"I can arrange that. Thank you, Susanna." The President got up and escorted her to the door. "Do you mind when we discuss things off topic?"

"Off topic?"

"Like my mother."

"Absolutely not. You can feel free to talk to me about anything. I enjoy it."

"So do I. Thank you."

When she left the room, the President was certain she was the most comfortable person to talk to in all of Washington. Maybe because she was older, or because he admired her so much; he didn't know why, but she seemed like a soul mate. He couldn't believe he had blurted out that he wished his mother would die, but it not only felt normal, it was a relief. The President also knew his own personality. If he got used to this, he would never want to let it go.

Los Angeles was deteriorating. Third-world diseases not seen in the United States in a century were breaking out in various parts of the city. In Echo Park, an underground drinking-water facility had been contaminated by broken sewer lines that were seeping through the aquifer, and three thousand people came down with cholera. In another part of the city thousands of people had developed whooping cough, a bacterial disease of the upper respiratory tract, and that origin was never found.

This once-great city was having a collective nervous breakdown. The people who had not left still numbered in the millions and were staying in broken buildings or sleeping in army tents or in cars. And they began to go crazy.

It manifested itself almost like a bad zombie movie. Each night large groups of people would roam the city. They weren't part of the Los Angeles gangs that had been in operation before the quake. Those gangs were still there, roaming outside of their territory, looting every store that had anything left to take. But the zombie gangs were something else entirely, just large groups of people who were losing their minds.

It began with them just walking through the city. Walking every night, sometimes singing, sometimes silent. But soon they started breaking into stores and then homes. Bel Air and Beverly Hills, where the mansions had all been destroyed, were overrun by the zombies. The owners of those houses were long gone. When they left they took their valuables, their diamonds and their Picassos, so the zombies would steal a grand piano. Watching a Steinway being pushed down Wilshire Boulevard by a thousand people singing a song no one had ever heard before was something to behold. The cops and the National Guard did nothing about it. They had to keep their priorities straight, and their first concern was violence.

Murder had gone up a thousand percent. Most of the murders were connected to armed robberies—people needed money, and those who had any were at risk. And then there was just plain crazy behavior. Men getting wildly drunk and fighting to the death. It was as if an entire city had post-traumatic stress disorder and no one was equipped to deal with it.

Those who were sent to a facility, as Brad Miller was, were considered the lucky ones, although no one in Pasadena felt lucky. But at least there they were protected from violence.

Brad never understood why he was picked to leave while others were allowed to stay, if "allowed" was the right word. But as time went on he understood. The people in the Pasadena tent were perceived as weaker than those who remained in the city. The very old, the very young, single mothers with babies, people who were disabled, those were who Brad was surrounded by. Men in their thirties and forties were nowhere to be seen. *So the tent people are the weaklings,* Brad concluded. But he had to admit when he saw the news pictures of the zombie gangs that maybe being weak was a good thing. *At least this is better than being attacked by roaming monsters.*

Still, Brad knew he had to get out of there. And once again, feeling like Lenny in *Of Mice and Men,* he took out the worn brochure of the retirement ship and stared at it, as if it were some far-off island. He knew this would be a burden on his son, but he was running out of options.

When Max Leonard got back to Indiana after his meeting with Walter Masters, something had changed in his personality. Kathy noticed it immediately. He was quiet, more pensive, kept more to himself. She tried to bring him out a bit, asking him all kinds of questions about the trip, but he didn't seem to want to talk about it.

He and Kathy had been basically living together—he spent almost every night at her house—but when he returned from seeing Masters, he slept in his own bed. Kathy would call and ask if he wanted to eat dinner or come over and make love, anything, and for the first time in their short relationship he said no. She thought it was her. *Did he meet someone in California? What happened out there that changed him? Is he falling out of love with me?* But Max assured her that that wasn't the case. He even bought her a beautiful bracelet and told her that he loved her more than ever; that if he seemed detached, it was only because he was in deep thought on how to "even things out," as he put it; and that he was only sleeping at home because he was up half the night thinking and he didn't want to bother her. She accepted this explanation.

Enough Is Enough didn't have any more meetings scheduled, although Max was in constant communication with the five people he considered the brains of the group. He encouraged protests when the members wanted to show up somewhere, as when a hundred people went to Chicago to march against the biennial Social Security bump, but other than giving his okay, Max was preoccupied. It was only when Kathy came by his place unannounced one day that she got wind of what he was up to.

When she knocked on the door and no one answered, she walked around the back and looked inside. Max was in his bedroom. He had not pulled the shades down completely, and the position of the sun allowed her to see in without him being able to see out. What she saw terrified her.

Max had made an entire wall of Sam Mueller's life. Pictures of his family, his parents, a flowchart of how he started Immunicate and all of the discoveries and patents he had been responsible for. He also had Mueller's current speaking schedule and what he was planning for the future. The information covered the wall. If this were a graduate thesis on the man who cured cancer he would get an A, but Kathy had no idea what Max was doing. She decided to leave before he discovered her, but she knew she would have to bring this up at some appropriate time. *Was he in love with the famous doctor? Did he want to become the famous doctor? Or was it something more sinister?*

When she got home she saw Max's face on her screen. He had left a message. "Hey, honey, do you want to have dinner tonight? Let me know. I'm working on something but I'm going to be hungry later. I love you."

He picked her up and they went to a small café they both liked. Twelve tables, one waitress, dark lighting, and Cuban music, although the food was a combination of Mexican and Chinese. Tacos with duck meat, pot stickers with beef and cheese inside. The restaurant's most famous dish was orange chicken enchiladas. When Max was hungry he could eat three of them.

As they were having sake, Kathy asked him what he had done that day. For the first time Max wasn't silent. He wanted to talk. "I've been thinking about how to make an impression. How Enough Is Enough can use their time and resources in a way that people will notice."

"What did you come up with?"

"When we went to see Sam Mueller speak it hit me, but I couldn't figure it out just then. When I couldn't convince Walter Masters to join, I realized we needed someone even bigger and more ingrained in the establishment. We need Sam Mueller to join our movement."

Kathy was relieved that Max had brought up Mueller's name, although she was still in the dark as to why someone would have to turn his bedroom into a shrine. "How would you get him to join? Why would he want to? He makes his living keeping people alive."

"That's exactly right. Here is a genius focused on one thing, longevity. But if a man that smart could understand the damage that that's doing, he could change. I just know it. I feel it in my bones. The bones, by the way, that now can live to be a hundred and twenty fucking years old, thanks to him."

At least Kathy knew that the man she loved wasn't having an affair. But this idea sounded a bit crazy. *Why would Sam Mueller all of a sudden denounce his life's work? And what about the wall?* She wanted to get it out in the open. Should she just bring it up? *Oh, by the way, I was sneaking around your house and looked in the window and saw your Mueller wall.* That wouldn't work. Then she had an idea. "Can I stay at your place tonight?" Max was surprised. She had never really wanted to stay there before.

"Why? You told me my place smells like socks."

"I just want to. I was sort of seeing my dad in everything today, and the house made me feel sad. I just want a change of scenery."

"I have a better idea. Let's take a drive and stay in a little motel. Just like an overnight vacation."

What could Kathy say to that? She tried one last time. "But maybe snuggling up in your place would be fun. I haven't slept there in ages."

"My place is filthy. Let's take a drive."

"Okay." At least they would spend the night together. She would find another time to ask about the shrine.

CHAPTER THIRTY

To get Chen Biao, the premier of the People's Republic of China, to come to Camp David without raising suspicion was a formidable task. Not that presidents and Chinese premiers didn't meet—they did—but the meetings were always planned in advance and were always tied to a bigger trip, something to do with climate or trade or a general peace mission. To tell the press that the premier of China would be coming to Camp David in two weeks had to be couched in some way that wouldn't arouse suspicion. There had never been a visit by the head of China to Camp David, especially not one that came out of the blue.

The President's press secretary, Elizabeth Foreman, and John Van Dyke, along with several other aides, worked for days to come up with a story. Van Dyke thought maybe a side trip for Biao could be arranged to Mexico and Canada to make it a North American visit, but the Chinese didn't like that. Then Van Dyke came up with another idea, one that might be difficult to pull off: Don't tell anyone. The Chinese were a little hesitant at first, but realized it was workable, and really, they loved this kind of mystery.

The one thing the Chinese premier would have to agree on was to be flown to the United States on an American craft. Surprisingly, there was no objection. The Chinese knew the plane couldn't be *Air Force One*, but they wanted it to be special, which wasn't a problem. The United States government had several smaller jets that were like flying penthouses. The one they sent to China was a pilotless Gulfstream, even newer and more advanced than what Sam Mueller flew, and certainly more opulent. And on this flight two Chinese pilots would ride along up front, even though there was nothing for them to do.

The Air Force prepared the inside of the plane to the exact specifications sent by the premier's office. They supplied the entertainment and food that he liked, special sheets for the bedroom, special accommodations for his wife and his dog, a specific color scheme, a masseuse, a psychic, a trainer, and a feng shui expert. When the plane was all prepared it looked as if it belonged in the Chinese Air Force. And when it landed in Washington, no one suspected a thing. Just another private jet.

The plan was that it would land, taxi into a hangar, and, after the hangar door was closed, the Premier and his party would deplane. They would be transferred to a waiting helicopter and then take the short trip to Camp David. Since helicopters routinely made that run, bringing staff or friends of the president for a weekend stay, nothing would be made of it.

And so, without raising any suspicion, the head of China and the head of the United States would now be in the same secluded location with no press and no fanfare. The President was pleased. Though he felt his position was weak, needing so much money as quickly as he did, he felt that he regained a small bit of power simply by having this meeting on his own turf. And by keeping it secret he wouldn't have to face the press afterward in case things did not go well, which was also a relief.

The Chinese delegation, which came in a separate American aircraft not nearly as luxurious, arrived two days ahead of the Premier. Susanna Colbert flew up Friday morning with John Van Dyke and Commerce Secretary James Gilford. Normally the Secretary of State, Bob Nugent, would be there, but he was in Korea at a trade summit and they thought that bringing him home would arouse suspicion.

Friday night, without the President or the Premier in attendance, there was a barbecue for the thirty-plus delegates attending the summit, and the two countries mingled over roasted pork, chicken, steaks, and vegetables. There was drinking and much laughter and a very good vibe. Nothing, absolutely nothing political, was discussed that night; it was just about setting a tone. A few of the Chinese got very drunk and told bawdy stories that made everyone laugh, even though the Americans did not always understand the punch lines. The Chinese had great stories about the former North Korea, as if it were the black sheep in the family. They had Kim Jong Il short jokes, and Dalai Lama fasting jokes, and even a couple of laundry jokes, thinking the Americans would still laugh at that.

By the end of the evening people felt quite friendly and ready to hear what the leaders had on their minds the following day. The Americans understood that the Chinese were as tough a group of negotiators as there were, and even though in their hearts they knew the barbecue would mean nothing once the dealing started, it still felt good to pretend everybody liked one another.

Bernstein and the First Lady arrived by helicopter on Saturday morning. Elizabeth Foreman told the press it was a simple weekend rest and that nothing but relaxation was on the schedule. The President was concerned that eventually the truth would get out, but he felt confident that if it did he could tell the press that it had had to be kept secret or else the complicated financial negotiations could fall apart, though when he thought of that excuse he had no idea what those negotiations were going to be. Then again, there might be a chance this would never leak, at least not while Bernstein was in office. The Chinese were the best secret keepers in the world, and if the American delegation took their secrecy oaths seriously, this could possibly remain private.

The night of the barbecue was also the night of the fourth act of terrorism against the olds. At eight o'clock on that Friday evening a bomb went off in a San Diego retirement community, killing twenty seniors and wounding a hundred more, including younger staff. What had started several years earlier as an isolated incident was now intensifying in frequency and magnitude. Paul Prescott was on the phone with Jack Willman as soon as he heard.

"What the fuck is going on out there?"

"This one I don't know about. It was a suicide event."

"You're shitting me."

"They've recovered the body, which will tell us something, but we had no warning of it and we don't even think it was connected to the others."

"Jesus," Paul said. "How vast is this?"

"I don't know. This one was scary. Maybe someone who lived there did it."

"Why? Someone was pissed because they never won at bingo?"

"I don't know. Maybe a relative or someone who expected an inheritance. When I get more information I'll tell you."

"You're being really great here, Jack. I feel like this is one-way. What can I do for you?"

"Do you have seats to the Redskins?"

"Are you a football fan?"

"Yeah."

"Gimme a week. I'll get you seats on the bench."

"Listen, Paul, if you did nothing I would still give you whatever information I have. This is scary shit. Did you see that some of the younger staff were also killed?"

"I saw that. What's that all about?"

"It just means whoever did this isn't particular. As long as enough elderly get it, whoever is nearby gets it, too. That's a bad guy."

"I appreciate whatever info you can get me."

"I appreciate the tickets."

"Did you hear?" Kathy asked.

"I heard."

"Where are you?"

"I'm at an art supply house," Max said.

Kathy still hadn't mentioned the wall. *What is he doing at an art supply house?* "Who do you think did this?"

"Someone with passionate enough feelings to take their own life. I sure would like to know who it was and what that's all about."

Kathy was on Max's side, of course, but she didn't condone a suicide bomber. "You don't think that was a good thing, do you?"

"Baby, I don't think killing indiscriminately is ever a good thing. And

I understand that some young people died, too. But I have to admire the passion that went into this. If it was for the same reasons that we're fighting for, then the idea was right, though the action was probably wrong."

"Probably?"

"Kathy, stop taking me literally. We're in a war. It can't always be bloodless. I would like to see things change without any violence, but that's obviously impossible. In any case, I think the killing here was bad. Okay?"

"Okay." Kathy needed to at least hear him say that. "By the way, why are you in an art store?"

"What?"

"Never mind. Call me when you get home. I love you."

"Love you, too."

CHAPTER THIRTY-ONE

The bombing was the talk of Camp David. The President was informed early Saturday morning and the rest of the delegation, both American and Chinese, heard about it at breakfast.

A decade earlier the Chinese had experienced similar problems, but they put them down quickly. There was no mercy in China for killing the olds. Though over the decades respect for the elderly had been dwindling in Asian countries, its origin was still there, and respect for elders was ingrained into the Asian culture, even if it was not practiced as it once was. And besides, the Politburo had so many old members there was just no tolerance for those kinds of actions.

Thousands of Chinese soldiers had been sent to put down this revolution before it ever got started. Young people were put in jail for life or killed or tortured, and it was shown to every schoolchild in the country. China was big on "this could happen to you," and, for all intents and purposes, it worked.

On Saturday morning, at a head-of-state breakfast before any negotiations started, the Premier mentioned to the President that his country had also experienced the younger generations "getting jealous," as he called it. He warned the President that in his humble opinion it was a bad idea to let this fester. Bernstein thanked him for his thoughts, and for a moment he was tempted to get into the discussion with the Premier about older people living too long. But Chen Biao was going to be eighty-eight in January, so the President decided to let that conversation go.

They had a nice breakfast, chitchatting about meaningless things like the weather and soccer and food, and then at noon everyone went into a large conference room and the real purpose of the weekend got started. Chen Biao spoke sufficient English, but he liked to mix the languages, starting a sentence in one language and finishing it in another. The Nextrons were out in full force, so that when he chose to speak to the President in English his own delegation could understand what he was saying.

The meeting started with Biao telling the President, "There is no way we can loan you twenty trillion dollars." Bernstein was a little taken aback at how quickly everything began, but he wasted no time, either.

"Well, Mr. Premier, we don't need that amount at this point. We are actually looking to borrow three trillion, which would be enough to get the massive Los Angeles project started."

"But what happens after that?"

"I don't know," the President said. "That would be enough for several years, I would imagine."

"But don't you see?" Biao answered. "You will come back to us for another seventeen trillion at some point and we will not be able to accommodate you." The President thought a moment.

"Maybe we won't have to come back for more."

"How would that occur?"

"We could issue bonds or borrow elsewhere; we would have a few years to figure it out."

"Unfortunately, Mr. President, you cannot borrow elsewhere. No one has these sums. And what you have borrowed already is putting an overwhelming debt load on your economy, as you know. To borrow another three trillion at this point, even if we could accommodate that, would be too much for you to bear. Am I wrong?"

He wasn't wrong, but the President did not appreciate being spoken to like a child. But, like a child, when someone needs more allowance he has to take the lecture his parents give him. And China certainly was the parent in this meeting. "Without the loan, Mr. Premier, we will see one of the great cities of the world go into severe decay. Imagine if Beijing was struck with a nuclear weapon?" As soon as the President said that, he realized it was a bad example. It sounded hostile and he didn't mean it that way. Chen Biao was gracious.

"I understand. One of your primary cities has been wiped out. The difference is, Mr. President, that in this time in history, if Beijing was in the same place, we have the funds to rebuild it. We would not be borrowing from you."

"That is true," the President said. "And I wish things were different, but at this time they're not."

"We will not be able to loan you the three trillion dollars. The most we could loan you, as we told your Madame Secretary, is several hundred billion. We feel, as I'm sure you do, too, that your debt is already too high, certainly regarding money you have borrowed from us." Before the President could reply, Biao continued, trying to be respectful but needing to say something that hadn't been said at this level ever before. "You are the most important country to us. You buy our goods and services and we try to supply you with reasonable labor and quality materials. We have always felt that loaning you large amounts of money was workable because that money was coming back to us. But this is a new day. You need more money than you have ever borrowed before to rebuild your city. Not to buy our clothes or cars or machines, but to make whole one of your biggest metropolitan areas. To simply take the money from our treasury and give it to you, no matter what the interest rate, would not generate enough for our country to make up for depleting our own reserves."

The President and the rest of the U.S. delegation were quiet. Bernstein thought to himself, *Why the hell did you come here, just to just say no in person?* But he forced a smile. "So there is no reason to even talk about an interest rate? Perhaps we could agree on a number that would make this worthwhile."

"We have never loaned money based on interest alone. We have loaned you money because your reasons for borrowing have improved our way of life in many areas, far beyond what interest could do by itself."

At that point the vibe in the room, at least from the American side, was that the meeting was over. Susanna Colbert had mixed feelings. She was upset that there didn't seem a way in, but at the same time she felt vindicated that even the President could not get China to budge. Then the Premier dropped the bombshell.

"We would consider another arrangement to help you rebuild one of the greatest cities in the world." The room was silent as the Nextrons spit out what the Premier had just said.

"What would that be?" the President asked.

"We would be your partner."

"Our partner? I'm sorry. I don't understand exactly."

"We would be your partner. We would help you rebuild your great city, we would shoulder most of the cost, and we would own the city with you when all was said and done. Fifty-fifty."

The President looked over at Susanna; Susanna looked at the rest of the delegation. The Chinese were looking straight ahead and many of them were smiling. The President wasn't even sure what he had just heard. "I'm sorry, Mr. Premier. Please tell me again what you are proposing."

"Mr. President, we have the ability, unlike any nation on earth, to do massive construction quickly and with high quality. We have manpower second to none, and I am sure you have seen the architecture and building results throughout China in the last two decades. Where one country might have five hundred men on a job site, we have five thousand. We would treat Los Angeles as one of our own great cities and take pride in helping you make it better than ever. We will supply the needed manpower and materials and know-how and do what you desire, and we will charge you next to nothing. All we want to do is be partners in the result."

"I'm not clear what you mean by partners."

"Partners. When Southern California is up and running, it can generate more revenue than almost any area in the world. My goodness, from Los Angeles alone, you must collect countless billions of dollars in federal taxes. Not to mention all the fees you charge. My people tell me that it costs more to bring ships into your West Coast than any other port in the world." Biao smiled. "So we would do the work and become your partner."

Everyone looked at the President. The American delegation was speechless. They had no idea what Bernstein's reaction would be. "Partners for how long?"

"Forever. Partners. Fifty-fifty. As we bring Los Angeles back to life and make it the income generator that it always was meant to be, we will split whatever revenue you collect from your people."

The President looked down the table. The Americans looked back. Bernstein couldn't read their expressions exactly, but he could tell there was some interest in this.

"Mr. Premier, if you asked me how this meeting would have turned out, I could have listed a hundred possibilities and this one would not have even been a distant thought. If you would be so gracious, I would like to break for a few hours and talk with my team and meet again this afternoon. Obviously we are not going to come back with specifics; it's only to see if this idea you propose is workable in *any* fashion. Do you have any problem with taking a break at this time?"

"Absolutely not," the Premier said. "I was told there was a fine horseshoe area up here. I love horseshoes. Could someone show me where that might be?"

"Yes, sir." The President turned to John Van Dyke. "Get him some horseshoes."

When the American delegation met privately, there was a shocking lack of being shocked. Many people, including Susanna Colbert, thought this was an interesting and possibly workable idea. "Talk to me," the President said.

"Let's look at raw facts here, sir," Susanna answered. "There is nowhere to get this money except from China. Nowhere else to borrow it from and no ability to print it without going under. If they will take the brunt of the cost in rebuilding the city, then sharing the profits might turn out to be an advantage for us. Even if we allowed them to take half, which I think is too much and can be negotiated downward, how long would it take Los Angeles to generate fifty trillion dollars, since half of that is what we would be borrowing? A hundred years? And maybe we don't make it forever. Maybe they will agree to a set period of time."

One of the undersecretaries, Mark Holmes, stood up. "Did we go insane? Are we really talking about letting the Chinese own one of our cities? Have we been drugged?"

"Is this any different from *borrowing* twenty trillion?" John Van Dyke asked. "Don't they own us even more by loaning us that kind of money? Maybe there is a huge advantage here."

"What would that be?" the President asked.

"Well, first of all, if they worked here and knew that in order to get their money back Los Angeles had to be profitable and peaceful and all that good stuff, then they would be working toward that goal. Hell, I don't think China would ever attack us if they had a fifty percent stake in our biggest city."

"Why not just give them half the country?" Mark Holmes shot back. "Then they would be sure never to attack."

People laughed, but Van Dyke was serious.

"Listen, they're not asking for half the country. We came to them, remember? They don't need our cash, we need theirs. So what are the choices? I see none."

The President stood up and paced around the table. "In a strange way, this could work in our favor. John is right. The biggest protection against a threat is having a long-term investment in your enemy. If we were just borrowing money, the Chinese could eventually call our debt or cut us off or have more hold over us than if we *were* partners. And they're right. They can build like no one else. From the worst disaster our country has ever seen, in a few years, we would have one of the greatest cities of the world. It would still be here, it would still be protected by our military, it would still be American, but its income would be shared. Why is that a bad thing?"

And most of the delegation agreed. They would bargain for a better deal, try and make it a fixed term instead of forever, and put in all the security language that was needed to make people feel safe. But it was this or nothing. And with gangs roaming the streets of Los Angeles, with the rest of the country's morale falling to a low never before seen as they watched Southern California rot, something had to be done and done quickly. If nothing else, the Chinese knew the meaning of the word "quickly."

And so it was decided. A new road was going to be opened in the history of the United States. The President authorized his team to take as much time as needed and work out a deal. "Try to get better than fifty-fifty and try to put a fifty-year term on it," he said, "but work it out. We have no alternative. Make it palatable and I will sell it to the country."

The President walked out of the meeting to find the premier of China throwing horseshoes, and unless he was placing them he was doing quite well. Four shoes were on the post and three were close by. "You're very good," the President said.

"And yet I hate horses," Biao answered, smiling.

"Well, you must like their shoes. In any case, let's work out your offer."

"I am very pleased. Do you require any more meetings here?"

"I don't think so. My team and yours will go to work immediately to hammer out the details. Be gentle with us, because I have to sell it to a nation."

"Of course. Do you mind if my party stays the weekend? We are enjoying ourselves."

"Stay as long as you wish. But we're not selling Camp David to you no matter how much you like it."

Biao laughed out loud. He was a sucker for a good joke.

CHAPTER THIRTY-TWO

The FBI had identified the San Diego suicide bomber as Jeffrey J. Anderson of Montgomery, Alabama, a man who had no previous criminal record but went nuts after he was fired from a paper mill. He drove out West to his father's retirement home, which he was paying for, and killed twenty people. He left a rambling note, and when Max Leonard read it, he got a chill.

> To whom it may concern. I loved my parents but I could not take care of them on the low wages I was paid. All of my money went to them and when my mom died the insurance company did not pay the policy claiming she drove a car intoxicated which she did not. My life was worthless only to get up every day to take care of my parents with no regard for me or the fact I will never become a parent because I cannot afford even one child. My father was greedy never offering to pay his own way and this country must take care of all people including the younger people and offer a quality of life for everyone. I hope my father is in heaven at least there I will not have to support him unless heaven is run by the United States and then I would be expecting to get a bill.

Max was floored. He showed the letter to Kathy. "Can you believe how articulate he was?"

"I don't know if I would call it 'articulate,'" she said, "but it certainly was heartfelt." And as much as Kathy did not like to see innocent people die, she had to admit she identified with this man's dilemma. She was going to be paying off her father's debt for years and years, and he wasn't even living. Still, innocent people were dead and she couldn't quite resolve that. "It's a good note," she said. "Although I don't think that kind of violence was necessary."

"And yet," Max told her, "people are reading this all over the world."

"Do you think it will change anything?"

"Not until these words come from someone hugely important."

"Like who?"

"The President. The Speaker of the House. A Nobel Prize–winning scientist. Someone like that."

"How's that going to happen?"

"Well, baby, that's exactly what I'm working on."

Older people were spooked by the rambling letter. AARP got almost two hundred thousand contacts from their members, who were, not surprisingly, petrified. There was obviously enough truth in the man's note that plenty of seniors thought it might awaken a sleeping giant.

Robert Golden requested an urgent meeting with the White House. He was invited to have breakfast the next morning with John Van Dyke, a measure of how important a political force AARP was.

Golden was furious. "The President needs to weigh in on this. He has said nothing. This could spiral out of control."

"The President knows this is serious, Bob, but we have to be cautious about speaking out too strongly at this juncture," Van Dyke said.

"They're shooting up buses, our building was bombed, and now twenty people just died and a note was left that our membership is shitting in their pants over."

"Don't they shit in their pants normally?"

"That's not funny, John. There's nothing humorous here. We need to hear from the top."

"Bob, we know from experience that as soon as presidential attention is given to something like this, then the kooks and the nuts get energized. We are working on this at the highest level. The FBI is all over it, but if the President comes out with a speech to the nation, he raises it to a national emergency and we can't do that."

"But it *is* an emergency."

"No, it isn't. Los Angeles is an emergency. This is not the same."

"We're scared, John. I'm scared. I go to work every day and worry whether I'm going to get shot."

"You won't get shot. You have protection. Do you need more?"

"No. I need the President to say this has got to stop."

"At this point that can do more harm than good. You'll have to trust me."

"You wouldn't say that if they bombed the White House."

"No, I wouldn't. But they didn't. I hear you, and I will convey everything to the President. But I will tell you that a speech to the nation is not going to happen at this juncture."

The President lay awake at night. Normally, he was blessed with the ability to sleep, and he had a doctor on staff with every sleeping medication known to man if he needed it.

Sleeping medications had taken great leaps in the 2020s. The only side effects associated with the new sleeping drugs were that once you got a good night's sleep using them, it was hard to ever go back. They put you to sleep, you didn't wake up in the middle of the night and eat or drive or make calls you were embarrassed about, and you didn't feel groggy in the morning. It was like an anesthetic in a pill, and once people tried them, they wanted them forever.

President Bernstein prided himself on his nonaddictive drug behavior. He used the medicine as often as needed but forced himself to sleep without it, just to strengthen his character. Betsy had taken them nightly for four years and had no interest in strengthening anything. She took them according to how many hours of sleep she desired. The pills were so specific that they came in six-, eight-, ten-, and twelve-hour doses, and they were amazingly accurate. In early tests, three thousand people who took the eight-hour dose slept within fifteen minutes of that time, most waking up on the later side. The time-release element in the medicine was brand new, a patent of a German pharmaceutical company. Their commercial had an animated alarm clock that looked at the pill to get the right time.

The President used to wake his wife up in the middle of the night when he really needed to talk, but once she was on the medication he stopped doing that. At three A.M. she was useless. She would pretend to listen and snore at the same time and remember nothing of the conversation the next day. And that was what started his late-night calls to Susanna Colbert.

Susanna slept without medication, only taking it when she traveled long distances. The first time the President called her was on a Thursday at one in the morning. It was the week after the Camp David summit. He wasn't sure if her husband was in town, but he thought the worst that would happen was that if her husband answered he would just say it was the President and it was important. After all, presidents are allowed to wake people up. But Susanna answered the call. She sounded out of it. "Yes?"

"Did I wake you?"

"Who is it?"

"The President." She jumped up.

"What is it? Is something wrong?"

"No. I didn't know if you were sleeping or how late you stayed up. I didn't want to wake your husband. I'm sorry if this is too late."

"My husband is traveling. We have separate bedrooms anyway. Actually, I fell asleep with tea in my hand and if you hadn't called I probably would have scalded myself."

"Well, then, I'm sort of a hero."

"Yes. Is everything all right? Is there trouble?"

"I couldn't sleep. I was thinking of so many things."

"Camp David?"

"Yes. And my mother. For some reason when I think of my mother, I think of you."

"Well, I don't know whether that's a compliment or not."

"It is. Why do you have separate bedrooms?"

"What?"

"Never mind. I was just curious."

"We've had separate bedrooms for years. I don't even remember how it started, I'm just so used to it now. I think because I would work in bed so late that it kept him up. It was something like that."

"I understand." And he did.

"Speaking of your mother, I was going to go and see her tomorrow, if that's still okay. I would just go alone."

"It's fine with me. And you're absolutely sure you want to?"

"Yes, I really do. I want to see it for myself. I didn't tell you before, but the people who own the facility she's in are former investors of mine."

"You're kidding."

"They own something like two hundred permanent-care facilities. It's a very big business. And they were also involved with The Card."

The President said nothing for a moment, but he was so impressed with her. *What is it?* Maybe it was seeing the softness of a woman with the cunning of a man that was so enticing. So many women in power came off as bossy or ballsy, at least to him, but not this one. "Well," the President said, "I think it would be very nice if you wanted to do that. You could give me your thoughts. In any case, I'll let you go back to sleep."

"You're going to wake me up and dump me?"

He laughed. "Okay, let's talk about Camp David. Am I going to be known for taking down the United States?"

"Quite the contrary. I know the pressure you must feel, but there is no other way. Change is scary and unpredictable and that is why most presidents don't want it. But fate has given this moment to you. In my opinion, sir, *not* doing this would cause a knockout blow to the country. I think the choice was handed to you and I have to say I think you reacted brilliantly."

"Will you tell Congress that for me?"

"Yes." Susanna laughed. "I'll take care of it in the morning. But you know something? You're not going to have trouble with them. Everyone in Congress knows the mess we're in. There's no more raising taxes or cutting loopholes. Without something this bold we're going down, and they know it. This is our rescue. And yes, if you need me to go up there and talk to every single one of them, I will be happy to, and quite frankly, I expect to."

The President's smile was so big he thought it would wake up his wife in the other room. "Thank you, Susanna. I'll see you tomorrow."

"Mr. President?"

"Yes?"

"Call anytime."

"I will. Good night."

Bernstein wanted to talk to this woman for hours. He hadn't had this feeling since high school.

CHAPTER THIRTY-THREE

Dallas, Texas, was the site of the annual stockholders' meeting for Immunicate. It was in October, a week before Halloween. Max Leonard knew he had to be there. He was now obsessed with Sam Mueller and felt this was one more chance to hear him speak and, possibly, put a plan in place. He was going to drive to Texas and asked Kathy if she wanted to come.

Kathy had never brought up the wall in Max's bedroom, but before she could drive to another Sam Mueller event she felt it was imperative. She decided to pay Max another surprise visit. She spoke to him early in the afternoon and he said he was working at home but would love to have dinner, so she waited a few hours and drove to his house at four o'clock. She would tell him she was starving and ask him if he wanted to go early.

When she arrived, she was tempted to walk around to the back to see if she could look through the window again, but she decided against it. She rang the doorbell. He answered, and he was in a very good frame of mind. "Hey, what are you doing here?"

"I was out doing errands and was really hungry. Do you want to have an early bite?"

Max looked at the clock. "You want to eat at four? Seriously?"

"Well, not at four, but maybe in an hour."

This was the moment she had been dreading. There she was, twenty feet from the bedroom. What would he do? How could he force her to leave? It would be so rude. Then Max said, "I don't mind eating early. Let me get a coat." Kathy walked in and looked at the living room.

"Your place is so clean."

"Yeah. The woman was here yesterday. My sink was smelling something awful." Kathy saw that his bedroom door was open a crack and decided to just get it over with. She walked toward the room; Max made no attempt to stop her. Kathy opened the door and there it was. Nothing. A clean room with clean walls and fresh sheets on the bed and a vacuumed carpet. It even smelled of a scented candle that was unlit on the nightstand.

Kathy thought she was going crazy for a minute. She knew what she had seen, but it wasn't there. Should she just ask him what had happened? But that would lead to a discussion of why she was snooping around his house in the first place, and what good could come of that? So she said nothing. In her mind she tried to spin this as a positive. Perhaps what she took as a dangerous obsession was no more than an old-fashioned way of doing research. Compile all the information you can, put it up on a board, and stand back and look at it. The more she thought about it, the more it made sense. It was temporary. It was nothing. As a matter of fact, she used to do something similar in high school when she was trying to learn where all the African countries were. As she was standing there lost in her own rationalization, Max touched her shoulder.

"Come on. If you're hungry, let's go. I don't care if it's early."

And then Kathy really felt stupid. Not only had she misjudged him but now she, a person who always thought she would be happier living in Spain where they ate at midnight, had to have dinner at four-thirty. It served her right, she thought; this was what she got for being paranoid about someone she loved.

As Brad Miller was eating his lunch, an administrator of the Pasadena facility asked him if he would come to the office when he was through. Brad had given up on trying to get his money, so he felt as if he was going to be reprimanded for something, that maybe there was some kind of problem. He finished his egg salad sandwich, which tasted as if it had been made a year ago, then got up from the table, left the tent, and walked the three hundred yards to the office complex. He went upstairs and sat down in a waiting area until someone called his name, then he walked down the same drab gray hallway, which still had no pictures on the walls, and into the same cubicle he had been in before. Except this time there was a woman there. "Please sit down, Mr. Miller. I'm Mrs. Yellin."

"You're new here?"

"I'm new to Pasadena. I have been working in Lancaster at another facility."

"Where's the fellow that had this office?"

"I don't know."

"Are you going to tell me I'm getting my money for my condo?"

"Yes and no."

Brad brightened up. "Yes? There's a 'yes' involved?"

"Well, no."

"You said 'yes and no.'"

"Mr. Miller, we need the space here in Pasadena. We have been more than happy to let you be our guest for these months, but now it's time to leave. To help you do that we can offer you twenty-five thousand dollars."

"Twenty-five thousand dollars? That's shit. That's all I'm going to get for my condo?"

"This is not a payment for your condo. We will advance you this money against the time when the payments will be worked out for Los Angeles property, which as far as we can tell is not in the near future. But with this money, which you won't have to pay taxes on, we would like you to move somewhere else, and free up space for others who haven't been as fortunate as you."

"Fortunate? That's a joke, right? Now I'm fortunate. Go figure. I thought when my entire life was taken from me that that was a bad thing; little did I know I was fortunate. I'll have to remember your way with words so if I ever deliver a eulogy, I can say how fortunate the person is to be lying in the dirt."

Mrs. Yellin smiled. She'd had to put up with people being sarcastic her entire life. She was used to it. This was still better than her last job, working for that crap airline in Louisiana that was never on time and had just five planes, with two always in repair. Oh, the bitching she heard all those years.

"Mr. Miller, I only meant that there are people like you whose lives were turned upside down who are still sleeping in parks. They have trouble finding food to eat."

"Well, if they come here, warn them about the egg salad. Personally, I would rather eat in the park."

Mrs. Yellin ignored his sarcasm. "So do we have a deal?"

"What is the deal?"

"We will advance you twenty-five thousand dollars and you will leave in one week."

"And if I decide to stay?"

"You would lose the money and be thrown out anyway."

"Deal," Brad said. "Let me try and make some arrangements."

As he walked back to the tent, he actually felt better than he thought he would. Hell, they were going to kick him out no matter what; at least he had twenty-five grand. He went back to his bunk, looked one last time at the worn-out brochure, and called his son.

"So you have a date?"

"I don't have a *date.* I'm taking a client to a football game," Paul said.

His partner, Owen Stein, was not buying it. They had not been getting along for the last six months. No sex, no laughing, just some quiet dinners with nothing to say. Owen thought something might be going on.

"Nothing's going on," Paul said. "We've both been under a lot of pressure, that's all. Life isn't always full of roses."

"What the fuck does that mean?" Owen asked.

Paul remembered the first time he saw Owen. He was shopping for a mirror and went into an antiques store, and the man who came up to him and asked if he needed help smelled so good. And he looked pretty good, too. He was younger than Paul by eight years. He had gray sideburns and blue eyes and thick hair that didn't seem styled. It just grew correctly. And he was tall. Taller than Paul by two inches. Normally Paul didn't go out with younger guys—he liked older men or men his own age—but he and Owen started dating.

Paul didn't like the effeminate type. He liked guys who could pass for straight, as he could, and he liked guys who kept in shape. Owen exercised religiously and at forty-two he looked thirty; the only thing that showed his age was the gray in his hair. They both went to the gym, and they liked the same movies, art, and music. There was nothing really wrong with the relationship, but Paul wasn't in love the way he wanted to be. When they had moved in together he'd felt that maybe that would do the trick, but years had gone by and the magic that was barely there to begin with was fading. Owen liked Paul more than Paul liked him. And Owen was the jealous one.

"So who exactly are you taking to a football game? What kind of client?"

"It's a guy who works at the Justice Department who is helping me with inside stuff. We're trying to see what these bombings are about and he's got information I need."

"What's his name?"

Paul should have just told him and left it at that, but he made a mistake when he said, "Why?"

"What do you mean, 'why'? I was just asking his name."

"Listen, Owen. He could get in big trouble for the stuff he's telling me. I don't know that he wants his name bandied about."

"Bandied about? What the fuck is wrong with you? It's me, for fuck's sake."

"Jack. Jack is his name."

"Fine. Have a great time with Jack." And Owen walked out of the apartment.

What's wrong with me? Why did I make the name such a big deal? Paul knew the answer. He just didn't want to think about it.

It was freezing cold at the Redskins game. Paul thought Jack Willman looked great that day. He had on a herringbone scarf, gloves, jeans, and cool retro sneakers. He didn't remember Jack being that cute, but maybe that had something to do with his argument with Owen.

Paul really didn't want to screw up this important contact. If they had a relationship and it went bad, who at Justice would ever give him this kind of information? But he couldn't help looking at Jack as someone he might really, really like.

"These seats are incredible. I've never sat in seats like this," Jack said.

And they *were* incredible. Robert Golden always got the best seats at every event. Golden wasn't even a football fan, but when Paul Prescott said he needed great seats at the Redskins–Bears game, Golden had them in thirty minutes. The seats were at the forty-yard line, two rows behind the Redskins bench. You could actually hear what the coach was saying to his assistants. It was so clear that Paul wondered if the other team didn't have guys sitting there, just to spy. "How long have you been a football fan?" he asked Jack.

"A long time. I wouldn't call myself a crazy fan, but it's like watching a car accident. I like that part of it."

"What do you mean?"

"When these guys run into each other, I'm just happy it's not me. I can't believe they take this abuse and I can't believe I get to watch it. I don't feel that way from any other sport. I don't know, sort of a vicarious thrill, I guess."

"I never looked at it that way," Paul said. "I'll watch it with that perspective from now on."

Jack smiled at him. "You know, we're finding out all kinds of stuff on that suicide bomber. I'm actually going to write something up and give it to you. Just so you can understand who these people are."

"That would be great. You mean like a profile?"

"Exactly."

"That's great. The more we know about these guys, the better chance we have of stopping them."

"Well, you may not be able to stop them without some big changes in the law."

"What do you mean?"

"Big cuts in medical for the seniors, less Social Security, the stuff that makes them crazy. That kind of thing."

"I don't think that's possible," Paul said. "Then we would have another issue that would get out of hand. The olds are capable of just as much violence."

"You mean an old guy might walk in and blow up a kid's birthday party?"

"Very funny, but there would be protesting and yelling like you never heard. They would throw any politician out of office who even suggested that stuff."

"Well, personally, I think you're going to have to throw a bone to these people. And a pretty big one at that."

At that moment, the Redskins scored and the crowd went crazy. Jack leaped to his feet and cheered and Paul followed him up, but he wasn't really paying attention. He was thinking, *What kind of bone could you throw a guy who's willing to blow himself up?*

The President's mother was now ensconced permanently at the Compassionate Care Facility in Baltimore, Maryland. Compassionate Care was a very successful business, housing thousands of older people who needed sophisticated machines to keep them in their comas. Hospitals certainly couldn't handle them and nursing homes had no place for people living on machines only. Plus, the equipment was so expensive that the investment was only possible for a few extremely rich entrepreneurs. Nate Cass was one of them.

The Cass family, one of America's richest, was based in Nashville. Ronald Cass, the patriarch, went into the termite business in 1945 and in ten years had the largest exterminator company in the world. Cass Exterminator was in forty states and twenty countries and by 1955 was clearing one hundred million dollars a year. Ronald's five sons took the family fortune and had turned it into thirty billion dollars by 2000, investing in industries as varied as snack food and fertilizer. They were one of the first owners of the modern-day factory farm. After Perdue, they had the largest chicken business in the world.

They then decided to go into health care, the only business they saw with no end in sight, and they played everything perfectly. The second eldest son, Nate, had a gift for this, and he invested in private health insurance, research hospitals, pharmaceuticals, and a small but growing area, life support, taking care of the people in irreversible comas who could still live many years.

In the 2020s, the religious right grabbed control of the life-death question. Evangelicals filled the courts with lawsuits, and doctors became even more afraid to pull the plug. The same mind-set that created the need for a Walter Masters made the Cass family more money than they had ever imagined. Their Compassionate Care Facilities were unlike anything that came before, beautiful surroundings where people could go and dream, if that's what they did, until their hearts stopped. Nate Cass invested in new equipment that was much smaller and designed in pleasing colors, so that when family members came to visit, everything looked normal. The old-fashioned heart and breathing monitors and pumps and drips were replaced with machines that were part of the bed frame, placed against the wall where visitors couldn't even see them. All tubes were under the gowns, which were no longer hospital-like but fashioned and styled by real designers. Whenever the family came to visit, the patients wore makeup. They were presented as if they had just been outside taking a stroll, wearing nice outfits and with a glow in their cheeks, and the result was that comatose people seemed just fine, as if they were only taking a short nap.

Of course there were people who were against all of this. President Bernstein, for one. But legally, the courts wanted proof that the brain was dead. If there was any activity at all, a doctor could not euthanize without everyone, including the patient, signing off.

The evangelicals didn't care what the brain was doing; they felt Jesus was in there no matter what. They went before juries and convinced them that even the slightest brain wave could produce a dream. One of their lawyers came up with a line that stuck: "These people could be enjoying a world that we will never know unless we are there. To end it is murder." And as a result, the Cass family cashed in. Thousands of people slept in their centers, sometimes for a decade or more, at great cost to the government.

The President's mother lived, if that was the right term, in a third-floor corner suite. There was pretty wallpaper in her room and a little writing desk and a small couch. There was even a ceiling fan. Air-conditioning was only turned on when someone visited, so the fan not only had a homey look but also saved the business a fortune. Why cool the rooms?

Susanna went to visit her that Friday, unannounced. When she arrived, the staff was miffed at showing anyone a patient before she was made up and prepared, but of course no one was going to keep the secretary of the Treasury out. She asked to see the President's mother alone, which the centers did not like. They always wanted a staff member in the room so they could tell the relatives and friends how well the person was doing. "I think I saw a smile the other day," they would say. Or, "He is doing much better today than last week." All the kind of garbage that made the living feel better.

Susanna got her way. She was escorted to the room, but she walked in by herself. *My God,* she thought, *this woman is dead.* She could see immediately that there was no life left. As far as dreams, Susanna didn't care; she did not believe in spending millions of taxpayers' dollars to perpetuate a dream. *How do we know the dream is even pleasant? Imagine years and years of being trapped in a falling elevator or never being prepared for the final exam.*

As she was leaning over the bed, she thought how happy the President would be if she could just end his mother's agony and his at the same time. She looked around for a switch, not that she would do anything. But the machines were so well hidden that she couldn't even be certain where the power was coming from. At that moment the door opened and the doctor on duty, Sharim Soulazo, stood there with a big smile on his face. "Madame Secretary! To what do we owe the honor of your visit?"

"Who are you?"

"I'm Dr. Soulazo. I am the day manager of the facility and I'm also a stockholder." He laughed a little at his joke. She didn't.

"I told the President I wanted to see where his mother was kept. I am here to understand the situation. That is all."

Dr. Soulazo was confused. *Why would the secretary of the Treasury be concerned with the president of the United States' mother?*

"Did you know her?"

Susanna was annoyed by the question. She decided a quick lie would end the conversation. "Yes. I did. We were friends. She was a lovely woman." Susanna then picked her bag up off the couch and made her way to the door.

"Do you want to know any specifics?" he asked.

"Like what?"

And then Soulazo gave her the standard speech. "She seemed to smile yesterday; she had a very good night. She seems better this week than last."

Susanna couldn't stand him.

"Thank you," she said. "I'm glad she is getting on so well."

CHAPTER THIRTY-FOUR

As October 21, the date of the Immunicate stockholders' meeting, approached, Max told Kathy how excited he was about driving to Dallas. Kathy didn't share his enthusiasm for this particular road trip. She had seen Sam Mueller's lecture and quite frankly did not want to sit through a boring stockholders' meeting, but she didn't want Max to go by himself.

"It's almost a thousand miles. That's a long drive. Do you really feel up for that?"

"You're right," Max said. "Let's fly. We can rent a car when we get there."

Now Kathy felt like she had to go. He was making it too easy. "I'm curious; what do you expect to find?"

"Kathy, I think Sam Mueller may be the key to everything."

"How?"

"Imagine if the man who is most responsible for keeping people alive reversed his philosophy. Imagine that. If this guy were to say that fixing old bones was not as important as improving the lives of young people, wouldn't that be amazing?"

"But that's his *business.* Is he ever going to turn on his own discoveries?"

"That's why we're going. Someone *must* bring this to his attention."

Kathy had to admit it was an admirable goal. How Max was going to get the master of living longer to acknowledge the inherent problem in it, well, that she didn't know. But damn it, she admired him for trying.

When they arrived in Dallas, they rented the electric Kar, made in Korea. If you had enough money you would never buy a Kar, but it was fun to rent just to check in and see how the frugal half lived. Max was impressed. It could seat five comfortably, could go one hundred twenty miles an hour, and got almost three hundred miles on a charge. There was an optional engine switch that gave it the sound of an old-fashioned race car if that was what one desired, and there was also a mock shifting knob that emerged from the center console when the driver got in, giving the feeling of shifting through gears, even though it did nothing.

What the Koreans did so well, Max thought, were the seats. These were one-piece bucket seats stamped from resin and cushioned perfectly. They could be adjusted by rocking them forward or back—the seat back itself would not move independently, which saved a fortune in manufacturing. The air-conditioning cooled the car to seventy-three degrees; the heater warmed it up to seventy-eight. It had no adjustment. And for the car's size it was considered very safe. The Koreans put the money in the metal and used a fusion of steel and resin that was almost impossible to destroy. They had actually had to add back weakness so the car would fold in a crash and not bounce off another vehicle and jolt the driver to death. The Kar didn't come in a luxury model, but Max thought that if the Koreans ever built one, it would be world-class.

Max and Kathy decided to stay in the finest hotel in the city because they assumed that was where Sam Mueller would be. The hotel was part of the Imperial group, a French-Italian lodging company that built small ultraluxury hotels. If Max hadn't been born rich, they would never have stayed there, but the chance of running into Sam Mueller and actually having *the* conversation was worth the expense.

Kathy was in awe. She had never seen a hotel like this before. Three hundred rooms, all suites. One-, two-, and three-bedroom configurations. A butler for each floor and food to die for, which was included in the price. There was always a buffet prepared by a world-class chef, and it could be served in their suite or they could go down to the mezzanine and eat at any time, even in the middle of the night. If someone called the concierge or room service or the valet, they would not only answer with their name but always on the first ring. They were known for that. And then there was the spa. The Imperial group was famous for its spas. Beyond luxury and with all the latest beauty machines.

For example, after decades of teasing women with false claims, a cellulite machine was invented that really did take the dimples away. Not permanently, but for up to a year. These machines were very expensive. They used a new laser technology along with a sound wave generator that got under the skin and massaged it from the inside. Each one was priced at two million dollars. The Imperial chain was the only hotel that had them in all of their spas.

Another impressive thing about the Imperial was that its hotels were the first to have virtual walls in every room. When visitors walked into their living room, the wall looked like a wall. But it was actually a picture of a wall. At the flick of a button it would turn into entertainment, or a babbling brook, or a famous artwork. Billionaires had these virtual walls first, but they were too expensive for regular people. When the Imperial group first installed the walls thousands of guests checked in just to see them. When Kathy pressed the Picasso button, the wall in the living room turned into the Museum of Modern Art. Six Picassos hanging there, so real that she wanted to go over and touch them. Something that was never allowed in a real museum.

Their gamble paid off. Max found a comfortable chair in the lobby and, sure enough, after about an hour he saw Sam Mueller come out of the elevator and walk to a waiting car. And who was with him? His son, Mark. The same kid Max met in Chicago. When the boy saw him, he smiled. Max smiled back. Mueller and his son got in the car and drove off, and Max just sat there, planning. When he finally pled his case to this man, how could Mueller *not* understand? Especially since he had a young son. *Doesn't he want a better life for his children?* Then he had to laugh. Mueller's children were going to have more money than God. Probably not the best example.

Max and Kathy were among the first in line the following morning to get seats at the opening of the Immunicate annual stockholders' breakfast. The stockholders' meeting was a two-day affair. On the first day they fed people, got them in a good mood, and showed them product reels, all before the actual meeting itself, which was on the second day. The company had figured out a long time ago that if they wined and dined everyone who showed up, made them feel important and gave them lots of free stuff before the actual meeting, people were in a far better mood and didn't complain as much when they were told the compensation of the company's directors.

When Immunicate started out they made the mistake of holding the meeting on the first day. People were tired and ornery and channeled all of that energy into bitching about one thing or another. "He's getting too much money." "Your advertising stinks." "Get rid of all the private jets." So the company looked around, saw how several other successful corporations did these yearly events, and copied the best of them. Some of the electronic and cosmetic giants gave out an abundance of free swag, understanding that if someone was sitting there with a new holographic picture generator, his mood was much improved. When a woman knew that she had just been given over two thousand dollars' worth of the newest cosmetic creams, her tough questions to the board faded away along with the spots on her hands.

Immunicate couldn't give out its products—they made drugs, after all—so they started out trying different ideas. At first they offered a free physical for every stockholder who showed up. That wasn't a big success. One year they even tried free MRIs, but the liability issue raised its ugly head. And telling someone he had a tumor and then sending him to the luncheon buffet really didn't go down that well. So the company settled on pampering. They didn't want to pick up the cost of the hotel because they would have too many freeloaders, people buying one share of stock just to get free lodging wherever the meetings were held. But they did offer world-class buffets, roaming masseuses, free use of the hotel spas, city tours, and small gifts like wrist phones, jewelry, and commemorative coins with the stockholders' names engraved on them.

Max Leonard owned a thousand shares that his father had given to him when he turned eighteen. He never paid any attention to them and in one decade they had made him almost a million dollars. But more importantly, it was enough shares to give him some cachet. The company was aware of who owned what, and even though they let small shareholders in for the free food, they had no respect for them. Those who owned a thousand shares were treated differently.

So Max and Kathy were told that first morning that they didn't have to wait in line for the buffet. They were escorted inside the dining room and given a lovely table, where they were served a delicious breakfast by waiters dressed in tuxedos. They were also given free use of a car service if they wanted to see some of Dallas's tourist sites. And someone privately told them that when they checked out of the Imperial, their stay there would be heavily comped. They were being treated so nicely, Max had to remember why they had come in the first place. Weren't they there to try to talk to the devil himself? *This is how the devil does it,* Max thought, *he plies you with goodies. Well, I'll take your goodies, but it won't work.*

Kathy and Max filled their stomachs with crepes and fresh fruit and the most delicious lattes they'd ever tasted, and then they spent the first day in Dallas just being old-fashioned tourists. The driver took them by George W. Bush's house. The former president was known to walk the neighborhood and talk to the sightseers. Bush thought that if he could hang around long enough, history would show him in a favorable light, but at eighty-four years old, history hadn't arrived yet.

Kathy had to admit she loved being a tourist, but all Max could think about was how to get Sam Mueller alone.

Over the previous month, the United States and China had worked out an unprecedented historic agreement that would change the world. No more borrowed money. Now they had full partnerships, and Los Angeles would be the beginning. Teams of negotiators worked out the minutiae. The agreement was more than two thousand pages long, covering everything from the rights of Chinese workers in the United States to what would happen if there was another earthquake. The Chinese insisted that their citizens who were going to come to the U.S. be given certain stature that other nationalities did not receive. They did not like the whole green-card routine. They wanted something new, something that was closer to citizenship than a work permit.

"What exactly are you asking for?" the United States team wanted to know.

"We want our people who uproot their lives to make your lives better to know how important they are. Our first choice would be dual citizenship."

"Well, if they stay here long enough and go through the process, we can certainly consider that."

"We need more than consideration. We need a guarantee. The only way for our people to accomplish such a great task set before them is to ensure that they will be part of what they build. Part of America. Most will take such pride in their workmanship that they will want to stay here. We ask that those who are approved to work on the reconstruction will automatically gain their citizenship."

"We can't do that," the United States said. "They can't just come here and become citizens immediately; that would be unfair to the rest of the world. They have to live here for five years minimum to apply for citizenship, like anyone else who comes here."

The Chinese were insistent. "All of the foreigners who have come to your country have come here because they chose to do so. This is not the case with us. You are *asking* us to come and therefore we do not feel it is right that we have to live under the same rules as those who come here uninvited."

The bargaining went on like that over many marathon sessions until the agreement was reached. As far as citizenship, it was agreed that after two years of work on the "project," as it was referred to in the contract, a Chinese-born person could apply for dual citizenship in America, providing his or her work record was clean and they had no issues with the law. The Americans thought they were giving up a lot on this point, but they gained a lot on another issue, that of the possibility of another great quake. At first the Chinese didn't want to address that, but finally language was put in the agreement that said, "Once China rebuilds and co-owns, they will take the responsibility of keeping the city from further decay, including any act of God, which will also include any further earthquakes." The U.S. was thrilled. If there was ever another natural catastrophe, the Chinese would shoulder the cost.

The part of the contract that dealt with disputes was a bit of a joke. If either party had grievances, it was allowed to bring them before a combined panel of American and Chinese officials that would then arbitrate. The Chinese asked, "What if there is a situation that cannot be arbitrated; how will that be approached?"

The Americans laughed. "That's called war, and we don't want to spell out an attack in the agreement."

As complicated as the contract was, the Americans were surprised by how quickly it was negotiated. Normally something like this would take years, but once the U.S. realized it was the only solution, everything was done in a matter of weeks. Many times the U.S. negotiating team went home at night imagining how beautiful and modern Los Angeles would be one day. Many of them had done business in China over the years and had become depressed leaving through one of China's modern and spacious airports, only to come back to the United States and land at an airport that had been built a hundred years earlier. And one of the U.S. negotiators who had lived her entire life in Los Angeles was overheard saying, "Just to get these decrepit water mains replaced is worth the price of admission."

The negotiations were secret, but word was slowly leaking out that something big was in the works. Brad Miller had moved in with his son until he was able to board the retirement ship *The Sunset.* Tom had taken out another loan on his small house to make this happen and he worried constantly about how he would pay it back, but he knew he had to do this for his father.

Brad was sharing a room with his eleven-year-old granddaughter, Melissa. He helped her at night with her homework and tried not to listen when she talked to her friends. When she was on her screen, he lay on the cot pretending to be asleep, staring at her posters of young hunks and looking at her falsie collection. The longer he stared at her pink wallpaper, the more he was ready to board the ship for the rest of his life.

One night at dinner, Tom asked his father, "Did you hear about the Chinese?"

"No."

"There's some deal in the works where they're going to rebuild Los Angeles."

Brad stopped eating. He wanted to make sure what he had just heard.

"Are you kidding? Does that mean I can get my condo back?"

"Do you want it back?"

"Well, I sure as hell want the money for it."

"I don't know what they're going to do. No one knows if they are planning to rebuild everything as it was or what. I just know a lot of Chinese people are going to be coming here."

"Who told you that?"

"I heard it at the post office."

"Like they know anything."

"But what if they *did* rebuild? Would you rather live there than on the ship?" Brad thought a moment. And the answer was no. It would take years to bring Los Angeles back and none of his friends would be there; they had died in the quake or moved away, and it only would reek of bad memories.

"I don't want to go back. I'm excited about *The Sunset.*" His son smiled. He then addressed the issue that was always on his mind.

"Dad, if you do get some money from your condo, you will help us pay back the loan, right?" His father looked at him. He glanced over at Tom's wife, Crystal, and both she and Melissa were staring at him, waiting for the answer.

"What do you think? That's a silly question. I know this is a hardship on you and if I get a goddamn penny it's yours. Didn't I give you the twenty-five thousand I got from Auschwitz over there in Pasadena?"

"No," Tom said. "You actually didn't."

"Well, I will. Just leave me enough money to live on. That's all."

"I don't want the twenty-five grand you just got. I just want to know that if you . . . never mind. I'm sure you know our situation is not so great."

"Tom, I'm sleeping on a cot in Melissa's room. I understand your situation. Yes, I'm good for the money. And anyway, you'll always know where to find me. I can never disappear once I'm on the ship, right?"

"You can leave the ship, Dad, you're not a prisoner."

"I'm a prisoner of poverty. That's the biggest prisoner of all."

And then the same discussion started all over again. "Do you not want to go on the boat?"

"You know I do. I'm just still shaken by having my life uprooted, but I know it will be a good thing. And I love you for helping me. As soon as I see real money it's all yours."

"Okay, we don't have to talk about it again."

His father got up. "I'm going to lie down for a little bit. Melissa, who is that naked boy on the poster?"

"He's a singer, Grandpa."

"Nice shoulders." Brad left the table. Tom looked at his wife. He was a little upset he'd brought up the money issue. She wasn't.

"Why can't he give us some of that twenty-five thousand now?"

"Honey, how is he going to live? You still have to buy things even if you're on the ocean. We can't say 'bon voyage' and not give him any money."

"He can have ten thousand."

"That's not enough for anything."

"What does he need? We're paying for everything. It's enough for snacks and souvenirs, isn't it?" Tom didn't want to have this discussion in front of his daughter.

"Let's see how it goes. I really believe we're going to see some of that condo money."

"That'll be the day," Crystal said. "Melissa, get up and take down that poster. I don't want your grandfather looking at that kid."

CHAPTER THIRTY-FIVE

When President Bernstein's press secretary announced that he would be addressing the nation, she gave no specifics. She just said it would be the most important policy speech given in this century. The White House wanted it to be seen in real time, as it was being given, not a day later or read about in a news blog. They handed out no advance copies. They wanted everyone to watch.

Bernstein was going to tell America that something was about to happen that had never happened before and he wanted to sell it himself, with his expressions and his voice and his speech-making ability, which was quite formidable. He had a relaxed way of talking to people he didn't know, as if he were sharing some information with a friend, and that was the way he wanted to let the country know that China was now a partner. If this was disseminated at a later time through sound bites and press clippings, he was afraid it would come off badly.

Weeks before, Bernstein had sat down with the three most important people in the House of Representatives and the three most important senators, four Democrats and two Republicans, to inform them of what was about to happen. He also asked John Roberts, now in his twenty-sixth year as the Chief Justice of the Supreme Court, to attend. Bernstein thought having Roberts there would give the meeting gravitas, since

Congress and the Supreme Court rarely mingled, except at the State of the Union.

White House staff had already cleared the idea with Roberts. They needed assurance that this was constitutional. Roberts said what they had hoped, that becoming a financial partner with another country was not even dealt with in the Constitution and therefore should not present a problem.

When the meeting adjourned, the President was pleased. There was virtually no resistance from anyone in the group, aside from perfunctory concerns about national security, but Bernstein convinced them that if anything, this would make America more secure, with two countries now having a stake in keeping the homeland protected.

When everyone left, the President said to John Van Dyke, "Ten years ago there would have been no way that those seven people would have signed off on this. This should prove to us more than anything what dire financial straits we are in."

The speech was scheduled for a Wednesday night at nine P.M. Eastern Standard Time. The First Lady and all of the president's cabinet accompanied him to the East Room, where the broadcast would take place. Bernstein was remarkably calm considering what he was about to tell the nation. But his calm came from the fact that he had grown to love the idea. Each day he was able to sell it better than the day before, and the fact that the U.S. had no choice—well, that made it easier. It was a little like surrendering in a war. You've lost, but at least it's over and there was no other way out anyway. But this no longer felt like surrender. Quite the opposite.

Bernstein sat down behind the desk that FDR had used when he announced the attack at Pearl Harbor. The setting was elegant and clean, with just the American flag and the Chinese flag behind him. The President had the speech on a prompter, but he didn't need it. It flowed out of him like conversation. At exactly nine P.M. he began.

> "Good evening. Tonight has been billed as a historic speech, and for once it might actually live up to the billing."

Bernstein smiled. He looked in control. He looked as if he was excited to tell the American people this information.

"As you know, one of the great cities of the world, Los Angeles, was destroyed on June twelfth of this year. Destroyed so thoroughly that it is now unrecognizable. It was as if nature turned back the clock to the time of the Old West. We now have huge swaths of land where great buildings once stood. Homes are gone, schools wiped out, lives ruined, commerce ground to a halt.

"Tonight I am happy to announce that all this is about to change. The United States, at this moment in its history, does not have the funds to rebuild a city of fifteen million people from the ground up. There is no way to give this a positive spin. The price tag to bring Los Angeles and the surrounding areas back to where it once was will be at least twenty trillion dollars. I repeat, twenty trillion dollars. With our debt load being what it is, there is no possible way to borrow this amount of money. No nation can afford to, or would be willing to, advance our country this sum. If we simply printed it, our economy would come to an end. Our currency would be worth nothing, so that has never been an option.

"The United States, in order to rebuild its largest city, had to come up with a new plan, something that has never been conceived of before. I am pleased to tell you that in this, we have succeeded. The richest country in the world, China, has agreed to become our partner in rebirth."

This was a particular phrase the President was proud of. He made it seem as if it were the United States' idea to divvy up Los Angeles.

"China would not loan us this money. They are aware of the fact that we would not be able to pay back a debt of this size for a century, if ever. So a new idea was born. The Chinese government has had phenomenal success in building great cities. Those of us who have been fortunate enough to visit Shanghai or Beijing or Tianjin have marveled at the magnificent architecture. The great area known as Southern California, the very same area that now lies in ruins, has the capacity, when up and running, to produce billions and billions of dollars each year in revenue. From its ports, to its farms, to its science, to its entertainment industry, what now lies dormant is about to change. And the Chinese are going to be a big part of it. They have formally agreed to help America bring one of her greatest cities back to life.

"In helping us with such a great task, they will, for the first time in history, become our partners. They will share in the cost and share in the revenue. The old-fashioned way of borrowing colossal sums of money and forever paying it back will no longer work. The amounts are too great. So we will give China a real interest in rebuilding Los Angeles.

"Chinese citizens will come and live here and work side by side with hundreds of thousands of Americans on the greatest building effort the world has ever seen. And out of this catastrophe will emerge a new friendship, a new partnership, and a new city.

"America and China have always had much in common: love of life, love of commerce, love of the future. And now we will enter that future together. Never in history have two great countries joined as one in such an ambitious project. But sometimes in life there comes a moment where a nation, just as an individual, must take a step that has never been tried. That moment for us is now. And so we welcome China as our partner in the rebirth of Los Angeles. We ask God to bless this historic moment and we ask all of you to give us your blessings as well.

"Thank you, my fellow Americans, and good night."

The reaction from the room was a sustained applause and a standing ovation. It was important that the nation saw this. The President believed strongly in first impressions and he wanted the country to see that at least *his* people were on board.

And now all they could do was wait. Wait for this to sink in and see how America reacted. Again, the President was calm because there was no other choice. He was surrendering. But it was an economic surrender, which had been happening for decades anyway. This was just the moment that made it official.

The audience for the speech was the largest ever for a presidential address. And the city with the biggest audience was, of course, Los Angeles. People watched there in huge crowds gathered around screens set up in the remains of parks and malls, on street corners, everywhere. It looked like a scene out of *1984,* thousands of people gathered around as a giant head spoke to them. The reaction was unanimous: pure excitement. No one whose life had been destroyed—which was everyone in that city—gave a shit about who or what was going to make it better. If the President had told them Nazis were coming to rebuild their homes, they would have cheered, so certainly the Chinese were welcomed with open arms, as they had a good reputation in the United States to begin with. They were smart, their gang activity was at the low end, they kept to themselves, and, of course, their food was great, which is very important in accepting people from another part of the world. It was the main reason why the Russians and Germans never had much success in America. Their food was lousy. But the Chinese faced no real resistance to begin with. Even the Aryans, who hated everyone, hated them the least. China was the perfect country to come to the rescue, and the reaction throughout America upheld that. Editorial pieces in both the right and left news outlets were positive. "It's about time," one said. "The United States has been living off China's money for decades. Why not stop the charade and bring them into our system."

The White House was thrilled. They hadn't known what the reaction would be since nothing like this had ever been done before, but this was beyond their expectations. The President, after all, was soon to start the third year of his first term. He was going to run again, and this looked like it would help him win. Obviously, it had to play out without unforeseen disasters, but this was a good start, and it was the best Bernstein had felt since taking office. If he couldn't get his world currency off the ground, if he couldn't get people to seriously question life extension, this seemed like the next best thing.

On the other side of the world, the reaction was even better. The Chinese were delirious. Even though they owned much of the United States anyway, this was something they could understand and feel proud of. "We are now part of Los Angeles," said *The People's Daily.* "We will bring our best to the United States and show the world that we are the most advanced and technically savvy nation on earth. When this is completed, we expect other cities of the world to line up. The Age of China has officially begun." The editorial was dramatic, but the Chinese people loved it. Pride was everywhere. And no one was happier than Shen Li.

From that first meeting with Zhou Quinglin, when it was alluded to that something big was going to happen, Shen had sensed that he would be heavily involved. And he was right. His company was chosen to handle all issues of health in the new city. He was overjoyed. All at once he was on the inside in the biggest way imaginable. He would show America how health care could work, and he felt the sky was the limit.

What he needed to do immediately was train people. He needed nurses and doctors and support staff who could run the new centers. He figured, given the population and the size of the area, that he would need at least forty health centers set up and running within twelve months.

When Shen Li arrived in Los Angeles for the first time, about two weeks after the deal was announced, he, like everyone who saw the city in person, was speechless. The images could not compare with the actual devastation. And images didn't convey the spirit of the people, which had been torn to shreds. But this was something Li had seen many times in China and knew how to fix.

He had always known that most health care in the world did not address the spirit, which he felt was the most important issue. If you had the right medicine and the use of robotic surgery, you could repair most physical issues, but to get inside people's minds and make them feel hopeful and realize that they should be happy to be alive instead of just existing—well, this is what Li felt he did better than anyone. And if there was ever a place that needed mental healing, it was Los Angeles. He almost felt guilty for being so excited about what could be accomplished. He would never wish tragedy on a scale like this just to show off his ability, but since it had been thrown into his lap, he was ecstatic.

The Army Corps of Engineers took him from triage center to triage center and he lied to them, telling them they had done wonderful work, while secretly amazed at how backward they were considering this was the United States. He knew that with very little effort he would surpass what they had done in a matter of weeks. And when he was through, the people of the United States would never accept anything less than what he was about to offer them.

Brad Miller watched the President's speech with his son and tried in vain the next day to get in touch with someone to see if the Chinese would give him his money. Of course, no one knew any details, but it was obvious that if this was ever going to happen it wouldn't occur for months, maybe years.

In one week Brad would board *The Sunset* and his life would take a new direction. He had to admit he was getting excited. He not only kept the worn-out brochure close by, but he watched the short movie about the ship and how great a life it was. The movie made it look so wonderful. People were happy, had great food, enjoyed activities, breathed clean air, took long walks, and had a constant change of scenery. Each day looked like an adventure. The movie had interviews with older couples and singles who had been retirement cruising for years, and all of them said they would never go back to the other life. Of course, these people were in the movie, so what else would they say? And maybe because Brad wanted to like it so much, or maybe because it was true, it was starting to look like the only life he could imagine. He thought of meeting a woman and falling in love and both of them cruising the world for the rest of their days. He didn't bother with details in his fantasy, like that the actual cruising time was only three months out of the year. But so what? The ports still offered adventure, and when fantasizing about love, none of the details are important anyway.

The one thing Brad had to admit was that in his old life, the one in which he lived in his condo and saw the same friends day in and day out, he never met women. He wasn't someone who liked dancing or other activities where women congregate, but now, he thought, he would be only a deck away from all kinds of activities women usually loved. Maybe he would meet someone by one of the five pools. Five pools! He wondered which pool he would like the most. So, as departure day came close, he was eager to board the ship. And it was mutual. His son and his daughter-in-law couldn't wait to get him out of their cramped house.

As he lay in his cot the night before he left, Melissa talked to him in the dark. "Grandpa, are you excited to go on your trip?"

"Yes, honey. I am."

"Were you as poor as Daddy is when you were his age?" What a strange question. He wasn't expecting it, had never heard it before, and didn't know how to answer. So he was honest.

"No, honey. I had a very good job when I was your father's age."

"Will I get a good job?" He didn't know how to answer that, either. This time he didn't want to be truthful because he didn't see the prospects being very good for her or anyone in her generation. Even worse than his son's, he thought. So he lied. There are times when the truth does absolutely no good and people who tell it then are just mean.

"You will do fine, honey. You're going to have a good life."

"How do you know?" He wished she wouldn't ask him any more questions. He didn't know how long he could keep this up.

"I just know, honey. I feel it in my repairable bones."

"What does that mean?"

"It's a joke. They've just come up with something that people my age can take if our bones hurt."

"Do your bones hurt?"

"Only my eyes, because you won't let them close."

"Grandpa, I hope you have a nice trip for the rest of your life."

What an interesting way to phrase it.

"Thank you, honey. And I'm telling you the truth; you are going to make a lot of money and be very successful. I'm rarely wrong about this kind of thing."

"Did you ever say that to Daddy?"

"Never."

CHAPTER THIRTY-SIX

Max and Kathy watched the presidential speech in a restaurant in Dallas, after several hours of sightseeing. Max was irritated. He thought that if the Chinese were going to start taking money off the top, it was going to leave even less for people, especially the younger ones. Kathy thought it might be an interesting idea. She had always romanticized Asia and wondered what Los Angeles would look like with its influence.

After dinner they took a walk, and on their way back to the hotel there he was. Sam Mueller. And his son. They were standing near the front entrance talking to a woman who was speaking into a recording device. She looked as though she was organizing something. "That's them!"

"Who?"

"There. Mueller. I'm going to say something."

Max walked quickly over to the lobby entrance. He waited until the woman sounded as if she was finished. "Dr. Mueller? I wonder if I might have a word with you? My name is Max Leonard and I'm here for the stockholders' meeting." Before Mueller could answer his son spoke up.

"Weren't you at my dad's speech?"

"Yes."

"Which speech?" his father asked.

"He was in Chicago."

"Are you from Chicago?" Sam Mueller wanted to know.

"No," Max said. And then realized he should have lied and just told him he was.

"What made you go to the speech in Chicago and also come here? Are you from Dallas?"

Max wanted to blurt out everything he was thinking but he knew this was not the right moment; he needed to get Mueller alone.

"Yes, I'm from here. I was visiting Chicago and happened to see you speak. I am a fan of your work and also a shareholder of your company. I was planning on seeing you at the stockholders' meeting tomorrow, but I wanted to speak with you beforehand."

Dr. Mueller was tired. He didn't want to talk business with an individual shareholder and thought that was what Max was getting at.

"Listen, what is your name?"

"Max."

"Max, I've had a long day and my son and I are going to get some dinner in our suite and hit the hay. If you want to ask questions at the meeting, I will look for your raised hand and call on you. It was nice to meet you." And before Max could say anything else, Sam Mueller disappeared into the hotel with his son in tow.

"Goddamn it! That was stupid," Max mumbled to himself.

"Why did you tell him you were from Dallas?"

"What difference does it make? He obviously doesn't want to engage anyone in conversation if he doesn't have to. I'll be right back."

Max walked into the hotel just as the Muellers were getting on the elevator. As the elevator door closed, he could see that they were the only ones in there, so when the pointer stopped at ten, the highest floor, he knew that was where they were staying. He nodded to the security guard, showed him his floor pass, and grabbed the next car. Max was smart to have stayed in the hotel. If he wasn't a guest, the elevator would have gone nowhere.

Max got out on ten and heard a noise at the end of the hall. He walked down and stood before a double door that said RONALD REAGAN SUITE. From the lack of other doors anywhere nearby, it was obvious this suite occupied half the floor, and that this was where they must be staying. He was about to ring the bell, but stopped at the last second. He had waited a long time for this moment, but now he had to think through *exactly* what he would say. He needed to prepare. He went back downstairs to get Kathy, who was in one of the gift shops, looking at what was very likely the most expensive watch in Dallas.

"What did he say?"

"I'm going to talk to him later."

"He told you to come back?"

"Sort of. I'm going to go to the room and jot down some thoughts. I want this to be perfect."

"Great. I'm going to window-shop down here. Look at this watch, isn't it beautiful?"

Max wasn't thinking about anything but his impending confrontation. "Yes," he said. "Buy it if you want."

"It's three hundred thousand dollars."

He didn't even hear her; he was out the door. Max's heart was racing. He finally had the chance to convince the one person in the world who could make a difference. The interesting thing about Max was that mixed in with his cynicism and bitterness, there was a naïveté. He still thought that if he could get someone to *really* understand, they would change. And now, finally, he could make Sam Mueller *really* understand.

When he got back to his suite he paced around the room, talking out loud, as if Mueller were sitting in front of him, listening rapturously. Max had made these speeches in the group meetings before to great response. He knew this stuff in his sleep, but now he was going to talk to the man himself. When Sam Mueller saw it the right way, he would spend his billions to reverse course. Max had dreams of sitting in front of Congress, with Mueller by his side, giving the "rights of each new generation" speech.

He looked at the time. An hour and a half had gone by. He was sure Mueller and his son had eaten by now and were probably relaxing; if he didn't strike soon, they might go to bed. He walked over to the minibar and downed two small scotch bottles. Then he pumped his fist in the air and downed a third. A little extra courage now couldn't hurt.

At five minutes to nine he walked out of the elevator. He was surprisingly calm, although the colors in the hallway seemed much more intense now. What was the worst that could happen? That he wouldn't quite make his point, but Mueller would find him compelling enough to have another conversation. As he reached the door he stood for one moment and took a breath. He pressed the bell. Nothing. He pressed it again. Nothing. *Did they go out?* He was about to give it one last try when he heard a voice. It was Mark Mueller.

"Who is it?"

"Is your father there?"

"Who is it?"

"It's Max Leonard. The man you met downstairs and also in Chicago."

"Oh, yeah. What do you want?"

"I want to talk to your dad."

"He isn't here."

"What do you mean?"

"He left. Come back another time."

"When?"

"I don't know, but he isn't here."

Max was frustrated. He was primed and ready. He didn't want to come back. "Can I wait for him in the room?"

And the boy, for no apparent reason, opened the door.

"You want to wait here?"

"May I?"

"I guess. I guess you can wait in the living room."

And the boy allowed him to enter.

Jesus Christ, look at this goddamn suite. This must be ten thousand square feet! The living room looked like a palace. It was divided into three sections. One corner was a den–office area with dark wood floors and the most magnificent desk Max had ever seen, like something out of Monticello. Another side of the room was a living area with beautiful oriental rugs and two couches from the Victorian period, and a love seat that looked as if it was so valuable that no one should ever sit in it. The remainder of the large room was yet another living area, but modern and welcoming with a holographic screen, a game center, and an automated chess set with hand-carved pieces that were made out of white jade. "How many bedrooms in this place?"

"Four," Mark said. "Do you want something to drink?"

"Yes. That would be nice."

"Help yourself if you want liquor or something. It's in the bar."

Max walked over to the bar, which was made from a combination of black slate and mahogany. *Jesus, the bar alone looks like it cost a million dollars.* He put ice in a glass and looked over the bottles of sherries. Max didn't know much about booze but he knew expensive sherry when he saw it. He poured a glass of Lustau and went back to sit down in the more casual part of the living room. He downed his drink and wondered if scotch and sherry mixed; he never really knew the liquor rules. The boy sat down opposite him. "I forget, how do you know my dad?"

Now Max had to figure out if he was going to make this lie go on or just tell the kid the truth. He continued to hedge.

"I'm a big admirer of his work."

"Oh yeah?" Mark had heard this a lot. It didn't mean much to him and it certainly didn't mean Max was his dad's friend. "Did you work with him?"

"No."

"So how do you know him?"

"Well, he's famous."

"So you're just a fan?"

"Yeah."

"I could get in trouble for letting you in. I'm not supposed to let strangers in here."

"Well, we met before, so I'm not really a stranger. I'm not going to do anything weird. It would be great if you let me wait for him. I really need to talk to your dad."

"What's wrong?"

"What do you mean?"

"Well, people who wait a long time to talk to my dad are usually dying. They want advice or something."

"I'm not dying."

"So what do you want to talk about?"

And before Max knew it, he was in deep conversation with this thirteen-year-old boy about generational injustices and how Mark and his friends were going to have a harder life because of the olds.

"The olds?" Mark asked.

"That's the name for anyone over seventy."

"Oh."

Max waited a moment before he spoke further to see if he had gotten any kind of a rise out of the son of the great scientist. *It would be so helpful to have a family member on board.* But the boy didn't bite. He didn't even seem interested, and he actually argued a little with Max. "My life is going to be better than my dad's. My dad was poor."

"I understand, but you don't count."

"Why? Why don't I count?"

"Because you're the richest fucking kid in the world."

"You don't have to swear."

"I'm sorry. But you're immune."

"Like my dad's company?"

"What do you mean?"

"You know, Immunicate."

"Right. Like that."

"Are you poor?"

"No."

"So why are you so upset?"

"Because I care about people and you should, too."

This was beginning to sound like a parental scolding and Mark wasn't too thrilled about it. And at that moment the front door opened and Sam Mueller was standing there. He was shocked to see a stranger holding a drink and talking to his child—shocked and angry. "Who in God's name are you? And why are you here?"

"I met you downstairs."

"Put your drink down and get out of here or I'm calling the police. What is your name?"

"I just want to talk to you. It's about something important."

"I asked you what your name is."

"Max."

"Max what?"

"Listen, sir, would you just talk with me for five minutes? You'll understand everything if you give me five minutes."

"Max *what*?"

"Max Leonard."

Sam Mueller walked directly to the intercom. "There is a gentleman who has come into my suite who was not invited and I need security up here immediately." Max was getting upset and frustrated.

"You don't have to call security. I'll leave."

"Then leave."

Max started to lose his temper. As he walked toward the door he turned to Mueller and yelled, "Do you know the suffering that young people are going through because their hopes and dreams are now buried under the debt of keeping old people alive? Do you know they do not get to have the same life their parents had? Do you know that? Why don't you work to make things fair for everyone instead of making all that money helping the olds?"

"That's what he calls the people over seventy," Mark told his father.

Mueller was livid now. "Get the fuck out of my suite or you will never reach an old age. I'm not kidding. I will prosecute you for breaking and entering and I will see that you are put in prison."

"Why can't you just listen to me? Do you understand what is happening with our country or are you too blinded by profits?"

At that moment two security guards appeared. "This man broke into our suite and he will not leave! I want you to arrest him!" Mueller said.

"I didn't break in, your son invited me."

"I didn't invite you, you said you knew my dad."

The larger of the two security men took Max's arm. "Let's go, sir. Now!" Max shouted as he was being led out.

"I'll see you at the stockholders' meeting! I own a thousand shares of your corrupt company!"

Mueller shouted back, "If you try and come to the meeting you'll be arrested! Do you hear me?" And then he slammed the door in Max's face.

Outside in the hall, when the guards realized that Max was also a guest in the hotel, they made a quick deal with him: Check out, go home now, and they would not call the police. And that's what happened.

Max and Kathy left the Imperial Hotel and he went back to Indianapolis with his tail between his legs, angrier than ever. Maybe Sam Mueller wasn't the right person to confront, or maybe he was. Max needed time to think. Now he was seriously confused.

CHAPTER THIRTY-SEVEN

A real feeling of success pervaded the West Wing. The polls on China were remarkably good, with sixty-seven percent saying it had been the right move. Only thirty percent disagreed, and three percent simply didn't understand or care about the question. Bernstein was pleased but still surprised by how many people welcomed this. He had underestimated how beaten down America had become.

There had been so many warnings to the people of the United States over the last thirty years that they were losing their place in the world. But what no one realized was that these warnings were being taken to heart. If you tell a child over and over that she's stupid, she'll eventually believe you. And it isn't any different for a nation. By the time the China plan was announced, the mood in America was "Save us. We need help." And while pleased with the numbers, the President couldn't help but feel a bit sad.

Born in the 1980s, Bernstein came into the world as a citizen of the most powerful nation on earth. But within his lifetime that had all changed, and now here he was, the president of the United States, at a time when the U.S. could no longer even borrow its way out of trouble. Sure, he put on a good face and told the world how exciting the new partnership with China was, but never before had a country been forced to sell one of its cities, which in essence was what they were doing. Would he go down as the president who sold out the country or saved it? Would history show him as a visionary or a fool? It was moments like this that he used to rely on his wife to tell him that it was all going to work out. Now he needed someone else.

"Madame Secretary, I have the President on the line." Susanna Colbert was always so happy to hear her assistant say that.

"Hi," the President said. "Did I bother you?"

"I live to be bothered. How are you?"

"Do you want to have a bite to eat tonight?"

"Of course. With your wife? Others?"

"No others."

"All right, I just didn't know how formal it would be."

"I'll be in my pajamas. You can wear what you like."

She laughed. Susanna was having an intellectual affair with this man, there was no denying it, and she was enjoying the hell out of it. It was something that had been missing for so long in her own marriage, and obviously it was missing in his. "I'll stop at the mall and pick up a nightgown," she said.

"Get one for me," Bernstein joked. "Betsy has a function to go to at six o'clock so I'll have some downtime until nine. Come to the Oval at seven."

The President liked eating dinner in the Oval Office. There were many places to eat in the White House; even the kitchen was fun to have a meal in once in a while. But for the ultimate in privacy, other than the residence, this was where he felt most comfortable. He didn't want Susanna to join him upstairs. That would be crossing a line, even though mentally he'd crossed it a long time ago.

As they ate a Chinese dinner—no special meaning given to that—the President let out some of his conflicting emotions. "Do you think I have sold out the United States?"

"God, no," Susanna said. "I think you made a brave and quite remarkable decision. Don't the polls tell you that?"

"The polls don't have a soul. And what the people think is temporary, anyway. Most of the time the real brave stuff gets the lowest numbers."

"Would you rather the numbers were bad? Would that make you feel better?"

"No. I'm a whore for numbers. We all are. But it still doesn't mean I'm right."

"Don't we have an 'out' clause?"

"Yes. After a year. But by that time it will be too late."

"Why?"

"Because the Chinese will front-load the project. At least a trillion will be spent early. They're not stupid. They're not coming here to work for a year and go home with nothing. So we would still be screwed. We would still owe them money with no place to get it."

"Well, Mr. President, it will work out."

"I wish I could tell you not to call me Mr. President. But I can't. That's for the spouse only. Even John calls me Mr. President."

"I understand. It doesn't bother me. I rather like it."

"I know, but sometimes the formality sucks."

"Well, I could call you MP."

"That's not bad. But don't."

They sat for a while, eating without talking, and then the President put his fork down. He hated the next subject but this was the one person he could trust. "Yesterday, I was asked again by some right-to-lifers about my mother. I can't stand that these fundamentalists are using her to their own advantage."

"What do you mean?"

"They know damn well what my views are on prolonging life. And now that it's happening in my own family, they think it's checkmate. I can no longer talk about it while she's draining the pot herself. And one of them actually said to me, 'When it's your own mother, it's a different story, isn't it?'"

"What did you say?"

"What *could* I say? That I want her dead and the machines were not my idea? I can't say that. Why couldn't she have just died? She lived almost a hundred years. Is that bad to say?"

"No. It's normal."

"What I don't understand about the fundamentalists is that their whole life seems to be about the kingdom of heaven. If the next world is so goddamn great, why all the hesitancy to go there?"

"They think God is keeping those people alive."

"I know. As if God is actually spending any time thinking about my mother. And what kind of a God is that? Did he allow man to come up with the respirator to counter his wisdom of taking breath away? Or is he so bored that he's playing a game? And if he *is* playing a game, why doesn't he just win?"

"You're talking to an atheist, Mr. President. I don't believe in a God game."

"You know, you never told me you were an atheist."

"Well, you didn't ask me. It wasn't in the interview."

"What were you born as?"

"Second-generation atheist."

"Wow. What was the religion when it was still there?"

"Catholic."

"Have you even been to church?"

"Weddings and funerals."

"Some people think they're the same thing."

"The funerals have better food."

The President laughed. "Did my mother look like she had any life in her at all? Anything?"

Susanna didn't answer right away. "Well, she looked peaceful."

"That's not what I asked."

"No, Mr. President. She didn't."

"So why can't they turn off the goddamn machine?"

"They want the income and they don't want the lawsuits. *Especially* because it's you."

"See? This is what I hate. I want her to rest in peace, I don't want the machines. But *because* it's me they'll keep her alive longer than anyone."

The President stood up and walked over to pour himself a drink. "I don't want to answer any more questions. I need to be free of this so I can do my work and make my decisions. They are prolonging life for profit, Susanna, and the young people know this and are resentful, and I don't blame them. That's what these uprisings are all about. How can I go out and publicly state that this violence is an outrage when I would be right there with them if I were their age?"

"I don't know. I just don't know. Maybe your mother will pass soon, naturally."

"How is that going to happen? With that equipment they can keep a cabbage alive." Susanna took a moment to think.

"Would you like me to talk to Nate Cass?"

"Talk about what?" And then the President realized what she was saying. He thought for a moment before he answered. "Yes. See what he thinks and ask him what he would do if it were his mother."

"I can do that."

At that moment the intercom buzzed and the President was told his wife was outside. "Get up. Walk with me to the door." He led Susanna out and as he opened the door he started a conversation they had not even been having. Susanna realized who it was for and went with it perfectly. "Talk to the Chinese counsel and see what their polling is. And ask John to get some feedback. Sorry for working you late, but at least you got fed."

"And Chinese food at that. Thank you, Mr. President. Hello, Mrs. Bernstein. It's great to see you."

"Hello, Susanna. Are you two finished? I didn't want to barge in."

"You're not barging in," the President said. "We were just wrapping it up. The public opinion on China looks great."

"I know. I hear it everywhere. Congratulations, Susanna."

"I had nothing to do with it, Mrs. Bernstein. This is your husband's accomplishment." And with that, Susanna was out the door, before any other subjects could be brought up.

Lee Dong Wo was chosen to be the grand architect of the new Los Angeles. Wo had only been twenty-seven when he was picked to design the Beijing Olympics. And over the last two decades, with an airport in Shanghai, a floating hotel in Abu Dhabi, and six thousand miles of a new highway design in China, Wo was the only real choice.

When Wo was a little boy he saw his father spending hours sitting in traffic, not moving, wasting what he thought was valuable time. And when there was an accident, things got even worse. *Why couldn't these cars simply be lifted out of here immediately?* Wo could never get that out of his mind and years later, when he was awarded the largest contract ever given for new highway construction in China, that's exactly what he did.

Every few miles, in heavily traveled areas, small cranes would lift any wreckage up and move it over the guardrail, off to the side, and get traffic moving again within ten minutes, as opposed to the hour and a half it took to get a tow truck and clear the area the old-fashioned way. The cranes would be spaced out so they could reach any accident in five minutes, and when they were not in use they disappeared, lying flat behind the rail.

The technology was imported to several crowded cities around the world, but never to America, which needed it the most. So Wo was going to use it in rebuilding the road system of Los Angeles.

He had also designed double-decker freeways in the downtown areas of China's bigger cities, areas where there were always traffic jams whether there was an accident or not. As he looked at the layout of Los Angeles he felt that having twenty or so miles of double-decker roads would eliminate seventy percent of the congestion. The roads would split into two levels where traffic would always slow, and then join back into one after the bottlenecks. Traffic jams were a mathematical problem, and if the worst areas could be helped, the rest of the road system would benefit exponentially.

Another area of Wo's expertise was high-speed rail travel. Wo had never understood why highways, which already existed, could not be used for trains, too. He put high-speed trains down the middle of many superhighways in China, and helped his country take its place as the owner of the most advanced rail system in the world. Wo's introduction of what were known as Road Trains revolutionized travel, and Los Angeles, he thought, was the perfect city in the world to build them.

Wo was also friends with Shen Li. They were both wealthy, young, and beloved in their home country, and they were not competitive, which in China was rare. Wo had no interest in the health business and worked with Li over the years on many issues involving greener and more cost-efficient ways to improve medical care. He loved Li's idea of putting a small health facility in each new building complex so people would have immediate access to care without having to travel. They were a great team and they both relished the idea of re-imagining Los Angeles.

The first jumbo cargo jets started landing at Los Angeles International Airport in late November 2030. Supplies were flown in from all around the world. Sometimes a skyscraper was constructed using materials from thirty different countries, and these materials arrived exactly when needed so they could go directly to the building site without having to be stored. Storage was the bane of construction budgets, and if materials could go from airport to installation without sitting for weeks and months, the savings were enormous. In order for that to happen, suppliers and transporters and builders and architects all had to be talking together 24/7, and that required a type of communication that the Chinese were the best at. Their logistic software was admired by every architect and contractor in the world.

When Lee Dong Wo constructed the world's first floating hotel in Abu Dhabi, it went up in sixteen months, a record for such a complicated build. And the Abu Dhabi government, which had experience with every nation's best construction companies, watched in amazement at the coordination of the Chinese, something that Los Angeles was about to see.

The first thing the Chinese needed to do was supply housing for its citizens. At the peak of the build there would be three to four hundred thousand Chinese people living and working in Southern California alongside their American counterparts. A total of twelve sites were picked initially, each one housing twenty to thirty thousand workers, and these would be like small cities, self-contained with shopping, schools, parks, health, entertainment, everything the workers needed. And they were all prefabricated.

Jumbo jets flew in the materials for the entire small city over a five-day period. In another six days, it was up and running. Eleven days from "take-off to shower," as the Chinese liked to say. The United States had never seen anything like it. Most people had the same reaction: "Thank God they're building and not attacking, because no one could survive this kind of coordination."

Shen Li had toured and become familiar with each army triage center. He also toured the hospitals to see if any were salvageable. They were not. Too many foundation cracks and, quite frankly, Li hated their layout. He was happy for an excuse to tear them down and rebuild to his liking. Even a hospital in San Bernardino that could have been repaired rather easily was tagged for demolition. When asked why by the city council, Li answered, "Look at it." The city didn't know what that meant, as it looked fine to them. But when the Chinese showed them drawings of what they intended to build, the city wanted the old hospital torn down immediately. As one city council member told the press, "I never knew this thing was so ugly. It was like seeing your wife for the first time without makeup." When he got home that night it was not pleasant.

Li knew that until the infrastructure was built it would be hard to put his style of health care fully in place. But he wanted to try. He started to integrate staff he brought from China, telling the Army Corps of Engineers, who had built and were running the temporary hospitals, that they deserved a break and, since he was going to be responsible for the health of Los Angeles anyway, he would be happy to start early while construction was just beginning. The Army Corps of Engineers was elated. There was no ego there. They hated this job, they wanted out, and they would have dumped every sick person on Li in five minutes if they could. So, of course, they agreed to whatever he suggested. Li introduced his Chinese staff to the triage units and asked them just to observe and be respectful of their American counterparts. But after a very short period of time, they began to take over.

Shen Li was right when he guessed that no psychological treatment was being offered to people on any meaningful scale. His nursing staff immediately made the temporary health tents more comfortable. They put in plants, played soothing music, and tried many different color schemes. The army watched with a degree of cynicism. They didn't really understand what a ficus would do for a broken arm, but they didn't resist. And, just as Li predicted, the patients responded positively. After living through one of the greatest earthquakes the world had ever seen, the people in Los Angeles thought no one would ever care about them again, so even these small measures made a huge impression. The Chinese were a breath of hope. And word spread quickly.

CHAPTER THIRTY-EIGHT

As the last bag was put in the trunk of the car, Brad Miller gave his granddaughter a big hug good-bye.

"I'm going to miss you, Grandpa."

"You are? You seldom give any indication of that."

"Is that you being funny?"

"Sort of. I'm going to miss you, too, honey. I enjoyed our late-night talks."

"What late-night talks?" Crystal asked.

"That's between me and her. Private stuff." Crystal looked worried. The last thing she wanted was for Tom's father to be filling her daughter's head with his ideas.

"Are you coming back, Grandpa?"

"Not for a long time, honey. Maybe never."

"Can we come visit?"

"That's up to your dad. Maybe when the ship rolls back into San Francisco you can drive up and say hi. Or come see me when it docks in Long Beach."

And with that Tom closed the trunk and told his father that they had to be going. Brad gave Crystal a good-bye kiss on the forehead. He had never liked her and the feeling was mutual.

Before long they were on Highway 101, heading to San Francisco. They had to allow two days for a trip that normally would have taken seven hours; until they got beyond Santa Barbara, the roads were a nightmare. As they were crawling along, leaving Los Angeles County, Tom said to his father, "You know what? I envy you."

"Why?"

"Because I think your life is going to be relaxed and fun and this will be a world-class third act."

"I've already had a third act."

"Let's not get literal. You know what I mean."

"You shouldn't envy me. I would kill to be your age."

"Believe me, Dad, you don't want to be my age. It's not the same as it was when you were my age."

"It breaks my heart to hear you talk like that."

"What can I say? It's a struggle. The idea of spending the rest of my life on a cruise ship is intoxicating. I wish I was you."

This made Brad so sad. This was not how it was supposed to be. A child should not long to trade places with the parent. Brad wished he could make it better, but he needed money to do that. "Tom . . . life can change at any moment. I feel something good is coming for you. And I have something I want to say." Tom looked at his father. "If the Chinese don't offer money but offer to rebuild the condo instead, I would allow you to live there with your family forever if that would make things easier."

"Thanks, Dad, but you would need to sell that place. You need your money."

"Well, maybe if you moved to the new Los Angeles you would find a much better job, and if you had a free place to live you could save something. And send a little to me."

"I appreciate the gesture. Let's see how it all works out."

Brad reached over and squeezed his son's leg, giving him a small bit of physical affection. Something that was rare between the two of them.

After spending the night in a cheap motel in San Luis Obispo, they reached San Francisco the next afternoon and went directly to Fisherman's Wharf. They sat in a little grotto having some clam chowder, and they could see the big ship in the harbor. Brad still carried the brochure and he had to laugh. The ship in the pictures looked a lot better, but what pictures didn't?

The departure time was five o'clock. They finished their meal at three-thirty and Tom walked with his father to the dock. When they boarded the ship there was not enough staff to show each retiree to his or her room, so they were given the room number, the deck, and the directions, and told the luggage would be delivered later.

Tom and his dad took an elevator to the third deck and walked down a rather dark hallway with what looked like two hundred doors. Toward the end of the hall they could see the number 316. This would be the place where Brad would spend at least the next ten years of his life, and they both were hoping their first impression would be a good one.

"This is it," Tom said. He touched a card on the door and it opened. Brad was nervous. If the rest of the ship didn't look like the brochure, he couldn't imagine the rooms would, either. And he was right. He stood in the doorway and stared at his two-room suite, if "suite" was the proper word. There was a small bedroom and a slightly bigger living room with a kitchenette in one corner and a shower and toilet in the other.

"Look at this," Brad said. "The toilet's in the living room."

Tom tried to make the best of it. "That's what they do on ships, Dad. You keep the bathroom door closed and it looks like a closet. I think the suite is lovely." His father didn't bother to answer. He looked at the green couch and the worn leather armchair and went over and sat in it. "How is it?" Tom asked.

"Not bad. Pretty comfortable."

Tom went into the bedroom. "Hey, Dad, come in here. Nice view." His father walked into the small room and there was a porthole that showed a speck of blue sky.

"Great. I see they make it small enough so you can't jump."

"Come on, it's nice."

Brad lay down on the bed and sank into the mattress. "Oh, it's one of those foams. I like that." Tom was happy that his father had said he liked something. He went and opened the small round window and let some air into the room.

"This is nice, Dad. It's perfect. I bet most of your day will be outside anyway, so this is very comfortable to come home to." And they spent the next hour convincing themselves that everything was fine. The ship did have five pools, although three were not currently in service. It had a movie theater and a large dining room, and a gym and a sauna. There were dance classes and bingo games. It was just that everything looked twenty years older than it did in the brochure.

At 4:45, two long loud blasts from the ship's air horn told everyone it was time for guests to depart. Tom and his father walked to the exit ramp and stood there for a moment, not saying a word. Then Brad started to cry. His son hugged him. "Stop it, Dad. Stop it. This is going to be great."

"How do you wind up like this? In a million years I would never have imagined this is where I would be."

"It's going to be great. I know it. And if it isn't, you'll leave."

"I can't leave. All the money is in this now. This is my fate."

"It's a good fate, Dad. You'll see. You'll make new friends. It's okay. You're going to love this. I know it." At that moment the air horn sounded one last time and it made both men jump.

"Jesus Christ," Brad said. "Is this the way they tell you to do things?"

"I think it's just for departure."

"It had better be. I don't want to be called to each meal like an air raid drill."

Tom laughed. He kissed his father on the cheek and then walked off the ship.

Brad went to the railing of the second deck, along with hundreds of other people who were saying good-bye, and waved to Tom as if he were just going to Hawaii for two weeks. The fact that this was permanent was too much to think about. Hopefully there were people here who loved to play bridge. Brad had not had a great game of bridge in years.

Susanna Colbert had gone to college with Nate Cass and had always stayed in touch with him. Nate invested in The Card at her suggestion and, like everything else he touched, it turned to gold. Her calling Nate was not unusual. But he had not heard from her since she had become the Treasury secretary.

"To what do I owe the honor?" he asked.

"I was thinking about you. How's your family?"

"No change. Still divorced. You?"

"I'm good."

"How's Washington?"

"It's exciting. A challenge."

"Pretty big news about the Chinese."

"I think it's going to work out well."

"It'd better."

"Are you free for a bite sometime this week?"

Nate paused. Normally whenever Susanna asked to see him it was about investing large sums, but he knew that as head of the Treasury she wouldn't be allowed to do that. Then he got curious.

"Susanna, don't ask me to bail out the country. I don't have that kind of money." She laughed.

"Really? I'm sorry. I'll call someone else."

"I would certainly have a meal with you. Do you want to tell me what it's about?"

"Let's do it over lunch. I'm coming to New York on Thursday for the weekend. Is Friday all right?"

"It's fine. I'll pick a place and let your office know."

"I look forward to it."

At one o'clock on Friday, Susanna and Nate met at Antonio's, a small, elegant Italian restaurant on East Sixty-third Street. The restaurant only seated seventy-five people and was frequented by advertising executives and designers. No famous people. No paparazzi. Colbert was, of course, recognized by some, but it wasn't a big deal.

They had a table in a reasonably dark corner near the kitchen, and what they gave up in foot traffic they gained in privacy. Nate ordered a fish stew and Susanna had an anchovy salad. They both had white wine. Nate raised his glass and toasted her. "To the first female secretary of the Treasury. May God guide you in getting us out of our massive debt."

Susanna smiled. "Even God can't do that, but thank you."

"So what is this all about? I'm panting with excitement."

Susanna played it down. "It really was about seeing you, since I was here anyway, and talking to you about something that I was curious about."

"Go ahead."

She paused. *How do you broach this?* She didn't know what Nate's thoughts would be and didn't even know if he was religious or not, although she never recalled him giving that indication. She also didn't know how fast she should bring the President into the conversation, but then again, Nate Cass wasn't stupid. So she simply cut to the chase. "The President's mother is in your facility in Baltimore."

"I know. We're taking extra good care of her."

"She didn't leave a living will."

"That I also know. Most people in our facilities haven't. Quite frankly, it's why our business is so good."

"Nate, I went to see this woman." Nate was surprised. *Why would she do that?* "I saw a lifeless old lady being kept alive by sophisticated machines and it broke my heart. It also is breaking the President's heart."

"I'm not clear on what you're getting at."

"Are there ever situations where the plug is pulled? Where your team finally admits to the family that there is no hope?"

"Of course. If someone is brain-dead, we don't want to just take the money. But that is not the case with the President's mother."

"Come on, Nate, I saw the activity. It's so minimal most medical experts think it isn't enough to even have a thought."

"I know, Susanna, but many *legal* experts say if you disconnect with a wave present you are committing murder. I'm not smart enough to know the real answer, but I know the law, and my people do not terminate when there is any activity."

She leaned in. Her voice got soft. She wanted to take his hand, but didn't.

"Nate . . . this is killing the President. He can't bear to see his mother like this. He knows her wishes. He wants her to rest in peace."

"Are the wishes written down anywhere?"

"No. Nothing is written down. But the President knows his own mother and he wants this agony to end."

"We don't know if it's agony, Susanna. She might be having a wonderful dream."

"Or a nightmare. And is a dream worth the cost of keeping those bodies warm?" Nate looked at her. He was not a fan of the President and he knew what she was getting at.

"Susanna, I know what Matthew Bernstein ran on, and I know when this happened to his mother it went against his promise to terminate life at first blush."

"Please, Nate. You know that's not what he wants. He wants precious, precious resources to be used for people who need it and can benefit by it. It's his opinion that the people in your facilities don't. That's all."

"And he's entitled to his opinion, but I respectfully disagree."

"Can you help? In this one case? Can you help? I'm sure the President would be grateful."

And there it was. It had taken a half bottle of wine to ask the plug question directly. Nate Cass had to admit he was intrigued. There were not many chances to do a favor for the president of the United States *and* the secretary of the Treasury in one fell swoop. And what a favor.

"Susanna, let me look into this situation more carefully. I will talk to some senior staff and see what we have here." Susanna was pleased, but she realized immediately how disastrous it would be if this went wrong.

"Nate, I have made you a lot of money and I consider you a friend, and the most important thing, the very most important thing is that this conversation did not happen. I appreciate that you will look into this, but if anyone, anyone at all, even an ex-wife knew about this it would destroy me. I know you're not crazy about the President but I am asking this as *my* favor. I came to you because I trust you and you have always been known for discretion."

"First of all, I'm only going to look into this. I knew the President's mother; I met her several times and liked her. I am doing this because I want the best for her. That's all."

Susanna was shocked. "You knew the President's mother? I had no idea!"

"I've never met her, Susanna. I don't know her from Adam."

"But you just said—"

"Quiet. I am showing you that there are ways to approach this that can come from me."

And Susanna got it. But Nate didn't want to give it up just yet. He had the White House begging him and he wanted to milk it for all it was worth.

"I am only saying I will look into the condition. Possibly it has deteriorated and possibly not. But she was someone I liked, so I will take a personal interest." Susanna now played along perfectly.

"I appreciate that. I'm sure since you were friends you know how much his mother would appreciate it, too."

"I will look into it. And by the way, Susanna, I don't talk to my ex-wives."

And that was the end of that discussion. For the rest of the lunch it was never mentioned.

Kathy had never seen Max really depressed before. After they got back from Dallas, he went into a serious funk. She still loved him, but now she was watching a man change before her eyes and she didn't know if it was positive or not. He was angrier. More easily upset. One night they were having dinner at her house and he bit into a prune and got part of a pit. He lost it. He stood up and threw the fruit at the wall. "Why the fuck do they call these pitted if there are still pits? What the fuck is that about?" Kathy got up and recovered the half-eaten fruit, cleaning off the mark it had made. Max left the table and walked outside. He sat on the curb, smoking a joint. Kathy followed him out and stood there, saying nothing, waiting for him to suggest that she sit down. He didn't. For almost a full minute he sat facing the street, getting high, and not saying a word. She turned around and walked back into the house, then closed the door, went to the kitchen, and cried. Really cried. This wasn't about the moment; it wasn't even about the relationship. It was about everything.

Max had taken her away from her problems, but they were still there and they were substantial. Kathy knew she had to sell her father's house at a loss to make any more payments toward the medical loan. She couldn't afford to attend college, only take some classes electronically, and that still was viewed as second class even though there were laws to make it equivalent. But employers always asked, "Did you *actually* go?" Kathy had been holding all of this in and now the floodgates opened.

Max walked back into the kitchen. He put his hand on her head and stroked her hair. "I'm sorry, baby. I'm just upset." Kathy said nothing. She actually wanted him to leave so she could experience these emotions in private. "I just got angry. I thought I chipped my tooth. I don't know how they can put 'pitted' on the package when there are still pits."

She wiped her eyes with her sleeve. "They also say that some may contain pits. Didn't you see that?"

"No. I didn't."

"Well, that's what it says."

And both of them just stood there.

Kathy walked over to the sink. Try as she might, she couldn't help but have *the* conversation. Without turning around she said, "Do you think we should be apart for a while?" She was surprised by how vehement he was.

"No fucking way! Do you think that? Just because I threw a prune? That's crazy."

"It has nothing to do with the prune. You've been down for a long time now, and it's getting worse. Possibly it's us and if so, I don't want to contribute to your anger."

Max got serious. He loved this woman more than anyone else he had ever known. Everything she said was right, but it wasn't about her. He walked over to the sink and turned her around and kissed her.

"Listen to me. You are not the cause of my despair. Yes, I'm in a funk because I want to make a difference. I thought that had something to do with Sam Mueller. But Dallas changed that. I need to do something bigger. So that's what you're seeing. I'm taking my frustration out on you and I'm sorry. Please, don't take it personally."

Kathy gave him a little smile and went into the living room. She sat down and felt like crying again. She believed what he was saying, but she didn't understand how this was going to translate into making her life better now. Max followed her.

"What's wrong? You believe me, don't you?"

"Yes. But when I first saw you speak and when we first fell in love, your energy was enough. I thought I could ride on that and it would carry me. But now I'm confused. My problems seem to be mounting and I can't escape them."

"What problems?"

"You know what. I'm going to lose this house. That's one of them. I don't want to get into the others now. I'll just start crying again."

"How much do you need right now to ease this?"

"I can't take that much money from you."

"How much?"

"I need a hundred thousand dollars. I could pay off several months of the loan and get some breathing room."

"I'll give it to you."

"I can't take it."

"Then consider it rent."

"But you don't live here."

"I will if you want me to."

Kathy looked at him. When people moved in together, it was supposed to be because they couldn't live apart; that was what she had always thought. Not to justify a loan. "I don't think you should give up your place. It's important for you to have your privacy and your work space."

"I can work here."

And then Kathy couldn't believe what came out of her mouth. Sometimes people hold something in and think it's locked away for good and then, in a moment they least expect, it comes sailing out all on its own. "I don't want you putting up hundreds of pictures on the walls here. It was creepy."

"What?"

Kathy wished she could take it back, but now it was out. "I came to your place one day when I was nearby, and I looked in the window. I saw the Sam Mueller wall. I got scared. It looked like you were crazy."

Max responded very tenderly. "Do you think I'm crazy?"

"No," she said, quietly.

"Baby, you should have just told me right away when you saw that. It was no big deal. Charts and photos on a wall are not crazy indicators, unless you're crazy to begin with. Tell me honestly, do you think I'm crazy?" Kathy had to smile.

"A little. It's why I fell in love with you."

"Okay, then. So what's the big deal with having a crazy wall?"

"Nothing, I guess."

"Here's what's going to happen. I'm going to give you the money to keep you from losing the house. We won't tie it in to living together. I'll keep my place and use it for an office. And when we have more meetings, we'll do it here. You can consider the money a payment in advance for the meetings."

"A hundred thousand dollars for a meeting?"

"There will be several."

"This is a loan," she said. "I'll pay you back."

"If you want."

"I do."

"Then consider it a loan." Kathy started welling up again, from a combination of relief and confusion. She knew she cared about this man, but she didn't want to think it had anything to do with the money. Was she just replacing one creditor with another? Then she looked on the bright side. At least she liked having sex with this creditor. And that's exactly what they did that night. They went into the bedroom and had a weird combination of makeup sex with some debt sex and crazy-wall sex thrown in for good measure.

CHAPTER THIRTY-NINE

One of the things that told people that a new Los Angeles was on the horizon was the smell. As the Chinese started arriving, people could smell the cooking in the air near the communities where they lived. Nothing smelled better than sweet rice as it was being steamed. It produced a lovely aroma, some said akin to pancake syrup, and all the other favorites of the Chinese table added something wonderful. That smell alone began to be associated with progress.

A century earlier, dirty smoke filling the skies told people that a city was growing, but now that was replaced by food steamers. Angelenos couldn't understand exactly what it was about that cuisine that smelled so good. Hamburgers didn't do that. Eggs didn't, either. Was it the spices or the fact that the American nose wasn't used to it? Whatever the answer, it was very welcome.

Shen Li officially took responsibility for the health of the city two months after he arrived. He kept some of the temporary centers the army had set up, but mostly he started on the ambitious plan of rebuilding the hospitals and urgent-care facilities and then adding his smaller health centers every five to six miles.

His mobile surgery units were not brought over initially, since people in Los Angeles had better access to operating rooms than people did in

China. But Li was still surprised at how infrequently robot surgery was performed in the United States. In addition to the AMA, hospitals also resisted the robots. They wanted local surgeons to use their operating rooms, nursing staff, and other facilities. But Li was determined to change that. He would prove to America once and for all that robots offered the best care at the best price. If a patient needed a heart valve replaced, would he rather have someone in his city do it, or have one of the best heart doctors in the world do it? And for the same price, maybe less. The fact that that doctor was in Johannesburg would be irrelevant.

But it was still the small health centers that were the centerpiece of Li's plan. He likened it to going to a good restaurant for the very first time. You had no idea what good service was until you got it and then, once you did, you never wanted less than that again. What Americans had given up on was the personal touch. And certainly one could see why. Emergency rooms were factories. Going to a private physician meant hours in a waiting room with only a few minutes spent with the doctor. Concierge medicine was more personal, but ninety-nine percent of people couldn't afford it. Li would change the whole dynamic.

His health centers would have nurse practitioners that could diagnose almost every problem and treat it immediately. And for what they couldn't diagnose, they had direct links to a doctor who could. These centers knew the patients' names, and their children's names, and what they did for a living, and they made everyone feel as if they lived in a small town. People loved the attention and as soon as they got used to trusting the live nurse–virtual doctor combination, they would never want to spend hours in a waiting room ever again. Li knew something else, too. When he showed how well this could work in Los Angeles, the rest of the country would be begging for it.

President Bernstein and his wife slept in the same bed. It was unusual in the White House. Most presidents had separate beds and some even had separate rooms. But thanks to the pills, Betsy slept so soundly that her husband could toss and turn to his heart's content without waking her up. Except this one night.

Betsy was sound asleep until she was suddenly awakened by her husband talking loudly. She looked over and thought he was on a call, that there was a real emergency, but he was sleeping, obviously having a dream. She was about to go back to sleep herself, when his mood changed from being angry. A smile crossed his face, and in his sleep he was kissing someone. He said, very clearly, "Susanna . . . Susanna."

Betsy got out of bed and went to the bathroom. She didn't know how to react. She was tempted to wake him up and have it out right there, but she decided against it. It was a dream, after all. But that didn't make her feel any better. She took a second pill and went back to bed. She would deal with this in the morning. And as she was getting drowsy and ready to fall off, she heard him again. "Love you . . . so much." Now she was furious. But the second pill was too strong, so she closed her eyes and, filled with rage, fell back asleep.

When morning came Betsy said nothing. The President was already downstairs when she woke. She sat up in bed and wondered if it had been a dream. No. She knew it wasn't. She decided to address it, nothing too heavy, just a comment at the right moment. *Screw the right moment.* After a shower, she went downstairs.

Bernstein was in the Oval Office with John Van Dyke and the French ambassador. Betsy asked to see her husband. She said it was important. The President's secretary never said no to Betsy, no matter what was going on, so she buzzed Bernstein and told him his wife was outside. "Please ask her to come back in an hour," he said. He heard his wife say, "I want to see him now." In a second, Bernstein opened the door and smiled. "I'm in the middle of something, can this wait?"

"No." His wife rarely said that. Maybe it was bad news. After all, what good news comes with the caveat of not being able to wait? Instead of asking the men to leave, the President took his wife into a side office.

"What is it? Is something wrong?"

One of the good qualities about Betsy Bernstein was that with people she knew, she wasn't a bullshitter. She performed her job well as First Lady and acted as if she were charmed by everyone she met, even if she felt nothing, but with the people close to her she always spoke her mind. "You told another woman you loved her in your sleep last night."

The President reacted as if a medicine ball had hit him in the stomach. He said nothing. Then he decided to laugh. "In my sleep? Who?"

"Susanna Colbert."

"I said two names? I said, 'I love you, Susanna Colbert'? That sounds odd and corny, doesn't it?"

"You didn't say her last name, but there is no other Susanna."

"Betsy, I can't take a position on what I say in my sleep. Sometimes I have dreams of monsters and war and people I have met just once, and if I said 'I love you' to someone in a dream, then that's where it should stay. In the dream. I don't feel like apologizing for a dream. Haven't you ever had a dream of another man?"

"Only sexual. Never love."

The President was surprised. This was going to turn into more information than he wanted to know. "Well, there you go. You could have easily said a man's name and if I was awake like you were I might have heard it. What *is* his name?"

"There are many of them."

"Many of them? Well, okay, there you go. You dream about having sex with many other men and I accept it."

"I am not in love with anyone else."

Bernstein could have and should have just said, "I am not, either." And for years afterward he wondered why he didn't. But he said nothing, which hit his wife like a ton of bricks. When he finally spoke, which was only a few seconds later but felt like an hour, he said, "It was a dream. I can't defend what I do in my sleep."

"Are you in love with her?"

"Who?"

"Goddamn it, Matthew, answer the question."

"I am fond of her. She is someone I need to talk to regularly. That's all I can say."

And with that Betsy left the office. The President thought about going after her but he didn't want an argument in the halls of the White House with everyone listening. He would deal with it later. Hopefully this would calm down. Hell, he hadn't slept with anyone. He hadn't embarrassed his wife publicly. He felt he could handle this. The one thing he *was* confused about was why he hadn't just said that Susanna meant nothing. Was he so involved that he felt loyal to her? *Did* he love her? Damn it, this was not something he needed now. Why the fuck wasn't his wife asleep when he was? It was her fault for being awake.

Susanna was in her office when Nate Cass called.

"How are you?" she asked.

"I'm fine. I have some bad news for you." Susanna's heart sank. If Nate couldn't do anything about the problem, then there was nothing left.

"Yes? What happened?"

"The President's mother passed away in the middle of the night."

"What?"

"At three A.M. They told me they tried everything but her body just quit. I thought you would want to tell the President first." Susanna had to literally pinch her leg so she wouldn't sound too excited. *How good is Nate at this?* To say he had bad news when he knew it was what she wanted to hear; well, he was just the best she'd ever seen. She was tempted to thank him profusely but decided to keep up the ruse as long as he did.

"Well, it's terribly sad, and I appreciate you letting me know. I will tell the President immediately."

"I will speak to you later, Susanna."

"Of course. Thank you so much. I mean, thank you so much for telling me."

Susanna wasted no time. She walked to the Oval Office and said she needed to speak to the President, that it was urgent. This time Bernstein was alone and when she walked in she just stood there with a stupid grin on her face.

"What is it? What happened?"

"Nate Cass called me. Your mother passed away last night."

The President simply did not know how to react. Jumping up and down was not an option. But in that one moment a huge problem had just been lifted. He looked at Susanna. He wanted to kiss her. He *did* love her. She had just taken care of the biggest problem in his life. And she'd done it perfectly. No one else could have accomplished it. But he decided to display no emotion. He thanked her as if she had told him some Treasury news and said he wanted to be alone.

"If you need anything else, Mr. President, please let me know."

"I will. Please tell John Van Dyke. He will prepare something for the press. Cass told you she died peacefully?"

"In her sleep. As peaceful as could be."

"Thank you, Susanna. I'll speak to you later."

Susanna left the office. The President was in emotional overload. He looked at the time. It was two-thirty in the afternoon. He hadn't had a drink before five o'clock in years, but today was going to be an exception. He pressed the intercom. "Get me a scotch and water."

And as he waited for his drink, he knew he needed to patch things up with Betsy. He would tell her he loved her and that he was overworked, and sometimes he got too dependent on people and Susanna was one of those people. She would have to understand. Betsy was a key reason why he had been elected president and he needed her. But he needed both of them. Why was that wrong? He was the president of the United States, for God's sake. If anyone was entitled to more than one woman, he was.

Lee Dong Wo, the grand architect of the new Los Angeles, and Shen Li, the new health minister, were not just good friends but had become a regular duo at gatherings, restaurants, and important meetings in the new city. They were like rock stars, photographed everywhere they went and written about daily.

Lee Dong was married and brought his wife and one child with him. They loved it. They were treated well and found the climate in Los Angeles, though it was hotter than in previous years, more favorable than their home in China.

Shen Li was still a bachelor. Forty years old and considered fairly good-looking, Li stood about five feet nine inches. He was a fit one hundred and fifty pounds, and one would describe him as friendly-looking. He smiled easily and often. He exercised every other day on one of the new virtual treadmills that rich people had in their homes and others could afford only at a gym. These treadmills were surrounded by moving scenery, so you could choose a mountain run, a run in the city, a run by the beach, whatever you wanted, and for the duration of your workout you felt like you were in that location. Scenery moved by you at any speed you chose, from a slow walk to a fast sprint, and when you added the wind, the sounds, and the smells, the experience was awesome.

Li had one in his temporary home in Santa Monica, a small house two blocks from the beach. The house had been severely damaged in the quake, but he had his men rebuild it quickly. His eventual home in the new city was going to be built to his specifications from the ground up, but for now, this would do.

He always had to laugh. Here he was two blocks from the ocean and he chose the treadmill "beach" setting instead. Of course, there were reasons for that. The real beach had an odor Li did not like. It was a combination of smells he couldn't really identify, something like fishy and trashy. Some people were sensitive to it, others weren't, but he couldn't stand it. So he ran on the perfect beach on his treadmill. He kept in shape, he dressed well, he was famous, and he was a catch.

Friends tried to set him up when he got to Los Angeles, but he was always too occupied with the great task ahead. He had dinner with a few different women and had sex with one of them, but it didn't amount to anything. The same way many American men liked Asian women, Li loved Americans. They were exotic to him. And he didn't go for the blondes. He'd thought that was what he would be attracted to, but as it turned out, he was nuts over the brunettes.

He liked women as tall as he was, not taller, and he liked a good figure. He had no real preference in religion, since he was not a religious man. He could tolerate most of the faiths as long as they didn't proselytize. He found Jewish women fun but a little annoying and he didn't care for Baptists, but other than that, he was fine with all types. And then one Saturday he went to a barbecue and met someone.

Laura Markum was the daughter of the senator from California, Stanley Markum. She had been married once, for three years, but had no children. At thirty-three years old she was simply beautiful. If Shen Li could have had a computer design the perfect American woman, this would be her. Five-six, long brown hair, a champion soccer player in school, dean's list at Yale, she was a prosecutor who worked in the DA's office and was known as "the killer." She had not lost a case in six years working for the city and now she was considering private practice, as she was being offered partner in one of the preeminent law firms in California.

Li was in the buffet line waiting for ribs when she came up to him. "I think what you are doing is fantastic. I was telling a friend of mine that the "big one" is going to turn out to be one of the greatest things that have ever happened to this country."

Li felt his face turn red. That normally didn't happen to him, but he was so taken by her.

"Well, thank you. Nobody would wish an earthquake this size on any city, but we are going to try to make it work in our favor."

They sat down and ate lunch together under an oak tree. They exchanged histories and anecdotes and genuinely had a terrific time. Li was wondering what the right moment would be to ask for her connections and to try to make another date, when she beat him to it. "Are you doing anything Monday night?" she asked.

"No."

"I'm having dinner with my father and his new girlfriend. Would you like to come?"

"Very much." So Laura gave him the particulars and they exchanged numbers. Li said what a great chance meeting this was.

"I don't believe in chances," she said. "I'm sure this was part of a plan."

"Well, that's okay with me. This is a good plan." Li reached out to give her a handshake good-bye, but instead she gave him a kiss on the cheek, and once again he turned red. "I look forward to Monday," he said.

"I can't wait," she replied.

And Li left the barbecue more excited about a woman than he had ever been in his entire life.

CHAPTER FORTY

Things had gotten back to somewhat of a normal relationship for Kathy and Max. When she accepted his generous loan she felt indebted, so she channeled that into more feelings of love. But what really made Kathy feel better was her new job.

Shortly after her twentieth birthday, she took the necessary courses online and got her real estate license. She started working for one of the larger realtors in Indianapolis, Premier Properties. When she interviewed with the company's owner, eighty-six-year-old Clyde Folsom, he liked her immediately, and the feeling was mutual. Clyde was shocked when Kathy said she had just turned twenty—he was sure she was ten years older—but he didn't care. There was nothing wrong with someone her age selling property, especially if she was good.

Though Clyde still came to work each day, he was slowly losing interest in the business. He didn't want to be doing this into his nineties. He had children, but none of them wanted to follow in his footsteps, which made him sad. He did not want to see the company that he'd built from nothing simply disappear. That was one reason why he was rooting for Kathy from the first day.

Kathy chose not to say anything to Max until she was hired. Her having a boss in his eighties wouldn't go over well with him. It seemed the more Max was frustrated, the younger the age group he hated. He used to hate anyone over seventy. Now he hated people over sixty. Kathy thought it was only a matter of time before he included fifty-year-olds, too. But when she finally told him, he was surprisingly supportive. "That's great," he said. "Maybe when he drops dead you'll inherit the business. I've heard of Premier Properties; I always see their name." Kathy smiled. She didn't want her boss to drop dead and she was certain she wouldn't inherit anything since he had plenty of children.

"I've got some good ideas," she said. "There's no reason he can't expand into other parts of the state. And his virtual showings are boring. There are better ways to show property without going there, and he's missing out." Max was happy she was involved with a new project, but his mind was really somewhere else.

He spent occasional evenings at Kathy's house but he mainly stayed at home, working there during the day and sleeping there most nights. They both were so absorbed in what they were doing, even though Kathy had no idea what Max was working on, that they started to lose touch on a daily basis. She still admired him for not living the life of a rich kid with his sizable inheritance. She also admired him for trying to make a difference, and she still loved him. Bailing her out of her immediate debt was such a grand gesture; how could she not love a man who would do that? But even though Max called it a gift, Kathy knew that if her job turned into anything at all she would repay him, just so she could feel good about herself.

About two weeks after she started work, Max stopped coming to her house altogether. They had not spent the night together for ten days. "Is anything wrong?" Kathy asked him.

"Absolutely not. I'm working on something that could be big and I've been working really late, so I just crash." Kathy was excited for him.

"What are you working on?"

"Just some ideas. You know what my goal is."

"Why don't you run for office?"

Max howled with laughter. "Right. Max Leonard. Congressman. I would rather kill myself."

"Okay. It was just a suggestion."

"I love you for it. I'll talk to you later. I have some guys coming over now for a meeting." Kathy was surprised. She didn't know Max was holding meetings.

"Anyone I know?"

"Yes. You remember Louie?"

"The biker?"

"Yeah. He's coming with another couple of guys. They're passionate. I like that."

"Is Louie smart?"

"He's passionate. That's more valuable. The whole point now is to actually do something, not just sit around and talk anymore."

"Well, it sounds like you're excited. I like hearing that."

"I love you, baby. I'll see you later."

When Kathy hung up, for the first time in ages, she thought about Brian Nelson. Brian had introduced her to this whole world through Louie. If it weren't for Brian, she wouldn't know any of these people, including Max. And that made her a little nostalgic. She didn't want Brian back, but she missed him, at least for a moment. However, Kathy's job was a lifesaver, not just because she needed to make money, but because now she had something to put her energy into. It was ironic that she was in love with Max Leonard and she was working for an old. But Kathy and Max were different in one major area: Max could write off an entire age group. Kathy couldn't. Try as she might, she couldn't hate Clyde Folsom. And why would she? He was taking on someone who had just gotten her real estate license and giving her a chance. So what if he was drawing more tax dollars than a younger person? Here he was trying to help someone younger. Kathy knew that Clyde wasn't doing it to spread the wealth; he was doing it because younger attractive women sold property. But selfish motives or not, Kathy finally had a job that might have a real future.

Selling real estate in the 2030s was quite different than at any time before. All properties were presented virtually in a compelling holographic style, so when a prospective buyer wanted to see the actual house or condo, they would go there already knowing they loved it. If the virtual tour was handled right, seeing the house was just a formality. Kathy even presented the "in person" visits as if the prospective buyer already owned it. She would say things like, "Are you going to paint this room?" or "Where are you going to put that beautiful painting?" If someone hesitated, she would say the house had a virtual buyer ready to close and they were going to do their "in person" tomorrow. Most people believed her and closed the deal on the spot.

Kathy sold eight properties in her first two weeks and made more money in a short time than she had ever dreamed possible. She was jazzed, and so was Clyde. He told her one day, "I've spent a lot of years building a business here and I would like to see it continue. My dream is that someone really smart will take this over one day and I will be a silent partner. Not too silent, mind you, but I'll go off and do some things I've thought about for years, and I could still count on an income. That's my dream. I just want you to know what my dream is."

"I appreciate it, Mr. Folsom. I like knowing the dreams of others. One day when I know you better I'll tell you mine."

"That would be fine, Kathy. I would be happy to hear it."

"Mr. Folsom, I had a thought. I think my success rate would be higher if I could be with the buyer on the virtual tour."

"Don't they do that at home, in their own time?"

"Yes, but there is software that would alert us and allow us to be present, which bigger cities are using but we still don't have."

"How much?"

"I think no more than twenty thousand." Clyde thought about it for a moment.

"How do you know they want us there?"

"I can be unobtrusive, but it certainly can't hurt. I would only know them better when they see the real thing."

"Okay. Do it. I trust you." Kathy was ecstatic. It felt so good to have an employer say he trusted her. And later that day, before she left, she stood in front of the building and looked at the sign, "PREMIER PROPERTIES," and she imagined herself owning this company one day. It was such a heady feeling.

The food was better on the ship than it was in Pasadena, but not by much. Brad Miller was two weeks into the rest of his life and his day pretty much consisted of getting up at seven A.M., going down to the second deck for breakfast, sitting outside until one, taking a nap until two-thirty, going for a long triple-deck walk or a swim until four, taking a steam, and then having dinner at six-thirty. After dinner he would take another walk, and if the weather was pleasant he would sit outside until eight-thirty and then either go to bed or watch some entertainment, or maybe play cards for small amounts of money.

After a while this routine felt like a job; he dutifully passed the time as if he were getting paid for it, but it wasn't so bad. However, he still wished the food was better. It was always buffet style on the ship. They had one fancy restaurant, which was never full because the meals there were not included; people would take visitors there or splurge on a special day, but most of the retirees did not like spending money, so the included buffet was where everyone ate.

The eggs at breakfast reminded Brad of when he was a boy at camp. They were too yellow, and though he was assured they were made from real eggs, he had doubts. The bacon was good, because how can you screw up bacon? The porridge was just okay. What he hated the most was the fruit. It was obviously from a can and it was always the same. Those peaches in syrup and those round things that must have been grapes but no one was ever sure. *Is it so hard to have fresh cantaloupe?*

Brad didn't really make any close friends for several weeks, but slowly he started to look forward to seeing one or two people he enjoyed talking to, and he even developed a crush. Her name was Barbara Nestor. Barbara was seventy-nine, but Brad thought she looked like a young woman. It had something to do with her body, which still was in nice shape, but more to do with his eyes, which weren't. She had a good sense of humor, loved to exercise, and one day, when they were in the pool, he actually got an erection looking at her behind. He felt wonderful. No pills, just thoughts, how great!

The President was giving his annual speech in front of AARP. The group had never really liked Bernstein. Some presidents gave the organization everything they wanted and some presidents had trouble with their outsized power. Bernstein was in the latter group.

His speech received polite applause with lines like "We must preserve the dignity of our senior citizens" and "No matter how old you are, you are still an American." But when he tried to hint about generational fairness, saying, "All Americans should feel they have the same rights whether they are one or one hundred," the audience just sat there.

Bernstein had almost lost the election because of his "generational fairness" platform. Fortunately for him, he was able to get an unusually strong turnout of younger voters, but those voters were fickle. After an election they disappeared. The older Americans had the lobbyists and the town halls and the time and energy to devote to politics; the younger people were too busy looking for work. And although the seniors were the parents or grandparents of the young, the older they got, the more selfish they became. They did not want to give up rights that were promised to them for any reason, even for their own children. Not one said, "My medical care costs too much, don't treat me, just give that money to my kids." It just didn't happen. So the question for any candidate dealing with equality was, Could you win without the seniors? And as time went on and the numbers of older people only increased, the answer was simple. *No.*

When he finished his speech, the President took ten minutes of questions. The first question out of the box was "Are you finding the people who have been creating the violence against us and putting them in prison?"

"We are making great progress in identifying the groups that are causing these problems," the President said. "The Justice Department is working vigilantly in this area."

The second question was about his mother. The President had delivered a heartfelt eulogy at her funeral and had hoped that she, along with the questions, would be laid to rest. But here it was again. She was dead and it was still coming up. "Mr. President, you campaigned against using excessive measures to keep people alive. But when your own mother was in that situation you seemed to have changed your mind. Don't you think that is hypocritical?"

"I have never said that if there is any chance of survival people should not be treated." Before he could answer further, someone blurted out the next question.

"Is China going to take over the country?"

"I hope so," the President joked. But realizing that these people did not have a sense of humor, he decided to wrap it up. "What is happening in Los Angeles is exciting. We are very hopeful as to the outcome. Thank you all very much for coming out today and have a great afternoon." And even though there were five minutes left for questions, he exited the stage. The applause barely lasted until he reached the curtain. They really did not like this man.

When the speech was over, Paul Prescott went back to his new apartment near Dupont Circle. He had moved out of his place with Owen Stein and was living alone for the first time in years. He had been dating Jack Willman, insisting that they still could see others, but slowly they were becoming an exclusive couple. And they were a good team.

Jack continued to feed Paul extraordinarily helpful information regarding the names of potential troublemakers, people who wanted to do harm to the seniors. Even though these were Americans who hadn't done anything wrong yet, and therefore were difficult to legally spy on, Paul took whatever names he could get and used his connections in Congress to alert representatives from those areas of the country about the potential troublemakers. A congressman, in turn, could talk to a local police chief and ask him, as a favor, to keep an eye on someone. It was never done officially, but it was at least something AARP could do preemptively, instead of just waiting for the next act of violence. One morning Jack reminded Paul about Max Leonard. "Remember that guy I told you about in Indiana? The rich kid?"

"The rich kid?"

"The one who started Enough Is Enough?"

"Yes, I remember."

"Well, there was a commotion in Dallas, where he was thrown out of a hotel."

"Why?"

"For harassing Dr. Sam Mueller."

"Why would he harass *him*?"

"I don't know. I'm just giving you a tip. This guy's name has been coming up more frequently. Have you seen a picture of him?"

"No."

"I'll send you one. He's handsome, like a movie star."

"Really?"

"If you saw him, you would stare."

"That's funny. A handsome terrorist. You don't see that very often."

"I've never seen it. The closest was Timothy McVeigh and he was ugly."

"Who?"

"You don't remember the Oklahoma guy?"

"No."

"Well, look it up. This guy's ten times better-looking."

CHAPTER FORTY-ONE

Shen Li had lived his whole life without falling in love, and now he couldn't stop thinking about Laura Markum. They had been almost inseparable since they met at the barbecue, and it was altering his life. He thought he had enough going on, being the most important force in health care change in the United States, but love was a whole different ball game. He hadn't realized the parts of him that were in hiding until they started demanding his attention.

Before Laura, Shen woke up each day and all he thought about was work. He was making great strides and the people of Los Angeles took to him like to a pied piper. Of course, he had an advantage. Anyone taking over from the army was going to look like Mother Teresa, but Li really did know what he was doing and it showed. He thought that his job alone would sustain him, which it did—until he met her. Now when he awoke, the first thing he thought about was calling Laura—that is, if she wasn't lying next to him.

He had been so nervous when they first made love. After all, Shen Li was a world-class nerd. He did have sex in high school, but he was the last boy known for his prowess. When he became one of the richest men in China, the ladies followed the money, and many of them told him he was a wonderful lover. He used to joke with a friend of his, "Isn't everyone good in bed if they have a hundred million dollars?"

But with Laura it was different from the first kiss. And the first time they made love, they really *did* make love. She thought he was the brightest man she'd ever met and she admitted to having an "Asian thing." She'd once had a professor at Yale who was from Taiwan and he was so brilliant, and she had had a mad crush on him, too. Laura loved smart. Cute wasn't bad, either, but with every ten points a man's IQ rose, she thought he was that much better-looking. And besides, Shen was always considered just fine in the looks department. He would neither stop traffic nor start it, but whenever he spoke he looked to her like a movie star.

As if falling in love with this woman wasn't enough, Shen fell in love with her father, also. It was mutual. Senator Markum obviously loved power and so did Li. The three of them had many dinners together and Li and the senator would talk nonstop for hours. Markum had been in favor of partnering with China in order to save his home state, and he thought they should partner up in all the other places in the U.S. that were deteriorating, too.

During one of their many nights out, when he was alone with his daughter for a moment, Markum said, "That is the best man you have ever dated. I'm crazy about him."

"I am, too."

"So don't waste any more time. Marry him, have children. He can go all the way and so can you."

"He hasn't asked me."

"Laura, the man would be your slave. He would sell his soul to marry you. Just make it easy. And do it quickly. Don't waste time like with that first one."

Laura left that particular dinner early, leaving her father and Li talking about steel prices and copper futures. When she walked into her house later that night the message center was lit up. She watched the screen as she got herself a glass of orange juice. It was Shen. "Sorry you left early. I love your father. I love you. I want you to marry me. I so love you."

Laura sat there. This was a new one. A proposal stored as a message. *At least the message center could have gotten down on one knee.* She got Li on the screen. "You ask me to marry you on a machine?" Li thought she was angry.

"I'm sorry. I couldn't help it. I love you."

"Well, I should give you my answer in a message, so disconnect and let me leave you my decision."

"Are you kidding?"

"No, disconnect." The screen went blank and Laura called him back. Li's face appeared in a recorded message.

"Hello, I am unable to talk to you now. Leave me the particulars and I will contact you." A red light went on and Laura looked into the camera.

"Yes."

Li called her back in thirty seconds. "Yes?"

"Yes."

"You make me the happiest man in the world."

"As you do me—woman—you know what I mean."

"May I come over?"

"I wouldn't sleep if you didn't."

"This is the happiest I have ever been."

"Me, too." And that was it. Laura Markum and Shen Li were engaged on a video link. It wasn't so uncommon anymore; there were even marriages performed this way. It was just something that Laura had never imagined when she thought of how the perfect moments in her life were supposed to unfold. Then again, her first marriage proposal *was* perfect. The restaurant on the beach, a beautiful ring, a violin player, the very best champagne, and the marriage stunk. So maybe this was a good sign.

The President had had his share of arguments with his wife, but he couldn't resolve this one. When Betsy was angry, she did not confront, she became passive aggressive. Her answers to questions were as few words as she could manage, and she didn't ask anything about her husband's day. If her husband had worked in a factory, that might have been understandable. But as president of the United States, his day was everyone's day, so not to ask about it was clearly hostile. This went on for about a week, until one night the President let loose. "Goddamn it, I have the hardest fucking job in the world, and I don't need the silent treatment in my own home."

"It's not your home. It's the people's home."

"Oh, screw you. What did I do?"

"You told a woman you were in love with her, and it wasn't me. *Comprende?*"

"In my sleep, Betsy. In my sleep."

"If it was only that, I would try to let it go. But we haven't been right for so long, that was just the icing. It took a long time to sink in, but I realize now that if it wasn't her, it would be someone else."

"That's not true."

"It isn't? You treat me like a secretary, and not the cabinet kind. I didn't run for this office. I serve as First Lady because you wanted to be president. I did this to support you. And now you seem to have left me behind. It feels bad. Can you understand that?"

"You have one of the most important jobs in the world."

"I never wanted it!" And Betsy walked out of the sitting room, trying to hold back her tears. The President followed her.

"You don't hate the job. Do you?"

"I wanted to be partners, Matthew. I'm all right with being a partner. Just like China. But if you're no longer there, what am I doing?"

"I'm here."

"No, you're not. We both know that. When was the last time we were physical?"

"Oh, stop it. It's hard to be physical in the White House."

"You're so full of shit."

Bernstein knew what he had to do at that moment to smooth this whole thing out. But he couldn't. He couldn't fire Susanna Colbert. He would look foolish having three people in that position in his first term. And he loved Susanna. That was the real issue. His head was throbbing. The person he wanted to call at that moment was the reason this was all happening. There were times like this when he was jealous of the religious presidents. *To be able to dump this in God's lap would be such a luxury.* But that wasn't an option for him.

Brad Miller had to admit he was adjusting well to his surroundings. He'd gotten used to the food, he liked his new friends, and he was falling in love with Barbara. He also liked the fact that the ship only moved about three months out of the year. Many of the passengers thought that being on the open seas was what it was all about, but Brad liked the ports. They would spend a few months in the Bahamas, then Mexico, Florida, and California, alternating between San Francisco and Long Beach.

The first time they dropped anchor in Long Beach, Brad got a chance to see what the Chinese were doing with the city, and he was amazed. What everyone on the ship noticed first was the construction on four large desalinization plants. It took a great earthquake to finally wean California off the Colorado. When these plants were up and running they would supply fresh water from the ocean to sixteen million people.

Brad even took a day trip to his old neighborhood, where everything was now cleared. As it turned out, owners of condominiums were going to be given first choice and a favored price on new development, and if they chose not to return they would be given money, though not anywhere near what they had invested. It was unfair, but that was the only way it was going to be, and now that Brad was safely ensconced in his new digs, he was less upset than he would have been if he had remained homeless.

His son, Tom, was not happy with this outcome. He had been counting on that money to pay back the loans he'd taken out to help his father. But even he had to admit that, if it weren't for the Chinese, these properties would have sat rotting for years and there would be no money at all, so something was better than nothing.

The activity over the month they spent docked at Long Beach impressed everyone on *The Sunset.* At any given time there were at least a hundred ships from Asia, mostly Chinese, unloading what was to become the new Los Angeles. Sometimes on the larger ships they could see already-constructed partial buildings, which were unloaded and put on the backs of supertrucks.

Brad and his friends would sit outside and play a guessing game of what the construction was and where it was heading, and he could never get over how much had changed within his one lifetime. He remembered the first Japanese car he ever saw when he was a boy. It was a Datsun and everyone thought it was cute. No one believed at the time that it would be anything more than a cheap alternative to the great American automobile. And now the American automobile was no more. Sure, people bitched and moaned, but the fact was that the consumer ran the world. And the same reason Jews bought Volkswagens was the same reason the Chinese were now partners in the greatest construction project the world had ever seen. People wanted it done quickly, and at a low price, and that was the way it was always going to be. It started with cars, went to food and clothing, and now it was the very places they were going to live and work. Resistance was not just futile, it was gone. As long as the name sounded somewhat American, what was behind it was unimportant. Wal-Mart had known that fifty years earlier, and now everyone did.

Brad and Barbara Nestor were taking a deck walk one particularly clear afternoon when they saw a group of people gathered around someone giving a talk. "Who is that?" Brad asked.

"It's a new fella who boarded yesterday. He took Marvin's room."

"What happened to Marvin?"

"He didn't wake up."

"I didn't know that. When?"

"A week ago."

"My God, I kept leaving him messages about a poker game. Well, at least it was a DIS."

"DIS" was an acronym for "died in sleep," the gold standard way to leave life. When someone died in their sleep, everyone thought they were blessed; it was almost as if they didn't die at all. Some people actually thought that if you didn't know you were dying, maybe you weren't really dead, so a DIS was what everyone wished for when their time came. "So who took over his room?" Brad asked.

"Some suicide doctor. Masters."

"Walter Masters?"

"That's it. You know him?"

"I know *of* him. He's famous. After the quake he was down in Los Angeles helping the suffering."

"You think he's moved here to up his business?"

Brad laughed. It wasn't so far-fetched, but Masters had never had a reputation as a murderer. He was someone who was there if you needed him. However, it was a little odd that he was now living right down the hall. "I'll have to be careful not to complain too much when I'm feeling lousy," Brad joked.

They walked over to where Masters was holding court. Twenty or so people were gathered around him, listening to his stories with rapt attention.

The few people who were known to practice euthanasia had become famous among the older crowd. It was as if they held the power of life and death in their own hands. And when people did meet Masters, they always liked him, because he wasn't anything more than a man with knowledge that others were afraid to talk about. It wasn't difficult to look up the information on what medications or potions could end your life, but when that information was one man's specialty, and he actually practiced it, it gave that man an aura. He was a celebrity, whether he liked it or not.

Brad and Barbara sat down while Walter was in the middle of what would be a thousand stories that everyone wanted to hear. "So I asked her if she was sure," Masters said. "And when she said yes, I took out my old laptop. I had designed a program where the individual had to press the 'return' button three times before the end."

"Three times?" someone asked.

"Yes. Three steps before the injection. That was to make absolutely sure that they chose this of their own free will."

"What did the steps say?"

"The first step said, 'Are you aware that what you are doing now will cause death?' The second step asked the same question but in a different way. And the third step said, 'If you press "return" now, that's it, you will never return.'" The people laughed. Walter loved that joke.

"Did anyone change their mind at the last minute?" a woman asked.

"No. Not one."

Someone else asked if he still performed the service.

"No. I came on this ship like you folks. This is my retirement. I no longer practice."

"But what if someone was suffering?"

Masters looked at the person who asked the question. He smiled. "I might help you throw them overboard, but that's it." Everyone laughed. And in a strange way they all felt safer than they had before Masters arrived. It was as if the man who could end their suffering was now one of them. Just the knowledge of that took away some of the anxiety of death. And how could that be a bad thing?

CHAPTER FORTY-TWO

Susanna Colbert was having dinner with her Chinese counterpart when her wrist tingled. She looked down and saw her assistant. Susanna was informed that Nate Cass was on the line. She excused herself and went to a corner where she could talk privately. It was funny; they'd finally come up with a working Dick Tracy device to communicate with, but no one had figured out the privacy aspect. You still had to either whisper into your wrist or walk someplace where you were alone. And even if people couldn't hear you, they could look over your shoulder and see the face on your watch. There was no privacy in the future. "Hello, Nate."

"Susanna. I hope everything turned out for the best."

Susanna knew that Nate Cass was not calling to chat. He had done her a huge favor, and she had been wondering when it would be called in. This seemed to be the moment. As soon as he said he needed to meet in person, she knew the favor would not be a small one. Nate said, "I'm going to be in Washington next Tuesday. I would love it if you would meet me for a quick lunch." Susanna pressed a button on her watch and her schedule was superimposed over Nate's image. She knew that whatever it said, she couldn't say no. The reason Susanna was so successful in business was that she followed the unwritten code of "You scratch my back,

I'll scratch yours." By the urgency in his voice, it seemed Nate wanted a total body rub with release. But she was going to keep her word.

"Tuesday is a monster for me, but I'll make time because it's you."

He didn't thank her, he simply said, "Noon or one, you pick. We can have a bite at the Emerald."

The Emerald was one of the newer hotels in Washington. It was designed like a monument: tall and thin, and if someone didn't know any better they might have thought that was what it was. It came to a point at the top and at that point there was a restaurant that overlooked the city. The restaurant had a number of private rooms that had their own entrances, so even though it was a tourist attraction, people could hold a meeting there and not worry about being seen. Except, of course, by the hotel staff, but that wasn't who people tried to avoid; they didn't like the gawkers and the tourists with their shirt cameras who could take a person's picture just by walking by.

It had been so odd when the first shirt that had a camera disguised as a button hit the market. The second button down from the collar looked no different from the others, except that it could capture perfect video and sound, and people had no idea when they were being photographed and recorded. Someone on the street could be taking your picture without holding anything or even giving any indication that they were paying attention. Basically, it was the clean underwear syndrome gone mad. Every time you left your house you'd better look like you'd want to if you were broadcast to the world, because that's exactly what happened, especially if you were famous.

In 2022 the first person caught on a shirtcam was one of the biggest male movie stars in the world. He was alone, or so he thought, sitting in his car with another man, with his pants down. Someone walked past and got into another automobile. The person didn't have anything in his hands and they didn't even seem to notice, and that night the image of two men having sex in a parked car, one of them a matinee idol, was everywhere in the world. It wasn't even the fact that the star was messing around with another guy, it was that he left his hair at home and he looked forty years older. The combination of bald and gay was a killer. It dropped his asking price by twelve million dollars.

Nate was waiting in a private room when Susanna walked in. "This is some hotel," she said, trying to make light conversation.

"Let's get to the point. I need a return favor and I need it quickly." Susanna didn't even have time to order.

"How can I help you, Nate?"

"My brother Charles—you know him, I'm sure—is in the middle of a very messy audit."

Susanna's face fell. She hadn't known what the favor was going to be, but she'd hoped she wouldn't have to interfere with another government agency. Nate continued. "Apparently he put a large amount of money offshore, not as a tax dodge but as a holding place until he could reinvest it. When the time was right he was going to pay his taxes, but they discovered the account and now they not only want the taxes but they are looking into his entire business. As you know, Charles is worth fifteen billion dollars. To have all of his businesses investigated would be a nightmare."

"Don't you think it's a little unorthodox to wait until you're profitable before you pay taxes?"

"Be that as it may, I would like to see the audit called off and I would like to see Charles left alone by the IRS. Just end this. He will pay the taxes due and that will be it."

Susanna thought about this request. Not since she had become Treasury secretary had an illegal favor been asked of her. Quite frankly, she didn't think she even had the power.

"I want to help you, Nate, you know that. You were helpful to the President and he knows it, but this could get ugly. I don't think I have the power by myself to stop an audit of this size."

"You don't, Susanna. It will take the President or John Van Dyke at the very least. But it can be done and you know it. This is what I am asking for in return for ending the President's, how shall we say, dilemma."

"I understand. Let me do what I can. I want to repay you for the favor."

"Thank you."

"Do you want to order?"

"Not really. I think we had a successful lunch and we saved a couple of thousand calories."

Nate got up and put two hundred dollars on the table as a tip. He gave Susanna a fake hug and then left. She sat there alone, her head hurting. Her honest government cherry was officially broken.

Over at AARP, Paul Prescott had a bulletin board where he put up the pictures of people who either had already committed crimes against the olds or were under suspicion. That morning he added Max Leonard. *Why would a guy who looked like that, and had money to boot, waste his time doing this?*

When Robert Golden walked into Paul's office and first saw the photos, he had no idea what Paul was trying to accomplish. "Why are you collecting these? Shouldn't the FBI be doing this?"

"Hopefully they are. But it doesn't hurt if we do it, too. I'm trying to see if there's a pattern here. Maybe if we can understand these kinds of people, we can figure out how to stop them."

"Well, that's a noble thought, but I think the only pattern you're going to find is that these people are all young. No old people are killing their own."

"But why would someone who's rich, like this Leonard guy, care so much about this issue?"

"Who knows? Maybe he had a grandfather who abused him."

"So you think he hates old people because of that?"

"Listen, Paul. I think it's great what you're doing. You're a smart guy, and if you can find something that ties this together, then that would be helpful, but this isn't your job. I think all of your time should be spent trying to get Congress in line so that if Bernstein ever decides he's going to keep his campaign promises on life extension, we'll be there to stop it."

"Does he even have the votes?"

"Not now. But the violence is having an effect. Did you read the editorial today from the mayor of Chicago?"

"No."

"I printed it out. Read it. Don't worry about catching guys or figuring out a pattern. Here is our clear and present danger." And Golden put the editorial on Paul's desk. It was titled, "Enough Is Enough."

"Jesus, does the mayor know there is a revolutionary group with the same name?"

And as Paul read the editorial, it sounded as though any one of the people on his bulletin board could have written it. It said the transfer of wealth was long overdue. That it was time to give young people a break.

And one line stuck with Paul because he thought it could catch on: *If we don't improve our youth's chances for a better life, we will one day hand this country over to a generation that does not want it.* Paul thought a line like that could only cause more trouble. It was time to ask a favor.

Paul knew a gay conservative writer he had once been set up with. They had had a pleasant evening but no connection. The writer had a sizable following, more so among Washington elite than regular people, but he was read widely. Paul had not spoken to him in almost a year. He appeared on the writer's screen. "It's Paul Prescott."

"My God," the writer said. "How are you?"

"Well, I'm hanging in there."

"A lot of shit going on with your organization, huh?"

"You can say that. I wondered what you think about the violence?"

"What I think? I think all these young people should be executed. Get a fucking job and stop whining."

"I *knew* it. I knew that's what you think. Will you write about it?"

"No."

"Why?"

"Because I understand it. I don't like it, but I get it. Don't you?"

Paul was silent. He couldn't really say he didn't understand it, but so what? There were a lot of things he understood but still wanted stopped. It was clear why all terrorists hated their targets, but that didn't mean you didn't try to kill them. "Are you there?" the writer asked.

"Yeah. I'm just thinking about what you said." Paul didn't have the energy at that moment to try to convince him. "Hey, if you don't want to write a support piece then so be it. I just love your writing and thought you could help the cause."

"That's cool. Listen, keep in touch. If I change my mind, I'll let you know."

"Thanks. Good to see you." And Paul clicked the man's face off his screen. The conversation made him glad they had never really connected. And anyway, Paul thought the guy wasn't aging well.

It's amazing how fast you can turn on someone when he disappoints you.

CHAPTER FORTY-THREE

The wedding was a big affair. Senator Stanley Markum let loose. Shen Li was gaining a great deal of fame, not just in political circles, but among average people, too. As health care in Los Angeles was slowly transforming and people started to feel that someone was really concerned about their well-being, Li was hailed as the one person who finally made a dent in a system that had frozen in time.

At first Li staffed the small clinics with Chinese nurses and doctors who'd been specifically brought over to get everything started, but it had always been his intention to train Americans to share in the work. So Li found himself speaking to medical schools and colleges and especially vocational schools. His English was near perfect, just enough of a challenge to make him sound cute. And he was a brilliant speaker. He not only had passion and a record of success, he also spoke with great love for America. He was becoming one of the most requested speakers at every big event. They billed him as the new minister of health. It wasn't quite true—there was no such position—but it sounded great and people lapped it up.

Markum held the wedding outside of Los Angeles, near Santa Barbara. It was on a rambling estate that overlooked the ocean. The main house had had to be torn down because of the quake, but the grounds were intact, and when all of the decorations were finished, it looked like a fairyland. It was a coveted invitation. This was the joining of a powerful American family with one of China's most successful men. The wedding itself represented exactly what was happening to the country.

Senator Markum had always wanted Li to meet Dr. Sam Mueller, so Mueller and his wife were invited, and had accepted. Li, of course, knew who Mueller was and was in awe. "I can't believe you are at my wedding. I would look at your picture when I was a boy in China and I would think that you are what I wanted to be."

"I'm flattered," Mueller said. "I heard you speak a month ago, not in person, but I watched it and I thought what you are offering this country is long overdue. I think you are going to have great success."

"Thank you, sir."

"I mean it," Mueller said. "I have always been in the business of miracle drugs, but without care itself taking a huge step forward, the health system can't survive. I admire that you recognize that."

Li could only grin. He was used to great things happening in his life, but once in a while you have to stand back and just gawk at your own existence. Here he was marrying an American princess and being complimented by the man who cured cancer. All in the same day. He just hoped he didn't wake up and find himself back in elementary school. *Please don't be a dream.*

After the dinner and some dancing and a lot of drinking, the senator took the microphone and asked everyone for their attention. He held up a glass of champagne and made a toast that was not expected.

"Ladies and gentlemen, it is not often that you can genuinely surprise someone. As many of you know, we have made a fast track to citizenship for the good people who are here from China helping Los Angeles rise from the ashes. Those who stay two years and want to continue living and working in this great country will have the opportunity to do so as a U.S. citizen. My new son-in-law will be one of those people, but I wanted to speed things up a bit and get him something for his wedding that he would truly remember for the rest of his life." Markum then reached behind him and brought out a plaque. "Shen, the Congress has voted you an honorary citizen of the United States of America." People applauded wildly. "Just so you know what an honor that is, the last person to receive this was Winston Churchill. On this, your wedding day, I give to you one of the best gifts in the world, full citizenship in our great country. Congratulations."

There was more applause. Li's parents, who had only been on an airplane once before when he brought them to Beijing, listened to their Nextron translate what the senator had said and wept with joy. From beginnings that were beyond humble, their son now looked as if he'd achieved everything there was in this life.

When the last person had left the party, Li and his new wife were finally alone. There was a guesthouse on the property that had not sustained irreparable damage and that had been fixed up just for this event. They sat together by the fire and Laura made another toast. "To my husband and my soul mate. Together we will conquer the world."

Li laughed. "What's left?"

"I have some ideas."

And they kissed and kissed again and both felt as if they were blessed by God, though neither believed there was one.

When Susanna Colbert told John Van Dyke of Cass's request, he was furious. "How the hell did I not know this was going on?"

"I don't know how much the President tells you, John. That isn't my business."

"So Nate Cass killed his mother?"

"Well, I don't think that is the way to phrase something as difficult as this."

"Susanna, don't give me this bullshit on how to phrase things. He pulled the plug and now he wants the IRS to do the same thing. That's what you're asking."

Susanna knew when it was time to stop the doubletalk.

"Yes."

"I'm really upset. I'm upset that this is illegal and difficult and I'm upset that the President did not confide in me what you were up to."

"That isn't my fault. I don't control who the President of the United States tells his business to. I did a favor and now the favor has to be repaid."

"And what if it isn't?"

Susanna hadn't thought of that. She'd just assumed this would be quid pro quo. Nate Cass was not just stupid rich but vindictive as hell.

"I wouldn't want Nate as my enemy, John, especially if I had to run for office again."

Van Dyke did not want to discuss it further. He had to make some tough choices. He could say no. He could ask the President to intercede, but that would be dangerous, bringing an illegal request directly into the Oval Office. He could try to handle this himself. He didn't know what the answer was at that moment, so he did nothing.

Susanna left the meeting feeling a bit betrayed. She presumed every single thing the President thought or did was cleared by John Van Dyke. If she'd known she was doing this alone, she might have corrected the situation while there was still time, but now she was in a bind. She didn't want this gesture to come back and bite her in the ass. Should she go to the President herself and explain? No. There was a chain of command and it must be followed. She didn't know the answer, either, so she also did nothing.

As time went on, Betsy Bernstein was feeling worse, not better. She felt she'd devoted her life to her husband, at the expense of her own ambitions. Something was changing inside of her, and each day she felt less like she could spend another four years in this charade. She finally broke down and shared her misery with her sister.

Her sister, Lori, was a child psychologist. They had never been very close, but as Betsy's world closed in when she got to the White House, she found her sister to be one of the only people she could really trust. And now that her husband was no longer serving in that capacity, Lori was essential for her well-being. Betsy called her late one night.

"Hi," Lori said. "I can't see you."

"I just wanted to do voice tonight, is that okay?"

"Of course. Are you all right?"

And Betsy just poured her heart out, telling Lori everything. Lori was one of those people who thought positively. She believed that things would always work out for the best. But as she heard her sister deep in pain, she couldn't offer much in the way of hope. And then Betsy said something that her sister didn't know. "Lori, I don't think I was ever really in love with this man. I respected him and I admired him, and I was willing to be his partner, but if that is no longer cherished, what am I doing? How many years do I have left? Don't I deserve better?"

Lori just listened. She didn't know where this was going. She knew Matthew Bernstein would run again, and she knew that no president had ever split up with his spouse, either in office or afterward. This wouldn't be a first that anyone would like to add to his résumé. But Lori heard Betsy's pain and, though she knew how she would advise her if she were just a friend, this was the First Lady of the United States, after all. And her sister.

"Honey, I hear you. I know how hard this must be. You just have to understand this is a very big decision given your public profile."

"You don't think I know that?"

"You will hurt his chances for reelection. That I'm sure you're aware of."

"Not necessarily. More people get divorced than stay married, he could get all *their* votes."

"Well, I don't know if people who get divorced want their president to get divorced. Do you know what I mean?"

"This is a tough job, Lori. I still have almost two years left on the first shift. There is no way I could sign up again feeling like I do now."

"I understand. I really do. You have to follow your heart, but maybe if you take a little time to yourself you can work this out. Can't you go to Camp David alone for a week?"

"I don't want to go to Camp David. It's the same as here; the beds are just more uncomfortable."

"Well, you can come stay with me for a week. We have no room for the Secret Service but we would love to have you."

And as Betsy listened to her sister's advice, she realized how few options she had living in the most public bubble in the world.

"Thank you for listening, honey. I'll talk to you later."

"Anything I can do, Betsy. If you want, I can come there for a few days."

"That would be nice. I would like that."

"Okay. Let me see if I can clear some time. I'll let you know."

"Thanks. I love you, honey."

And Betsy disconnected, not feeling an iota better.

CHAPTER FORTY-FOUR

"Would you like to see the house in person?"

"Yes. That was the best virtual tour I've ever taken. Unless there's something I missed or the inspection turns out negative, I see no reason that I won't buy it."

Kathy Bernard was beaming. The extra expense to upgrade the virtual business had resulted in five additional sales for the month. For the first time she made enough money to pay back some of the medical loan. She felt like an adult and it suited her just fine. She was also growing very fond of Clyde Folsom. Kathy realized that this was the first older person she'd had any major contact with. She had lumped them all in the same group as Max did, but knowing Clyde made her wonder if that was such a good idea.

"You sold another?" Clyde asked.

"Well, I have to meet her there to close but she certainly bought virtually. And this house, unlike some, reads even better in person."

"Any inspection issues?"

"I had the inspector come out when we took the listing. There was some termite damage, but I fixed it."

"You know, Kathy, one would think all Realtors would do that, but you'd be very surprised at how many people I've had working here who wait until the sale to inspect. And how many sales get reduced or simply go away because some cranky guy with a tool belt says a floor is raised or there's a water spot. You're really on the ball to do that first. Who paid for the termite fix?"

"We did. But I added it back in the price. Actually, I tripled it."

"So we made money on the termites?"

"Yes, sir."

Clyde sure did like her. He had a daughter ten years older than Kathy who'd gotten hooked on downers, and he'd spent a lot of money and worry trying to get her clean. His daughter finally moved to Canada and married a waiter, and Clyde hated to admit it, but he was happy when she became someone else's problem. He saw her once a year at Christmas and she always looked fine, but he stopped asking if she was off drugs. When she had a child, Clyde just assumed she'd cleaned up, but he didn't want details. And the funny thing was, he usually loved asking personal questions. He thought it was the one thing that made him successful at his business. He used to say, "The better you know someone, the better you can sell them the right house." It just didn't apply to his daughter.

Clyde met Max Leonard only one time and, of course, hated him. Even though Max feigned politeness for Kathy's sake, Clyde saw right through it. When Max left, Clyde couldn't help himself. "How long have you known that man?"

"A while."

"I see. Are you in love with him?"

"Am I in love with him?"

"When you repeat a question it always means no."

"It means no?"

"Boy, you *really* don't like this guy."

"I am in love with him. He has been very good to me and I love him."

Clyde smiled. "Okay. What does he do?"

How could Kathy get into this with Clyde Folsom? What should she say? *He's head of an organization that wants people like you dead?* That wouldn't come off right. "He's an organizer."

"What kind of organizer?"

"He works with the younger generations. He's trying to make things fair." Kathy hoped that would put an end to it, but of course it didn't.

"What's unfair, exactly?"

Kathy knew the answer and was capable of having this conversation, but here was a man who was giving her this terrific shot at independence, and what good would it do to get into this with him? Fortunately, as she was thinking of a way out, her wrist vibrated. "It's my client. We can discuss it later, but it's pretty boring."

"That's okay. Go back to work. But if you feel like talking I'm always here."

"Thanks. I know that." And when Kathy walked away, she realized how much Clyde made her miss her dad. This was the first time since Kathy lost her father that she felt like she was standing on her own two feet. She felt that Brian and Max, the men who had filled up the last few years of her life, were there primarily to lean on. And Kathy didn't even know who she was when she wasn't leaning. But that was changing. One of the things she was looking forward to the most was paying Max back the money. He kept saying it was a gift, but she didn't want that; it made her feel like a child, which she hated.

Late that afternoon, when she closed the deal on the house, she wrote a check to Max Leonard for fifteen thousand dollars and decided to surprise him. It was only a small part of what he'd loaned her but it was a start, and that was important. Checks were not really used that much anymore, but they were still accepted, and it was still a meaningful way to hand someone a large amount of money.

Ever since Kathy had come unannounced to Max's house and looked in the window, ever since she'd seen the Sam Mueller wall, she always called first before coming over. She didn't want any more surprises. But this time she thought it would be great to appear at his door with a check and a kiss.

When she pulled up to Max's house there were two motorcycles and three other vehicles parked in the driveway. There was also an electric scooter by the front door. Loud music was coming from the inside and Kathy froze for a minute. *Is he having a party? Is he cheating? Maybe coming here was a bad idea.* But before she could change her mind, Max saw her through the window and came outside. "Hey, what are you doing here?"

"I was driving home and I had a surprise."

"A surprise? Great. Come in."

He gave her a quick hug and told her he was having a meeting with his associates but she was welcome to stay, at least for a little while. When Kathy walked inside there were six guys sitting around the living room, drinking and obviously in the middle of some kind of discussion. There were pictures and maps and what looked like a large model of a ship.

"What's that?" Kathy asked.

"That's a boat. Andre built it." Max pointed to one of the men. Kathy didn't know any of them except Louie. Louie looked bigger than she remembered. Whatever drugs he was taking, they made his head look huge. The other men looked foreign, either from Mexico or Europe or somewhere in Asia, Kathy couldn't tell.

"Why did he build the boat?" she asked.

Max's smile left his face. He wasn't in the mood for Twenty Questions. "He's a model maker. It's what he does."

Kathy sensed she was not welcome. She said she was sorry to interrupt, that she would call Max later. As she headed for the door, Max followed her, and when they got outside she gave him the check.

"What is this?" he asked.

"It's the surprise. I'm going to be able to pay you back. I just wanted you to know."

"I told you it was a gift."

"I know, but I want to pay you back." Max looked at the check and tore it up.

"I don't want the fucking money back. It's yours. You don't return a gift. That's rude."

"Max, it was too much money. I'm doing well now; I want to pay you back."

"I don't want it back! Give it to that old fuck you work with. It will be that much less he'll steal from us!" Max was on something. His temper was too short and he looked irritated. She gave him a quick kiss on the cheek and walked to her car. She had a terrible knot in her stomach.

When Kathy got home there was a message from him. She always thought Max acted phony on his messages. Some people forgot they were being recorded and were just natural and other people acted for the camera. Max always seemed so theatrical whenever his face appeared on her screen. "Hey," he said. "Sorry if I was rude, but I really don't want the money back. It was a gift and let's leave it at that. I'm also going out of town for a few days and I'll see you when I get back. Take care."

And that was it. No "I love you" or any other salutations, just "take care." Kathy played it back, zooming in on his eyes. His pupils were like saucers. He was loaded. Some sort of speedy cocktail. She had noticed this months earlier, but before she could say anything, it stopped. Now it was back. These friends of his were obviously bad influences.

Kathy was tempted to get him on the screen and have it out at that very moment, but she didn't. This had been her best day at work and she didn't want to ruin it by having a big argument. She erased his message—she never liked to keep messages, anyway—and decided to treat herself to a bath and a glass of wine. She would make an effort to keep the good part of her day going as long as she could.

Laura Markum was now officially Laura Li. Over the decades women had vacillated between keeping their name or using their husband's name, or using some combination of both. But she didn't like Laura Markum-Li; she didn't like hyphenates, for one, and she had another reason. She thought her husband was capable of almost anything and that it would only help him to have a world-class American dame by his side, and with a Chinese last name at that. "Confuse 'em all," she would say.

Laura was a born producer. She was known as a brilliant prosecutor, but what gave her the most pleasure was pulling strings behind the scenes and watching the results. She had always been attractive and had a strong ego, so she wasn't looking for public validation. When she watched her father in the Senate she saw how some of the senators were always in front of the camera and others stayed in the background, but the ones in the background seemed to have all the power. That was who she wanted to be.

Li, on the other hand, loved the limelight. He loved the fame he gained in China and loved it even more in America. He thought that the more people knew his name, the easier it would be to get his ideas across. And Laura agreed. The first thing she did was to increase the number of his speaking engagements and also to raise his fee.

It was Laura herself who called Paul Prescott and suggested her husband be the key speaker at the big AARP winter meeting. It was going to be in Florida, and was the biggest event they held all year.

"I'm sorry, the vice president is already booked," Paul said.

"Shen will have a greater impact on these people. He will address their health concerns directly, and you can't tell me that any of them are not dying, excuse the pun, to know how Los Angeles is reshaping their lives." Paul thought a moment.

"May I get back to you?"

"Quickly. We have more offers during that time period than we can even consider. My husband would rather speak to the Economic Forum but this is my idea. I think AARP needs to hear what he has to say."

"I'll get back to you no later than tomorrow."

"I will hear from you then." Laura disconnected. She was no-nonsense about this kind of thing. She knew who her husband was and knew what a hot ticket his lectures had become. But she also knew how powerful AARP was in Washington, and she wanted this engagement.

Paul Prescott walked into Robert Golden's office and told him about his conversation. "Don't we have the vice president?" Golden asked.

"I think this is a better choice. We already had the president; the vice president might seem like a letdown. I think Li will address their needs directly, and he *is* married to a senator's daughter and *is* becoming world famous. I believe we can make his appearance sound like a much bigger event than the vice president."

"But we've already told people what a coup getting the vice president was. What do we say now?"

"We say that because of what is happening in Los Angeles and all of the success out there that we have just found out that Shen Li has canceled his speech in China and is able to come to Florida and speak to us."

"He'll cancel the China speech?"

"There is no China speech. You asked me what we would tell people and I gave you an example."

"Hey, you're good! And what do we tell the vice president?"

Prescott thought a moment. "We tell him we got someone bigger. He's used to that."

The Sunset had left the port of Long Beach and was cruising to Miami through the Panama Canal. The canal was still one of the wonders of the world and people aboard the retirement ship loved moving through the locks and watching it all happen. Brad Miller likened it to sitting in his dad's car going through the car wash.

The Panama Canal had had a major reconstruction that lasted twenty years, and now the widened locks could handle all cruise ships and most supertankers. A new class of supertanker had at first been too big for any canal, but the Koreans had had an idea: Their new supertankers would actually be two ships, joined in the middle. The ships could separate and both navigate on their own, or join up and form one ultralong vessel. This not only worked great going through canals but allowed the huge ship to travel the ocean as one and then break up and dock in two separate ports to unload cargo. It was known as a SplitShip and it became the new workhorse of international trade.

The day *The Sunset* was moving through the canal there was a SplitShip from India. Everybody gathered on deck to watch. It looked so funny. Half a supertanker moving slowly through the locks, while the other half was waiting on the other side. To watch them join up was really something. When the two halves came together, they made the same sound that blast doors at NORAD made when they closed, a low, massive thud that could be heard for miles, and then, as if by magic, the ship was one again. People sat on the deck of *The Sunset* and applauded when it happened. And it was all they could talk about at dinner.

Brad Miller was pleased that everything was turning out better than he thought it would. He liked his friends and looked forward to seeing them each day. And he loved having a lady in his life. There were no younger people around, except some of the crew, and they were paid to smile at the seniors. But no one missed young people. It became very easy to forget about the real world and just live on this floating universe.

"Let the young folks have the land," Brad would say. "We'll take the ocean."

When the ship pulled into Miami the residents were warned to be careful. They were told that when they went ashore they needed to go in groups, as there were youth gangs that would prey on the olds. They were always given that same warning, but this time it sounded more serious.

Another retirement ship that had just pulled out of port had had a homicide: One of its residents was knifed at a local restaurant. But the people on *The Sunset* weren't too concerned because they really didn't leave the ship very often and, when they did, they went en masse. Sometimes a hundred people would go together and cling like a school of fish. It was almost impossible to get robbed if you moved around like that, but the truth was, the longer they lived on board, the less they wanted to get off anyway. They got tired of buying the stupid hats and T-shirts and other souvenirs in the Bahamas or Mexico. Unless there was a big event or some unusual attraction, the residents of *The Sunset* enjoyed just staying "home."

CHAPTER FORTY-FIVE

The time had come for Matthew Bernstein to make a decision. Would he run again? It was never really a question, but it had to be addressed officially so fund-raising could start in earnest.

Normally, this would be a conversation he would have with his wife, but they were not communicating. Though Betsy was fulfilling her duties as First Lady, she had moved to another bedroom, and for the first time in their marriage she and her husband no longer slept together. This was not unheard of, but usually when presidents and their spouses slept separately they had been doing so before they reached the White House. When they started out sleeping in the same bed and then wound up in separate rooms, well, that caused people to talk.

John Van Dyke assumed they would patch things up, certainly before the President officially decided to run again, but it had not yet happened. They were sitting in the Oval Office late one night when Van Dyke broached the subject. "Matthew"—this was not something he called his boss often, it was always "Mr. President," but he used the President's first name when he wanted to get serious—"we have to make a decision. I assume we're going for another term. We don't have to announce it officially, but you and I have to be on the same page. You haven't mentioned it once." The President didn't answer. He stared at a painting of George

Washington on the far wall. Van Dyke thought he hadn't heard him. "Mr. President?"

"I heard you. I would like to continue in office." He paused. "I don't know if my wife feels the same way."

Van Dyke felt as if he had been hit with a right hook. What was his boss saying exactly? "I don't understand. She doesn't want to be First Lady any longer?"

"I don't think she wants to be my wife any longer."

John Van Dyke had dealt with everything imaginable, or so he thought, but was he really going to be the first chief of staff in United States history to deal with a divorce? He sat there trying to find something clever or witty or soothing—anything—to say, but he could think of nothing. Finally he mumbled, "I think a divorce would be hurtful to your reelection."

The President laughed. "You're telling me!"

"Does Betsy not enjoy the job of First Lady?"

"Betsy does not enjoy the job of being my wife. If she was married to someone else, she might tolerate being First Lady, but she has made it clear she does not want to do this again."

"So if you don't run, would that make her happy?"

"If I didn't run, the way I see it, I think she might divorce me anyway. She has fallen out of love with me. If she ever was really in love with me in the first place."

"Well, sir, that's bad news. I'm sorry you're going through this. Hopefully you will find a solution, but if worst comes to worst I think we can still work around it. After all, more Americans are divorced than married. Maybe we can spin it in a way that makes you sound like one of them."

"One of whom?"

"One of the divorced many."

"Great. Sounds like a campaign slogan."

"Mr. President, would it help to talk to someone? A professional?"

"Marriage counseling? Is that your idea?"

"What's wrong with it?"

"I'm in love with someone else and she knows it, that's what's wrong with it."

Van Dyke was not expecting that answer. He knew of his boss's affection for Susanna Colbert, but he had never heard the President say the words "I'm in love" until this moment.

"Susanna?"

"Of course. You know that."

"I know you like her very much. I didn't know you were officially in love."

"Officially in love?" The President laughed. "That's a good one. Maybe another slogan."

Van Dyke got up from the couch. "I have to think about this. I don't think it's insurmountable, but it certainly will depend on how this goes down, if it does. Would Betsy cause trouble or just leave?"

"How the fuck do I know?" The President started to get upset. "Will she give me her blessing with Susanna? I doubt it very seriously."

"I just meant that sometimes these things are done quietly and sometimes they are public and messy."

"John, for God's sake. I'm the president of the United States. How quiet do you think this will be?"

And of course he was right. No matter how this played out, if it actually happened it would be a national scandal for months. But in a strange way Van Dyke thought it might not be as damaging as it appeared. "Sir, would you marry Susanna Colbert?"

"Would I marry her? Why do you ask?"

"I don't know. If you were to leave your wife because you were in love with the brilliant secretary of the Treasury, well, it might make you seem like you care about the country, in a way. At least she's in the government. And the fact that she's older, well, if I may say so, it makes it sound like the love is real. That you didn't just go after some young assistant. Does that make any sense?"

The President hadn't thought about marrying Susanna Colbert. It was the farthest thing from his mind at this moment, but he couldn't blame his chief of staff for trying to think ahead.

"Listen, John, I don't know anything now. Let's not discuss it anymore tonight. I'm going upstairs to my separate bedroom and I'm going to read. Maybe everything will work out."

As Van Dyke was walking to his car, he started to think about his own future. He had worked for Matthew Bernstein for twenty years. What would he do without him? Not that a president couldn't be reelected if he were divorced. Just because it hadn't happened didn't mean it couldn't. But it would be such a hurdle. Perception was everything in politics, and even if you were the leader of a country with more debt than it could ever pay back, even if you were the leader that had gone partners with China within your own borders, even if you were the leader at a time when the youth had never hated their elders more, it still could seem all right if your wife loved you. If that went away, people might think something really was wrong.

No one gave serious thought to Nate Cass's proposal. No one except Nate, that is, who was running out of patience. A grand jury was going to be called to hear his brother's tax evasion case, and Cass knew that if this went on much longer, it couldn't be stopped.

Susanna Colbert had put it on the back burner. That was the advantage of being the secretary of the Treasury: There was so much on her plate that she could let things slide; something more important would always replace it. So when she looked at her wrist and saw who was on the screen, she got an uncomfortable feeling. "Hello, Nate."

"Susanna, there is a grand jury scheduled in two weeks."

"I didn't know that, Nate." And she wasn't lying; she didn't.

"If he goes before a grand jury, then stopping this will become messy and possibly unobtainable. Something has to be done now. Do you understand me?"

"I do. Let me see what I can do."

"That's exactly what I said to you. Except I delivered. I expect the same courtesy."

"I will get on it immediately." And she disconnected. She didn't have to be told that time was of the essence. The very fact that a man as careful as Nate Cass had had this discussion over a device, and not in person, showed how urgent this was. Susanna reached John Van Dyke.

"I just got a call from Nate Cass."

"I don't have time, Susanna. I have bigger fish to fry."

"John, he's upset. Did you talk to the President?"

"No. And I won't. He has other issues that are more important."

"But this could rear its head. Cass would be someone to contend with in a reelection. He wields a lot of power."

"Great. Maybe he can convince the President's wife not to leave him."

"What? What did you say?"

"I have to go now, Susanna. I'm sorry."

This was the first Susanna had heard this, at least the first time someone other than the President had mentioned that the Bernsteins were in serious trouble. She was at a loss. She had no idea how to proceed.

Max Leonard called Kathy and invited her to dinner on a Wednesday night, the day before he had said he was leaving town. She hadn't talked to him since he refused the money, but when she saw his face on her screen she knew she wanted to go. He picked her up and they went to Gino's, a family-style Italian place that had been her father's favorite, and she wondered if Max had chosen it on purpose. But Max had no idea. He'd even forgotten that they had eaten there before. He seemed very scattered.

"Why did you choose this place?" Kathy asked.

"I don't know. It was close. I let the car choose it. I put in 'Italian' and the car said this was good."

"Oh. I thought it was because of my dad."

"No." They sat there in silence and Kathy knew that something was wrong with him. He ate nothing, drank several glasses of water, and had trouble looking her in the eye. He was on something, but she wasn't sure what. Finally she addressed it.

"Are you all right?"

"Yeah. Why?"

"You're speedy and you're not eating and you're weird." Max didn't try to argue. He admitted it.

"I'm taking something for my testosterone."

"What's wrong with it?"

"It's too low."

"Is that safe?"

"It's fine. At my age your testosterone levels are supposed to be high; mine aren't."

"Did a doctor give you that?"

"Sure. Where would you think I got it?"

"In the mail."

"So what if it came in the mail? It came from a doctor. I sent my fucking blood in and he told me this is what I needed. Why are you giving me the third degree?" It took Max only a few moments at the table to lose his temper. Kathy felt depressed. She still loved this man, but she was watching someone leave her life and she didn't know how to stop it or even if she wanted to.

"I don't want to fight with you, Max. Maybe you should take me home."

"I'm sorry. I'm sorry I lost my temper. I have a lot on my mind."

"Like what?"

"I can't tell you because you won't approve. Ever since you started working for that old fuck, you're different. I'm still fighting the fight, Kathy. I still want equality."

"And you don't think I do?"

"You're working for *them* now. They've got you. Your principles have been compromised." Kathy got up.

"Take me home."

Max didn't seem to care whether they stayed or not. They left the restaurant and got in his car. He continued his rant. "You were once someone who saw the injustice and now your paycheck is coming from them. Do you realize that?"

"My paycheck is coming because I sell houses better than other people and I am earning it. I wasn't born rich like you!"

"I resent that. I gave you the fucking money to pay your father's medical bill so you wouldn't have to work for a fucking eighty-year-old."

"Stop the car."

"I'm sorry."

"Stop the car!" Max pulled over to the curb. Kathy got out even though she was miles from home. "I never asked for that money and I tried to pay you back and I'm going to pay you back even if I never see you again. I will put the money in your account whether you want it or not. Do not contact me. Something is wrong with you and you should see a doctor. And not a fucking doctor somewhere in Mexico who is giving you pills that are making you crazy."

And with that she walked away. Max pulled up next to her. He rolled down the passenger window. He just looked at her for a moment and then said, "I love you, baby. You'll understand soon enough. You will be proud of me." And he drove off.

Kathy sat down on the curb and cried. *How could such a strong flame burn out like this?* But that's what people always said. Too hot. Too hot to handle. Maybe there would be a miracle and he would come to his senses, unless he was already there. Her heart was breaking, but for the first time in her life she had something else to turn to. Not another person. A job. A career. And for Kathy, that was huge.

CHAPTER FORTY-SIX

Almost ten thousand people at the Miami Dome had paid to see Shen Li. Paul Prescott, who organized the event, was over the top with excitement. "This is much better than the vice president," he said to Jack Willman.

Paul and Jack were still dating, although Paul hated that word, but most importantly, they talked daily and Paul relied on him heavily for information. Sometimes Jack would say, "You only love me because I work at the Justice Department." Paul didn't even disagree. People love other people for what they do; there was nothing wrong with that, and if Jack got fired, Paul would deal with it then. In the meantime he was invaluable in helping Paul ease the fears of AARP.

A whole section of the monthly AARP news blast was called "Protecting Yourself." It contained everything from how to carry concealed weapons, to naming safe places to live, to suggesting the kinds of younger people to stay away from. The Justice Department had done sophisticated profiling trying to figure out who hated the olds the most. The disturbing result was that it was millions of younger people, such a large number it scared the hell out of everyone. But the Justice Department always made a distinction between the people who showed up for a rally and the people who organized it. And as with all protests throughout history, they thought that if they could bring down the organizers, they could contain the rest.

Max Leonard read the AARP news blast every month and expected to see his name under a section called "Troublemakers." He had mixed feelings when he didn't. Part of him thought he wasn't doing enough, and the other part thought he was being clever by flying under the radar. That part wasn't true. The Justice Department knew Max Leonard well and so did AARP, but until there was an arrest, his name would not be published. They chose not to warn him that they had him in their sights.

AARP membership demanded that their organization publish as many names as they could get their hands on. There were other groups vying for their business and one of them, the Association of Older Americans, promised it would spend whatever it took to stop the violence. It said it would hire private police in order to catch and prosecute anyone hurting the seniors. Its slogan was "We'll get 'em before the cops do."

So Paul Prescott had to match that promise, which was why the names that Jack provided him were so important. Even if they were bogus.

The night that Shen Li was scheduled to speak to AARP was also the night *The Sunset* pulled into port in Miami for its two-month stay. Over a hundred of the ship's residents had planned to see the event and had secured tickets weeks in advance. The ship's director organized three buses to take them, and everyone was so excited. Including Brad Miller.

Li was getting a reputation as a kind of health god. His legend was growing as fast as older people liked to gossip, which was constantly. And in a world where there was so much hostility toward those who had reached a certain age, to see a young man who liked the older people and could also improve their lives—well, it was like seeing the biggest rock star in the world.

Max Leonard and his five associates took a flight from Indiana to Chicago, and then on to Miami. They also planned to see Shen Li speak, but that was not the real intent of their visit. Leonard had come to the conclusion after his embarrassing confrontation with Sam Mueller that he had to do something really big. Something that would finally capture the attention of the country, maybe the world. Something that would change laws and redistribute wealth. Something that would give younger people a reason to hope. That was his dream. And he felt he was about to accomplish it.

In a strange way it was what Matthew Bernstein wanted, too. Bernstein had campaigned on taking the burden off of the younger generation, but he was unable to accomplish anything in that area. If going partners with the Chinese in the rebuilding of Los Angeles was a success, he would go down in history as a great president and he would certainly be reelected. But he couldn't help but think of what he'd wanted to do before the earthquake. It seemed that every action he'd taken since that fateful day was a reaction to what nature had thrown him. But his ambitions were still there, even though the China deal had put everything on hold.

And that was one more reason why the Max Leonards of the world were fed up. They were willing to work within a system if there was one. But now all anyone could talk about was California and how great China was and how maybe China would build up the rest of the country. The idea of a new America had now become only about its buildings and infrastructure. It was like someone had detonated an intellectual neutron bomb. What happened to the new America that was going to let younger people breathe and dream and not be saddled with debt? Younger people now felt as if the earthquake had set them back even more. And Max was determined to do something that even the president couldn't do: change the focus.

When Shen Li took the stage in Miami, the audience went wild. The older folks thought he looked so handsome, especially for a Chinese man. He showed them holographic images of the new Los Angeles, and he explained his ideas of putting "care" back in health care, showing people exactly how it could be done. When he asked, "Can you remember the last time someone knew your name as soon as you walked into a clinic?" the people in the audience broke out in applause. "Never," they responded.

And then Li turned to the elephant in the room. Their protection. And for the first time he sounded more like a lawmaker than a health minister. He told the audience that in his opinion, violence toward older people was simply unacceptable. He used facts and figures to explain to them how China had stopped this kind of violence in its tracks, and said he thought America should do the same thing. Then he uttered one line that would make people love him forever: "Getting old is a right, not a privilege, and young people must treat their elders with the respect and the dignity that they would want for themselves."

The audience stood up and applauded for a solid minute.

At that moment, Max and his group, who were sitting in the back row, had had it. This man was the anti-Christ. *What is he saying? That these old fucks need even more care? Great. Let's keep them going until they're two hundred and then young people can work in labor camps to make the money to feed them.* They didn't stay for the end. They went back to their motel and felt more empowered than ever. Someone had to stop this madness.

When Li finished his speech he received another standing ovation. Laura was backstage and felt as though it was her accomplishment, too. Her idea of getting him in front of this crowd had turned out perfectly.

Later that night Paul Prescott and Robert Golden held a small dinner for the Lis at one of Miami's most exclusive restaurants. At the dinner was the governor of Florida, the mayor of Miami, Laura's father, and another senator from Illinois.

It was Christopher Martin, Florida's governor, who said something in jest that planted the seed that evening. After a few drinks he toasted Shen Li and said, "If Congress can finally amend the Constitution and let this guy run for president, he'll win!" Everyone laughed and drank to the toast. But Laura Li had one of those moments that people dream about, a moment when the future is clearly laid out and all one has to do is follow it. She looked at her father, and it seemed from his expression that he had the same exact moment.

Watching Betsy Bernstein go through her daily duties as First Lady of the United States, one would never suspect that her marriage was ending. She had made a decision that she would not leave during the first term, even if it meant staying in separate bedrooms or spending more time away from the White House. But she knew she could not do this again.

She had to ask herself if it would change the way she felt about her husband if he did not choose to run for a second term. The answer was no. It wasn't about his job or her job, it was about the feelings that had disappeared from their marriage years ago, and Betsy wanted those feelings back, even if it meant finding another person.

No one on the President's team wanted this separation to happen, including Susanna Colbert. Susanna knew that Bernstein relied on her for emotional support and she knew that they probably were in love with each other, but she was practical. She loved her job, more than she had thought she would, and she wanted another four years. She was smart enough to know that if Betsy left her husband, everything would change, most of all her relationship with the President. And the fact was, she had no real desire to share the President's bed.

Susanna liked the arrangement she had with her husband and did not want to leave him. She rather enjoyed the sneaking around, having moments with the President of the United States that no one else was having. It was enough for her. But unfortunately, she did not get to choose.

And there was still the Nate Cass problem. John Van Dyke had chosen to do nothing. Susanna was on the receiving end of what were becoming more frequent and more threatening calls. Finally, Nate Cass came to Washington and insisted on one last meeting. This time he asked to come to the White House.

Susanna agreed to see him, and when he walked into her office he was blunt and quick. "I am not used to being ignored. Especially after doing a favor as big as this. I don't know what is going on, but the investigation is continuing. I will make it as difficult as possible for the President to have another term if something is not done immediately. That's all I can say."

"Nate, I'm doing what I can. I have to go through channels; this is not something I can bring directly to the Oval Office, and you know that. I'm doing what I can."

Nate Cass had no more sympathy and no more tolerance for excuses. "I want the favor returned and I want it returned *now*. That's it. You won't hear from me again. But I will be there when it's time to get this man reelected, and believe me, Susanna, you will want me on your side." Then he left her office.

Susanna thought for a long time. *Could he really use his money to keep the President from being reelected? After all, he wasn't a big Democratic supporter to begin with, so what would the loss really amount to?* Then again, she never wanted that kind of man as an adversary. So the problem was clear. Get his brother off the hook or endure his wrath. Either one seemed unpleasant, but if the Treasury Department was ever caught stifling an ongoing investigation, wouldn't that be worse than having Nate Cass as an enemy? That was a question that had to be answered immediately.

CHAPTER FORTY-SEVEN

They were in the middle of dinner when Jack Willman looked at his wrist. He spoke to someone but Paul Prescott couldn't tell who it was. The way Jack was whispering, Paul jokingly accused him of having an affair. "Can I see?" Paul asked. "Share with the whole class."

Jack motioned for him to be quiet. Whatever this was, it was serious. As Jack looked at the person on his watch and spoke softly, Paul could make out only a few words. Words like "When?" and "How?" and "How reliable is this?" When Jack disconnected he was white as a sheet. He said he had to go back to Justice, even though it was nine o'clock in the evening.

"What is it?"

"You know I tell you everything, but I can't talk about this until we're sure."

"It's me. Don't do that. Sure of what?"

"There could be an attack in the next twenty-four hours. Somewhere in Miami."

"Old people?"

"What else?"

"Jesus. I was just there!"

"The people we're tracking came to the AARP event."

"Come on! And you didn't tell me?"

"We didn't know it beforehand. They were seen leaving and going to a motel. If I'd known they were going to be there, I would have told you."

"Well, they didn't cause any trouble at the event. How do you know they're planning something?"

"Listen, this might be nothing, but they don't ask me to come back at this hour for the fun of it. If there's something planned that I can warn you about I will, but they're trying to catch these guys. If too many people know it too early it can ruin the sting."

"Jack, I'm not too many people. I'm in charge of the largest senior group in the world. I have to protect my membership."

Jack got up.

"I wouldn't even know what to tell you now if I did know something. The target isn't clear and nothing seems set in stone, it's just what we're hearing. Let me go to my office, and I swear to God if there's anything that can help you, you'll know first."

"How bad is it?"

"Paul, I don't know. This is early information. It may be minor."

"Can I come with you?"

"You know you can't."

"I'll be home," Paul said. "Anything, *anything* at all, you have to contact me immediately." Jack gave him a kiss on the top of the head and left the restaurant. Paul wanted to call Robert Golden—he wanted to be a hero with some secret information—but he didn't have anything concrete and he didn't want to be responsible for a sting going badly.

Max Leonard and Louie were in one van driving toward the port of Miami. Behind them were the four other associates. All of them were wearing uniforms that could help them pass for the retirement ship's personnel, the same generic white uniforms that everyone from the waiters to assistant captains wore. What made the uniforms look official were the pins.

The pins had a small holographic model of *The Sunset* that, when first made years earlier, had been hard to duplicate. But they had never been changed and Andre, one of the men on Max's team who was good at everything technical, easily made fakes that couldn't be distinguished from the original.

Each night in port, from eleven P.M. to four A.M., maintenance was performed on the ship. Garbage was removed and food supplies were loaded for the next day. Twenty-five people came and went, and some of them had uniforms and others didn't, but all had identification, which Max and his associates had also successfully duplicated.

They knew that if all six of them went on board together it would cause suspicion, but if two went with the garbage team, two went with the kitchen staff, and another two walked on board as if they belonged on the bridge, they could pull this off.

Andre, the one who built the model that Kathy Bernard had seen, knew these ships inside and out. He had the plans, he knew the nooks and crannies, and he had also worked on one for four months. He knew there were several easily opened storage rooms that people rarely used. One room, on the same floor as the infirmary, held extra medical supplies, everything from oxygen and spare beds to canned food and batteries. During the entire time Andre worked on board he never saw anyone go in that room. He even set up little traps, like leaving toilet paper on the floor just inside the door, something people would disturb if they walked in. After a week, the toilet paper was still there. So not only was this particular room viewed as safe, but it was large enough for the six of them and had food and bottled water to boot. Their plan was to board the ship in small groups and meet in this room at exactly three-thirty A.M.

The next morning at eight o'clock the ship was scheduled to move out of port and go three miles north to the berth where it would stay for the next two months. The retirement ships always overlapped each other. One would pull in while the other was nearby, ready to depart. That would allow people a day or two to mingle with their friends from other ships. The retirees always liked to see how the other groups were living—who had the cleaner pools, the better deck chairs, and the prettier women.

Max and his associates knew if the ship was tied up in port it would be difficult to accomplish their goal, but as soon as it was at sea, even if it was only going a few miles north to the permanent dock, they could execute their plan.

They were shocked at how easy it was to board. They had gone to all the trouble of trying to look like the real crew and no one, not one person, asked them for ID or anything. People who saw them smiled and walked right by. *Jesus, we wasted ten grand on these pins for nothing,* thought Max.

By four A.M., all six of them were safely ensconced in the storage room. Max congratulated Andre on his precise information. Max had never believed those movies about heists and bank robberies where there was always one guy who knew everything about the technical stuff, but that's exactly who Andre was. Born in France, Andre moved to America when he was sixteen, and was still a teenager when he watched his father lose everything. His father was so broke he just split, too embarrassed at being a failure.

Andre and his brother had to work instead of going to school just to keep their mother and sister from being thrown out of their crummy apartment. But Andre didn't need school; he was a genius at mechanical stuff. From the very first video game he ever played, it was as if he saw how things worked from the inside out. He was short and wiry and not very attractive, and girls didn't really take to him, which gave him even more time to bond with the machines. And when he first met Max at one of the early meetings, he felt like his purpose on earth was clear. He didn't want to make the big statements—he would let Max do the talking—but he loved being the technical guy, and he was perfect at it.

Max passed out speed patches. An hour before the takeover they would place them on the insides of their thighs. The concept was simple, but highly effective. Snorting methamphetamine was too much of a rush; it was too fast and then too steep of a drop. The speed patch, as it was known, delivered a steady amount of the drug for twelve hours. Then they could either sleep or put on another one. They felt the rush, but it was even, and sometimes it was mixed with newer steroids, which made them feel almost like Superman.

Without the drugs none of this would ever happen. It was a simple fact that nobody ever hijacked anything on the natch. Something was always used to pump up these kinds of people, even if it was just booze, and Max and his group loved the patches. Earlier in the year, when they first bought them, they used them far too frequently; it was just so much fun. Andre built the model of the boat on his first patch and did it in ten hours. "Jesus Christ," he said in his French-Belgian accent, "this would have taken me a week!"

Kathy Bernard had known that something was in Max Leonard's system when she came to the house that day, and then a week later when he took her to dinner. It was more than Max being jittery. It was a look. A look of abandon. He didn't even have that look when he climaxed; only the drug could produce it. But Kathy had no idea that these patches even existed. Then again, why would she? She wasn't the one who was trying to make history.

Senator Markum took a late flight from Miami to Washington after his son-in-law's triumph in front of AARP. His office was already deluged with communications regarding the appearance. When someone could arouse such large groups of people the way Shen Li did, everyone in politics knew about it instantly. The same way that political convention speeches used to make stars overnight, now the omnipresent delivery systems made it happen anywhere and anytime, providing the moment warranted it. And Shen Li's speech did. With countless millions of viral videos always in the air, only one currently showed a five-minute standing ovation given by thousands of older people. And Li's was it. People watched it over and over, only adding to his growing legend.

Markum was good friends with the Speaker of the House, a slight man named Henry Roman. Roman was from Oregon, and Markum had helped him get elected a decade earlier and was a big booster in his rise to Speaker.

The ebb and flow between the two houses of Congress never changed. There were periods when they hated each other and periods when they worked closely together. If Shen Li had come to prominence ten years earlier, it would have been impossible to even raise the possibility that Markum had on his mind. But with everything that was going on, with Los Angeles rising higher each day, looking more modern and beautiful than any other American city, what Stanley Markum was thinking did not sound crazy at all.

The two of them had a six-thirty A.M. breakfast in the Senate dining room. Markum simply told Roman that if the Constitution was changed, his son-in-law could be elected president. Roman didn't act surprised. In fact, he agreed. "He's a genius, that boy. And the people love him."

"So don't you think it's about time to amend the damn thing?" Markum asked him.

"I don't know. Maybe."

"There's no 'maybe' about it. When the founding fathers wrote the thing, China was on another planet and every other country was a threat. Wasn't the whole point of the United States to get *away* from the world?"

"Yeah. It sure was."

"Fine. So that's over. We're partners now. You watch. Los Angeles is the first one but other cities are going to follow. Hell, if I were Michigan, I would beg the Chinese to fix Detroit. And if this is going to happen, what the hell's wrong with letting a brilliant Chinese guy run things for a while? We still have Congress. We still can veto. We still have the Supreme Court. The whole country's not going to turn into Chinese, it just finally might make sense to let a brilliant guy take charge."

Henry Roman did not disagree. Finally, after a moment, he jokingly said, "Would you feel this way if he wasn't your son-in-law?"

"Damn right I would. But he *is* my son-in-law, and it wouldn't be the worst thing in the world to have the ear of the president of the United States."

"It's an interesting idea, Stanley. And maybe the time is right. Maybe it's exactly what we need."

Stanley Markum got up from the table. "Let's do this, Henry. If it can't happen now, it will never happen. The people love this guy; his country is saving our ass. Let's do this."

CHAPTER FORTY-EIGHT

The investigation of Charles Cass, Nate's brother, continued. A grand jury determined there was enough evidence for a trial. When Susanna Colbert heard the news she expected a contact, but Nate Cass was a man of his word and he did not talk to her again. Hopefully the trial would not go badly and Nate would have other things to do in his life that were more important than getting back at Matthew Bernstein.

What Susanna had not thought through was how much Nate Cass loved revenge. When someone has that much money, there are few things left that give real pleasure, and they usually involve either giving or taking. When giving gets boring, some of the very rich only get their rocks off by depriving others. One would think that after someone has made enough money to last several lifetimes this would dissipate, but the individuals who love revenge love it even more when they can afford it.

Susanna was tempted to contact Nate one last time to see if she could still smooth things over, but her days were too busy, so she let it go. She not only had the responsibility at Treasury, but the President wanted her to travel with him whenever possible.

At the moment they were on their way to Denver for a fund-raising event. Normally this would be a function that John Van Dyke would attend, not her. But Van Dyke said he needed to stay in Washington, that there were some pressing issues, and the President didn't really care. As long as Susanna was with him, he was happy.

When Bernstein left town, Van Dyke knew it was the right moment to finally have a private conversation with the First Lady, something he felt was long overdue. Betsy invited him to the residence and they sat in her upstairs office. She was very friendly, feeling almost sorry that he had been put in a position of marriage counselor. She pretended she didn't know why he wanted the meeting. "What's the problem, John? Something wrong?"

"Betsy, I haven't said anything to you earlier because I didn't know if it was my place, but I know how serious this is and I know that I would hate myself if I didn't give it the college try."

"How serious what is?" Now Betsy was playing with him. She couldn't help it, it was just too easy.

"You and the President."

She smiled. She gave a little nod as if to say, "Oh, that."

"Do you mind if I give you my opinion?"

"Of course not. I like you, John, and I respect you, and I respect what you have to say."

"You two are a great couple. The country voted for both of you, even though his name was on the ballot. You're half the team. I think the President needs another four years to accomplish his goals and I fear that without you he won't get it. I can't be more direct than that."

She didn't say anything. She poured herself a cup of coffee and drank half of it before she spoke. "I appreciate your loyalty to my husband and to the office. You have done your job well and my husband is lucky to have you."

"By the way, Betsy, I swear to you he doesn't know we're talking. This was my idea."

"I believe that, John. But this is bigger than you think. If this were a spat that could be fixed, don't you think I would be the first one to do it? I never loved this job, but I did it for my husband. Obviously that no longer seems important to him."

Van Dyke had no immediate reply. She had thought this through more carefully than he'd imagined.

She continued. "I think it would cause more harm to his mental state to stay in this marriage just to have another four years in the White House.

As far as my mental state, I'm trying with every fiber in my body to make it through *this* term. Do you think I don't know that he's in Denver with Susanna? How should I feel about that?"

"You aren't going to finish out *this* term?"

"I didn't say that. But eighteen months, even living separately, is going to be difficult. I offer no guarantees."

This was worse than Van Dyke expected. He could do nothing more than make a joke. "So fund-raising for his library is out of the question?"

Betsy laughed. But she was sad. And she had lied just now. Telling him she didn't know if she could continue was not the truth. She did know. She was slowly reaching a decision that there was no way she could stay in this marriage for another year and a half. But telling John Van Dyke that with certainty would accomplish nothing. And then, there was still a very, very small part of her that thought her husband would come crawling back. Fire Susanna. Beg her forgiveness. Tell her that he literally could not live without her. But what bothered her most was that she wasn't sure she even wanted that to happen.

Paul Prescott was sleeping when the small screen by his bed started buzzing. He could have chosen a more pleasant sound or whatever music he liked to alert him to an incoming message, but he was a deep sleeper and if he didn't pick the most annoying sound the machine offered, he wouldn't wake up.

"Yes?" he said, still groggy.

"I promised I would give you information before anyone else. I didn't want you to wake up and have it waiting for you on the screen." Paul sat up quickly. He was staring at Jack Willman.

"What? What happened?"

"Six men hijacked the retirement ship *The Sunset.*"

"What?!" Paul leaped out of bed, threw on a robe, and switched on the wall screen. "What the fuck is going on?"

"It isn't on the news yet but six guys snuck onto the ship in the middle of the night. They're holding it right now. There. It's on. Turn to News-One."

Paul switched his screen to one of the many twenty-four-hour news feeds. NewsOne was a combination of professional and amateur video capture. It had no commentary, just raw footage from wherever it originated. Paul saw shots of the large cruise ship, out at sea, stopped, with several smaller boats around it. "What are they doing?"

"I don't know. It's pretty confusing. The ship was going only a few miles north to port when it just stopped. There was an SOS and all we know is that there are hijackers aboard."

"Do you know who they are?"

"We think it's Max Leonard and his group."

"Son of a bitch! You should have arrested him."

"On what grounds? You still have to do something to get arrested."

"On planning to hijack a ship! That's a fucking crime, isn't it?"

"I didn't call you to get into legal arguments. I just wanted you to know what happened and that we're on top of it."

"How are you on top of it?"

"All those tugs you see are either police or Navy. They've surrounded the boat."

"Well, what are the hijackers going to do? They could kill a lot of people."

"I don't think that's the intent. They want something. That's what we're waiting for."

"Shit, Jack. This is scary. How many seniors live on that thing?"

"Currently, twenty-five hundred."

"Fuck. This is just great. Let me call Golden. Let me at least try to tell him this is under some kind of control. Our membership will go crazy. This goddamn country can't protect them anymore."

"Don't make it worse than it is. There's a good chance this will end peacefully."

"How?"

"I don't know. I've got to go." Jack disconnected and Paul switched his screen from one news outlet to the next. Everyone was covering this now. This was being seen worldwide.

Max and Louie had tied up the captain and three of his assistants. They waited until eight o'clock in the morning, when the ship was making its way on the short journey up the coast to its permanent berth. Four of them walked onto the bridge and it was easier than they had imagined it would be. These ships were not considered targets since they didn't carry large amounts of cargo or money, so the crew wasn't trained in combat. There was security on board and they had weapons, but they were caught off guard, and Max and the three others had no trouble subduing the men. They touched them with a sleep gun, which injected enough chemical to put down a horse but didn't kill anyone.

Andre knew how to steer the ship, but they didn't want to move it. All they did was stop and drop anchor. They waited a few minutes until they heard a controller ask what the problem was. Max turned off the video, deciding that he was going to communicate the old-fashioned way, just voice. "My name is Max Leonard. I have taken over as the captain of this ship."

"I have no picture," the controller said.

"I have disabled the picture. Voice communication will be sufficient."

"Have you hijacked this ship?"

"I wouldn't say that. I don't want to take it anywhere. I want to talk to the President."

"The President?"

"You heard me."

While this conversation was going on, the remaining men in Max's group had gathered all of the crew members and put them in five different rooms. They locked the doors and one of them stood guard. The residents didn't know what was happening until many of them showed up for breakfast and nothing was prepared.

Max and his group had carefully thought through what would be done with the residents. They would all be assembled in the large dining room. This was the biggest single space on the ship and even though meals were staggered, it could hold everyone, if necessary.

So while Max and Andre remained on the bridge, the other four men, after locking up the crew, went from room to room and told everyone there was an emergency. They needed to come to the dining room immediately. Since Max's group was wearing uniforms, the residents thought they were staff and did what they were told.

In less than thirty minutes, all of the rooms were empty and the dining room was filled to capacity. The residents, including Brad Miller and Walter Masters, sensed something was wrong. The very fact that there was no breakfast prepared told people that there was trouble.

There were not enough chairs in the dining room, so hundreds of people stood against the walls or sat on the floor. When everyone was assembled, Max addressed the residents over two large screens. He had rehearsed this moment very carefully, as he wanted as little panic as possible. "Hello. My name is Max Leonard and I am talking to you from the bridge. My men and I have taken over this ship for a short while as we wait to speak with the president of the United States."

Several hundred people started to panic. Max had known that would happen. His associates, standing at the entrance to the dining room with automatic weapons, yelled for everyone to be quiet. Max continued. "Listen to me carefully. You will not be hurt. I repeat, you will not be hurt, unless you try to escape. The ship is lined with explosives." Max paused again while twenty-five hundred people screamed at once.

Of course, there were no explosives, but that was the beauty of it. The threat was everything. He continued, trying to calm people down. "These explosives will *not* be used. They will not be used if you do what you are told and let us accomplish our goals. When we are finished, we will leave this ship and you will all be safe. When I speak to the President you will be allowed to hear the conversation as it is happening. As you will see, what we are asking for is fair and long overdue, and unless people like ourselves take a stand, nothing will ever change."

When they were told that Max was going to talk to the President, people calmed down somewhat, thinking that maybe the President would be in control and there would be negotiations, and that this would end peacefully.

"I know many of you are hungry," Max continued. "And we will allow certain crew members to feed you and keep you comfortable. You may use the bathrooms in the dining area but you may not leave to go anywhere else. Again, you will not be hurt. And some of you may even agree with what we are trying to accomplish."

Brad Miller was sitting next to Barbara, who for some reason was ultracalm. "What do you think they want?" Brad asked her. "Are they going to blow up the ship?"

"He said no. He doesn't seem to want to hurt us."

"He hijacked the goddamn ship, honey. That's not a good way to say, 'I like you.'"

"I'm not going to panic yet. And I don't know about you but I'm starving. I wonder if they'll set out the buffet?" Brad couldn't help but smile. Barbara was so Zen. But she had a point. At least maybe while they were being held hostage they could get the eggs Benedict they liked so much.

Walter Masters recognized Max Leonard the second his face came on the screen. And Masters was probably the only one in that room who had a real sense of what this was about. How interesting, Walter thought, that his conversation with Max Leonard those many months ago had led to today. In a strange way, Walter admired him. Whatever was going to happen, Max *would* make his point. And that took guts.

CHAPTER FORTY-NINE

While Kathy was driving to work, very early, Clyde Folsom's face appeared on her windshield. She could see through it without being distracted from the road, and it provided a safe way to communicate while driving an automobile. "You heard what happened, I'm assuming?" She didn't know what he was talking about. Her first thought was that a new seven-bedroom house that she was sure she would sell this week had gone to someone else.

"I don't know what you mean."

"Your boyfriend hijacked a boat."

"What? What boyfriend?" For a minute Kathy thought Clyde was talking about Brian Nelson, but that was impossible, he didn't even know him. Then it hit her. "Oh my God! What happened?"

"Why don't you turn to the news and you can see. Thank God you're not with him."

Kathy reached for a button on the wheel to cut off the conversation and put a news channel on in its place. She continued to drive, looking through the story as it unfolded. Even though she could focus on the road, she had to pull over. She started to feel sick. She stopped the car on the right side of the highway and sat there, just watching it unfold. It looked so confusing, there was so much going on, but it took only a minute to see Max's name and his picture. She heard a commentator say, "That is all we know right now. There are six of them and this one seems to be the leader."

Kathy turned it off. She didn't know whether to go to work or go back home, but she didn't want to be alone.

Clyde Folsom and the other two employees were at the office, watching the news on the big screen in the waiting area. Kathy walked in and sat down with them, and Clyde could see she was in shock. He told the others to go back to work, leaving him and Kathy sitting by themselves. "I hate to say it," Clyde told her, "but I knew he was trouble. Did you suspect this?"

Kathy could barely speak. She was hoping this was a bad dream. "I don't know. I just don't know. He was passionate, but I didn't think . . . I just don't know." Clyde really liked Kathy and wanted to comfort her, but he also thought the FBI could come charging through the door at any moment, assuming that she was part of this.

"When was the last time you saw him?"

"A few days ago."

"The authorities might want to question you, wouldn't you think?" Kathy was smart. She knew what he was afraid of.

"I won't let them question me here, if that's what you're worried about. I've got nothing to tell them anyway."

And at that moment Clyde's fears were realized. Without any warning, five men, looking very official and very scary, came into the real estate office. It was all Clyde could do to keep from saying, "You want her!" But he didn't. He played it cool. "May I help you?"

The men didn't need him. They knew who Kathy Bernard was and what she looked like and they asked her to come quietly. Kathy didn't resist. She could have asked for an official warrant, but she didn't. She wasn't on that ship and had never known about it, so she had nothing to hide. But the questioning was going to be tough.

She was taken about twenty miles west to an army base in Plainfield. She was escorted into a conference room where there were several screens on the wall, and on one of the screens was a man who looked very important; certainly he had more medals on his uniform than Kathy had ever seen. He was introduced as Major General Mark Allen.

"First, Ms. Bernard, we brought you here only to get as much information as possible. No one is accusing you of anything."

"My God," Kathy said, "I can only imagine what this would feel like if you *were* accusing me."

The general smiled, but immediately got down to business. Over the next hour and a half he asked her a hundred questions about Max Leonard. How did they meet, what was he like, what drugs did he do, what were his plans, what was his family like, who were his friends. It went on and on and on. Kathy had been deposed when her father was shot, and she'd thought *that* was the third degree, but this made that seem like kindergarten.

Fortunately for Kathy, she had had no idea of the plan. And since that was the truth she didn't act as though she were hiding any information. The only things she didn't tell them were that she'd seen a model of the boat and that Max Leonard had made a Sam Mueller wall. They would never know that. Somehow she felt that those could be taken the wrong way, that someone might think she should have called the authorities as soon as she discovered either one of them. But she was forthcoming in every other way. She told them that she was part of the group for youth equality, but she always went back to the truth, which was that she never, ever participated in violence and she hadn't known Max Leonard would, either. That last part might have been a lie, but so what?

When they drove her back to the office three hours later, she felt as if she'd been verbally raped. Clyde Folsom was waiting there to see if she was okay and if his business was going to suffer. But it became apparent that, at least for now, Kathy Bernard was not a suspect. And even after all she had been through, she *still* sold another house before lunch was over. That was good enough for Clyde. *Hell, maybe this will even turn out to be a plus somehow.*

Sam Mueller was in Switzerland when he saw the news. He turned to his wife and said, "That son of a bitch accosted me in Texas. I thought he was going to kidnap Mark."

"Jesus," Maggie said. "Did you think he was capable of doing this?"

"How could I? I knew something was wrong with him, but who would know this?"

"You should have had him arrested."

"I suggested it. They threw him out of the hotel. Go figure. Thank God we don't know anyone on that ship."

And because they were a world away and the skiing was particularly good that afternoon, they turned off the news and went back to their luxuries.

Matthew Bernstein was trying to get two hours of sleep as *Air Force One* made its way back to Washington from Denver. The night before he didn't get to bed until three-thirty. After the fund-raising event he went back to the hotel with Susanna Colbert and two longtime friends from Colorado. His friends left at one in the morning. Susanna got up to leave, too, but the President asked her to stay a little longer. She did and they talked. For two and a half hours.

As always, it started out about business and before it was over Bernstein was telling her what his current demons were and all the other things that one should tell only a psychologist or at least one's very best friend. These conversations were becoming so necessary for the President, he didn't know what he would do without them.

When they were finished, Susanna got up and wished him a good night. They still had never kissed, only hugging a few times in a friendly way, but she kept wondering if that was going to change. She wouldn't refuse, but she knew that once it happened, it would alter the dynamic, and she didn't really want that. But that night at least there was no kiss. Just another friendly hug and she was back in her room.

Susanna was doing work at her seat on the plane when she noticed a conversation of some urgency near the front. Before she could find out what was happening, an assistant to the chief of staff came to her and told her that the President was being woken up, that there was an emergency.

"What's going on?"

"There has been a hijacking of a retirement cruise ship."

"Oh my God! Where?"

"Miami."

"In the *United States*? Oh my God!" Susanna could see two people standing at the open door of the President's sleeping quarters. Within moments he was dressed and walking down the aisle, reading something, drinking a cup of coffee, and talking into a device. He stopped at her seat and asked her to come with him. They went upstairs on the aircraft to the heart of the communications center. Susanna had to wonder if this was something that a normal secretary of the Treasury would be asked to do. But it was her. And he wanted her there.

The room upstairs was, as it had been for decades, one of the most sophisticated control centers in the world. It was not large, about two hundred square feet. There were several people sitting at their stations, monitoring secure and regular communications.

The President, Susanna, and the assistant chief of staff sat on a couch in one corner, looking at the screens. On one screen was John Van Dyke. On another was the chairman of the Joint Chiefs, General Mike McGuiness. On a third was Admiral Boyle, secretary of the Navy.

"He wants to talk to you," Van Dyke said. "I don't think that's a good idea."

"Why not?" the President asked.

"It's too easy. You can't just hijack a boat and get to speak with the president."

"For God's sake, John, it's not a boat. It's a ship with almost three thousand people on it. Isn't that good enough to talk to me?"

McGuiness spoke up. "Mr. President, I think John is right. If we give in now to this demand, it will appear weak."

"So what do we do?" the President asked.

"I think we stall as long as we can and see if we can overtake them."

"How are we going to do that?"

"Sir, we have the best snipers in the country only about an hour away now. They will soon be on those tugs surrounding the ship, and if there is any way humanly possible of getting them, these guys can do it."

"What about the explosives?" the President asked.

"That's what they say, but all satellite data at this time show none of that. If they lined the ship with what they're claiming, I think we would know."

"Are you sure?"

The general paused. "I can say ninety percent."

"Not good enough," the President said. "If you're wrong and they kill all those people, it won't be worth keeping me from having a conversation."

Van Dyke had an idea. "Sir, you're landing in an hour. Let's see if we can stall until you get to the White House."

"I think that's a good idea, Mr. President," McGuiness said. "In the meantime, the SEALs can get sophisticated equipment under the ship that can detect explosives with ninety-nine percent accuracy." The President looked unhappy.

"What am I hearing? How many trillions of dollars do you people need to get me to a hundred percent?" No one answered. "Okay. I would rather have the conversation from the White House anyway. It would be less dramatic for the American people than having me talk from the plane. Tell him I am on my way back to Washington and I will speak to him when I get there. If he thinks that will happen, then hopefully we'll buy more time. But if you can't assure me without any doubt that they won't blow this thing up, I am telling you now I am going to speak to this guy."

"I understand," the general said. "We will tell him what you said and make him think that a conversation is imminent. I'll keep you posted every few minutes on any changes, and I look forward to seeing you here, sir."

"That's fine, General. John, are we in sync?"

"Yes, sir."

And with that the President got up and walked downstairs. He asked the steward to make him a mushroom omelet. He went back to his office and told Susanna to come with him. When they were inside, he shut the door and locked it. "People forget to knock in an emergency, I don't like that. Are you hungry?"

"I ate."

"What do you think I should do?"

Susanna sat in one of the big chairs opposite his desk. She was surprised by the direct question. Bernstein talked to her about everything, personal issues and work and life, but this was the first time he had asked her opinion on a national security crisis. She was flattered and a little uncomfortable. She also knew John Van Dyke would be furious if he ever thought that her opinion had been factored into the President's decision. Susanna thought carefully before she answered. "If it were me, I would talk to him. If the worst happens and you never do, you can be blamed for not trying. And if you do and the worst happens anyway, at least you made an attempt. That's my two cents."

"I'm crazy about you." The President just blurted it out.

That was the first time he had come close to saying he loved her. She had no immediate response. She couldn't think of a reply. Several were swirling around in her head. "Me, too" almost came out, but sounded trite and too forward, so that was edited. "I'm flattered" sounded too formal and too distant. While she was thinking, he got up and walked over and put his hands on her face. He kissed her. Not long and passionate, but on the lips and lasting more than five seconds. She wound up saying nothing. She put her head on his shoulder and they stood there as if they were slow dancing without moving.

A loud buzzer on the President's desk broke them apart, and when he went to answer it, she mouthed, "I'm going back to my seat," and blew him a little kiss. Then she forgot the door was locked and pulled on it until the President motioned for her to release the bolt. She felt like an idiot.

When she got back to her seat, she was lightheaded. This was where it was leading now, that was apparent. The one thing she didn't want was for them to become awkward. But it was just a kiss, not enough that everything had to change. At least that's what she was hoping. She would continue to be there when he needed her and to be the same person, but whatever was going to happen, it obviously had already started.

CHAPTER FIFTY

Even though there were at least six hours left on the speed patch, Max Leonard pulled down his pants and put on another one on the opposite thigh. He could feel his teeth grinding, but he needed all of the artificial energy he could get now. He paced on the bridge waiting for an answer. As he was rehearsing what he would say to the President of the United States, a voice came on the speaker. "Mr. Leonard, this is General McGuiness."

"Where's the President?"

"First of all, would you please allow visuals again? We can accomplish more if we can see each other."

"No. I don't want to see you. This was good enough for hundreds of years; there's no reason to see each other. Where is the President? I will look at him only."

"The President is on his way back to the White House. He was in Denver. He should be there within two hours."

"Where is he now?"

"He's en route. I believe they are still in the air."

"I want to talk to him *now*. I don't want to wait two hours."

McGuiness had his story prepared and was about to see if it would fly.

"There is something wrong with the satellite that lets us see the President in the air. It has to do with the sun and the time of year. There is no consistent visual with him until he gets to the White House, so we're going to have to wait." Max was livid.

"You are fucking kidding me! You're out of touch with the President because of the *sun*? What do you think, that I'm five years old?"

"Mr. Leonard, there are some things that are out of our control. There is only one way to have a solid visual with the President when he is in the air, and right now that is being disturbed. I could not see him myself, but all that will be restored when he returns to the White House."

"And how long will that be?"

"It should be under two hours."

Max thought a moment. He had a few options. He could bluff and tell them he wouldn't wait, or he could ask to speak with the President using voice only, but he didn't want that. It had always been his plan to look Bernstein in the eye. He knew that this conversation would make its way around the world, and the best way to succeed was to have a one-on-one, face-to-face, with the President of the United States. Anything short of that would not accomplish his goal.

The second speed patch was now kicking in and it made him feel invulnerable. "I'll wait until he is at the White House, but if there's any more delay you can say good-bye to the people on this ship. Is that clear?"

"I hear you," the general said. "Are you sure you cannot speak to me? I have great authority, you know."

"You're nothing, General. Even the President is weak, but you have no power without him. But there is one thing you can arrange. When my conversation with the President is over I will want a helicopter to take me and my group, along with five hostages of our choosing, to Cuba. When we land there safely you can fly the hostages back. So you might as well plan for that now."

This was the first time anyone had heard that demand. McGuiness was impressed. If these guys could get to Cuba they would be heroes. And even though over the decades the relationship with Cuba had softened somewhat, there was still no extradition and there was still no love for America. The Cubans would take these men and allow them to escape with their lives, and that would create even more problems. McGuiness acted as though he didn't understand the demand. "I'm sorry, what are you requesting?"

"Play the fucking transcript back if you didn't hear me. I want the chopper to land on the boat before my conversation with the President. And if you try anything foolish . . . well, you'll probably kill me, but I will definitely take every last person on this ship down with me. Is that clear, General?"

McGuiness had no more negotiations up his sleeve. All of this would buy him at least two hours, which was enough time to try to end this the military's way. "Yes. It's clear."

Laura Li and her husband were watching this unfold like every other person in the United States and in most of the world. A crisis like this was like a worldwide police chase; everyone watched it in real time, glued to their screens of all sizes, waiting to see what would happen next.

They were still in bed, looking up at the ceiling. The projector in their bedroom would put visuals wherever they wanted, and Shen and Laura had found that their favorite position was lying on their backs, staring straight up. It was like looking at the stars. They loved the holographic video of a planetarium show, which was even more fun after a little hit of the organic weed grown on their windowsill. They'd probably watched that at least twenty times, making love and getting lost in the colors and the depth.

As they watched the hijacking unfold, Shen was a bit surprised by how angry it made him. "Do you know the last time this kind of thing happened in China?"

"No," Laura said.

"Never. It would never happen and if it did, it would never get this far. Those men would be dead."

"What about the people on the boat?"

"This is going to sound harsh, honey, but the people on that boat are less important than giving the people who are holding them worldwide attention. In the overall scheme of things, if you stop this in its tracks—if people who are prone to this behavior know that not only will they never survive, but they won't even get an audience—this kind of thing will go away. Nobody will do this if they can't find the reward in it."

Laura smiled. "You know, it's funny, the way you say that. It's almost exactly what my father says. He believes in tolerance, only up to a point."

"That's because he's brilliant, and I'm lucky that I fell in love with his brilliant daughter."

They turned off the crisis footage and put on Niagara Falls. Shen loved this video, too. Niagara Falls was one of the few places on earth where the water showed no indication of drying up. Glaciers were dying, the Himalayas looked bare, but Niagara was still as forceful as ever. And they could almost feel the water as they watched the falls pour down from the ceiling. "We have to go there one day and see it for real," Shen said.

"I've been there, darling. Believe me, this is better."

The twenty-five hundred residents of *The Sunset* were fed, which helped them calm down somewhat. One of the advantages of old age was that the threat of dying was a bit less scary to them than to those who had not experienced a long life. But also the vibe in the dining room did not feel as if they were about to be killed. They believed that if Max Leonard could talk to the President, this would work out. "I wonder what he wants?" one of the older women asked her friend.

"Money. Everyone wants money."

"How much would they pay for us?"

"Nothing. Who would pay for us? What are we worth?"

Someone else said, "But they don't want the ship ruined. How much do you think the ship cost? Wouldn't the ship company pay a lot of money so they don't blow it up?"

That made sense and many of the people who heard it suddenly felt encouraged. They knew they were not worth a lot, but the ship certainly was.

And conversations continued like that all throughout the dining room. Some people weren't that concerned; they were just uncomfortable and didn't want to wait in the line for the bathrooms, a line that was now stretching around the corner and into one of the kitchens. And to make matters worse, one of the toilets had stopped up, so not only was there a long line, but the smell was horrible. People weren't used to that here.

Brad Miller made his way over to Walter Masters. He noticed an empty seat next to him and asked if he could sit down. "It's fine with me," Walter said. "The guy went to the bathroom, but he hasn't been back for an hour."

Brad really liked Walter. They had played cards often and he liked Walter's sense of humor, which he considered to be a mixture of playful and dark. He could never get over the fascination of what Walter did to allow people a dignified death. He thought it was so noble. "Are you worried?"

"I'm not unworried," Walter said. "I could think of better ways to spend the afternoon, but there is a bit of adventure in this and that is always somewhat exciting."

"I agree. As long as it ends okay, then the experience isn't that bad. It's going to make for a lot of good stories. How much money do you think they want?"

"I don't think this is about money."

"What's it about?"

Walter smiled. "Well, we'll see, but I think this young man's demands are going to be different than what they think."

"Will they be able to meet them? These demands?"

Walter thought about that for a moment. He wasn't a man to bullshit and he thought such a good question deserved an honest answer, at least an honest opinion. "No. I don't think so."

Now Brad's mood changed. If the demands were not going to be met, what was the answer? "So what do you think will happen? Will he blow up the ship?"

"I don't know. I sure hope not."

At that moment the man who had gone to the toilet came back to his seat. Brad got up and thanked Walter for the chat. "I sure hope you're wrong," Brad said.

"I often am." Walter smiled.

"Wrong about what?" the man asked.

"Nothing," Walter answered. "Mr. Miller and I were just playing a guessing game."

As Brad walked back to where Barbara was sitting, Max Leonard appeared once again on the big screen. "I hope you all are comfortable," he said to his captives. "I am in the process of making contact with the President of the United States. I don't know how many of you voted for him, but if you did, then you know more than I do whether he will act sensibly and listen to what we have to say. I know that several of you have been communicating with the outside world, telling them what is going on, and quite frankly, that is fine. You might tell them to contact their representatives and convince the President to do what we ask so you all can go back to your comfortable existence. This was never meant to hurt you and it should not hurt you if your government listens to us. When this is over I will leave this ship and you will go on your merry way, hopefully with a new outlook and a new appreciation of the generations that are following you. That's all for now."

And the screen went dark. It didn't really put anyone at ease, but some of the older folks had to admit that Max was rather charming. And he would have been more so without the two speed patches.

At around two-thirty, Kathy asked Clyde if she could go home early. "Of course. Absolutely. You've had a very, very rough day. I'm sorry if I seemed so worried, Kathy, I just know how publicity can help or hurt a business and I didn't know what this would do, but it's obvious you're innocent, and I'm so happy you're here."

Kathy smiled and gave a halfhearted thank-you.

As she was heading home she couldn't stop thinking about Max. She was still in love with him. He might have done something stupid, but so many people never do anything at all. At least he was trying. *Just don't kill anyone.* That's all she could think. *Make your points, but don't kill anyone and don't you get killed.* She kept saying it to herself as if she could make it come true. But the truth was, she didn't know how this could end peacefully. She knew Max was not going to sit in prison the rest of his life. That was certain.

All of a sudden her car slammed on its brakes and stopped itself. Kathy came out of her trance and saw that she was driving toward the back of a pickup truck. She'd never been a big fan of cars taking over control from the driver—she always thought it was intrusive—but today it prevented a crash that would have made the afternoon even worse.

When she got to her house she had a message waiting for her. She played it back and watched as Max Leonard talked a mile a minute, licking his lips, looking tired and crazy, but it was still him and she was happy to see his face. "Hi, baby. I love you. I'm sure you know what's gone down and I want to say to anyone who cares that you had nothing to do with this. You didn't even know what I was up to for the longest time and I don't want you blamed by association. I still love you but you are not part of anything that I am doing and it's important for people to know that." As Max was about to continue with his rambling someone pulled him away and he finished up by saying, "Gotta go. Love you, baby. Love you so much."

And the screen went blank. Kathy knew that everything Max did once he got on that ship was going to be monitored. But at least he said exactly what she had told them. She was not part of this. But of course she was. Here was a message, after all, from the man holding thousands of people hostage.

She made a decision at that moment to try to save her own ass. Knowing the FBI would have already seen the message, even before her, Kathy knew that *not* telling them would look as though she was hiding something. She decided to contact them first. "My name is Kathy Bernard," she said to the man she was put through to. "I received a message from Max Leonard when I arrived home and wanted to make sure you were aware of it." Of course the FBI man acted as if he knew nothing; what else was he going to say? He asked Kathy to forward it to him and said that if he needed to he would contact her for further questioning. She did what she was told and then left the house, deciding just to drive and think. *You were so smart, Max. You could have run for office or something. Don't be stupid now. Make your point, but don't be stupid.*

CHAPTER FIFTY-ONE

Air Force One landed at two forty-five in the afternoon. The President took *Marine One* to the White House and brought Susanna Colbert with him. When the helicopter landed on the White House lawn, both John Van Dyke and General Mike McGuiness were waiting. Thcy walked with the President, who glanced back to see if Susanna was following. She chose to let them go ahead and went back to her office, alone.

The President went to the bathroom and then headed downstairs to the Situation Room, which by now had every person who was involved with this crisis in place and waiting to brief him. McGuiness started.

"In the last hour we have been able to send twenty SEALs to scour the area. They have been all over the outside of the ship. Under it, behind it, everywhere, and there are no signs of explosives. So our satellites tell us there are no explosives and the SEALs confirm it. It would be highly unlikely for both to be wrong." The President felt somewhat encouraged.

"So you put this at what? Ninety-nine percent?"

"Yes, sir."

"Have we been wrong before?"

"Not with both, sir."

"Let's say you're right. What does that allow us?"

"It allows us to board the ship and to try to take these men out."

"And the hostages? If they see us, they'll kill hostages, won't they?" Admiral Boyle had an opinion on this.

"Mr. President, there is always a chance they will kill hostages. But if they are lying about explosives, then there is a good chance they are lying about other things as well. It's one thing to take over a ship, but to kill thousands of people takes a certain kind of mind-set, and that mind-set would have used the explosives." The President thought this over. It sounded so pat.

"Where do you get this opinion, Admiral?"

"From experience, sir. I'm not saying that some individuals may not be shot or even killed, but if we're talking about blowing up the ship, I don't think that's going to happen."

"But if they kill ten people, isn't that ten people too many?"

"Mr. President, if the goal is to end this without compromising you, then I think losing a few people would be considered a success."

"What do you mean, compromising me?"

General McGuiness was quick to answer. "I think that we board this ship before you talk to them. Take them out without having you humiliated." John Van Dyke agreed with the general's assessment.

But Matthew Bernstein agreed with Susanna. Of course, he would never let on that he had had this conversation with her, but he didn't understand why talking to Max Leonard, especially if it could save lives, would be the worst outcome. "Explain to me again why talking to this man would be so humiliating?"

Van Dyke answered. "Mr. President, if every hijacker thought they could give their opinion to the president of the United States, it would embolden them. People would see that as a reward for committing the crime. It would be a means to an end. Hijack a ship and you can talk to the president."

The President turned to General McGuiness. "When was the last time a ship with almost three thousand Americans was hijacked by another American?"

McGuiness looked at Admiral Boyle and then at John Van Dyke. "Never, sir."

"Okay," the President said. "So it's not like this is a daily occurrence. I say that I talk to him if he will assure us that after that, he will leave the ship and leave the people unharmed. If he guarantees that, then a conversation would be worth it, don't you think?"

"He's a hijacker, Mr. President," Van Dyke said. "We can't believe him just because he says he'll do that."

"Well, you're giving me mixed signals here, gentlemen. First you tell me that a man who is faking about setting explosives is not a man who would blow up a ship, and then you tell me that a man who gives his word will never keep it because he's a hijacker. That is not a personality profile that I can work with. He either is someone who will act in a certain way or he isn't. Aside from the conversation, what are his demands that we know of right now?"

"He wants a helicopter to take his group to Cuba and he will take five hostages with him that he will release when he has landed and is safe."

The President thought for a moment. "Admiral, do we have a clear shot at the bridge?"

"Yes, sir. From a drone we could get anyone who was standing there."

"And where is this Leonard fellow right now?"

"When he was speaking to us he was on the bridge; that's where the communications are. Then he leaves and we don't know where he goes."

"So if I did speak to him, wouldn't it be the best way to keep him in one place?" General McGuiness looked over at Admiral Boyle. Boyle had an expression on his face that could be interpreted as, "I guess so, what do you think?" McGuiness looked at the President.

"Yes, sir, that would be the best way to keep him on the bridge. But the other five men could be anywhere. They are probably with the hostages."

"So here's what we do," Bernstein said. "I will talk to this man. That is the best way to get his attention. While I am talking to him, you will get men aboard the ship. If you have older men who can do this job, I would say dress them like passengers, but get them aboard. I will draw out the conversation until you tell me that we have a presence. I don't see any other way to do it." General McGuiness gave a quick glance to the admiral. He then did what he was supposed to; he followed the order.

"Yes, Mr. President." The general decided that he would let the President make all of the decisions now, since he was not being listened to. "Do you want to land the helicopter as if we are willing to get them off?"

The President thought for a second. "I think we can land the helicopter, but I don't want it taking off again with hostages. But if it will buy us more time, then getting a chopper there is fine. It would be nice if men could come in that way."

"I think they would be expecting that, sir," Van Dyke said.

"Exactly," the President replied. "So one would think at least two or three of their men would be waiting for it. That should help us in locating them, don't you think?"

General McGuiness looked at the others. He didn't agree with *any* president talking to hostage takers, but he had to admit he was impressed that Bernstein had thought it through to this degree.

Max Leonard was getting impatient. The drugs were making it worse and for the first time he worried that this could go badly. That he wouldn't be able to make his arguments and he would be forced to kill people without the world understanding anything. Then he got a communication that made him feel somewhat better.

"Mr. Leonard, this is Admiral Boyle. I have been authorized to tell you that the President has agreed to talk to you." Max was pleased, but why wasn't the President just on the line? Why was a new person now telling him this?

"Just put him on the screen; I don't want to talk to anyone else now but him."

"It isn't that easy," the admiral told him, stalling for as much time as possible. "He is on the way back to the White House and we are setting everything up at this moment. He will speak to you as soon as he gets there."

"Where is he now?"

"He is en route."

"You told me this two hours ago. How long does it take the fucking President to get to his house?"

"Mr. Leonard, to get him to agree to talk to you was a big job. It is not a decision that can be made in an instant. I hope you understand how unusual it is that you are able to speak to the president of the United States. I hope you appreciate that."

"And I hope that you appreciate that I will blow up this ship if I don't." There was silence. Admiral Boyle's delay tactics were working, at least for the time being. Even having *this* discussion gained precious minutes, while thirty of the best Navy SEALs were in the water, surrounding the boat, ready to try to board when given the order. "I want the helicopter on this ship *before* my conversation begins, is that understood?"

"It's understood," Boyle said. But that was not what was going to happen.

Soon they were going to say that the President was ready to talk, even though the helicopter had not landed yet. They were banking on the fact that Max Leonard, having the President of the United States staring him in the face, would be thrown off, and they would say that the helicopter was in the air and would land during his conversation. Something happened to people when they faced a president, even if it was over a screen. People became unglued, and the military was relying on this to execute the plan.

The admiral concluded the conversation by saying, "The President will be in the White House very shortly. The helicopter is being readied and will take off as soon as it is fueled and prepared." Max didn't argue. He had never done this before and had nothing to compare it to. It sounded as though his demands were being met and they weren't stalling anymore.

"I am here and waiting. Don't keep me waiting much longer." And he disconnected. And when he did the drone could clearly see that he left the bridge.

The camera was set up in one of the press rooms. The President did not want the background to look official or important. It would be him alone sitting in front of a blue curtain. No flags. No United States symbols represented in any way, except, of course, for its President. Bernstein wanted this to look as if he was forced into it. As if *he* was being held hostage.

He entered the press room and sat behind a small desk. Facing him was a screen, ninety-five inches in diameter, with a camera on top, pointing at the desk. Bernstein had given consideration to what he would wear. No tie. He wanted to have an open shirt with the sleeves rolled up, a look that would suggest that Max Leonard was not important enough to get dressed up for.

As he took his seat, he asked that Susanna Colbert come down to the room as quickly as possible. Only General McGuiness and John Van Dyke were present, and when she walked in, neither smiled or greeted her in any way. The President asked her to sit next to the two men. Van Dyke could barely contain his contempt. It was one thing for the President to spend his private time with her, but asking the secretary of the Treasury to be present at a crisis that had nothing to do with finance or business was unseemly.

Bernstein took a sip of water, then signaled that he was ready to speak. An important decision was made that this would not be aired. Max Leonard had not demanded it and the White House certainly did not bring it up. It would be shown to the hostages in the dining room, but that was it. No other broadcast was going to take place. The President knew it would get out—everything did—but the fact that they could stop it from airing live around the world felt like an accomplishment. They had been worried that Leonard would insist on that and they had prayed that it would slip by. They were thrilled when it did.

Max was informed that the President was ready to speak with him. As expected, he was so nervous he didn't realize it was happening before the helicopter landed. The drone saw him enter the bridge and go to the screen. And there it was. Matthew Bernstein looking directly at Max Leonard. For years, Max had tried to get his point across. Meetings and confrontations with all the wrong people. Now he was speaking to the President of the United States. It overwhelmed him for a moment. His heart raced with the anticipation of what he was going to say. The President spoke first.

"Mr. Leonard, this is Matthew Bernstein. I have agreed to talk to you providing you keep your end of the bargain and no harm comes to the people you have taken hostage." At that moment Max realized the helicopter was not there.

"Where's the helicopter?"

The President knew what to say. He didn't need to look at the three people sitting opposite him, although the one person he glanced at was Susanna. More for support than anything else. "The helicopter is on its way. It will be there before our conversation is through. Now why don't you tell me what is on your mind?" As Max launched into his tirade, the SEALs got into position. The plan was that they would wait for the helicopter to approach. As it landed, which would happen as slowly as gravity would allow, they would split up and rush the helipad, the dining room, and the bridge at the same time. All of them prayed that they were right about the explosives.

"You have made this country no longer livable for the younger generations," Max began. "You have saddled us with debt and all you care about is extending life for those who have already lived. The rest of us are stuck with the bill with no hope of getting out. Your priorities are backward. You should be helping the young, not the old. The old have lived already. What about *us*? Being young in this country means that you don't count. We're not here to service you, do you understand that?"

Max knew he was speed-talking, but at least it made sense to *him*. And Matthew Bernstein was impressed. *So this is what it's all about?* Obviously this was something Bernstein had thought about himself. Now he was going to have to argue a point that he actually agreed with.

The hostages were also seeing this conversation. Almost three thousand of them stared intently at the two big screens. And many of them, for the very first time, were hearing it articulated as to why people were killing them. They knew there was resentment in the country, but very few thought that it had gone this far. And they were nervous. To them, Max Leonard started to look like a man who *would* blow them up. They hoped the President had an answer of some kind.

"Mr. Leonard, I hear your frustration." Before the President could continue Leonard launched into another speech. He was becoming more agitated.

"I want this changed right now! I am speaking for all young people in this country, and the world!"

At that moment the helicopter came over the horizon and approached the ship. The chopper dropped slowly, making as much noise at it could, its two large blades causing everything in its wake to blow frantically. When it was just twenty feet above the ship, the SEALs went into action.

Max Leonard could see the helicopter from the bridge and looked away from the screen for a moment to make sure he didn't see any armed men aboard. He didn't. He turned back to the President and continued. "I want your word that you will change the laws in this country. You don't allow people to vote until they are eighteen, and yet once they do, you allow them to vote forever until they die. There *must* be a law that ends the voting age the same way it begins. After seventy there should be no more voting allowed. It will be the only way to make sure that the generations share power. The old people have too much power and that must stop!"

At that moment Max Leonard was shot almost thirty times. The drone had let loose a hundred small laser bullets that didn't even break the glass. They passed right through and stopped in Leonard's body. It was like being electrocuted. As soon as they hit him, he dropped to the ground.

The President had guessed correctly. Three of the remaining five men were waiting for the helicopter with drawn weapons. But the SEALs were not in the helicopter. They came from the sides of the ship and took out the men with four shots. Other SEALs rushed down to the dining room. The last two men were guarding the entrance there and Louie was one of them. The other man, a Mexican named Santos, was taken out before he knew what hit him. Louie thought he was going to be killed in the next few seconds, so he panicked; he turned and fired into the crowd. Before they could kill him he shot fifteen people, including Brad Miller.

Brad fell off his seat onto the floor. People around him were screaming. Barbara was holding him, yelling for help. But there was too much confusion, everyone running in all directions. People trying to escape with their own lives.

Walter Masters saw that Brad was shot and rushed over. As soon as he saw Brad up close, he knew it was too late. The blood was pouring from his heart and his head. He took Brad into his arms and held him while he died. Barbara wailed uncontrollably and Walter Masters realized that not since his wife passed away had someone died in his presence whose death he had no control over. All he could do was witness it, and he broke down in tears.

Matthew Bernstein got up from his chair and walked to the Oval Office. General McGuiness and John Van Dyke were congratulating him. The ship had not blown up and most of the people were saved, but the President felt that those who lost their lives were his responsibility, and he felt no joy. He was also haunted by what Max Leonard had said. He knew there was truth in it, but he didn't know how to react. He certainly could not publicly acknowledge that this madman, who was responsible for killing innocent people, could be right in any way. For now he had to act as if the military had saved the day, and he would have to make it seem like the people who died were heroes. That their deaths somehow saved everyone else. It wasn't true, but it was what you said when you were the president; that's what the job required. You had to keep your real thoughts inside. It's why he was in love with Susanna. She had become the only safe person to tell what he was really thinking.

CHAPTER FIFTY-TWO

The story broke around the world. So many of the ship's residents had recorded every moment that Max Leonard's demands would eventually be seen by billions. It was why the Joint Chiefs of Staff had been opposed to the President having this conversation in the first place. Even though the lives of thousands were saved, everyone would now get to hear Max Leonard. And that couldn't be good.

Will this create a revolution? Now Bernstein was questioning himself. *Had I known what Leonard was going to say, would I have talked to him? What did I think he was going to say? Could the SEALs have stopped it without me intervening? What if they really had had explosives?* The President put his head in his hands and sat there. He had a blinding headache. He called Susanna. "What did I do?" he asked her. "The whole world is hearing this guy. Did I make a mistake?"

She came down the hall to the Oval Office, and walked in and stood by his desk. "You were a hero. You saved the lives of almost everyone on that ship. There is no telling what they would have done had you not chosen to speak with him. You are a hero."

The President stood up and kissed her. "I want you to stay with me."

"I'm here."

"I mean forever. I want you in my life. I can't do this without you."

She didn't answer. He looked so worn out. This was not the time for that discussion. "I'm sorry to be so weak," he said.

"You're not weak. You just went through a crisis that most presidents never face and I think you did it brilliantly. I will stay late tonight if you need me, but now, if you're all right, I have to get back. I left people sitting in my office. Is that okay?"

The President nodded. "Of course. I'm sorry if I pulled you away from something. I just needed to talk."

"Stop it. I'm here for you. I support you."

As Susanna left the room, she knew that something was coming to a head in their personal lives, but she didn't know what. What she did know was that the President needed to remain strong and she wanted to remain in the White House.

The news was filled with the hijacking and the rescue for days. It was all anyone talked about. There were commentators who thought the President had been wrong in talking to a terrorist, there were people who thought he handled it well, and there were others who agreed with what Max Leonard said, but couched their words carefully so they wouldn't sound like they approved of his actions.

Robert Golden and Paul Prescott had their hands full. Thousands of AARP members were panicked, flooding their offices with communications, wanting assurances that the government would put a stop to this violence once and for all, saying that the idea of a voting age limit was ridiculous and that even the talk of it had to stop.

There were some editorials that agreed with Max Leonard and said the idea of an age limit should be considered, or that maybe the voting age should be lowered to fifteen, a gesture that would even out the electorate. But that was going to go nowhere. The power of the older generation was too great. And just to make sure, Paul Prescott went into action.

Paul went to Congress and lobbied himself. Stopping by the offices of the influential senators and congressmen, he made it clear that anyone who would even entertain the idea of putting a limit on voting might as well clean out their desks now. Not only would it never get passed, but simply bringing it up would assure that person a one-way ticket back to his or her district. And no one argued with him. They knew he was right. Still, Paul wanted more than just assurance. He wanted speeches on the floor of the House and Senate about how the oldest Americans were national treasures. About how with age comes respect and how if older people could not be assured a good life, then life itself would lose meaning.

Paul found his greatest support in Stanley Markum. Senator Markum, who was consistently elected by older Americans, not only found what Max Leonard said reprehensible, he believed that giving Leonard center stage was criminal and blamed it squarely on the President.

Markum gave a speech on the Senate floor that was one of his best. He used phrases like "God wants man to live as long as he can, that is why he gave us the knowledge to do so," and, "What should we do next? Get rid of all the species that live a long and healthy life? Maybe we should kill all the turtles and chop down the redwoods." It was meaningless, but it sounded great and it stuck. It was forwarded all over cyberspace. So much so that Shen Li called his father-in-law to congratulate him on such a wonderful sound bite.

"That was just great, Dad," as Li now called Markum. "I love the turtle line."

"Did it get good play out there?"

"Yes. Everywhere. And what I agree with the most is that Bernstein should have never spoken to that guy. That made us seem weak."

It was funny, after Shen married Laura and after he made such an impact in California, he started to use "we" and "us" whenever he talked about America. He had adopted the country completely, even though China still considered him one of its greatest citizens.

As time went on Li spoke less and less Chinese, unless he was talking to others from China who were rebuilding the new city. Initially, he would mix the two languages, using phrases in Chinese when he could think of nothing comparable in English, but Laura gently guided him toward an English-only mind-set. She would say, "They love you, but if you want them to think of you as their own, speak English." And of course, as with everything else, she was right.

Kathy Bernard stayed home for a full week. She was due time off and had been planning to take it in a few months, but she asked Clyde Folsom if she could have it now instead. He wanted no press at his place of business and was more than happy to oblige. If she were not as good a saleswoman as she was, he would have let her go. But Kathy was his best and, personally, Clyde liked her more than his own children. He believed her when she said she had no involvement. Unfortunately, the FBI was not as convinced.

On a Tuesday morning, when Kathy was making herself some cereal and fruit, there was a knock at the door. She looked at the monitor and saw three men standing outside. One was a uniformed policeman; the other two were plainclothes. She pressed the button and asked what they wanted. They said she needed to open the door. She said she was not dressed and asked if they could come back later. They told her they had a warrant for her arrest and that if she didn't open the door they would come in anyway.

Kathy opened the door. One of the plainclothes cops told her to get dressed while they waited, that they were going to drive to Chicago to the FBI offices there. Kathy was confused and scared.

"Chicago? That's three hours, when will we get back?"

"I would pack for a few days, miss."

"I'm sorry. I'm not following. Why a few days? Where are we going?"

"Miss Bernard, you're under arrest at this time as an accessory in the hijacking of *The Sunset*." And then the uniformed cop played her a recording of her "rights" on his watch. She was completely in shock.

"I'm innocent! I told you I had nothing to do with this!"

One of the men smiled and said, "Ma'am, I don't make the decisions, I just carry out what I'm told. Please pack a small bag so we can get on the road. I'm sorry."

Kathy went into the bedroom and packed her suitcase. She knew that whatever was going to happen now would most likely be more expensive than even her father's illness. And she didn't have the funds.

The aftermath of the hijacking was not going as well for Matthew Bernstein as he had hoped. In hindsight, people were upset that so many had to die, even though six of them were the perpetrators. This also became the straw that broke the camel's back in regard to the violence that older Americans had been subjected to over the last several years. Congress, fearing the power of the olds, got tough, enacting new laws that would come down hard on attacks on the elderly. Stanley Markum wanted automatic life sentences for anyone attacking seniors. That didn't quite fly, but the vote was close.

The President had to play both sides of the fence. He had to make older people feel safe, but he also needed to convince younger Americans that what Max Leonard said was wrong, that America loved them and that their lives were going to be better than those of their parents. It was tough, especially since it was a lie. But Bernstein did the best he could.

He spoke to colleges and gave them his "This country is yours, too" speech, and he spoke to seniors and gave them his "The rights of Americans are good until they die" speech. Neither speech elicited the reactions he was hoping for. It felt as if he was just treading water. A little bit for everyone and not enough for anybody. And then Betsy left.

CHAPTER FIFTY-THREE

Betsy Bernstein woke up one rainy morning in February 2031, and knew from the moment she opened her eyes that she was finished. The first person she called was John Van Dyke. They met for coffee and she told him that she was leaving the White House for good and would announce the official separation later that day. Van Dyke was not really surprised, nor did he even care that much. As Susanna Colbert became closer and closer to the President, Van Dyke had felt his job was threatened, culminating in the President's decision to talk directly with Max Leonard. Van Dyke had been strongly against that, as were the generals, and he was convinced that Susanna was the one who made it happen.

Van Dyke knew the President's feelings toward Susanna and was willing to accept them, until they got in his way. So as he listened to the First Lady telling him that this was it, he almost wanted to say, "I'm with you. I hate her, too." But he didn't. He told Betsy that he was sorry it had come to this, but he understood how frustrated she was. And he asked her why she told him first. She didn't really have an answer. "Maybe just to hear how it sounded," she said.

She waited until her husband had an hour free and walked into the Oval Office. She had not been there for weeks, so when Bernstein saw her standing at the door he knew the rest of his day would most likely be terrible. "Hi. What is it?"

"You know what it is, don't you?"

"No. Tell me."

"I'm leaving tonight. I'm not coming back. We'll be officially separated and we'll start divorce proceedings. I have no plans to make it a problem or drag it out and I'm assuming you feel the same way."

He felt a lump in his chest. It was one thing to no longer communicate, one thing to be in love with another woman, but when that moment came that rips your life apart, it hurts and it's scary and you're the president. And this moment had never happened before. It was not a historical first that Bernstein had thought about when he took office. Being the first Jew, or half Jew, whatever they would call him; that was enough. Now he was the first divorced half-Jew president who sold America's biggest city to China. *Wow. How would history judge this?* "Betsy, I don't want you to leave. I don't know if we can work it out, but maybe you should stay and we should try."

She laughed out loud. "My darling, I'm not a labor union or a country demanding more aid; there is nothing to work out. You're in love with someone else and I'm not in love with you. That's a bad combination. Let's cut our losses and try to salvage some happiness. Don't you think?"

"But no First Lady has ever left the job. That might come across as a slight to America."

Now Betsy got angry. "Fuck America. I didn't marry America. America didn't cheat on me and I'm not leaving America. I'm leaving you! You can have your bullshit speech people say it anyway you want. I've already had mine write something and if you want to use it, it's already approved."

And with that, feeling herself about to lose it, she threw the short speech she had prepared on his desk and left his office for what would be the last time. Bernstein looked down and read her statement.

> After twenty-two years of marriage, Matthew and Betsy Bernstein have decided to go their separate ways. They both love and respect each other, but sometimes in life two people, no matter how close they were, drift apart and need to start fresh in a new direction. Betsy Bernstein has loved her time as First Lady and will continue to love and support this wonderful country, a country that she has

had the privilege to serve. But now the time has come for her and her husband to each seek a new path in their personal lives. Please respect their privacy in this matter.

The President looked at the last line and ran his hand through his hair. *Right, everyone's going to respect our privacy.*

Susanna Colbert was giving a speech at the Wharton School of Business when one of her aides told her the President wanted to speak to her. She was told it was urgent and for a moment she had no idea what to expect. She was, after all, the secretary of the Treasury, and in a normal relationship with the White House, the word "urgent" would mean some kind of financial problem, possibly one that was very serious. But this relationship was anything but normal, so she contacted the President on a secure link. As soon as she saw him she knew what "urgent" meant. He looked terrible. He had either been crying or sweating or doing something that made his face look moist and his hair messed up, and he had circles under his eyes. "What's wrong with you?" she asked him. "Are you sick?"

"She left." Susanna didn't need to ask who. "She's gone. It's over. Can you come back here?"

"Of course. I'll be back tonight."

"I'm sorry to sound like a wounded child. I haven't told anyone but you. She gave me a statement and I wanted your opinion."

"I'll look at it as soon as I get back. Is that okay?"

"Yes." And then the President asked her, "How did your speech go?"

Goodness, there was something about him that Susanna really *did* love. Something allowed him to ask that question at a moment when it was the last thing he cared about. It was probably why he had been elected president. He knew how to make people feel important—everyone, that is, except the woman he married. "It was fine," she said. "They love you here."

CHAPTER FIFTY-FOUR

When she arrived in Chicago, Kathy Bernard was booked and formally accused of aiding and abetting a terrorist activity. She was put into a holding cell. There was no bail allowed, and even if there were, the amount would have been astronomical. Any arrest with the word "terrorist" in the accusation—either of being one, helping one, or knowing one—carried such a stigma that judges were hesitant to grant any bail at all, and if they did, they set the amount beyond the ability to pay.

Kathy was taken to a communication room, where she realized that she had no one to contact. No one except Clyde Folsom. That fact alone made her so sad. Clyde's face appeared on the screen. He was at home. "Hi, it's Kathy."

"I see," Clyde said. "Where are you? Are you in the office?" Kathy just started bawling. In one second she turned into a little girl.

"I'm in Chicago. I've been arrested. They're accusing me of helping Max and I had nothing to do with it." Clyde was torn for a second. He thought about the reputation of his business, but he saw how scared she looked and he knew he had to help.

"Is there bail set?"

"No. No bail."

"No bail? What the hell is that about?"

"I don't know. No bail."

"Did you contact a lawyer?"

"I don't know any lawyers. I contacted you. I'm sorry."

"You need a lawyer, Kathy. Let me talk to someone and we'll find you the best one."

"I can't afford that."

"Don't worry about that now. Let's see if we can get you out on bail. I'll do what I can, I promise."

"I'm so sorry to involve you. I didn't know anyone else. I didn't do anything, Mr. Folsom." Kathy had not called him Mr. Folsom for months. He was always Clyde. But now she had been reduced to a child, and a child never calls an adult by their first name.

"I'll help you, Kathy. I'll do everything I can."

"Thank you. I'm so sorry. I'm so sorry to bother you."

Clyde Folsom's life had been going pretty well, or so he thought. Healthy into his mideighties, not a great relationship with his kids, but this new young woman who worked for him was bright and the best salesperson he'd had in decades; he actually had been planning to let her take over the business so he could finally retire, knowing that she could continue to generate income for him for many years. Now she was in prison. *Damn it.*

When Susanna got back to the White House she went directly to the Oval Office. When she walked in the President got up and put his arms around her. She didn't resist. The funny thing was that even though he was president, and even though she was immensely fond of him, this was now officially a rebound relationship and she hated those. It was one thing when the First Lady was there and they were sneaking around, talking at all hours, but now she was the only woman in his life and she didn't know exactly how to deal with that. After all, the world had not even found out yet that Betsy Bernstein was gone. So Susanna broke the hug and led the President to his chair. She sat opposite him and they talked. They talked for five hours straight. And they talked about everything.

"I've been coming off so badly since the rescue of the hostages," he said. "My actions probably saved thousands of people from being killed. And yet all they say is that I'm soft on these youth brigades or whatever the hell they're calling them."

"So punch them back. Tell them they're idiots. Stand up to them."

"That's something Betsy did so great," the President said. "She knew how to attack." When Susanna heard that, it was all she could do to keep her anger in check. She spoke sharply.

"You don't have Betsy now. That's not an option. You must use your cabinet and John and as many people in Congress as you can. You've let them get the lead on this and playing catch-up is too tough."

Bernstein knew she was right. He also knew that when the sun came up the next day, the whole world would know that the President and his wife had separated, and the timing could not have been worse. "No one will listen to me about the hijacking or anything else," the President said. "All they are going to talk about is the divorce. There is no precedent for this. I can't even go to the history books to see how other presidents handled it. I am in a weak position, Susanna. I don't know what to do." Susanna took control. She believed him when he said he didn't know what to do, so someone needed to take over. It might as well be her.

"Matthew." It was the first time she called him by his first name and it sounded strange. "You need to address the divorce yourself and keep it separated from everything else. One thing has nothing to do with the other and you need to make that clear. If it were me, I would address the issue with your wife in a national broadcast tomorrow night and give it your spin and leave it at that. I also think you can talk more about the hijacking in the same speech. As a matter of fact, it might say to the people that business goes on as usual. And that you are in control."

At that moment the door to the Oval Office opened. Standing there was John Van Dyke. The President's assistant was standing next to him, looking upset. "I told him you were in a meeting, but he didn't care."

"It's okay," the President said. Van Dyke looked at Susanna, looked at the President, then turned around and left without saying a word.

"What just happened?" Susanna asked.

"I'm not sure," the President said. "I think when it rains it pours. I'm afraid you're going to have to stay late and help me with the speech. Is that all right, will you do that?"

"Of course."

And at that moment Susanna Colbert realized she was now unofficially the second most important person in the United States.

CHAPTER FIFTY-FIVE

When the country found out the next day that Betsy Bernstein and her husband were no longer together, it was as if an atom bomb had dropped. By that evening, when the President spoke to the nation—against John Van Dyke's advice—the whole world was watching.

He presented their marriage as that of any man and woman and said that even the president was not immune to the problems of the heart, that sometimes people were better off not being together. He said he related to the average couple who had gone through these problems and he wished his wife well, and told the world he would always love her. He also assured the country that even though he might be lonely for a while, the government would run as smoothly as ever and life must go on. He cut short any talk about the hijacking, only telling the relatives of the deceased that they were always in his prayers, and he signed off by saying that his love of his country was the greatest love in his life and America had won in the battle for his affections. He ad-libbed that last part and was rather pleased with it. All in all, he thought the speech was a success. He was wrong.

When the address was over Stanley Markum called his son-in-law and asked if he saw it. "Of course," Shen said.

"He's through," Markum declared. "He will never be reelected."

"Why?"

"Because if a woman won't stay with you then she knows something. You have a defect and you shouldn't be president."

"Is that true?"

"It's true if you say it's true. The trick is saying it so it doesn't sound mean."

"I guess you're right," Shen said. "Now that I think about it, it does make a man look defective."

"You're damn right. We'll find a way to use it against him, you mark my words."

Shen didn't know exactly what the senator meant. It almost sounded like Stanley Markum was going to run for president. But that wasn't what his father-in-law had in mind.

The thirties had become a decade of firsts. The first glimmering of a health care system that might actually make sense. The first time a country invited another in to help with its problems and agreed to share its wealth. The first time a president and his wife split up while in office. There was one more first that was long overdue, and Stanley Markum felt that time had come.

It had been talked about decades ago when it looked as though Arnold Schwarzenegger was the most popular man in America, but as his approval rating sank, so did the movement to amend the Constitution. But now it was different. Shen Li had taken America by storm. His ideas were smart, he was charming, he'd married the perfect woman, and his father-in-law had the power, the desire, and the ability to get this amendment finally passed.

Shen had already been made a citizen; he was the best representative of the country that had come to save America. Why couldn't he go all the way? It was always Laura's plan and now, finally, it seemed possible.

Senator Markum anticipated no problem with Congress. The only issue was whether the states would ratify it, but why wouldn't they? They were all lining up to get their *own* makeovers. All that was needed was money. And a lot of it. This needed an expensive and well-organized campaign. Enter Nate Cass.

Charles Cass did not go to prison, but the embarrassment of his trial and the publicity that ensued only hardened his brother's position against Matthew Bernstein. Nate didn't know how or when he would pay the President back for not "thanking him," but the stars aligned perfectly when he met Stanley Markum one evening at a charity event in the summer of 2031.

Cass never considered himself a conservative; he played the field and supported candidates he thought would be good for business. But he liked Shen Li. Li's smaller health centers were catching on and Nate, who was big in this industry, saw a windfall in building and running these kinds of places; to him it seemed an even bigger idea than Compassionate Care.

After several umbrella drinks, Nate Cass and Stanley Markum bonded, and Nate thought that allowing a foreign-born naturalized citizen to run for president of the United States was a fine idea, especially if it was Shen Li, and especially if it was against Matthew Bernstein. It was at that dinner that Nate Cass realized exactly where he could spend his money and exactly how he would get even. He would contribute the lion's share to the fifty-state campaign to ratify the twenty-eighth amendment to the Constitution.

All they needed were thirty-eight states, but both Cass and the senator thought they could get all fifty. If Los Angeles had not worked out, none of this could have happened, but because it was being perceived as a major success, it would show the other states what was possible with a man like Li. A massively expensive ad campaign, if it was handled right, would have Americans begging for the amendment. Cass was so enthused that night when he left the event that he almost felt sorry for the President. He said to his new wife, "If that son of a bitch had only helped me, I wouldn't bring him down like this, but I have no choice. And it'll be good for business."

Three weeks after going to Chicago, Kathy Bernard was transferred to a state prison in Illinois. She shared a cell with another woman who was accused of murdering her husband. Kathy felt like her life had ended. Even the murderous cellmate looked at her with disgust because she had the label "terrorist" attached to her crime. The women in that prison were strangely conservative. You could kill another person, especially if it was a man, but try to take down the country and you were some kind of child molester.

Clyde Folsom had secured an attorney who came highly recommended. He took the lawyer to meet Kathy in prison and afterward she felt extremely depressed. She was grateful that Clyde would help her out with what would certainly be enormous fees, but she didn't like the lawyer and thought he wasn't smart. She couldn't say anything—beggars can't be choosers—but when Clyde came to visit her alone a week later, she expressed concern that the attorney was not good enough. Clyde was insulted, but he listened. He thought the lawyer was just fine and was a little miffed at Kathy for complaining.

"Kathy, he comes highly recommended. He has friends in the government. A lot of strings are going to have to be pulled to get this resolved. You know that, right?"

"Of course. I'm sorry. I just felt he wasn't as passionate about it as you or I might be. I guess I was expecting something else."

"Listen, dear, it's not about passion. It's about who you know and what favors you can call in, and from what I understand he is very, very connected. My God, he certainly is charging enough."

Kathy realized that Clyde was right. Of course the lawyer would be fine. And without Clyde, God knows what attorney she would have gotten. Some shitty public defender. She apologized for even questioning it.

And as it turned out, Clyde Folsom chose well. It took almost six months but the attorney convinced the prosecution that Kathy Bernard was not an accomplice; she had merely chosen her friends poorly, which even in 2031 was not yet a crime. The good news was that Kathy got her job back and continued to be Clyde's very best employee. The bad news was that after adding the attorney's fees to the medical loan, she was now well over a million dollars in debt. But Clyde reassured her.

"Don't worry," he said, "there're a lot of houses out there to be sold. You'll be fine." And even though Kathy wasn't much for irony, as she arrived at work each day she could not ignore the fact that her very best friend in the world was about to turn eighty-seven.

When the President announced that he would run for another term, it wasn't a surprise. There was no Democrat who was going to compete with a sitting president. But when John Van Dyke turned in his resignation and said that he would not be part of another Bernstein administration, it caught the President unprepared.

Van Dyke had seemed to accept the new order in the White House. He seemed willing to work for a President who was divorced and in love with a cabinet member, willing to be third in line, after Susanna. But it wasn't true. And one Friday, before he left for home, he came to see the President and put his letter of resignation on his desk.

"Do I have to read this?" Bernstein asked.

"I will not be helpful to you any longer. I have loved our relationship, but it's time for both of us to move on. You and I have always seen eye to eye, but no more, I fear. You deserve someone who is always on your side."

The President looked at the letter. It was simple, just two sentences stating that Van Dyke was leaving. He asked John to sit down. He would accept the letter, but after twenty years this at least deserved a conversation.

"You are my right arm. You know that, don't you, John?"

"I was. Not anymore."

"It's not true. I know you're jealous of Susanna, but it's silly. You both are helpful to me. Why is that wrong?"

"It's not wrong, Mr. President. But when you were married to Betsy, your decisions came from *our* discussions, not the discussions you had with her. It no longer runs that way. I now wait to find out how you're going to approach each day. I'm not the first one in the loop any longer and it doesn't make sense anymore."

The President didn't have it in him to convince Van Dyke to stay. He could see that the decision was made, and he had learned a long time ago that if someone actually wrote a resignation letter, they had reached a point of no return. He recalled years earlier when his chief aide in Congress had resigned, but Bernstein had begged him not to leave. The aide stayed and the next year was miserable for the both of them. He didn't want that to happen again. "John, I will miss you. You are a really good man and I know you will do something great. I hope I at least have your support in the next election."

"I'll vote for you, if that's what you're asking."

The President smiled. He got up and gave his chief of staff a bear hug. He whispered in his ear, "Don't turn on me, John. Don't write a book."

CHAPTER FIFTY-SIX

The opening of the new football stadium in downtown Los Angeles was a major event. It was a beautiful site with monorails providing transportation directly into the arena. And it was surrounded by ongoing construction; new condominiums, office buildings, and three hotels that looked as though they would be finished within a year. It was the kind of downtown that Los Angeles had always dreamed about, but never could accomplish.

The rest of the city was taking shape and it was equally magnificent. No other American city looked like it. Finally, America had made a leap into the future. It had taken a disaster to make it happen, but it happened nonetheless, and the rest of the country was jealous.

The Chinese who were in charge of the project became folk heroes. The architect, Lee Dong Wo, and the health minister, Shen Li, were idolized everywhere they went. It was lucky for Li that Wo had no ambitions to run for office. It would have been hard to pick between the two of them. But as it turned out, only Shen Li was primed to make a historic move.

On September 9 and 10, 2031, both houses of Congress unanimously passed the twenty-eighth amendment to the Constitution of the United States, allowing a naturalized citizen of foreign birth to run for the highest office in the land. With Nate Cass's help, ratifying it with three-quarters of the states was easy. All they did was make an ad campaign that showed

Los Angeles and said, "This can happen to you if you allow the best and the brightest in the world to love America."

Before this, the fastest a constitutional amendment had ever been ratified was the amendment giving the vote to eighteen-year-olds, and that had taken three months. But with Cass's money and the country's desire for China's help, the twenty-eighth amendment was ratified in three weeks time by all the states except Alabama and Mississippi. And by Thanksgiving of 2031, the die was cast.

With his wife and his father-in-law by his side, Shen Li announced his candidacy for president of the United States. It didn't really come as a surprise. People knew they were amending the Constitution for a reason and that Li was that reason. But from the moment he announced, the crowds he attracted were humongous. Not for decades had people seen such enthusiasm. Latinos, who were now in the majority in the United States, loved this man. He represented something that they thought was long overdue. Since many of their relatives had come here from other countries, to finally see someone who was not born in the U.S. be allowed to participate at the highest level—well, it was about time.

But it was the health issue that really put Li over. He could point to China and now Los Angeles and promise the people something new. He promised that if he were president he would work to get his smaller clinics in every city in America. He promised that the nurses that ran these centers would know the patients' names and care for them like relatives. And he promised that if they needed surgery, the robots would allow the greatest doctors in the world to perform the operations at a lower cost than ever before. Whether it was all true made no difference; everyone believed him. Millions of people wore holographic buttons with Li's picture and the slogan "A President Who Cares." He equated the president of the United States to the health of the country and it was powerful. And it was something that caught Matthew Bernstein by surprise.

Bernstein had not married Susanna Colbert, but he did make her his chief of staff, and she was now with him eighteen hours a day. They slept together six times, but it wasn't meant to be. She didn't want to leave her husband and she convinced the President that they both could get everything they wanted from each other without having sex. And he understood.

She would work until two in the morning if he needed her and then be there for him at eight A.M. This arrangement allowed the President to not appear as if he had ditched one woman for another, though that was what the opposition was trying to make people think.

One day, out of the blue, the President asked Susanna Colbert if she had any thoughts why Nate Cass had supported the twenty-eighth amendment. Wasn't he a friend? Why would he campaign for something that could only hurt her? Susanna decided to come clean. She had held it in for so long, it felt good just to tell him the truth. But Bernstein was not happy with what he heard. "I appreciate that you were concerned about getting me involved in his case," he said, "but you leave that for me to decide. You don't make any decisions that could come back and bite me in the ass, like it's doing now. You will always consult me in the future. Is that clear?"

"Yes, Mr. President." Susanna thought about trying to get out of this by telling him that she had informed John Van Dyke, but she decided to take the blame and be done with it. "I'm sorry I made the decision without telling you. It just seemed like it was the last thing you needed to hear at the time. I did not want you involved in something illegal." Bernstein gave her a nod.

"It's okay, Susanna. You might have lost the election for us, but it's okay."

Susanna knew he wasn't kidding.

It was clear who Robert Golden and Paul Prescott supported. Shen Li was the no-nonsense candidate when it came to stopping the violence toward the olds. They loved his Chinese roots; they loved the fact that China stopped these kinds of protests before they ever got started. And so did their members.

Though the elderly had it rough in every part of the world, the mystique of the Asians treating them with respect was still alive, and AARP kept up the legend by advertising that message heavily. One ad said, "Only Li knows how to treat you right; it's in his blood."

Violence against the elderly did not disappear during the election year, but Li's strong comments forced the President to play catch-up, and before Bernstein knew it, he was campaigning on the defensive. He was spending time at his rallies answering charges from every group. *Yes,* he was tough on elder abuse. *Yes,* he did want more personalized health care. *Yes,* he did think that China had done a brilliant job with Los Angeles.

But the Li campaign raised more money, had the support of the seniors, and even courted younger voters, telling them that if anyone was capable of getting China and the other foreign countries to forgive some of the massive debt, it was him. He was *from* there, after all. He could accomplish what no American-born president had ever been able to. He could speak to much of the world in their own language. And young people were so desperate for any kind of hope, they believed him.

When Li won the Iowa caucus, Matthew Bernstein knew he was in for the fight of his life. He begged John Van Dyke to come back and help him, but that relationship was over. Bernstein did assemble the best team he could find. They forced him to change some of his liberal views, and what he hated the most was that he wound up campaigning on scare tactics. National security issues. It was all he had.

During one speech in Nevada he actually said the words, "Do we want a president who was not born and raised in our country? The founding fathers knew this was a bad idea, that's why they wrote it into the Constitution. Maybe we should ask ourselves what they knew that we are now trying to forget." He came offstage and smashed his fist into a wall. "Goddamn it, they've reduced me to sounding like some right-wing asshole. How did that even come out of my mouth? I'm the goddamn liberal one!"

And that was the way the year went for Bernstein. He didn't know what side to take. Finally, in the fifth national debate, which he felt he was losing, he turned to Shen Li and said, "*I'm* the one who invited you here. Let's never forget that." And Li smiled, took a long pause, and looked directly in the camera. "Mr. President, *that* was the best decision you have ever made. And on *that,* I congratulate you."

The audience applauded for one whole minute.

CHAPTER FIFTY-SEVEN

It was a beautiful day in January 2033. A light snowfall covered Washington, and the crowds that were brought in for the inauguration were enormous. The entire world watched as Shen Li was sworn in as the forty-eighth President of the United States.

After he took the oath of office he approached the stand, which was entirely enclosed in a transparent material that was invisible to the eye but could stop a laser from three hundred yards.

Li had memorized his speech. No prompters and no papers. That alone made him look different from any president before him. He thanked the appropriate dignitaries, including Matthew Bernstein, who was sitting alone and still looked shell-shocked. He thanked his wife, the new First Lady, who looked radiant and powerful, almost as if this were a copresidency. He then began his speech as the entire world listened.

> "My fellow Americans, and my fellow citizens of the world. Today marks a historic beginning of a new era. A man who was born outside of the United States can finally stand before you as president of this great country. This man is not measured on where he began life but where he chose to live that life and how he chose to live it, and how he chose to make your lives better because of

that decision. It is not just a change in a law that has enabled this man to stand here. It is a change in the very world we live in. For the first time we are recognizing that we are not simply a collection of nations with borders that let some people in and keep others out. We can no longer be a world filled with isolated countries that only care for themselves. Our borders divide land, but they do not divide people. And until we understand that, we will never reach our potential as human beings and we will certainly never reach the stars. If one day we are truly to take our place in this universe, we cannot do it as America or China or Russia or Japan. We must do it as Earth. And today you have elected a president who understands this and can work toward accomplishing that goal.

"The last year of my life has not just been the most exciting year that I have ever experienced, but it has also been the most gratifying. The people I have met across this great nation, the debates and the conversations and the disagreements, they have all showed me that people deep down are the same. They want a good life for their family and their friends and their fellow citizens. They want peace and they want prosperity. They want health and they want longevity. They want to replace fear and suspicion with security and trust. And I believe that time has come. It is finally within our reach. And as president of this great country, I will do everything in my power to lead the United States into this brave new world. We have seen what cooperation can do in just one of our great cities, and this is only the beginning. If the world works together, there is no stopping us.

"It can't happen all at once. There will be setbacks along the way. But it has begun. And as America and China have now shown, we can break down barriers that have divided our species since the beginning of time. We can finally understand that color and size and nationality and personality are all just parts of what it means to be human. And if we truly understand that fact, we can spread peace throughout this world, the peace that has eluded mankind since the dawn of civilization. And in the distant future, when we colonize new planets and then new galaxies, we can hold our heads up high and say, 'We are from Earth. We are One.'"

The crowd went wild. The cameras took pictures of the bused-in fifty thousand high schoolers standing arm in arm with fifty thousand senior citizens, a sight that had never been seen before. And even though it was staged, it still looked hopeful. Chances were these two groups would not speak to each other after the election, but it was a great image and one the whole world talked about the entire next day.